RED SKY AT NIGHT

A Novel By:

Bill Bigelow

Published by:

AUTHOR HOUSE
1663 Liberty Drive
Bloomington, Indiana 47403

Library of Congress Control Number: 2004191760

ISBN 1-4184-2161-8

Printed in Hong Kong

Second Printing

January 2006

Cover Design by Rick Terwilliger, Red Monkey Graphics, Honolulu

Dedicated to the men and women of the United States Navy.

Your daily contributions to the defense of our country will be

forever appreciated. Thank you for your service to America.

ACKNOWLEDGMENTS

This book is written as a work of fiction, although many of the locations and settings are based in fact. All characters' names are fictitious, with the exception of certain references to past or present government leaders or other historic persons. Statements issued by such people are fictitious, except those highly recognizable quotes or acts by former world leaders. Actual U.S. Navy ships and weapons are depicted to authenticate situations created for this novel.

Completion of the book would not have been possible without the superb contributions of several U.S. Navy active duty and retired officers and chief petty officers. The details of life on a nuclear submarine, its thousands of working parts, its daily routines both at the pier and during battle, require a specific and proper description. Knowing the exact language used by various crewmen and the ship's officers, and the particulars of how things actually happen during a for-real attack on an enemy ship or shore position, required much investigating on my part. Just remembering my Navy days on the USS FRANCIS MARION, or watching old movies about WW-II submarine battles with the Germans, didn't cut it!

To my old broadcast news colleague and former shipmate Dr. Bob Basso: Thank you! for giving me the motivation to sit down and put on paper the story that was in my head. You also convinced me that re-writes are the only way to achieve a truly great book. Your positive attitude about my ideas and your support will, no doubt, lead to future literary efforts on my part.

From former Navy Commander Scott C.S. Stone, one of my favorite authors and long-time colleague on various Hawaii news reporting ventures, I learned the lesson of how to focus on characters.

And to my San Diego partner, editor, friend and fellow Hawaiian music lover, Hal Hodgson, very special thanks for your editing genius, insight and ability to cut out the large amounts of chaff in my field of words.

My most sincere and loving thanks go to Nancy Bigelow, my wife and daily source of encouragement. Without her unique skills, encouragement and help, my first novel would still be waiting to be written.

RED SKY AT NIGHT

PART I

THE CONSPIRACY

CHAPTER 1 - REBELS WITH A CAUSE

January 6, 2000 - Shanghai, China

The most dangerous revolution of the 21st Century was about to begin.

Captain David K.Y. Wong peered at the restless group, with the quiet delight of a tiger about to pounce on his prey.

"Comrades and fellow Red Dragons, I thank you for your show of support for what we must do. Each of you has pledged your lives to maintain the secrecy of this great moment in Mother China's history. Our Chinese people have been forced to accept great loss of face by the leader of the world's oldest civilization, the head of our own country, who caves in to the decadent West. President Zemin is now too afraid of American consequences to declare war on Taiwan, and certainly doesn't have the *chun toy* to initiate a surprise attack on the ships of their Navy's Seventh Fleet."

The clique of People's Liberation Army officers and civilian leaders cheered Captain Wong. To anyone old enough to remember World War II, or to have seen the old movie-house newsreels, he resembled a modern day version of Adolph Hitler in one of his early 1930s speeches to a group of young Nazis in Munich or Berlin.

Wong was ramrod tough, in control, and those in the jammed meeting room hung on his every word. This is the way it should be, he thought, recalling the past 20 years he'd spent clawing his way up the ladder of power in the Chinese PLA Navy, but having to do it within the bounds set by those now in control of the People's Republic.

The hard, chain-smoking old world Communist was preaching the doctrine believed but rarely spoken by his peers. "Bringing down America is the key to our future success. We here tonight will agree to take the battle directly to the Americans, when and where they least expect it, and without any form of advance notice, from either our own political

9

leaders or our fellow comrades in the PLA. When our actions are successful, we will be heroes of Mother China."

A thunderous roar of approval shook the flimsy walls of the unassuming Shanghai waterfront building that housed the Chinese American Friendship Society, CAFS, a front for Chinese intelligence experts training new agents for assignment to various PRC agencies in the U.S., including embassies, consulates, trade missions and anywhere else Beijing's spymasters might obtain useful information.

"We and we alone have the means for new China's deliverance. Our HAN submarine is Chinese designed and built, but it will be re-configured and modified with secret stealth capabilities we are currently borrowing from the U.S. Navy. It will also be armed with the latest nuclear missiles and torpedoes, and then sent to sea to deliver our message directly into an American Aircraft Carrier Battle Group."

He paused to light another cigarette and quickly put it down next to two others still burning in the ashtray, and continued: "Naturally such a devastating blow will call for massive retaliation. Naturally, our feeble leadership will respond with all out war." A huge roar went up in the crowd.

When the room quieted again, David Wong turned slowly back to the group of about 35 dedicated combatants, all of whom were ready and willing to lead the battle or face the bullet, and continued his charge to the soon-to-be martyrs:

"With the element of surprise, and our superior commitment to this mission and to the future of China, we will seek out the U.S. Navy in *our* South China Sea, and strive to send them all straight to the bottom of the ocean. The world will know that China is alive and well: the premier international force of the 21st Century!"

His fellow Red Dragons sprang to their feet and pounded the table to the frenzied cries of "Leader Wong, Leader Wong, Leader Wong!" The steely-eyed rebel captain raised his arms, quieted the room and offered another chant.

It was quickly enjoined by the young blood hawks and soon wafted along the ancient cobblestone streets outside and rose to meet the early red sky at night: "China Forever!"

CHAPTER 2 - GENERAL QUARTERS

January 16, 1998:   At Sea Off Pearl Harbor, Hawaii

"Holy shit!   What the hell did we just hit?" I yelled as the klaxon horn screamed General Quarters.   The fuzzy-cheeked petty officer next to me jumped up and like the hundred or so others on the Pearl Harbor-based nuclear attack submarine USS NASHVILLE (SSN-727) scampered down the passageway to his assigned battle station.

As the sleek boat surfaced I watched the captain grab the periscope, spinning it around nearly 360 degrees, pausing a moment almost where he started, but then backing up ten degrees.   A consecrated feeling of focus fell like a damp fog across the control room.   Officers and men went about their assigned GQ station duties, passing orders and situation reports back and forth.   The entire crew anxiously waited for the skipper's report on what they'd hit. "Lord, don't let it be another Navy ship," whispered the XO.

"Bridge, Conn.   All engines stop.   Prepare for emergency surface rescue. All rescue parties to your lifeboat stations and prepare to launch lifeboats. Make note of the time; 13-thirty seven.   We've hit some type of medium-sized fishing vessel. It appears to be sinking and I don't see any lifeboats near the ship but there's a lot of activity on her decks."

"Bridge, Aye. All engines stop.   Rescue parties to lifeboat stations. Launch boats and search for survivors."

For me, then Military Editor of The Honolulu Times, what had begun as a day at sea observing routine operations as the guest of the submarine's skipper was about to turn into one of the biggest stories of the year, if I could get it off the ship and filed with my city desk.

"Mister Watkins, didn't you see that fishing trawler when you did your periscope scan prior to surfacing?" the captain growled at his Officer Of the Deck.

"No sir, Captain, I did a full 360 like you did just now, and saw nothing, sir."

"There's a lot of swell out there. Waves are five to ten feet. Could you have missed the trawler in the waves?"

"There was no fishing boat anywhere near us, believe me, Captain."

"Well, there is now, and it's starting to break up. Are those rescue teams getting the rafts into the water?"

"Getting them over the side now, Captain, and ready to head for the fishing boat," replied Damage Control.

"That's one very odd fishing boat, gentlemen. She's rigged to tow nets and looks like a tuna trawler, but I'm seeing some very sophisticated radar and sonar dishes on topside masts, and what looks like several radio antennas for long range transmission. And her flag is red with yellow stars in the left corner!"

"All rescue party boats away, Captain. They can see several men in the water."

"Very well, Chief. Keep the reports coming."

"Gentlemen," the submarine commander said solemnly, "if I'm not mistaken the ship we just hit is from the Peoples Republic of China. It may look like a fishing trawler but I bet a case of macadamia nuts that she's a ChiCom spy ship, watching U.S. Navy Ops and hoping to get something new to send back to Shanghai."

Holy shit, I muttered to myself, realizing that was the second time in less than five minutes I'd said that!

"Mr. Watkins, take over here. Keep me posted on anything that comes in via the radio."

"Aye, aye, skipper. This is Mr. Watkins. I have the deck and the conn."

"XO, get off a Flash message to COMSUBPAC and CINCPACFLT that we've hit a fishing trawler upon surfacing, and believe it to be a Chinese Communist spy ship. Give our position and inform them we've started rescue operations. When you finish that, join me on the open bridge."

I stayed quietly out of the way during the emergency, but knew now I had to get word of the incident to my city desk fast. Anxiously I waited until my golfing friend Commander Matson left the control center for topside and the XO was engrossed with the radioman in getting the emergency signals off to higher authority.

I slipped out of the control center saying: "I need to use the head," to anyone listening. The XO gave me a nod and I walked the few yards down to officer's country, into the head, and locked the door. If Chuck knew what I was about to do he'd have locked me in the brig instead of the head. My cell phone was always with me. I started dialing, but before I could get the times I shut off the phone. Something inside me said: Wait one, Dan. Is this really what you want to do?

I left the head and went to the wardroom where I'd wait until Chuck or one of his key officers came to let me know the final outcome of the incident. The XO came in five minutes later, poured a cup of coffee and sat down.

"Appears the boat broke up on collision when we surfaced. Several men are in the water and our rescue teams in life boats are searching for survivors and victims. The skipper is up on deck supervising the rescue efforts."

"The big question is what the hell are the Red Chinese doing in our front yard? That's not their normal method of operation. It seems to me that this could be the tip of a very big fortune cookie."

Realizing I didn't have a shred of hard evidence the sinking vessel was a spy ship, reluctantly I decided to pass on filing a story for the moment. As a guest on a U.S. Navy warship I was hard pressed to avoid the implied censorship I accepted, and being a former sailor myself I know how the game is played. The Navy won't be releasing anything in the next few hours so I'll be able to get a story written when I get back to shore.

On the way to his cabin the skipper passed by the open wardroom door and gave me a quick wave. "Everything okay, Dan?" I nodded affirmative. "I'll join you in a few minutes after I finish my initial incident report to COMSUBPAC."

Twenty minutes later Chuck flopped down in his wardroom chair, breathed a sigh and muttered: "We got eight of the crew, and think there may still be one or two more on board. Our guys and a Coast Guard chopper are still on the scene, but the boat is taking on water real fast. I say she'll be gone by sunset. We took relatively little damage. I can't imagine why we never saw that trawler, what with our pre-surfacing periscope sweeps; she had to be right over us when we broke the surface."

"Chuck, I'm really sorry that it had to happen on your watch. I know you'll be raked over the media coals for this one but you can count on my support in what I'll file. I was right there when we came up and I know your crew saw nothing ahead of time."

"Thanks, Dan, I appreciate it and that you didn't call your office." I gave him a quizzical look and he replied: "Our equipment detects any cell calls made from the boat, and my communications guys would have let me know if any transmissions were exiting NASHVILLE."

A third-class radioman knocked on the wardroom door and handed the captain a clipboard crammed with messages. Signing for them Captain Matson took the top signal off the clipboard, and reviewed it before tossing it over to me. It was a copy of the initial incident report he'd just sent to Pearl Harbor. None of us could have known we had just witnessed round one of a titanic heavyweight battle that would soon rock the world. And in my wildest dreams couldn't imagine I would have a ring-side seat for the entire fight.

CHAPTER 3 - TRICK OR TRAWLER

January 20, 1998 - Honolulu, Hawaii

For the next week the LOTUS MOON sinking was the major local news event, dominating every radio newscast on KSSK, KHVH and any other station using the AP wire feed. The TV crews from channels 2, 4, 8 and 9 were trying to get interviews with Chuck Matson, but to no avail. They did talk with crew of the Chinese ship but got little or no useable quotes.

I was assigned to do follow-ups to my initial story. The best news for everyone involved was that the entire crew of the boat made it off alive. Because the ship sank that first night there was no real evidence left to check out, other than a few fishing nets and the crew's stories about the collision and details of their rescue. They wouldn't talk about what many believed was the ship's real mission.

A few accounts alluded to the possibility that LOTUS MOON was really a spy ship and not just your every day Chinese fishing boat. But without a big protest from Beijing, and with the ship's crew and skipper flown back to China, the incident was soon bumped out of the first section of most papers and by the end of January it was all but forgotten.

The State Legislature had just convened and was grabbing most of the local headlines. Simon Cardigan, my Honolulu Times buddy, had the Leg beat along with some investigative material he'd been working on for what seemed like years. The legislature notoriously keeps most reporters very busy with endless night sessions but Simon had built up a long list of contacts in leadership circles so he was able to get the stories well before they were actually being made. The Hawaii State legislature was almost entirely Democratic, so you had half as many people to talk with to get your story!

Simon was a most interesting guy. He was English, that's a good beginning right there, and for eight years had

15

worked on the London Evening Standard before coming out to Hawaii. A very skilled journalist, and with the British method of tabloid writing, he could get to the point of a story quicker than any of his Yankee colleagues. About three years after joining the Times he confided to me that he was uncovering all sorts of stories that the local reporters knew nothing about or seemed uninterested in seeking out.

Over a few beers one evening, he casually hinted that he was working on a tip, and said it would stun the free world if it proved to be true. He also indicated that the Chinese fishing trawler that was hit and sunk by the NASHVILLE during my daytrip on her was an integral part of what he was working on. Pressing him a bit, I asked what this meant but he refused to go into any detail saying only: "You'll read all about it under my byline, in the not too distant future."

One day early last fall, Simon stopped by my desk and slipped a large manila envelope in front of me. He casually tossed a one-hundred dollar bill on top of it and murmured quietly: "I'd greatly appreciate it if you'd open a safe deposit box in your name and put this in it. If anything should happen to me open the envelope and read the contents. You'll know what to do."

I chuckled and said: "Who have you killed and what do I do with your confession!"

Simon waved off my attempt at humor and demanded I do as he said. I agreed and that week rented a box at the Kahala Mall branch of First Hawaiian Bank. Nothing has happened to Simon, the box is paid for three years, and I've gone back to my routine.

My LOTUS MOON story garnered some kudos from the Pearl Harbor brass, especially several senior officers in the submarine service who discovered I was aboard NASHVILLE during the collision and that I did not file any story from the boat, nor did I suggest any possibility of spy ship activity. This was how they liked press coverage, but rarely saw it, and that action allowed me to get interviews and view actual training exercises that I would never before have been allowed to experience.

In the weeks after the big incident I flew with Coast Guard sea rescue missions; landed on a Windward Oahu beach during a Marine training exercise; and went to sea on the guided missile destroyer USS RUSSELL for about a week. I was able to create enough stories to keep my editor smiling for weeks.

That story probably helped immensely in getting my new job in Washington. I got an offer I couldn't refuse, so come springtime I said Aloha to the Honolulu Times, sayonara to my many friends in Hawaii, and moved lock, stock and barrel to the nation's capitol. My new assignment: staff reporter for the Washington bureau of Pacific & Asia News Service, affectionately known as PANS.

Early April weather in D.C. was certainly nothing like Hawaii but it wasn't as bad as I feared. Quite a bit of rain but daytime temps in the 60s and 70s. I loved my new job, co-workers and especially my boss Bennett Huntley. He was kind of a father figure even though I'd been there only a few weeks. On my first day at PANS I was summoned to his office and motioned to sit down as he began:

"You have some good credentials, but don't ever try to bullshit me! I've pulled that routine on the best of them. I'm no shrink but if you've got a problem, or need a shoulder to cry on, I'm a good listener and can probably come up with something that will help you. This can be a mean town, Danny, and it'll eat you alive if you let it. It's also the greatest place in the world to be a newsman. Holler if you need help." Abruptly he shooed me out of the office and went back to his stack of paperwork.

Ben was a newsman's newsman; married right out of college and started his career on a small-town weekly in Iowa. He then made it to the Sun Times in Chicago as a beat reporter, and a dozen years later landed at the Washington Post. After a few years as Kathryn Graham's Metro Edition editor, Ben missed the day-to-day activity of reporting. Even though he knew squat about Asia and the Pacific he stumbled onto a new wire service just being created which was going to specialize in that region. Being a great writer, editor and administrator easily snagged him the job as PANS Bureau Chief.

My household effects from Honolulu arrived a week after I did, so I asked Ben for some time to look for an apartment. On a map he and some of the other office regulars showed me which neighborhoods were good and which I didn't want to even consider. Within several days I found exactly what I wanted; first class digs in a first class section of town.

Growing up in a middle class district of suburban Buffalo where all the houses on our street looked alike, and all the families, including mine, thought the highlight of any week was the Saturday night bingo game at the local church, I had vowed to never live or associate with people who had what I believed are limited goals.

I signed a one year lease on a two bedroom apartment in The Attaché, a recently renovated 1920s six-story building on 23rd at I Street, NW, just south of Washington Circle, in the area occupied mostly by diplomats and government executives, easy walking distance to the Foggy Bottom/George Washington University Metrorail station.

I loved the neighborhood. The apartment overlooked a tree-lined grassy front yard and the street. On April 8th the movers came, off-loaded and unwrapped my stuff, and by 4 pm that day I was fully moved into the Attaché, suite #404. I made the smaller of the two bedrooms into a den and home office, and my big brass bed fit perfectly into the other sleeping and I hoped playing room. Books and the rest of my junk would be unpacked later, but basically I was now home.

I established a daily routine at PANS and began enjoying springtime in D.C., a great city with lots to do and see and great places for dining and entertainment. Hawaii was out of my mind in a month. Well, maybe not out but moved to the rear echelon of my brain. I'd forgotten about the weather, the beach and Simon Cardigan's safe deposit box, and was now totally immersed in the big time world of international politics and journalism.

CHAPTER 4 - IN SEARCH OF *THE* STORY

May 10, 1998 - Washington, D.C.

Our watering hole, a cozy gin joint across from our building on Pennsylvania Avenue, lost the urban renewal battle and shuttered a week ago. We quickly adopted The Capitol Connection, just a short stroll from PANS, which our gang would grow to lovingly call the C-C. It resided in a wonderful neighborhood, a block from the old Ford's Theater.

Archie McNichols, the tall-drink-of-water owner, was creating a buzz with his flawless photographic memory. Word was the CIA came to him to do their background checks. A shrewd operator, he knew our rat pack of newsmen and P.R. types regularly left hefty tips at the old pub and would do the same for him. He promised to build a special nook for us, including a Roundtable, in a cozy rear corner.

Savoring a cold MGD, I noticed Archie leave his office and amble toward me. "You must be Dan Lincoln, the new guy with Pacific and Asia News Service. Been in D.C. just a few months, right?"

"Right. You don't happen to know my mother's maiden name by any chance?"

"Give me a week. Hi, I'm Archie."

"Your reputation is well deserved, Archie. Maybe I ought to do all my story research right here."

"You're looking at the king of leads, facts and unnamed sources."

"I hear you're putting a Roundtable in the back for us?"

"Hey, believe me, it's not altruism. From the info I get, your bar bill is gonna put my kid through Harvard."

I liked Archie's easy east coast openness. He spoke the way a good reporter should write, unaffected, to the point and always on the issue. We chatted awhile and I learned that he had bought the pub in 1995 from an uncle who had won it in a poker game from an ex-Congressman back in the sixties.

"Now, tell me about you. I want to know it all."

He meant it. The guy who called a few thousand customers by their first name and remembered their kids' birthdays was the real deal. I never open up to strangers but Archie was an immediate old friend. I gushed out the whole story.

I told him I had been a reporter, correspondent and journalist since I left the University of Washington and the University of Missouri Journalism School in 1986. "I can't think of ever not wanting to do exactly what I'm doing now, holding a non-nine-to-five job, doing investigative reporting on politics, the military and Asian affairs, and getting paid damn well for it!"

Most of my family was surprised when I chose journalism, although I don't know what they thought I would do for a lifetime career. I guess it all started back in Seattle when I volunteered to be a reporter on the UW college paper The Husky. The newspaper bug bit me within a month and I couldn't get enough assignments to keep me happy. However, a year of dumb stories and the daily association with other staff, all a bunch of geeks, and I wanted out.

My editor Nancy, a dark-haired sultry senior, told me that doing my course studies and homework were more important than the paper at that time in my college career. She assured me saying: "Look, don't throw in the towel. I like your style and dedication." That was enough to bring me back in my junior year. Before she graduated I had learned a few other techniques from Madame Editor.

I don't know why but I had no interest in journalism during high school. I grew up in Hamburg, New York, right on Lake Erie, and my teen interests were water skiing, basketball and girls, not necessarily in that order. My tall six foot frame, supporting 140 pounds, lent itself to all three activities. I'm still six foot, but time and a few hundred beers after work have added another 40 pounds.

"What you working on these days, Dan?" my new buddy and fellow staffer Jack O'Neill queried, coming out of the head, sliding onto a barstool and nodding to Archie.

"Ah, the same old Pentagon jive. Trying to figure out this year's defense budget. When Uncle Sam doles out 2.2 billion dollars to the military and 5,000 defense contractors there's got to be a story hiding somewhere."

I was still beaming from being asked to join the big Washington news service after my notoriety from the Chinese spy ship story for the Honolulu Times. Ben Huntley, affectionately known as Big Ben, had assigned me the Pentagon beat right after joining them.

I was in hog heaven, quickly making contacts and friends, and reveling in being in the middle of the biggest power movers on planet Earth. Jeez, I said to myself, thank God I'm not still back in Hamburg facing the same kind of life that has entwined my parents for so long.

The fact that I was a Navy veteran with active duty in the submarine service probably sealed my Pentagon assignment. I had joined the Navy right out of high school in '76 and was riding high on my first sea-duty assignment, a nuclear attack boat based at Pearl Harbor, Hawaii. My specialty: sonar operations.

After two and a half years aboard the USS LA JOLLA, patrolling 600 feet under every ocean on the globe, I was devastated when my annual physical turned up a problem in my left kidney. The ship's doctor told me it couldn't be handled with just a few pills, and so four years into my enlistment I received an honorable discharge, for medical reasons, and began my civilian career.

The Capitol Connection reminded me a lot of the late Columbia Inn in Honolulu. It was a classic watering hole, busy but intimate, where blue and white collar types mixed easily. Dark wood-paneled walls, comfy seating, friendly management and female bartenders who allowed you to run a chit, hoping it would be paid up by week's end. I was so busy scanning my new neighborhood and sizing up the crowd that I didn't notice Archie slipping up behind me.

"A hundred and eighty two bars in the metro area, including Georgetown, all with the most colorful clientele in

21

the world. Congressmen, bureaucrats, ambassadors, high-priced hookers, mistresses..." I completed his list: "terrorists, traitors and con men."

Archie smiled; "Them, too! All the major stories of our time, one way or another, start in a quiet corner in a place just like this, even that big scoop you'll be looking for."

"I'm counting on it, Archie." I didn't have long to wait.

CHAPTER 5 - THE IDEA MAN

September 12, 1987: The Western Pacific Off Taiwan

Robert Bernard Sharpe had dreamed about submarines since he was a kid. He'd seen every World War II submarine movie ever made, and delighted his wardroom officers with verbatim dialogue from the 1957 classic The Enemy Below, with Curt Jurgens skippering a German U-Boat going mano-a-mano with Robert Mitchum, commanding officer of an American destroyer. Bernie reached his top form imitating Clark Gable in Run Silent Run Deep. Gable, as the skipper, gets injured in a battle with a Japanese destroyer. He turns to his XO, Burt Lancaster, who wants to take the boat back to Pearl, and says: "You once told me you were the best XO in the Navy. Now your first order as captain is to retreat!"

Young Mr. Sharpe longed to join the brave brotherhood of undersea celluloid sailors. But it's a long way from Indianapolis, Indiana to any ocean. To become a naval officer he needed an iron will and a total devotion to academics. He'd have to finish in the top three percent of his class at Broadmore High School, ace all the college entrance exams and hope it was good enough to win an appointment to the U.S. Naval Academy. It was.

Hoosier became his nickname at the Academy where he placed in the top ten percentile in every class. He did find time to meet, date and fall in love with a Navy Junior Barbara Buchanan, daughter of a Navy captain serving at the Academy. After graduation, Hoosier Sharpe and Barbara were married in the traditional Navy wedding ceremony, complete with a canopy of swords held high above the couple by a dozen very green ensigns.

Their lives were typical of thousands of other young Navy officers: sea duty, schools for technical training, more sea duty, more training, transferring from Norfolk to Honolulu and to mid-rank tours at the Pentagon. Like their peers the Sharpe's coped with the life, and by the time Ronald Reagan left 1600 Pennsylvania Avenue they had three girls, had lived in eight different sets of quarters, and were moving up the Navy career and social ladder.

From the start of his midshipman year he had set his sights on the silent service, and to his great pride served with distinction in submarines since graduation. Three tours in Norfolk, two at Pearl Harbor, plus a stint as Submarine Base Commander in Bangor, Washington qualified him for just about any job on the Navy's newest nuclear boats. Fate continued to work in his favor when he was personally selected for the program by the brilliant but ornery father of Navy nuclear power, Admiral Hyman G. Rickover. As Sharpe recalled, "In those days, if the old man didn't like the cut of your jib you just didn't get into the nukes."

Seventeen years after leaving Annapolis, and now known by his colleagues as Bernie, Commander Sharpe was fast tracking to captain and flag rank as the skipper of USS GEORGIA, one of the large OHIO Class SSBN ballistic missile submarines that currently projected U.S. power around the world.

"Bring her up smartly to one-five-zero feet, maintain your speed and come left to course three-three-zero," Sharpe ordered his Officer Of the Deck.

"Aye, aye, Captain. Come up smartly to one-five-zero feet, maintain speed and steer left to course three-three-zero."

The 150 man crew of the GEORGIA, like its skipper, was the most professional and highly trained group of sailors in the Navy. It had spent years of study and constant OJT, arguably the most rigorous in the Navy, and was justifiably proud of the role they played in the cold-war years of the 80s. Home for seven months at a time was this sleek 18,700 ton ballistic missile firing nuclear submarine, the most deadly killing machine the world had ever devised.

Four times the size of World War II destroyers, boats of the OHIO class patrolled the oceans of the world with almost infinite endurance, not needing to refuel for over ten years.

Their only limit was the stomachs of their crew, forcing them eventually to put into port to replenish their food inventory.

"Level at one-five-zero feet and baffle cleared, Captain. Steady on course three-three-zero," called out the OOD, LTJG Frank B. Russell, Buzz to his fellow junior officers.

"Very well. I have the conn," said Sharpe. "Let's see if we can find any Chinese out there looking for trouble today. Diving officer, bring the boat to periscope depth."

"Come up to periscope depth, aye sir," answered a young chief petty officer currently being trained as one of many who would perform in this position. "Leveling off at six-five feet, Captain."

"Very well," the skipper responded, taking the periscope controls in hand and scanning the surface of the South China Sea.

The Red Chinese Navy had made itself a force to be reckoned with recently, buying a dozen submarines and destroyers from the Soviets, and designing new classes in their own shipyards. A large part of their modern fleet had just completed a Teddy Roosevelt-like show of power, circumnavigating the globe, conspicuously taunting and badgering Western navies whenever they could.

"Sonar, Conn. Keep a sharp ear for anything that sounds like a sub. Assume it will emit the sound pattern of a Soviet diesel boat. These Commies are getting good at their jobs and we're finding them farther and farther away from their two main bases every month. So far they've been easy to detect and shoo away from allied waters, but they're anxious to take us on and become numero uno. We never know when they'll come up with something new that could make them a real threat out here."

Slowly moving his muscular six-foot frame around the periscope platform, scanning the surface, he called out: "Bingo! Company. A newer class Jiangnan Class frigate and two old Soviet destroyers eight thousand yards dead ahead."

"Sonar, Bridge. Any pinging?

"Bridge, sonar. Nothing, sir. They don't even know we're here."

"Ripe to be picked off, wouldn't you say, Buzz?"

"Yes sir, Cap'n. Are we ready to jump-start World War III?"

"I don't think so, Buzz. I doubt COMSUBPAC or the boys back at the Pentagon would approve."

Crewmen chuckled at the banter, understanding full well that this mission was strictly snoop, not shoot.

"If those tin cans are up there I'll bet there's a submarine or two down here with us," Bernie said. "School's in session. Everyone, be alert. Let's sharpen our skills in finding their boats and recording their sonar patterns. Mr. Russell, take the conn. Dive her down to four-zero-zero feet."

"Aye, aye, Captain. This is Lieutenant Russell; I have the deck and the conn. Dive the boat to four-zero-zero feet, maintain your course and speed."

"Aye, aye sir. Diving to four-zero-zero feet, maintain course three-three-zero degrees, all ahead standard."

Bernie Sharpe knew that today's drill would be no real challenge. Chinese boats were relics, diesel powered hand-me-downs from their some-time Russian friends. While highly motivated the PRC Navy was not so highly trained, at least for the moment.

Designing submarines had been Sharpe's forte for years. His passion grew into an obsession to develop a totally new type that could go anywhere, do anything its crew wanted, completely undetected, right down to sailing into enemy infested waters, firing missiles and torpedoes that could not be heard by any known sonar device now in operation.

"Someday there will be stealth subs," he whispered to himself, "giving us the ultimate advantage over every other Navy in the world. An overpowering deterrence to guarantee world peace. Some how, some way, I *will* figure out how to make it happen!"

Two hours after it began the exercise ended, GEORGIA going undetected. Two Chinese destroyers sunk and one submarine torpedoed with a bow attack. Another turned tail and ran away as fast as her screws could move her. All on paper, of course.

The skipper exchanged hand shakes with the men in the control room and quickly added more fuel to the euphoria: "I assure you, gentlemen, in a few years we'll have a weapon so powerful it will paralyze the aggressive plans of any enemy we face, because we'll have a total stealth submarine."

"You really think it's doable, skipper?" asked Buzz.

"It's been sitting right in front of me for months but I can't seem to connect all the dots."

"Well, if anyone can make it happen, I'm sure it'll be you."

"It better be us, Buzz. God help us if it isn't."

CHAPTER 6 - MR. ANDERSON GOES TO WASHINGTON

November 6, 1992 Minneapolis, Minnesota

As the sun broke over the horizon that crisp Tuesday morning, Henry B. Anderson, Jr. prepared to cast his ballot for the U.S. Representative from the suburban Westside of Minneapolis and Hennepin County. The 30 year-old candidate he would vote for was....himself.

The son of wealthy grain and farm supply dealer and loyal Democrat Henry B. Anderson, Sr., Hank Anderson was a four-year veteran of the Minnesota State Legislature. He had been prepped throughout his career for politically bigger and better things. During campaign visits to the district, the senior Anderson ushered Hank into all the right offices, factory lunchrooms and farmyards. This time, however, the focus was on Hank Jr. His wife Linda, mother of their three small children, was always at his side ready to talk about her young JFK-handsome husband and hopefully soon-to-be national politician.

By the time the sun fell over this sprawling mid-west city, election victor Henry Anderson the younger was headed to Washington, D.C. as Minnesota's new Democrat Farmer Labor (DFL) Congressman.

Winning the election, in this often-Republican district, was no minor feat. And to be elected in1992, during the popular Bush Republican administration, was a feather in his political cap, one to be quickly noted by the power brokers leading the Democrat Party in Congress.

When the TV cameras from WCCO, KSTP, CNN and others came rushing to the family compound near White Bear Lake, Hank and Linda were surrounded by well-wishers and family. He gave the usual victor litany: "Thank you for your support and you can count on me" type of acceptance speech, then settled in with his father and some newly found DFL

28

party friends to discuss what had to be done when he got to Capitol Hill. He knew only too well there would be strings attached to this election victory.

As the party regulars and campaign volunteers relaxed with drinks on the heated verandah of the lakeside house, the broadly beaming state party chairman raised his glass in a toast to the new Congressman:

"Here's to great success for Hank and Minnesota!"

"Here, here!" responded the group of loyalists. "Here's to Hank and Linda!"

Hank returned their toast saying: "You can count on us. I believe in the basic rights under the Constitution, and will fight to defend those principles and get those who support these freedoms heard. Give me a year or so and I'll be ready to turn our party ideas into serious legislation."

His mind flashed back to his high school years, in the early 70s when Richard Nixon made his historic trip to China, and to career diplomat George H.W. Bush named America's first permanent envoy to Beijing in 1974. They put China in the forefront of our national thinking. Bush was one politician he really did admire and whose early work with the Chinese he hoped to expand upon. "Too bad he was a Republican," Hank thought.

Henry B. Anderson, Jr. wanted to be remembered for bringing the Peoples Republic into the mainstream of world politics.

"One of the things I'm really keen on is getting China a far better shake. They've been living from year to year on the issue of trade relations but not getting our most favored nation or MFN designation. That I hope to be able to change." A few whistles accompanied the loud applause for that pledge, making Hank feel more confident he was on the right track with his China issue. After all, Minnesota farmers stood to make big bucks on the export of their grain and other products to that huge Asian market, especially if China was named a most favored nation.

"The Chinese are being kept from playing a key role in the search for world peace, and if we just give them a chance in the halls of international diplomacy I'm certain they will become trading partners and strong allies for us."

Forebodingly, the applause was now barely polite. The state party chairman thanked Representative Anderson for his lofty goals and solid Democrat liberal thinking: "You're on the right track Hank," directing his remarks more to the assembled loyalists than to Hank himself, "we'll be watching you with great expectations. Don't forget, Hubert Humphrey started as mayor of Minneapolis and then in the U.S. House before going on to greatness. There's no reason why you can't do the same thing."

Hank promised Linda, his father, and his new party allies that Minnesota would not regret electing him to Congress. He also knew the U.S. House was just the first stop on a long and ambitious journey.

CHAPTER 7 - THE NOT SO BARGAIN BASEMENT

January 3, 1993:   The Pentagon, Washington, D.C.

Bernie Sharpe continued climbing the promotional ladder swiftly and unimpeded. A captain for the last three years he was transferred to the Pentagon in late summer 1992 to work on developing new submarines.

He hoped that during this tour his life-long goal of finding a way to build a stealth sub might be accomplished. It turned out easier than he thought and after only a few months on the job he was able to sell his idea to top Navy brass, including ADM Edgar R. Lynch, Chief of Naval Operations.

By January 1993 the CNO was also acting Secretary of the Navy, and took the stealth sub idea to the Chairman of the JCS. Not surprisingly the chairman, another Navy admiral, liked the concept and said he'd take it all the way to outgoing President George Bush. We'd later call him Bush #41. After weeks of refining numbers and presentations, Captain Sharpe and the two senior officers presented their concept, and the need for funding this special project, to Mr. Bush. POTUS, the Secret Service's handle for the president, bought off on it immediately and authorized money for the one-of-a-kind project to be included in his final fiscal budget.

Preparing to leave the Oval Office, Bernie shook hands with the Commander in Chief and said: "I can't tell you how pleased I am with your decision, Mr. President. It's my sincere hope that if you visit us in a few years I'll be able to show you our first stealth submarine, and unless some politician beats me to it the first one will be named after you! Now, all I have to do is work out how to fit the money you just authorized into our Navy budget."

Actually the funding would be buried in some non-scrutinized category, since the Navy was already spending billions on new and improved versions of LOS ANGELES class submarines. Typically creative, Sharpe suggested the monies

31

be included in a semi-secret rarely questioned budget for technical development that Admiral Rickover had set up for some of his favorite projects. It was approved and from that day on Sharpe's office would be known as OpNav N-771, reporting directly to the CNO. Bernie began staffing on the day the money was released, May 1st.

He was jubilant, and felt certain that with the support he now had his stealth boat was just around the corner. His team was three submariners specializing in nuclear propulsion, ship design and sonar, two computer gurus and a CIA intelligence expert on the Russian and Chinese navies and their submarine programs. They brainstormed in their Pentagon basement offices, drafting dozens of plans and tested some of the most unique submarine inventions ever seen. However, total stealth remained totally elusive.

Sea trials were held in the summer of 1995 on improvements to propulsion shafts and props, aimed at finding the quiet CAPT Sharpe sought. Torpedo experts tried new techniques with wire guidance, but to no success. After several totally unsuccessful tests COMSUBLANT in Norfolk was becoming cold to Sharpe's requests for tests on his submarines for fear N-771 ideas might sink a boat!

Bernie was forced to say so-long to his precious stealth project when he was deep-selected for the rank of rear admiral (lower half) in the fall of 1996. His new duty, upstairs in the Pentagon's E-Ring offices, was to supervise construction of improved LOS ANGELES class subs. He would also oversee the start of the Navy's nuclear submarine program for the 21st century, called VIRGINIA class attack boats.

Before leaving the basement digs he gathered his team for one last challenge: "Ladies and gentlemen, thank you all for your superb efforts and ideas, and the start you've given our dream. This isn't the end, but merely an intermission. I've dreamed about and worked on this concept for twenty years and many of you have too. Today I say to you: Don't give up the dream. Keep your ideas coming. Keep striving to achieve. *It will happen* and you will be a part of it. And in some unknown way, so will I.

CHAPTER 8 - MATA HARI SHIN

June 6, 1998:   Hong Kong, B.C.C.

The 20-year-old government sedan chugged up the hilly streets of Hong Kong Island, several blocks out of the business and tourist sections, to an area frequented mostly by those knowledgeable of Chinese antiques.   If they had cared to, the two men in the sedan could have viewed the hectic activity below that is Hong Kong Harbor and the bustling tourist destination of Kowloon across the harbor. No worry, they weren't looking for tourists or antiques.

A tiny bell over the Hollywood Road shop door tinkled as the men entered and strode purposefully through narrow rows of vases and plates, pots and pans, rugs and hanging tapestries. It was similar to dozens of antique shops along this popular and well-known street, but these men cared little about the merchandise. It was the shop proprietress they were here to see.

Madam Lily Shin's long porcelain-like fingers glided over the computer keys, finishing a report and then pushed the Cantonese-lettered version of the enter key was on most PCs, storing it in a secure file. It was typically hot and humid in Hong Kong, slowing most people but not this sleek woman of purpose. Hearing the doorbell she moved quickly to close the polished rosewood bookcase that was her thinking room, and returned to the standard office desk that looked just right for an antique shop owner.

As several customers left, the two men moved quickly through a door marked Private at the rear of the shop. They entered a small office where Lily sat behind what one of them thought was a most appropriate Government Issue desk.

"Good day, Madam Shin," said the taller man, bowing politely and extending his hand. "I bring regards from your husband, in Shanghai. He is well and speaks of you often."

"I am honored, Admiral, and request you relay my

regards and love to him. Please tell him I will try to arrange a visit to Shanghai in the very near future."

"I shall do so, Madam Shin," said Rear Admiral T.K.S. Loo, head of the Chinese Navy's Southern Sea Fleet.

"May I serve you tea?" the proprietress asked.

"Thank you, no. We must be brief. This is my assistant Captain Chang. Our government has a new challenge for you. You have served your country and our party loyally for many years, and it is time for a new assignment we feel only you can accomplish."

"I am prepared to do whatever is required of me to further the cause of our great nation," she responded.

"You will move to America," the admiral said noticing a certain spark in Madam Shin's eyes, "and augment the cadre of intelligence agents already in place. You will be a liaison between our Embassy and several Americans of Chinese ancestry who are also supplying the Motherland information about their companies, especially those involved in defense projects."

Taking a long drag on the cigarette in his right hand, Admiral Loo snuffed it out in an ashtray on the desk and continued his instructions.

"You will set up a shop, just like this one but perhaps on a bit more expensive scale, and do exactly what you have done the past five years since graduation from PLA intelligence school. Your most important assignment will be to gather information about the American military plans for this part of the world. And you'll do so from the enemy's very heart, Washington, D.C."

Lily Shin was taken aback by the enormity of what she was being told, but realized this was a great promotion in the Chinese intelligence service. Bowing respectfully, she said: "I am deeply honored, Admiral. Your faith shall be rewarded. You can count on me to make our country proud."

"We shall help you sell this shop for a most reasonable profit, and assist you in getting established among our friends in the Washington art and antique marketplace as a major new importer of Chinese goods sought by wealthy Americans."

"The task sounds very challenging, Admiral Loo. I will need a list of a few people in Washington who are friends of China and who can give me some names to contact in government. And, of course money to set up a shop in the right area of the city."

"Consider your every wish a completed request, but remember the shop is but a minor part of your assignment. You will make contacts in the very highest levels of U.S. business and government. Their Pacific Fleet has been making life impossible for our Navy, and we do not wish to be left playing catch-up to some new weapon system that further strengthens them. Is this something you're sure you can handle, Madam Shin?"

"You can rely on me, Comrade Admiral. It will be my honor as well as my duty. My husband has given me a very good overview of America which I am sure will come in handy. When do I leave?"

"Captain Chang will contact you about the sale of this shop and details of your move. You should plan on flying out of Kai Tak by July 1st, and be in Washington ready to set up your new life by July 4th, a major American holiday they call Independence Day."

CHAPTER 9 - THE FIRST CONTACT

June 25, 1998: The C-C, Washington

It was a three-shirt day; two for the office and a spare for after hours play time. The temperature and humidity were threatening to break into triple digits. "You're going to miss those Hawaiian trade winds in June, July and August," Jack O'Neill, a PANS buddy had said. "Summer in Washington!"

"Hi ya, Dan," Archie called out as I entered the Capitol Connection. My grandfather used to tell me about his favorite radio program Duffy's Tavern, and the lead character that opened the show each week answering the telephone: "Duffy's Tavern, where the elite meet to eat. Archie the Manager speaking, Duffy ain't here." I didn't hang that moniker on my new pub manager, even though it certainly fit.

"You will forever be my main man Archie, if you produce this very minute a frosty pint of your finest lager."

"Your wish is my command, Sir Daniel," Archie quipped, drawing the beer. It was 4 pm, a bit early for any of the gang so I sat at the bar and chatted with Archie. It wasn't long before the Navy Times guy joined me at the long bar.

"Howzit, Ray. Too hot even for an old Washington-hand like you?"

"Goes with the territory, Danny boy," Ray Kinny quipped, pointing at my half-finished beer and adding: "and make it a pitcher will you please, Guv?" Archie placed the cold beer in front of us, and Ray picked it up signaling we retire to our table in the back. It was an infinitely better place to talk than the now rapidly-filling bar.

Ray, like me, was a military reporter, but had twice the experience and about ten years more in Washington than my meager four months. He knew all the right contacts and where the bodies were buried, both at the Pentagon and on the Hill. I found out early on that anything I could glean from him would be career helpful in a big way.

We weren't competing on major stories. He wrote for the weekly paper that was the bible for all USN types, not the kind of media that was looking for controversy or situations that might put the Navy in a bad light. For that reason he had been very generous in sharing some of the contacts he felt may help me in my new routine.

"How're you doing with the new job and the folks over at the five-sided building?" he asked.

"I've been spending most of my time breaking down the Navy budget, trying to see how much is going to maintaining current ships and developing new ones, to personnel living conditions and wages, and antiquated projects with no real value in our new digital world. Being a former submarine sonarman, I'm always interested in what the Navy's planning down below."

"Well, there's one good old boy at the Pentagon you've got to get to know, and probably interview. Rear Admiral Bernie Sharpe," Kinny said, downing his first beer before I'd finished half of mine. I poured him a second mug full, topped off my own, and asked to hear more about this Admiral Sharpe.

"I don't know him all that well, although I did a profile about him for my paper about four years ago. He had just taken over a real hush-hush research project in the Office of the Chief of Naval Operations, and although he couldn't tell me much about it he was pretty chatty about his pre-Pentagon career in submarines. He's absolutely *the* source when it comes to secrets of the deep, both theirs and ours. And that means any enemy Navy you ask about."

This was a man I needed to know. He could lead me to others here in Washington and specifically at the Pentagon who are in a position to give me access to the kinds of stories I knew existed in this one-of-a-kind people city.

Monday morning I called the Navy information operator at the Pentagon and asked to speak to Admiral Sharpe. Shortly a voice came on the line: "Office of the Chief of Naval Operations, Chief Brown, this is not a secure line, how may I help you, sir or ma'am?"

I stifled an outright laugh because I knew this wasn't a top-secret scrambled-code phone, and in a controlled voice said: "May I speak with Rear Admiral Sharpe, please?"

"Wait one, sir."

I did and soon a professionally cool but polite female voice came on the line and introduced herself as Lieutenant Commander Cannon. She asked my name and my business with Admiral Sharpe.

"I'm a reporter with PANS, new to the Pentagon beat, and Ray Kinny at the Navy Times suggested I meet the admiral."

"Mr. ah, Lincoln? I'll forward your request to our Public Affairs Officer for CNO and someone will contact you if Admiral Sharpe can see you. "Is there anything else I can assist you with?" LCDR Cannon asked, rather exotically I thought. What the hell, I'm always imagining sultry intriguing women at every turn.

"Yes, what is Admiral Sharpe's current job title?"

"I think he would prefer to tell you himself," the lady said in a definite 'that is all' tone. "Thank you for your call, Mr. Lincoln."

Nothing new there, I said to myself, hanging up the phone. My first top brass encounter had gone just about the way I expected.

Looking back to my Honolulu news reporter days, I recalled it taking several months to get on speaking terms with the CINCPACFLT brass at Pearl Harbor, and nearly a year before I could interview the commander of all forces in the Pacific, CINCPAC at Camp Smith. But after passing muster and writing stories that were factual, on the money and noncontroversial, I found access to the major commanders was just a matter of setting up appointments through the proper channels.

Surprise! Just three days later LCDR Cannon called, but this time identified herself as Janice Cannon, a nice touch I didn't miss.

"Your request was forwarded to Admiral Sharpe, Mr. Lincoln, and he is available for 30 minutes only this Friday at sixteen hundred hours. That's 4 pm civilian time."

"I remember. We had that same clock on my submarine several years ago," I replied. No answer came from the lady commander, but then none was expected.

"Thank the admiral for me and tell him I'll be there promptly at 1600. Where exactly?"

Commander Janice gave precise directions to the proper CNO office, but her sharp military voice couldn't disguise a sexy hint of mystery. I thanked her for the info and said I looked forward to meeting her. She didn't know, but I really meant it.

CHAPTER 10 - MR. SUBMARINE

July 1, 1998: The Pentagon

Friday afternoon came quickly. I left for Virginia about 3 pm on the Metrorail's Yellow Line. I was sort of familiar with the Pentagon's crazy labyrinth of floors, or rings, after covering some major news conferences, so finding Admiral Sharpe's offices was pretty easy. My credentials were in order. I was early but decided to go in and ask for LCDR Cannon, she of the sultry pipes.

I hope, I thought, she's half as gorgeous as that voice. Suddenly the stale air of room 4097-E filled with an unmistakable scent from my past. It was like being back in the lush green of Manoa Valley, high above Waikiki on Oahu's south shore. The early mist had lifted releasing the most delicious combination of plumeria, white ginger and one distinct sweetness rising above it all, pikake, my favorite Hawaiian flower.

I turned slowly toward the source of the fragrance as a stunning high-fashion model with gleaming brunette hair pulled tight into a bun legged through the door. I caught myself in mid-gasp, eyeing her from head to toe.

Her properly loose-fitting regulation whites were fighting a losing battle to conceal her taut, athletic body and had given up altogether on her substantial round breasts.

Princess Pupule have plenty papaya! I said to myself. I couldn't imagine what Navy uniform regulations have to say about nipple protrusion on its female officers.

Extending a hand and beginning a glistening smile, this vision of loveliness purred at me: "I'm Janice Cannon. It's a pleasure to meet you Mister Lincoln." Trying to control my surprise at finding such a beauty at the other end of my phone calls I muttered something like: "It's my pleasure, ma'am. I truly appreciate the efforts you've made on my behalf."

"You're early, so why don't we go into the conference room and have an iced tea."

Like a small puppy I trailed after my future wife. Hey, a guy can dream, can't he? I've had some success with the fair sex but this was one I wanted to get to know real well. We dispensed with the usual small talk when my journalist streak entered the conversation. I quickly learned she was originally from Daytona Beach, Florida, home of my favorite NASCAR racetrack.

I thought: Keep it on the professional side for now, Danny boy. Don't kill something good by jumping all over it. So, I said: "What got you to join the Navy? I don't recall anyone in uniform looking quite like you?" Blushing, I mentally kicked myself for acting like a rookie.

But LCDR Janice Cannon was one very cool kitten, with everything under control. "I was a Navy junior, grew up in San Diego, Norfolk, the Bremerton area of Seattle, and here in D.C. My teen years and early adulthood were spent in Asia where my father served as a Naval Attaché. In the mid 80s he was at the U.S. Embassy in Hong Kong. After retiring from the Navy he joined a big U.S. manufacturing company's home office in Hong Kong, overseeing their China-based manufacturing operations and sale of electronic equipment."

My enthusiastic nods at her story didn't register any better than my initial stumbling conversation. It was like suddenly being back in high school, awkwardly fumbling for the words to ask Terry Lou Olson to the Junior Prom. Having always hated the time-consuming traditions of the mating dance, I was about to blurt out: "Commander, you're the most beautiful female I've seen since coming back to the Mainland," when the door opened. Janice stood quickly at attention and if I didn't know better it could have been John Wayne himself, in a rear admiral's uniform, who strode into the room.

Well over six feet tall, he moved with all the easy confidence that announced the obvious: *Don't snow me, pal, or you're dead!* His broad friendly smile immediately won my attention, as he shook my hand vigorously and told the commander to be at ease and sit down with us.

"Nice to meet you, Mr. Lincoln. I see you're in the very capable hands of Commander Cannon, here. She's been a member our submarine family since she joined me back in '93, and before coming to my current team she did a stint with COMSUBPAC at Pearl a couple of years ago. You were at the Honolulu Times while she was out there, I believe."

Nodding in the affirmative I said: "I can't thank you enough, Admiral Sharpe, for taking time to speak with me. As you know I'm relatively new on this job but expect to be around the Pentagon for quite awhile. I need to know people like you for my coverage of the Navy."

"Relax, Dan. I know you're a former submariner and I have a thick file on your journalism career. I've followed many of your past stories as they were faxed to me from my colleagues in Hawaii."

I was impressed and extremely flattered. He had a way of putting one at ease. "Your superb coverage early this year of the NASHVILLE collision with that Chinese fishing boat, or shall we truthfully say spy ship, is the kind of journalism we appreciate and hope to see more of."

"Thank you very much, sir. I guess I'm from the old school; just lay out the facts that I found, as long as they don't jeopardize national security, and then leave the story's interpretation up to the readers."

Although one of the top military leaders in the world, he was definitely easy to get to know. He responded with good, quotable answers to the questions he accepted, making it clear he was involved in classified projects which were off-limits for comment. "Make no mistake; we're working on real and not make-believe submarines here." I leaned forward and he took the cue to elaborate.

Slipping back into memory the admiral recalled: "A few years ago I did the initial research into a future class of boats that was to be called NAUTILUS, named after America's first nuclear submarine built half a century ago. That original SSN left Norfolk in February 1955 on her maiden patrol after sending a terse but historically significant message to the Pentagon; Underway on nuclear power. I'll never forget it."

I don't use shorthand, but I do take notes quickly. However, not quick enough to keep pace with the admiral's rapid fire dialogue. "May I use a tape recorder, Admiral?" Without missing a beat he nodded yes and continued.

"The NAUTILUS sub program was scrapped in favor of an interim class of fast attack boats called SEAWOLF, far quieter and faster than the current or earlier LOS ANGELES class ships. For example we made great strides recently when shipyard crews gave SEAWOLF a new high power propulsion system that is focused on delivering lower RPMs, decreasing chances of detection thus giving greater stealth to the boat. Sea trials were very successful and that system has been designated standard on most of the Navy's new submarine construction. There was another successful project where some of our engineers came up with newly designed diving planes for our attack subs. They work better in shallow waters since they can respond to very small depth changes common in such seas as the Persian Gulf and waters off the shores of Red China."

Sharpe continued for another ten minutes, outlining the non-classified details of the Navy's submarine programs for the next couple of decades. The new VIRGINIA class fast attack boats, huge and very technically advanced, in both systems and armament, would enter the fleet in 2004. They would be built using a civilian budgeting model guaranteed to save in the neighborhood of $600 million on the first four subs over the upgraded costs on USS JIMMY CARTER, the last of the three SEAWOLF class boats. I thought, why can't my savings account be in that 'hood?

Admiral Sharpe was ending our interview and he said: "My Pentagon colleagues do lots of interviews and most of them feel reporters are just looking for an angle, something to hang their stories on, or are just trying to stick it to us. I hope what you've learned here today will be taken in the spirit it was given. We in the Navy want the public to know what we're doing and how we're preparing to defend this country during the next century within the bounds of security. I'm sure you see it this way and I look forward to reading your stories."

"Thank you, Admiral."

"Good luck, Dan. I know we'll meet again. And if you don't mind, Commander Cannon will show you out."

I hated for the interview to end because it meant saying goodbye to the enchanting Commander Cannon. Geez, I never dreamed I'd get the hots for a sailor, but I felt the earth tilt just looking at her. I know, I know. Think above the belt!

NAVY IN MIDST OF MAJOR
21ST CENTURY SUBMARINE BUILD-UP

By: Dan Lincoln

Washington D.C. July 4, 1998 (Pacific & Asia News Service):

The Navy is embarked on a major buildup of nuclear submarines, and is ready to unveil a new generation of attack boats to be called the VIRGINIA class. In a wide-ranging interview with Rear Admiral R. Bernard Sharpe, USN, it was revealed the Navy's latest super-submarines will be the second largest non-SSBN boats ever built. The VIRGINIAs will utilize the newest computer systems, torpedo and vertically launched missiles, and be the quietest subs ever constructed.

Admiral Sharpe, head of the Navy submarine development program for the Chief of Naval Operations, is a veteran submariner and a 1970 graduate of the U.S. Naval Academy. He said Congressional debates and political arguing during the early and mid-1990s had stopped progress on any new class of subs, including the proposed NAUTILUS boats. "The Navy has put everything it has into making sure these new boats will be the best America has ever produced," said the two-star admiral.

The contract for $4.2 billion has finally been approved for four new boats to join the fleet. The class leader, USS VIRGINIA, is to be operational by 2004, followed by TEXAS, HAWAII and NORTH CAROLINA by 2015. To date, funding is for these four submarines only.

"The prime contractors, General Dynamic's Electric Boat Division in Connecticut and the Newport News Shipbuilding Co. in Virginia, are committed to building the finest and quietest submarines ever to leave their shipyards, with the latest in combat control, and all the bells and whistles the techies can design," RADM Sharpe added.

VIRGINIA class submarines will be 7,700 tons submerged, 377 feet long, 34 feet wide, with a crew of 134. They can attack, surface, undersea or land targets several miles away. They have four torpedo tubes, a Vertical Launch System (VLS) for Tomahawk missiles, and will be able to lay advanced Captor mobile mines thousands of yards into enemy harbors or in known submarine patrol paths. They'll be the quietest boats ever built and have the ability to maintain U.S. undersea superiority anywhere in the world.

They will be cheaper to build than earlier SEAWOLF class boats, which cost over one billion dollars each. The Navy reports the two shipbuilding companies, working together, will save up to $600 million on the first four boats in the new class.

"If these boats are as good as we believe and if Congress gives us the funding, we hope to have 24 VIRGINIA submarines in the Fleet by 2015, replacing the older LOS ANGELES class which is being retired from active duty," the admiral concluded.

The Navy's total operating budget this year is about $85 billion dollars. That is part of the overall $288 billion dollar budget proposed by the Defense Department.

-end-

CHAPTER 11 - THE CHINA CARD

August 18, 1998: Washington, D.C.

Sliding onto a stool at the nearly full C-C Roundtable, I was immediately given a cold empty mug by a smiling waitress named Lisa, and in a matter of seconds Tom Miller, a news producer from NBC-TV's Capitol bureau, filled it from a large pitcher of golden brew.

"G'Day Mr. Miller, Mr. Kinny and you too, Mr. O'Brien. And how has the world treated you this fine Washington week?"

Ray said "Nice piece on the submarine admiral last month. I knew you'd get a good story from him."

I thanked Ray and chatted briefly about my reactions to Admiral Sharpe. He wanted to know what the veteran submariner was working on, but I said I knew only what ran in the piece.

I did, however, tell him and the others who were listening that I had been assigned to sit in on next week's House Armed Services Committee hearings into the new fiscal year defense budget. My editor was particularly interested in me keeping track of young Congressman Henry Anderson, Jr., from his home state, who was on the committee. Anderson had recently announced his intentions to run for the U.S. Senate this fall. The budget sounded more interesting to me than just another politician on the move, but my editor said this fellow was a bit different. He was also a strong supporter of Communist China.

Before I could ask Ray what he knew about Anderson, a short Oriental chap approached the Roundtable and said: "May I join you? Understand this is journalist new favorite bar!" He extended his hand to us introducing himself: "I am from Beijing. Sung Jiang, New China News Agency, NCNA. Or as you Americans would call me, Jiang Sung. How you do?"

"Welcome, Mr. Sung. Pull up a stool and join us. I'm Dan Lincoln with Pacific and Asia News Service. They call us PANS."

Laughing he replied: "What is requirement for working at PANS, a master's degree in POTS? And, please call me Jiang."

I avoided commenting on his humor, asking him: "How long have you been in Washington, Jiang?"

"Four years. Very good post for journalist since many good stories and lots of juicy politics. My service loves stories about America and its leaders. They make headlines on dozens of papers in China and other countries friendly to us. I know all your compatriots in press and many TV journalists. They want go China on assignment. I help them cut red tape!"

He laughed again, this time sounding more like he meant it. And that was about the only thing genuine about this little man doing a lousy Charlie Chan imitation. He wasn't fooling anyone. The NCNA was nothing more than a cover for Beijing's spying operations. The only question was why he was cozying up to Roundtablers like me. What could we have on our plate of possible interest to the Big Bear from the East?

Monday morning held great promise as I was off to Capitol Hill and my first major Congressional committee hearing. As I entered the hearing room several Congressmen and staffers were spreading out paperwork on the long raised committee table above a relatively small witness table, centered below the members. The press and public gallery sat behind them all. I quickly learned each of these hearings creates its own unspoken image. Sometimes it's burn 'em at the stake; other times they just go through the motions.

I sensed a David and Goliath battle with Congressman Anderson as Goliath, and David in the person of Navy Secretary E. Thomas Wetzel of New Jersey. The CNO sat behind the Secretary and Admiral Sharpe next to him.

Bang! Bang! Bang! The committee chairman gaveled the hearing to order and recognized a senior member of his party who, with few civilities, began questioning the SECNAV

47

about details of how his department's money is spent. It was surprisingly close to the numbers Admiral Sharpe gave me a month ago.

After his time was up the GOP senior yielded the floor to his distinguished colleague from Minnesota, Representative Anderson. Even the dozing news types snapped awake at his name. I quickly pulled out my pocket tape recorder to be sure I recorded this line of questioning to the letter.

"Mr. Chairman, ladies and gentlemen. Thank you Mr. Secretary for your very detailed explanation. I am sure you will judiciously use those billions of dollars to strengthen our defense. But, Mr. Secretary, may I ask how many dollars you will be spending to develop friendly relations between our Navy and those of other nations who seek to work with us, such as China?"

My brief on-line research into Congressman Anderson and his hot buttons had alerted me to this Navy friendship trip he was on, and his intention of turning it into a piece of legislation known as the Chinese American Navy Friendship Agreement.

David aimed his verbal slingshot squarely between the intense blue eyes of the young Minnesota hot shot. "Congressman Anderson, we maintain cordial relations with all navies of the world who do not seek to do us harm. I am familiar with your efforts to promote a so-called Navy friendship agreement, but at this time my job, and that of the U.S. Navy, is to fight and win wars with those who would be our enemy. And in winning any such wars that might arise we will be sure to destroy, to the best of our ability, the entire fighting power of any enemy naval units we encounter, this means ships, aircraft, submarines and personnel. If such an event was to arise, and I sincerely hope it does not, there will be no need for any Navy friendship agreement with any enemy country."

The entire room erupted with everything from cheers and applause to boos, plus a drone of individual conversation. Bright lights filled the hearing room as TV cameras rolled, switching shots between Anderson and Secretary Wetzel.

I knew what had just concluded would be tonight's big news story and source of follow-up stories with the key players in the future. One thing I kept thinking about was how correct Ben Huntley had been when he told me to cover this aspiring politician from the plains of what he called Swede-e-sota.

NAVY SECRETARY AND MINNESOTA CONGRESSMAN TANGLE OVER PROPOSED U.S. CHINA FRIENDSHIP PACT

By: Dan Lincoln

Washington, D.C. August 22, 1998 (Pacific & Asia News Service):
U.S. Navy Secretary E. Thomas Wetzel today told Rep. Henry B. Anderson, Jr. (D-MN) the chances of the Congressman getting approval for a Navy friendship agreement between the U.S. and China are approximately zero.

When queried during a House Armed Services Committee hearing about what portion of the Navy's budget would be spent on building better relations with various world navies, including that of the People's Republic of China, Wetzel said the Navy's mission was "to fight and win wars with those who would be our enemy, and in winning such wars that might arise we will be sure to destroy to the best of our ability the entire fighting power of any enemy navy we encounter. This means ships, aircraft, submarines and personnel." Wetzel continued his testimony by saying: "If such an event was to arise, and I sincerely hope it does not, there will be no need for any friendship agreement with any enemy country."

Representative Anderson has been a vocal advocate for most favored nation trading status for China, and the Navy friendship agreement concept. He has stressed the importance of the MFN trade measure to farmers in his state and several others.

A three-term House member, Anderson recently declared his intentions to run for the U.S. Senate in the

upcoming November elections. He faces moderately stiff opposition from the veteran incumbent Republican Senator, Robert T. Larson.

Today's confrontation came during House hearings into the FY-1999 Defense Department budget, currently proposed at $288 billion dollars.

-end-

CHAPTER 12 - MING & CHING THINGS

September 7, 1998: Georgetown

Admiral Loo lived up to his promises setting up Madam Lily Shin in a first class shop at 35th and Prospect Streets, NW, the heart of Washington's swanky suburban Georgetown. Named Ming & Ching Things, it had an inventory of the best and most expensive original Chinese art treasures, antiques and collectibles.

New but affordable antiques occupied one section. Basically knockoffs of the real ones, Chinese workers turned them out daily and they looked as if they had been around for 200 years. Claiming that she was certain these goods were original, Lily had no problem passing them off as originals.

The desk phone rang; she answered and smiled, recognizing her daughter's voice. "How nice of you to call, my dear. I know you are busy at school work, but I can not wait to see you again and show you what I've done with the shop since you were here last."

Brief family conversation was exchanged, and then Madam Shin said: "Yes, most of my customers are rich Americans. A rude lot, always pushing their way around the shop and demanding to bargain, just like they told me they did while on vacation in Asia. Ugly Americans abroad, still ugly Americans at home. They probably think those Filipinos are just more Chinese," she laughed and listened to more about her daughter's apparently exciting life in Washington.

"Okay, Cheryl, you can tell me more at dinner on Sunday. Be at my apartment at five and we shall chat about things before we dine. Fine, see you then."

Madam Shin didn't bother with the regular customers, except the really wealthy ones who knew what merchandise was original and what wasn't. With them she would spend as much time as necessary, ordering quality art treasures from her best contacts in Hong Kong, Shanghai and Beijing.

51

She spent most of her time at local civic group meetings and Chinese functions, but concentrated on cultivating new contacts in the U.S. government. Her training a decade before had stood her well, gaining her a most highly respected post in the worldwide Chinese intelligence organization, a post she was most proud of. Most importantly, she knew her business.

She reported locally to the Chinese Ambassador at the PRC Embassy in D.C., but Madam Shin took great pride in knowing that ultimately she reported to none other than the deputy director of all PRC overseas spies, a close friend named David Wong.

At 5 pm Sunday Cheryl arrived for dinner and a little mother-daughter chit-chat. Sharing a typical Chinese dinner the two brought each other current on their lives and then Cheryl said she had to leave. Busy school day tomorrow.

After picking up the few dinner dishes they used, Madam Shin returned to her Chinese-character equipped computer, and reviewed a short list of U.S. Navy Intelligence Service and government personnel she had been ordered to get to know. Each of them she had met either socially or at her shop, and the relationship with them was, at this point, strictly business. Luckily for her, their impressive dossiers indicated each was single, divorced, separated or just unhappy in their current relationships. A cat-like smile crept across her face as she thought: that makes stalking my prey far easier. Everyone knows American men lust after enchanting Asian women!

She wondered which of the two men she had selected would become her best top-secret source; a smart young lieutenant commander in the CNOs office who was also a computer geek qualified in submarines, or that very vocal U.S. Congressman the Embassy identified as being pro-China who was also running for the U.S. Senate in November.

She had reviewed each man's file, had photos of them on and off their jobs, was familiar with their habits and was now trying to find any Achilles' heels they might have. "Eeney, meeny, miney, say! Which man will agree to play? It will be Hank."

CHAPTER 13 - BACK TO THE WELL

October 9, 1998: The Pentagon

"I'm really getting to like this town," I told Ray Kinny as we sat at the Roundtable nursing a full pitcher of beer. "D.C. during Indian Summer is really very nice, and if winter is as mild as you say it can be I could call this place home."

"Enjoy this lull in the action, Dan. With all the politicians back at home making last minute Congressional campaign appearances, this is a decent place to be right now. But believe me, they'll be back in full force in a few weeks, organizing for the new session, with several new players or some of the old ones in new jobs."

"Like that wild man from Minnesota, Henry Anderson? I won't soon forget that confrontation between him and Navy Secretary Wetzel. There was no love lost between those two!"

"Anderson's support for Communist China will get him in bigger trouble, mark my word," Kinny said, as he polished off his mug of beer. "And if he returns here as a Senator, which all the polls say he will, he'll be hell bent to introduce legislation to get his military friendship bill passed. That MFN trading recognition for China appears to have enough votes to pass and the President supports it, so look for more Made-in-China labels in your shoes, on cameras, your jock straps and most any piece of electronic gear."

It really is ironic, Dan thought to himself. All this MFN business and how China has become a major player in world trade is just so much crap to cover-up the fact that the loot they've raked in has helped put the U.S. in its current trade deficit, and has mostly gone to upgrading their military and purchasing or building the new ships and hardware needed to become a global military force.

Noon arrived, four more Roundtablers joined us, and we talked baseball playoffs and World Serious speculation as we devoured lunch. Pulling Kinny out of the baseball discussion, I asked: "This China business is really important, isn't it?"

"Priority number one, buddy. My editor is forever asking for more pieces on the Chinese Navy buildup. Makes for good copy, gets the troops motivated about 7th Fleet duty, and, frankly, it has the makings of a real live shooting war if we don't watch what we're doing."

"I think I ought to call Admiral Sharpe again, and see if he's willing to give me a backgrounder on the Chinese Navy and what we're doing about it, if we are doing anything."

I said so-long to everyone and headed back to my office. As soon as I got there and had returned the two worthless messages left on my voice mail, I dialed the Pentagon and asked to speak with Admiral Sharpe. He came right on the line, greeting me like an old friend.

"How you doing, Dan? Nice piece you did on us. Got all the facts right and did what you said you would; leave the interpretation up to the reader. What can I do for you today, young man?"

"Well sir, as you know the Chinese Navy seems to be in the news a lot these days. I got my first interest in them when I was invited to spend a day on the USS NASHVILLE. You know that story. From then on I've come to learn that these guys are really up to no good, worldwide. Ray Kinny from Navy Times, who says to say hello, suggested I ask you to give me an off the record backgrounder on the PRC Navy so when story opportunities come up I can write from a far more knowledgeable point of view."

Silence prevailed for several seconds before Sharpe firmly said: "I'll do it on three conditions. Number one; only you will be privy to what I say. That means no sharing of information with any of your colleagues even if they work with you at PANS. Number two; I will never, repeat never, be attributed as your source."

"So far, no problem, sir. I imagine the third condition is I give you my first born and half my retirement pay," I quipped, hoping the admiral would take it in the lighthearted manner in which it was offered.

"The Navy pays me what this old sailor needs to live on, and you should definitely hold off with that extra kid stuff. However, I'll save the third condition until our meeting. Then you can either say yes or no."

We agreed and set next Friday afternoon, the 9th at sixteen hundred hours, for the meeting. Must be the old man likes to leave the Pentagon early on Fridays, I figured.

Arriving ten minutes early at the CNO conference room, I was getting my tape recorder set when Janice Cannon strode into the room. Damn, I thought to myself, how can one sailor be so alluring? Through her uniform I could see her legs started down there and went all the way up...never mind! I jumped up and greeted her: "How ya doin, Commander Cannon?" She smiled, took my hand with both of hers and said: "Just call me Janice, okay?"

"That works for me. I'm currently researching some stories about Asia and maybe you can give me a more human look into the area. Perhaps over dinner? Soon? You know, some details about your time in China? I've been to Hong Kong many times and I'll bet we've got lots of things of mutual interest to talk about."

"Sounds like fun, Dan. Call me Monday morning after I've checked my calendar and we'll set a date."

The admiral arrived precisely on time, saving me from saying anything stupid to her like: "Maybe we can have breakfast the next morning, too." With a wink Janice quietly excused herself.

Nonchalantly I said: "Afternoon Admiral. And that third condition is? Or is it that I'll have to learn about the PRC Navy by volunteering for a tour on one of their ships?"

"No, nothing as drastic as that. I'm not at liberty to go into certain areas of submarine development. However, from articles you've written on the Air Force stealth bomber I know you're aware that a stealth submarine is an on-going Navy goal. But just what we're doing about it, what our designers have done, or if there even is a current stealth sub project underway, I can not confirm nor deny, officially."

"That's fine, Admiral, I have no problem with security and the need to prevent such developments from falling into the wrong hands." Sounding like John Wayne in one of his movies about World War II, I said: "I'm an American first and a journalist second, so don't worry that I'll ever leak anything classified in my stories."

The admiral smiled and went on: "Because you're an ex-submariner, with top-secret clearance when you were on active duty, you should know about a recent success. So here comes condition number three. Promise that you'll not use this information in anything you write until I give the okay."

Nodding affirmative I said: "Agreed."

"Very well. Earlier I told you I could not confirm or deny that the Navy is developing a stealth submarine. Well, for five years we've been doing just that. Prior to my current assignment I headed that operation and although we've made some headway we haven't come up with the final answer. Several news people have speculated about us but their guesstimates about how it would work are just that, guesses."

After taking detailed notes for thirty minutes, I knew much of everything there was to know about developing an undetectable submarine and also had the real story about China and its growing Navy. Both topics would give me a wealth of info for future stories. After putting away the tape recorder and closing my notebook I got up to leave.

"Dan," Sharpe said, waving me back into my chair, "there are a couple more things you could do to help us out. Great ideas come from all sorts of places, and as a former submariner you might just have an idea that would help with a stealth submarine design. It may only be a wild dream, but if you think it should be evaluated, let me know.

"You talk with lots of interesting people, and learn about projects we might not know about. If it's within the bounds of journalistic ethics, I'd like to hear about anything regarding submarines or activities with navies other than our own, particularly China. This is purely voluntary, mind you, and you're to tell me only if you feel it's something we'd not be getting from other sources."

"I can't imagine Intel doesn't know everything about every project in the world already, Admiral, but I will do it. If I learn of anything that sounds remotely interesting on the subject, you'll be the first, after me, to know about it."

"I can't ask for anything better than that," Bernie Sharpe replied. "We'll talk again soon, I hope. So long, Dan."

CHAPTER 14 - DATE WITH AN ANGEL

October 12, 1998: Washington, D.C.

"Dan, I'm glad you called," Janice murmured in that soft voice. "But I'm drafting a message that has to get chopped by the captain in 30 minutes. Can I call you back after I finish?"

"Fine. I'll be waiting. Bye."

I puttered around, updating my list of future feature stories. The mail came and contained only bills and solicitations from experts who wanted to show me how to make a million dollars by investing in gold, soybean futures, or some other such scam. When my private line rang just before 11 am, I grabbed it and blurted out "Dan Lincoln!"

"It's me, Dan. The message is done and things are a lot quieter now. Sorry for not being able to talk with you earlier."

"Understood Janice. I'm glad you're not at GQ anymore. I know how Monday morning madness goes. How was your weekend?"

"Oh, I slept most of Saturday morning, did a little shopping and lounged around the rest of the time. This job keeps me spinning to the point where some weekends I just crash and then get ready for it all to begin all over again on Mondays."

"Well, let's break the cycle. My dinner offer still stands. I'd very much like for us to get to know each other a little better." I was flying now, visualizing us together first at dinner, later over a brandy and some soft music, and finally making love in my big brass bed.

"This week is chock-a-block and Saturday I fly out to San Diego, but my plane doesn't leave until 3 pm. So, does Friday night sound good?" she cooed.

Trying to be casual I still blurted: "You bet it does. I'll pick you up at 6:30 and we'll dine at the Irongate Inn. Ever been there?"

"I was there once and loved it. Sounds great to me. I live in Braddock Heights in Alexandria. I'll e-mail you the directions."

"I'll be there with bells on. Well, actually, I'll be there in a dark green Mazda Miata. See you then."

Janice's directions proved easy to follow and when she opened the door I felt the gates to heaven had swung wide open. Her clingy hunter green sweater suit left little to my already over-worked imagination. The drive back into the city was a breeze, since all the traffic was coming out and our lanes moved right along. There was some of the perfunctory first date chit-chat, but I couldn't stop taking sidelong glances at this lithe lovely woman.

Arriving at the Irongate, the maitre'd Bertrand greeted us saying: "Nice to have you with us again, Mr. Lincoln." I discreetly slipped him a bribe as he took us to a secluded dimly lit booth. I noticed him giving Janice a good look, then nodding toward me his approval. This guy sees hundreds of Washington's finest females so she must really be something special.

We made small talk about our jobs and the Navy until the waiter arrived and we ordered dinner. As we ate Janice turned the tables becoming the inquiring one, I the interviewee. She wanted to know everything about me from journalism school to my Navy days and right up to PANS. Not being exactly shy and retiring I regaled her with tales from my somewhat colorful past. Realizing I was hogging the spotlight I maneuvered conversation around to Janice's Asian experiences.

As it worked out both of us had dined at several of the same Hong Kong restaurants, gone to many of the same clubs and even knew a few friends of friends, mostly on Navy or embassy staffs.

"My father got an average-only fitness report from the ambassador in Hong Kong, preventing him from making admiral. Shortly after that he retired and took a local sales job exporting electronic products from mainland China, eventually becoming a major player in China-America trade.

Mom died five years ago and he's retired but still lives out there. He's got a great flat on the island overlooking the harbor and Kowloon."

"One of these days I'll get to China. I know there are a ton of stories I could do that I can only get if I actually go to the PRC."

"Work on it, then. Let your bosses and maybe some other folks know of your interests, and perhaps Beijing will become closer than you think."

When the dinner, dessert and wine were gone, we were too. Outside, my Miata had miraculously appeared, and the valet had the door open for Janice. We both had a nice glow on, but nothing that prevented me from driving. With heart pounding I suggested we go to my place, which was close, for a nightcap and more conversation about Honolulu, Hong Kong, and the Navy. To my delight she agreed.

As Janice settled her limber body on my sofa drawing those long legs under her, I put on a new CD by a terrific Italian singer I had recently discovered, Andrea Bocelli. His singing was the perfect setting for what I hoped would be a perfect ending to our evening.

"What can I pour for you?" I asked the lady.

"I'm really not a big drinker, but perhaps just a small snifter of brandy?"

I poured a Courvoisier for each of us. In a few minutes Bocelli was into his fourth song: 'E Sara' A Settembre,' Italian for Someone Like You, and about my favorite song on the CD. By the time the brandies were long gone we had soared into the wild blue yonder. Unfortunately what I had hoped would lead us straight to my big brass bed, didn't.

"This has been great, Dan, but I'm not ready to take our new relationship to higher ground, yet," Janice said in a low and slow voice. "I like you very much, and want to spend more time with you, but tonight is not right for me. Give us some time to know each other better, and then we'll see about other things. I've got that flight to San Diego tomorrow so I'd better go home now and get a good night's sleep before the trip."

Manfully concealing my disappointment I gallantly said: "Your wish is my command. Home it is and we'll talk about other things when you get back from the Coast."

The ride to Janice's apartment was quick and after kissing her good-night I headed back home. Picking up the place from dinner could wait until morning. I couldn't believe how exhilarated I felt, having just entered the presence of an angel so I restarted the CD, poured myself another brandy and sat back listening until Mr. Bocelli had sung his last song.

CHAPTER 15 - PRAIRIE HOME POLITICIAN

November 3, 1998: Minneapolis, Minnesota

By the autumn of 1998 Linda Anderson had endured all the politics she could and longed to return home to Minnesota permanently, to resume a simpler family life with their children on their ranch.   On the way back from the election victory celebration at the Minneapolis Hilton she let Hank have it with both barrels.

"I can't take this life anymore, Hank. They're all so phony in D.C., not just the wives but all the players in that big game of politics. I feel myself being dragged down to their level of clawing and conniving and I will *not* allow myself to join them. I want out, Hank. Just let me come home and you can stay in Georgetown and become a huge senatorial success. You can say I'm ill or had to be here to help my elderly mother, or whatever, but let me out of this horrible lifestyle."

Coldly, Hank snipped: "Nicely put, darling, but neither you nor I are leaving. We will keep up on our social contacts and smile when in public. I will *not* allow you to run back to the land of milk and make believe. You *will* maintain our Georgetown home and you *will* be Mrs. Senator Anderson anytime the occasion calls for it!"

Don't ever forget: you are Mrs. Senator Henry B. Anderson, Jr., and you *will* love being a part of anything I wish to do in this city. You *will* love the Senate, my people and what I do for my country." He was now yelling at his cowering wife: "*We love Washington.* Understand?"

Hank felt a surge of power rush through him. He was now a United States Senator, one of only 100 select politicians in the nation to make it to the top of the legislative branch of government.   After six years in the House he had been encouraged by none other than the President himself to run for the higher chamber. "If a good old boy like me can make it to the White House, you can make it across the Capitol to the

Senate," he told Anderson. Hank enjoyed broad support from the party and his newest political friends in Washington. There were also new and truly outstanding social contacts in the city, contacts that could help the soon-to-be senator move up the steps of power in the U.S. government. Perhaps even greater things awaited Hank, or at least that's what many of his new friends, who had a lot more experience than he did, told him.

MINNESOTA ELECTS PRO-CHINESE SENATOR BEIJING BEEFS-UP CHINA'S NAVY

By: Dan Lincoln

Washington, D.C. November 8, 1998 (Pacific & Asia News Service):

Former Representative Henry B. Anderson, Jr. was elected to the U.S. Senate last Tuesday, ousting conservative G-O-P incumbent Robert T. Larson.
Anderson has been making headlines recently with his calls for immediate Most Favored Nation trade status for the Peoples Republic of China and his clash with Navy Secretary E. Thomas Wetzel before a House Armed Services Committee hearing last August. Then Rep. Anderson had asked Secretary Wetzel what portion of the Navy's budget would be spent on developing military friendship agreements with current enemy countries, including such an accord with the Chinese Navy. Wetzel's response basically suggested that hell would freeze over before the U.S. would negotiate such an agreement.
At the same time Americans are being asked to seek better relations with mainland China, the Beijing government has called for new efforts to expand its current Navy, particularly in the area of surface warships and nuclear attack submarines.
The Chinese have reportedly held talks with the French and Russians about design and building of new aircraft carriers, and have bought three former Soviet

carriers, the *KIEV*, *MINSK* and the *VARYAG*. So far, they have not refurbished or made any attempt to operate them.

They have also bought two Russian SOVREMENNYY class guided missile destroyers. These 8,500 ton warships carry surface to air missiles, an anti-submarine helicopter, torpedo tubes, mine launchers and the latest radar and sonar equipment. The first of the two, the *HANGZHOU*, is expected to be delivered to Shanghai late next year and the second, the *FUZHOU*, will enter their fleet in 2000. It is expected that they will also soon unveil two new Beijing-designed DDGs, with what they call Type 052B and 052C hulls. These ships will add the capability of vertically launched surface to air missiles with a range of about 50 nautical miles.

Equally as important is the Chinese submarine program. They reportedly have under construction two of what they say will be four XIA class ballistic missile nuclear subs. To be home ported at their Qingdao Navy base, these 7,000 ton boats will carry 16 submarine launched missiles, each with multiple warheads.

An equally ambitious program is their HAN class nuclear attack submarine. These are the first to be totally Chinese designed and built. Five of them have been completed over the past decade. They will be augmented with four KILO class submarines purchased from the Russians and now in the active Chinese Fleet.

Probably the biggest threat to U.S. Navy and allied control of the Western Pacific would come from the proposed sale of two of Russia's latest nuclear submarines. They are known as AKULA class subs and are capable of speeds up to 35 knots and a reported diving depth of approximately 1,800 feet.

China's military forces are called The People's Liberation Army, and include over one million soldiers, and another 360,000 in the PLA Navy, Air Force and Marines.

-end-

CHAPTER 16 - A MOMENT IN HISTORY

January 10, 1999: Capitol Hill

The icy chill of January was at its peak, while the political climate was heating up fast. Congress was back in session, and though it wasn't an election year, Hank stood to garner a big prize next year. Senator Randall Potter of Rhode Island, the current ranking minority leader of the Senate Armed Services Committee, would probably lose his bid for re-election and Hank could vault to the number one minority position on this most important committee.

Hank was due in the committee hearing room for another top secret Pentagon briefing about the Navy's newest submarine developments and requests for additional funding. With his House Armed Services Committee position and earlier Navy briefings, he felt qualified to view the materials and make decisions on funding.

"Morning Senator Potter," Hank greeted his superior colleague and soon to be a former senator, he hoped. "I trust you had a most happy holiday season? Sounds like this should be an interesting session today!"

"Good morning, Henry," said the smiling Democrat from Providence. "We did indeed enjoy being home with the winter snow, the grandchildren and all the parties, but it looks like I'll have my hands full when the election rolls around. I need all the exposure I can get with the electorate so I best get involved in what the Navy is planning, do some research on which way the voters are thinking and get on that bandwagon." Hank took his seat at the committee table, the chairman gaveled the session into order and turned the floor over to the Navy.

"Good morning, gentlemen, I'm Rear Admiral Bernard Sharpe from the Office of the CNO, and today's briefing will be limited to new developments in submarine design and weaponry. When I'm finished, you'll be briefed on the Navy's requests for special funding for FY-99/00. I ask you to hold your questions until the end of our presentation."

The room was quiet, more from politeness than interest. These senators had heard hundreds of military briefings, all sales pitches for this new missile or that super carrier. Why would this one be any different?

The one star admiral began: "Let me first outline some of the reasons why we're proceeding in the direction we are, toward achieving a totally new submarine that can defy detection by any person, sonar, radar, computer or other listening device on the face of the earth or below it. We're not there yet but we are making great strides."

He continued: "The major opponent will be China, with its huge navy and a program they call Sea Denial to challenge any other fleet. Today they have three major fleets: the North Fleet, headquartered at Qingdao, with responsibility for the Yellow Sea ops area; the East Sea Fleet, operated from Ningbo which is near Shanghai; and their South Sea Fleet, based near Hong Kong at a place called Zhanjiang. This is the fleet we most often deal with as they patrol the South China Sea where our Seventh Fleet CVBGs operate. The PRC Navy also maintains a basic coastal defense posture along a line from Korea south to Taiwan, and we expect China to extend that area on to Japan and the Philippines by 2015, giving them their Sea Denial Navy."

Several senators chatted quietly, or signed bills, and then returned their attention to Admiral Sharpe.

"They have 52 submarines and are planning on having a blue water SSBN and SSN fleet, but they're behind schedule on design and construction. They currently have one SSBN and five HAN class SSN boats in the fleet. The HANs are of their own design and construction, and quite a good boat, if not a bit noisy. They've also been plagued with high radiation levels which stopped production on several occasions. The PRC has over 100 shipyards, the key ones being in Shanghai, Guangzhou and on Yulin Island. They have submarine bases at the first two locations and at Bohai and Hainan Islands, the latter only four miles off their coast. They acquired several new yards when they recently took over Hong Kong."

The stoic faces around the table gave Sharpe no indication which way his message was being received, if at all.

A Navy Lieutenant JG quietly adjusted the final focus on a slide projector and nodded to her boss. A color map of the region appeared. Sharpe used a laser penlight to illustrate his next point. "Gentlemen, this is a map of the South China Sea area, above Singapore, between the Philippines and Vietnam and below China. Not very important to the U.S. in the overall scheme of things but vital in two specific areas are the Spratly Islands, right here. Making matters worse is the fact that five countries lay claim to the Spratlys; Taiwan, the Philippines, Vietnam, Malaysia and the Peoples Republic of China. Also, the tiny but oil-rich Sultanate of Brunei has filed a maritime claim to the islands as well."

"These strategic islands have potentially a huge reserve of natural gas which the Philippines has been exploring for years, and may someday be of importance to us. It's currently of vital interest to many of our Asian allies. More important to the U.S. right now is the strategic location the Spratlys play in the trans-Pacific shipping of oil from the Middle East, through the Straits of Malacca, and up to the key cities of Southeast Asia, then on to our allies in Japan and even to Hawaii and the U.S. West Coast.

The waterways around the Spratlys could be barricaded by a belligerent Navy such as China, forcing container ships, oil tankers and even U.S. warships to go thousands of miles out of their way instead of via a direct sea crossing."

Now the senators were listening. No more business as usual atmosphere as their stony faces were coming alive.

The committee chairman, Senator Donald M. Walther of Arizona, a highly decorated Navy fighter pilot during the Vietnam War, interrupted: "Admiral, are our ships now being held up when sailing past the Spratlys?"

"No, Senator. But we can't allow this ever to happen, and for that very reason we regularly send 7th Fleet ships down that channel even with Chinese warships in the same waters."

"Gentlemen, let me now share with you the latest developments in achieving a total deterrent advantage over the PRC, and all enemies for that matter; a total stealth submarine."

That did it. Bernie Sharpe had them. Eyes widened and bodies leaned forward as if on cue. This was a supernal moment in history. Slides came onto the screen showing a cutaway of a nuclear submarine. The admiral continued:

"I'm sure it is not necessary to remind you that what I am about to show you is top secret and for your eyes only. We understand that you are aware of the importance of what we're doing, but it would be catastrophic to national security if any of this leaked out. What I show and tell you today must remain in this room."

They all acknowledged agreement by pushing the aye voting button on their desks, and the admiral continued. "Here's one of our SEAWOLF class boats. Only three of these will be built but we're madding them the quietest subs ever by adding a new high powered propulsion system focused on delivering lower engine RPMs to give us greater stealth on the surface and especially when submerged.

"With our new 21st century VIRGINIA class boats, under construction as we speak, quiet will come incrementally. Each boat we commission will have taken advantage of new efforts to achieve maximum quiet that are being developed. What's new today will be updated by something even better and harder to detect in 2002 and 2005, etc."

All nineteen senators were measuring the admiral's every word now. One was writing them down; Henry Anderson knew full well that the man who was going to lead the call for closer ties with Red China had to understand every move being made in this giant and rapidly unfolding political chess game.

"By the time we commission the sixth VIRGINIA class boat it will have electric drive, be very very quiet, use more powerful propulsion and have both moving and stationary propellers to force water through the props. We've created props that have a baffle around them, much like an aircraft jet engine, that allows the water to enter, be propelled out, and directed in any direction by turning the baffle. You might compare it to an Everglades water boat with those big enclosed fans they use to propel the boat."

"And finally, gentlemen," Admiral Sharpe concluded, "the Air Force has the stealth bomber. Soon the Navy will have the stealth submarine. We recently developed what we call laminar flow and are testing it on boats in both fleets. Basically, it's a procedure where we discharge a gel-like substance from several spray heads in the submarine's bow and the gel flows back over the boat's exterior, reducing friction and making it quieter as it runs through the water. The Russians tested a similar compound a few years ago but their gel didn't work. Some say the problem was they used toothpaste gel, not stealth gel!"

A few titters filled the room, and Senator Walther gaveled it quickly back into silence. He then turned to the naval officer and said: "Thank you Admiral Sharpe for a very significant briefing. You can be assured this information will remain with this committee. Let's adjourn for 15 minutes and when we come back I am sure there will be more questions for you. This committee stands in recess."

CHAPTER 17 - KUNG HEE FAT CHOY

January 23, 1999: PRC Embassy, Washington, D.C.

The Chinese Embassy, originally a typical red brick estate, stood on a quiet Georgetown street. The exterior had been altered to look more like a landmark than a historic old D.C. residence. It boasted red painted exterior trim, arch-like entrance, and oversized portraits of current Chinese leaders and a few old revolutionaries like Chairman Mao. The embassy's facade was the perfect winter overcoat for the inside; a Chinese-flavored Circle de Soleil.

A light snow fell as Senator Anderson got out of the cab. He thought of the clamor and chaos often surrounding this place. Pickets, human rights advocates, D.C. police and the ever-present parade of the anti-China lobby. Tonight all was quiet outside.

Inside it was lively theater, with the noise of drums and cymbals, the din of firecrackers and the forty foot long dragon dancing around the huge ballroom. This was Hank's first Chinese New Year's celebration and he was enjoying the attractions. As he drank heartily from a flute of champagne, his host appeared and bowed politely to China's staunchest new ally on Capitol Hill.

"Great party, Ambassador Wu. Thank you for inviting me," Hank said bowing to the impeccably dressed silver-haired Beijing diplomat. "I particularly like all these great hors d'oeuvres, especially those little dumplings with the red pork inside."

"Those are dim sum, Senator, steamed cakes and dumplings that have become very popular here in the West, especially in Hawaii. A very large Chinese population there, as you know."

"I've been looking forward to this evening for quite awhile, sir, and I'm sure the new year will be great for both our countries."

Draining his glass, Hank proclaimed: "I have accepted Beijing's gracious invitation to visit your great country this spring. I'll be there for the May Day parade and hopefully will get to see many of your beautiful and interesting cities. Being somewhat of a Chinese history buff I'm looking forward to the great museums of Beijing and perhaps Shanghai as well!"

"History we can give you Senator, thousands of years of it. After the lion dance please sit at my table for dinner."

"I would indeed like that, Mr. Ambassador."

Only three other U.S. senators were invited tonight, two from the majority party, his colleague the minority leader of the Senate Armed Services Committee and the Under Secretary of State for Chinese Affairs. Also a few people who would be with him on the trip, including the head of one a big California farm worker union.

Strolling around the ballroom, enjoying the activity and tasting everything offered by the lovely young Chinese waitresses, he thought to himself: these people are sharp as a tack. I believe they want to be our friends, but we'll no doubt have to pay a price for that public show of mutual affection. Next week I'll give Charlie Finkel, head of the Chinese American Friendship Society, a call and see what his group is all about.

Dinner was announced and Senator Anderson was seated next to Fred Y.Y. Tong who identified himself as the embassy's cultural attaché, and who in turn introduced Hank to the woman on his left, a stunning Asian beauty named Madam Lily Shin.

The attaché said Lily owned Ming & Ching Things, one of Washington's finest shops featuring rare Chinese art sculpture and other collectable items. He added that Madam Shin had emigrated from Hong Kong last summer and considered Georgetown her new American hometown.

The senator turned to the lovely lady and said: "My honor, Madam Shin. I'll have to visit your shop one day soon?" Lily gave him a knowing bow of her head and a very welcoming smile indicating she understood he was looking forward to much more than just learning about Oriental art.

Hank pegged her at about 40, plus or minus a couple years, height 5 foot 5, weight near110 pounds and he marveled at her deep black eyes, coifed hair and perfect skin. She wasn't very large in the chest department, he thought, but then how many Orientals were?

The evening proved to be more than Hank could have hoped for. He chatted briefly about his job in the Senate and then pushed the conversation to talk of Madam Shin and her antique shop. By 10 pm Henry Anderson was thoroughly entranced with everything Chinese, including the marvelous Madam Shin.

She left Hong Kong in 1998 when Fred Tong, who she knew through art business friends, suggested she move to Washington. Now living in what she described as a delightfully decorated and furnished apartment above my shop at 35th and Prospect, Madam Shin had become very westernized in a very short time.

From the moment they met Hank craved her body, and since they lived only six blocks apart he suggested they share a cab when the evening at the embassy ended. The idea met with a favorable smile, but unknowingly the new senator had opened an Asian floodgate he would later deeply regret opening.

When they arrived at her combination shop and upstairs apartment about 11 p.m. they were effortlessly on a first name basis. Lily suggested a brief tour of the store and after a quick walk through, Hank said: "Obviously, the antique business is doing well and good luck seems to be with you in this brand new year. It must take a very smart lady to have done so well so quickly. Many of my friends would envy your success."

"We are gaining prominence. I'm very committed to the shop and have several contacts in China from whom I get my merchandise. But after living here, even for less than a year, I know I can never return to China. It's just too different for me now. I love America and I'm filing the paperwork to become a citizen."

"That's great! What America needs now is more knowledgeable businesswomen. I'm in favor of China becoming an even better friend of our country. Lily, you're going to be very happy as an American. Is there anything I can do to get your citizenship paperwork moving along?"

"I don't know just yet. But if I do need some help or guidance could I call on you for advice?"

"Of course! Here's my card with my private phone number on the back. Call me any time you need me."

What Hank really wanted to say was "call me right now to your bedroom," but knew that wouldn't work. Thanking her for the tour, he bowed politely and headed out into the fresh air and the walk back home. An overnight over the antique shop would have to wait for another time. Little did the naive Hank suspect what Madam Shin had planned for him.

CHAPTER 18 - OPERATION QUIET

March 14, 1999: The Virginia Capes Operations Area

It was over two years ago, in a brief ceremony at the CNO's office, that Captain F. B. Buzz Russell had relieved Captain Bernie Sharpe as head of N-771. A veteran submariner, Russell served in fast attack and ballistic missile submarines in both fleets, and had been on the list for deep selection to captain last year. A 1978 graduate of Annapolis, Russell was the perfect choice to head this secret operation because he thoroughly knew submarines and nuclear propulsion, but most importantly he knew how to keep his mouth shut. Now, after nearly two years in this job, he was reflective.

He'd been Sharpe's XO on the USS SCRANTON, an L.A. class attack boat home ported in Norfolk, Virginia. Like his mentor, Captain Russell was committed to the quest to develop the world's first stealth submarine and missile delivery system. Buzz knew the cat and mouse game of how the original funding came about, privately thanking Admiral Rickover, and made sure that each year's Navy budget included a renewal of funding for his little development project.

So far no nosy Navy brass or Congressional committees had learned of or shown any interest in the project, and he was able to keep it alive with little or no opposition.

But now with so many secret Navy projects going on and so many other problems surfacing for the President, Captain Russell figured he really didn't need to worry about his operation. He was right.

His staff had grown to 20 people including active duty personnel and civilians, a dozen at a computer software company in Alexandria, and the ever-present intelligence types. Buzz had code-named the project *Operation Quiet*. After reviewing the work by Sharpe's team, he knew at that point any truly silent boat didn't exist, and he also knew making major structural or even propulsion modifications to the current fleet was a waste of money.

Buzz was determined to build a submarine that would do for undersea warfare what the Air Force's stealth bomber had done for air-to-air and air-to ground combat. If he couldn't achieve this by end of spring, he would propose closing N-771 and retire.

The new hull design he wanted was the most recently modified version of the SEAWOLF class boats because Buzz knew they were the quietest available. Only three would be built, serving as a bridge between the older LOS ANGELES class and the now approved VIRGINIA class fast attack boats. The last of this interim trio of submarines, USS JIMMY CARTER, was due to be commissioned in 2003 or 2004. Buzz got approval to try some of his experiments on the SEAWOLF itself.

A few million dollars and 18 months had been spent redesigning the boat's propeller shaft creating a one-foot wide tunnel around it. The tunnel would be permanently flooded with oil so the prop shaft could not be detected while spinning, thus denying the enemy any sonar contact. In a simulator mock-up of the proposed system the shaft floated in its bed of oil but the props still generated enough noise to be picked up by an average sonar operator.

Another project involved building torpedoes to magnetically home in on a target, ostensibly a steel hulled ship or submarine, but they failed miserably during testing off Norfolk. One was fired at a target ship five miles away but also sensed another steel target ship three miles away and took it out rather than the programmed vessel!

Buzz Russell and his *Operation Quiet* team found themselves persona non grata with CINCLANTFLT. He didn't look forward to providing reports of these episodes to those who regularly briefed the Senate Armed Service Committee, knowing the details would draw a huge laugh from those experts on the Hill.

Disheartened but not defeated, his team continued to come up with new ideas.   One was based on the fact that private industry was constantly working on improved communications because they had more engineers and scientists and bigger budgets than the Navy.   So, N-771 set up a new program called Advanced Replacement Commercial Installations, purchasing the newest of what private industry had on the shelf.   In other words, don't waste time trying to develop what the private sector already had in the pipeline. Buy theirs and don't try to re-invent the wheel.

CHAPTER 19 - AN UNEXPECTED INVITATION

March 26, 1999: Washington, D.C.

Winter had finally melted. The cherry blossoms along the Mall were about to pop with the expectation of a million tourists over the next four weeks. If Courier and Ives did springtime this was the perfect place for their work.

Growing up in Buffalo you got to know the best and the worst of that season. This winter was a lot warmer for me, what with sharing frequent overnights with Janice because after her return from San Diego we hit it off perfectly. We both enjoyed our independence so a long-term commitment never entered our minds.

The thought of being paired up with the same person for life, as my parents did, was just not acceptable. I'm sure Janice remembered that she really never had any family life, what with her father moving all over the world for the Navy.

We dined out once in a while but most nights she'd cook dinner for us, either at her place or mine, and we'd pass the evening listening to CDs and talking shop. I soon got the needle from my mates asking why I wasn't on my C-C Roundtable stool as much these days. "Why should I sit in a dark gin joint with a bunch of yahoos when I could be in the arms of my femme fatale?"

I had pumped out three dozen by-lined stories in three months, my star at PANS was rising, and Ben Huntley was springing for my lunches. Hell, the time was ripe for a risk. I knocked on Ben's office door and laid it on the line. "Ben, I want a week's leave to go back to Honolulu, get some sun and surf, and talk story with my old friends. My batteries need a charge!"

You could have knocked me over with a ti leaf when he said: "Fine but wait a month so I can cover your beat."

Setting what must have been record for tying up loose ends, I locked my desk, turned off the computer, and told

Rhonda the Receptionist that I'd be at the C-C, not to be disturbed unless the government fell or the Pentagon burned down.

It was only 4 pm but the long bar was already SRO. I recognized a couple staffers from congressional committees, an Air Force guy I had met a few times at the Pentagon, and a hopefully growing number of ladies. Janice and I may have been close but with no long-term commitments party-loving females were still high on my list of favorite pastimes. Pushing through the C-C to our Roundtable I grabbed the last empty barstool.

Apparently at least two of the guys had been there since lunch; the empty glasses and MGD bottles were jammed in among today's papers, menus, salt & pepper shakers, phony sugar packs and a paper napkin-filled mug.

God, I thought, if my conservative parents saw me now in this gin mill with these clowns they'd revoke their support for my journalism career.

I shot the shit with the guys for awhile and then Sung Jiang gave me a forced smile and said he had a surprise for me. The other guys laughed when the Washington Post warned me to "be wary of Chinese bearing surprises. It may be an invitation to visit one of their prisons for foreign correspondents!"

Jiang motioned for me to follow him and we lucked into a table up front just as two women were leaving. Jiang said: "I see you are filing many stories. Good stories and very much balanced. I sent several, especially those that have anything to do with China, to the Chinese Ambassador here and to my government back in Beijing. They are all most impressed with your work and style."

I nodded my thanks.

"Dan, Ambassador J.C. Wu and the Government of the Peoples Republic of China have asked me to present this to you."

I took the small ivory envelope Jiang offered and saw the flag of the People's Republic on the front of what appeared to be a formal invitation:

The Peoples Republic of China requests your presence at the May Day Celebration and Parade in Beijing, May 1st, 1999.

You shall enjoy a special charter flight from Honolulu to Beijing on April 29th.   All hotel accommodations and meals, guided tours of Beijing, and hosted lunch with the President are provided.

I wanted to immediately accept the invitation, but Sung Jiang suggested I read further.

You will travel with U.S. congressmen and senators, labor leaders, educators and longtime Chinese-American business people. You will spend a week in China, including visits to the Great Wall, the city of Canton, and Hong Kong.

The return flight to Honolulu is on May 10th, 1999. Your RSVP to the Chinese Ambassador to the United States by April 15, 1999, will be greatly appreciated.

The smile on Jiang's face grew in direct proportion to my own. He added: "You will be only American print journalist on the plane. Since PANS specializes in stories about Asia that makes you the logical choice."

Before I could comment, Jiang went on: "Being aware of your journalistic inquisitiveness I have asked the Ambassador to put in special request to visit our Shanghai Navy base.   If approved you might have to miss the Canton side trip and perhaps one day of the weekend in Hong Kong. Would that be acceptable, Dan?"

"Of course," I said and then began blurting endless questions.   Jiang told me to write down anything else I thought of and he'd answer all that he could.   We agreed to meet here next Friday. Before parting he gave me a flyer he said I should look over. I glanced at it, put it in my pocket, and then the little man from NCNA quietly slipped out of the pub.

I was on such a high I scurried back to the Roundtable and ordered another drink. When asked why the Cheshire cat look on my face, I told the guys that Jiang had a friend who owned a Chinese antique shop in Georgetown and was having a sale on some items I'd been looking for. "He gave me a chit worth 25% off," I said.

With as many beers and mixed drinks as they had consumed, my explanation sounded plausible and so we all resumed our conversation with no further reference to my little Chinese friend. I got back to my apartment around 7 pm and thought about the Chinese antique shop. I looked at the chit Jiang gave me and saw the name of the shop was Ming & Ching Things.

CHAPTER 20 - ALOHA NO 'O HONOLULU

April 21, 1999 - In Flight and In Hawaii

Janice took the news of my China trip positively. "Remember I said if you worked hard enough on it Beijing wasn't that far away. Now, you're taking the first step to the world's greatest civilization." I told her I was looking forward to the trip, would miss her loads, but be back in her sweet arms by mid-May.

Tuesday was my last day of work and my reservations were for Wednesday. I got up early and caught a cab to Ronald Reagan National Airport for the 8 am shuttle to Newark then transferred to a 10-hour Continental Airlines non-stop flight to Aloha Land. I wanted to reach Hawaii as quickly as possible, and with the six hour time gain we landed in Paradise at 4:30 pm Hawaii time. After a quick taxi ride to Waikiki I checked into the Royal Hawaiian at 6 pm and 17 minutes later was in the Pacific Ocean! Ain't life grand?

"Now, this is the way to spend a Wednesday evening," I said to the attractive woman bobbing next to me. "I was in Washington, D.C. when the sun came up and now I'm in Waikiki five thousand miles away, watching the sun set."

"We owe it all to Boeing," she replied with a beaming smile, showing off her cover girl pearly whites. My trained eye revealed her baby blues, her light brown topsail and a more than ample pair of water wings! "I'm from Seattle and here on a week's vacation. What do you do?" she asked.

"Well, I'm on vacation, too, but this used to be home for me, working on The Honolulu Times. Name's Dan Lincoln, now a reporter for Pacific and Asia News Service."

"Nice to meet you, Dan. Nancy Regan, not Reagan, and I'm in aircraft design at Boeing."

"Well we really do owe it all to Boeing then, don't we? Will you join me for a drink at the Mai Tai Bar after I cleanse my soul in the Pacific?"

"Meet you there in ten minutes," she said, turning to swim back to the beach.

We enjoyed a couple drinks at the Pink Palace's oceanside bar and she agreed to dine with me if I had her back at the hotel by 10 pm. "I have no problem with that since it's already past midnight body time. Even Boeing can't eliminate jet lag. We'll go to my favorite Thai restaurant over at Ward Center and your chariot will return by 10 pm promptly, I guarantee it."

Nancy Regan, without the extra a, and I hit it off brilliantly. It didn't take long to learn that she was a native northwesterner, lived in Renton and had gone to the University of Washington. Go Huskies! Once I mentioned that U-W was also my alma mater she seemed to warm up even more. But she said that when it came to journalism she felt more comfortable on a CAD program than writing even the simplest letter to the editor. So much for future occupational conversation.

The evening flew by. We returned to the Royal a minute before the 10 pm witching hour and agreed to meet at the Mai Tai Bar for a drink again on Saturday night. I gave her a brief kiss on the cheek and said good night.

When he picked up the phone I said to my old City Editor Bruce Ferguson at the Times: "Howzit? You up for lunch, a few beers and a lot of conversation at the Columbia Inn today?"

"Dan? Is that you, Dan Lincoln?" he replied, sounding somewhat skeptical. "Are you in Honolulu, or still climbing that Washington press corps ladder?"

"It is me, I'm here at the Royal and I am definitely climbing the ladder just as fast as I can take the rungs. How about you?"

"I'm fine and it's great to hear from you. We miss you around here. Nobody's been able to fill your shoes since that NASHVILLE story last year. Yeah, I'll be happy to down a few browns with you at lunch. See you at the Roundtable at noon."

Since World War II, the Columbia Inn had been the favorite hangout for news types and others. It squatted next to the building housing the two daily papers and the A-P. I got there a little before noon and recognized a few of the regulars who were already into the suds. Taking a familiar feeling stool at the Roundtable it felt like old   times. "Did I really want to leave this place?" I asked myself.

Noon arrived and one by one so did the Roundtablers: the currently non-practicing physician still up on all the recent medical magic; the former City Councilman cum Hawaiian lobbyist; the veteran three-dot columnist; the business writer from Kiwiland; the publisher and former stock broker who always had a story to tell; and Wee Freddie. This guy was so old that few people even remembered what he did when he was doing what he used to be so good at!

Bruce arrived just a few minutes after I did and he, along with everyone else, was interested to know how I liked D.C. and what it was like to cover Capitol Hill. After about 30 minutes of questioning and conversation we moved to a booth where I ordered a bowl of ox tail soup, my favorite Columbia Inn dish, as Bruce filled me in on the Honolulu news scene. Not much had changed but there were some indications that one of the dailies was going to be sold within a year or so. After finishing the soup and working on my third beer of the day, I said:

"Bruce, I'm here for a week's vacation, true, but I'm not going straight back to D.C. I'm heading for Beijing."

The instant look of envy on his face was replaced with one of happiness for me.

"The Chinese government has invited me to attend their May Day celebrations. I'll also get to see the country and best of all I may be allowed to tour their big Navy base and shipyard at Shanghai."

"I've been to Beijing, but I never got to the Navy base at Shanghai. How'd you work that invite?"

"It's not totally approved yet but I'll know before we leave here next Wednesday. Apparently the Chinese have seen several of my recent stories on the U.S. Navy and their developments, and some of the backgrounders I've written about the growing and modernized Chinese Navy fleet."

"Some have come across my desk. We subscribe to PANS. Didn't you do a piece on that new senator from Minnesota and his committee confrontation with the SECNAV?"

"Indeed I did. What a hearing that was! He'll be on this trip with a few politicians, businessmen and a bunch of lobbyists as well."

"By the way, Bruce, what became of Commander Matson from the NASHVILLE? Was he court-martialed, or just spanked?"

"Spanked, as I recall. Think he's still at Pearl Harbor but he's not driving submarines anymore. Last I heard he was pushing a desk at COMSUBPAC."

"I should call him. He's a great guy and that fishing trawler/spy ship episode was obviously planned from the start by the Red Chinese to sway world opinion their way."

"Tell you what," Bruce said looking straight at me. "You come up with some good feature stuff about the Chinese Navy when you're in Shanghai, tie it to the Pacific situation in general and Hawaii in particular, and I'll run it on the front page of the op-ed section on the first Sunday after you've filed. If you stumble onto some hard news, especially relating to the Navy or Pearl Harbor, I'll push for page one, above the fold. Now, how's that for going to bat for my old buddy?"

Bruce and I shook hands and said Aloha. I returned to the hotel to call a few other friends. I also scheduled some surfing for the Pipeline, a round of golf with Chuck Matson at Navy Marine Golf Course, and hopefully enough time left to spend a day scuba diving off Lanai's Manele Bay.

"I can't tell you how sorry I was to hear they transferred you off the NASHVILLE," I said as we stood on the first tee.

"Goes with the territory, Dan," the former sub skipper said. "I'm still Navy and I didn't get a written reprimand so I might make Captain yet, and I'm still a submariner. Who knows, maybe there's life after my day job at COMSUBPAC!"

We dined on hot dogs and cold beers as we played, and talked openly while riding from shot to shot in our cart. The round of golf was over in what seemed like an hour. He beat me by a few strokes but I charged him with year-round golf advantage. Over one more beer at the 19th puka we traded e-mail addresses and went our separate ways.

Before the week could slip through my fingers like the sands of Waikiki, I had another date with Nancy, this time at the cozy Hau Tree Lanai right on the ocean at the small and quiet Kaimana Beach Hotel. I gave serious thought to going for a one-nighter, but couldn't do it. I had to admit, it certainly had a lot to do with my relationship or whatever it was with Janice Cannon.

Wow, I was beginning to really miss being with her. She was just mysterious enough, while totally charming, to keep me slightly off-balance. I wondered what is it about this lady that so captures me? Probably those *loong* legs that make her so statuesque. I wanted a pet name for Janice and after pondering for awhile her description became her moniker: Triple L; long, lean and luscious.

By Wednesday the 28th I was ready for Beijing. The tour group, under the watchful eye of Red Chinese government escorts, gathered at the Sheraton Waikiki for our bus transfer to the airport. On arrival I instantly saw on our plane's tail the PRC flag, a red rectangle with yellow stars in the upper left corner. Stepping aboard the long-range Boeing 737, a Chinese flight attendant holding a small envelope bowed and asked: "Are you Mr. Rinkon?"

I should have told him it's Lincoln like in the car, but not wanting to hold up the rest of the passengers I thanked him, put the envelope in my pocket and boarded the plane

Smiling cabin attendants, both male and female, welcomed us. Champagne was offered and our host escorts said they and the flight deck crew would get back to us with details of the trip after we'd taken off. I settled back in my seat for what I knew would be a very long, but very comfortable flight.

And then I met my seatmate

85

CHAPTER 21 - THE SEATMATE FROM HELL

April 28/29, 1999: In-Flight Honolulu to Beijing

I recognized him from newspapers TV interviews and that House Armed Services Committee hearing. My heart sank.

"Senator Henry Anderson, Minnesota," he said extending his hand and almost knocking over my glass of champagne on the small center tray between our seats. "And you are?"

"Dan Lincoln, Pacific & Asia News Service in Washington."

"You seem to be the only reporter from home, right? Why didn't they include the really important press, like the Washington Post or the New York Times, and all the TV boys?"

I suggested: "Probably because those papers and most TV networks have Beijing bureaus with regular feeds whenever a story breaks from there."

"Of course they do. I knew that. Just slipped my mind. Well, we've got a long trip, so let's get real acquainted. Even if you're not from a big wire service."

I thought what a pompous ass this guy is. It was all downhill from there. I tried many excuses to let him know I just wanted to read my book and catch some sleep. At first I politely listened to his farmland to senate story, and his every tale from Minnesota politics to life with Linda and their kids. He extolled his great respect for The Peoples Republic of China and related his plan for the bigger role he would soon play on the Senate Armed Services committee.

Finally exasperated, I said I was in the hearing room when he and the SECNAV had their face-off. He thought a minute and then said he recalled the story I did on that incident. I could tell he was searching his brain to remember whether the story was favorable to him or to Secretary Wetzel, but the answer wasn't there.

The chief steward came on the intercom giving details about the trip, our hotel and some specifics about the May Day parade and celebration. The briefings kept Hank Anderson quiet while he too digested the details.

Drink orders were taken and the Senator ordered two gin and tonics, telling the stewardess he didn't want to bother her again while she was busy with other passengers. Sure!

A menu was presented; its cover was a reproduction of a classic Chinese watercolor showing a man and small boy stopping at a stream to drink water before resuming their journey.

When our cocktails arrived we made our lunch choices. Looking for further escape from the Senator's babbling I put on the headphones and found Western music, talk shows and cockpit in-flight transmissions.

Our flight path initially took us over historic Midway Island then northwest toward Japan and Korea. In the long hours between lunch and land we had two movies, more cocktails and dinner. The sun raced with us since we moved through at least five time zones.

Following lunch I watched the movie Saving Private Ryan, and loved it for the second time. After the film I headed aft to an unoccupied row and stretched out for a couple hours of sleep. Suddenly remembering the envelope in my pocket I took it out. It was a note from Bruce Ferguson. It read: Dan, I couldn't get you on the phone so I will rely on the airline people to get this to you. Simon Cardigan was found by the Honolulu Police shot dead at a small upstairs club on Hotel Street in Chinatown. Call me when you return. Aloha, Bruce.

I hadn't seen Simon for over a year but knowing he was murdered in Chinatown quickly brought back our discussions about his investigations into what I knew would be a real life spy story. Then it came to me; the safe deposit box. At that moment I planned to spend whatever time needed in Honolulu to learn about Simon's death. Perhaps the contents of that box held some answers to what were now at least a dozen questions.

My body clock said sleep. I heard it and lay back to rest for as long as I could. Sleep came but it was capricious. When the flight attendant woke me for dinner the lights of Japan twinkled below meaning we'd soon be over South Korea. As we got near Seoul I saw bright lights all over the land below and to the left of us. I also saw a most distinctive demarcation almost as if you had drawn a line across the peninsula between North and South Korea. There were next to no lights at all above the 38th parallel.

We passed over North Korea, the Yellow Sea, and shortly entered Chinese airspace beginning a descent from our cruising altitude. Beijing was an hour from here. My excitement level began to grow. Senator Anderson had fallen asleep after dinner and numerous brandies, and was snoring so loudly the stewardess had pulled a blanket up around his face to soften the noise. I didn't want to disturb him, since to me the snoring was a respite from his constant braggadocio.

When he had to be jolted awake as we neared Beijing, Hank seemed a bit out of it, but docilely followed orders, asking the female flight attendant if the president was going to meet him upon arrival. She said she didn't know but there would definitely be a welcoming party. That seemed to satisfy him and he dozed off, this time properly buckled up and ready for landing.

Beijing and its sprawling suburbs surged into the countryside below, over 12 million people crowded into its metropolitan borders. As we touched down, I set my watch for local time and figured it had been almost an eleven hour flight. Any ground, U.S. or Chinese, would feel good to step on, and the thought of a full night's sleep figured even more prominently into my first thoughts upon entering the Peoples Republic of China.

Tomorrow, it would be back to the realities of the day, and I would be spending that day and the next week in the largest and most communist nation in the world.

CHAPTER 22 - POWER TO THE PEOPLE

May 1, 1999: Tiananmen Square, China

"This will be a May Day Parade to remember," Chinese President Jiang Zemin told the assembled Cabinet members and journalists from all over the globe, "and the West will be forced to accept the Peoples Republic of China as the leading military power in Asia and the Pacific, not the United States."

Thundering armed vehicles missile launchers and tens of thousands of men marched in Tiananmen Square, startling a worldwide TV audience with the realities of the real 1999 China and its growing military might.

"The world today witnesses the strength of China's military forces, and if they could see beneath the waters of the Pacific and Indian Oceans they would know the strength of the modern Chinese Navy. Our nuclear submarines will soon match anything the Americans possess, including any so-called stealth submarine or their pitiful attempts at drenching their undersea boats with stealth gels."

A few yards from the reviewing stand, a small band of Chinese government officials was hosting dignitaries from the United States; witnessing the new China first hand the Americans were impressed. Most were politically liberal, eager to work with new and old Chinese friends to achieve lasting peace and friendship between the two world powers.

Although it was impressive I couldn't get Simon Cardigan out of my mind; lying dead in a Chinatown club in downtown Honolulu, probably because of what he knew. I was positive these damned commies were involved and I vowed to expose them for the thieving spies they really were.

"It really is a new China," Senator Anderson cheerily told a legislator next to him. In the 20 years or more since the deaths of Chairman Mao and Zhou En Lai, China had moved through the 80s and 90s led by temporary leaders Hua Guofeng, Deng Xiaoping, Li Ping and Zhao Ziyang.

Never forgotten, but long put out of their minds by the new regime, were the 1988 independence uprising in Tibet and the student riots at Tiananmen Square a year later.

Today a new crop of Chinese Communists, better educated and understanding the importance of a technological economy, had been mainstreamed into the government leading China into a world of international trade and global politics.

Big changes came swiftly to the Peoples Republic during the 1990s. Tourism opened up and increased trade brought Chinese-made goods to every home in the western world.

That was also the case with the development of China's military and naval forces. Hank realized that what he was seeing today was similar to what he had learned during his tenure on both Armed Services Committees. These guys really have their stuff together. No wonder our top brass is always crying about the Chinese Navy getting too big.

"What do you think of the parade, Senator?" asked a PLA naval officer, introducing himself as Lieutenant David Wong.

"It's terrific Lieutenant Wong, very impressive. Where did you learn to speak English so perfectly?"

"Well, sir, my father was a professor at Beijing University and sent me to the U.S. for my education and to broaden my philosophical horizons, which it did! My undergraduate years were at Purdue University in Indiana, with a degree in electrical engineering. And thank you for the compliment about my English."

"You and your countrymen," the senator pontificated, "have been most gracious to us and we do appreciate it. I'm sure this will go a long way toward improving the friendship between our countries." LT Wong nodded politely.

"You know, we have millions of Chinese in America in leading positions in many of our best computer companies, and I hear they're very sharp as stock brokers and Wall Street financial analysts."

Wong smiled, saying: "A cousin of mine owns a Chinese art and antiques shop in Washington. It is called Ming & Ching Things. Do you know of it?"

Oh shit, Hank said to himself. It must be Lily Shin. Better let this one slip under the rug.

"No, lieutenant, but maybe my wife does. I'll ask her when I get back. By the way, is this your permanent job escorting invited visitors?"

"Definitely not, Senator. I am only assisting your group while you are here. It is better than many of the routine tasks in my position at the Shanghai Navy shipyard. I imagine it's a lot like some of the paper pushing and constant campaigning you have to do to keep your constituents happy!"

"You can say that again. It's unbelievable and since I moved up to the Senate the volume has tripled. But then, you 'gotta keep the people happy, right?"

"Yes sir."

"Philosophically I believe our two nations need to work closer together, develop more friendship between us. I'm certain you seek the same peaceful world we do. Am I right?"

"Absolutely, Senator, and will you take that message to your countrymen?"

Hank smiled nodded yes and turned his gaze to the last of the parade. His thoughts flashed back to the Senate committee hearings where top Pentagon brass and their staff officers positioned China as a major world threat. He felt they were over reacting to current events, but he did recall his surprise at finding out just what a juggernaut the Chinese military was becoming.

It's known as the PLA; Peoples Liberation Army, said that Pentagon briefer. From a fleet of coastal cutters and old Soviet destroyers in the 70s and 80s, China has expanded its bases at Shanghai, Hainan Island, and in the northeast of the nation to support a fleet of former Soviet diesel submarines plus newly purchased Russian nuclear subs. They also have their own new classes of guided missile destroyers, frigates and nuclear submarines.

Hank knew about the Russian boats and how Gorbachev sold them to get revenue into the lousy post-Soviet economy.

The lieutenant commander at the briefing podium had said: By early 1997 the PLA Navy was a force to be reckoned with in the Asia-Pacific area. Patrolling Taiwanese waters, defending their alleged claim to the Spratly Islands, harassing U.S. Navy ships in the South China Sea and expanding skills learned from the Russians, the Chinese Navy now boasts quite a fleet.

"Senator Anderson. Senator?" Lieutenant Wong interrupted Hank's train of thought. "When the parade ends our Minister of Cultural Affairs has invited your group to lunch in the Great Hall of the People, followed by a tour of Beijing. You will join us, I trust?"

"Oh yes, for sure. Sorry for my inattention. I'm just disappointed we didn't see anything of your Navy today."

"Begging the Senator's pardon, but I thought your government didn't have any interest in our Navy," teased Wong. "They turn down our suggestions for mutually exchanged port visits, and if we ask for access to simple non-classified information to help our ships become safer for our crews, we're refused with no answers at all."

"Please be more specific, Lieutenant Wong," Hank replied in a low voice, "or I must be forced to take offense at your allegations."

"Sir, my superiors contacted your Office of the Chief of Naval Operations asking about a new type of GPS device used by General Motors in its Cadillac cars that tells the driver where he is currently located to within a city block. This would be a most welcome addition to some of our smaller craft manned by sailors less trained than our submarine and destroyer crews. Such an exchange of information could be a step in the direction of those friendly relations your group says they want to establish."

"You have a point there. When I return to Washington I'll look into the matter and find out why you got no answer. That, Lieutenant Wong, you can count on."

The parade ended and the group was taken to the Great Hall for lunch, followed by a bus tour of the city and ultimately delivered to suites in the latest western brand name hotel.

The naive senator didn't comprehend that his party was being given very structured glimpses of what Beijing's conniving leaders wished them to see.

CHINA CLAIMS IT IS LEADING MILITARY POWER IN ASIA/PACIFIC

By: Dan Lincoln

Beijing, May 1, 1999 (Pacific & Asia News Service):

This year's May Day Parade had the traditional ranks of soldiers, tanks and armored personnel carriers, ballistic missiles towed by the latest battlefield vehicles, and one new element: a claim by Chinese President Jiang Zemin that "this year the West will be forced to accept that the Peoples Republic of China is the leading military power in Asia and the Pacific, not the United States."

China has been building its defensive military forces over the past few years and the Peoples Liberation Army, PLA, includes an army of over one million and an Air Force, Marine Corps, a home defense force of millions, and a growing and increasingly modern Navy. Recent purchases of surface ships and submarines from Russia give the Chinese a fleet of attack warships in excess of 100. Added to those are nearly 300 fast gun and torpedo boats and mine warfare ships, plus another 500 amphibious ships and coastal defense craft.

President Jiang Zemin stressed that the PRC has a major program of Chinese designed and constructed SSBN and SSN nuclear attack submarines. He told the Tiananmen Square crowd: "Our nuclear submarines will soon match anything the Americans can put up against us, including any so-called stealth submarine or their pitiful attempts at drenching their undersea boats with stealth gels."

-end-

93

CHAPTER 23 - SHANGHAI SIDE TRIP

May 2, 1999:   Beijing, China

RING! RING! RING!   Long loud knocking and the obnoxious sound of the door bell of his suite jolted Hank out of a deep sleep at 7 am. "I'm coming," he called out, heading for the door. He was surprised to see LT Wong because this was supposed to be a free day for us to wander around Beijing.

Groggily Hank muttered: "Morning, Lieutenant.   To what do I owe the pleasure of your early morning visit?"

"Good morning, sir. I apologize for my early call but I have news I believe will make you happy. May I come in?"

"Certainly. I like being happy."

"Senator, after our discussion about the Navy and our problems making friendly contacts with your Washington people, I spoke with my superiors and they have invited you and a journalist in your group to visit our Shanghai shipyard. We will look over some of the ships and perhaps see the city. How does that sound?"

"Impressive, lieutenant. I didn't expect to see your Navy up close but that would greatly improve my ability to make better input into anything my Senate committee gets involved with regarding the PRC. By the way, may I suggest the journalist?   His name is Dan Lincoln and he seems very interested in learning all about China."

LT Wong nodded his agreement. "Yes Senator, he is the one we have already selected. You have several free days left in Beijing, but if it's convenient we would like to leave for Shanghai the day after tomorrow. That will give us enough time to see most everything at the Navy base and still get you to Hong Kong on Friday afternoon."

"I'll be ready at 9 am sharp on Tuesday."

"Very good, Senator."   LT Wong bowed politely, and left the suite with Hank asking himself: How did I get so lucky? He would quickly find out this really wasn't just so much 'luck.'

CHAPTER 24 - THE DRAGON'S DEN

May 4, 1999:   PRC Navy Shipyard, Shanghai

A very bumpy four hour flight on a Chinese Air Force transport plane carried Senator Anderson, the ever-present LT Wong and me to Shanghai, a city we Americans found immense from the air. "It reminds me of 19th Century photos of Paris I've seen; I seem to remember this city was referred to as the Paris of the Orient," I said to Hank.

The plane touched down at an Air Force base in the city suburbs and taxied up to a VIP reception area and hanger. At the bottom of the ramp a highly decorated officer waited. He was short, but had the kind of physical demeanor that clearly indicated he was in control of his base and his men.

"Welcome to Shanghai, Senator Anderson. I am Rear Admiral K.J. Kwock, commander of the Shanghai Naval Operations Base. It is an honor to meet an American of such important stature."

"Thank you, Admiral Kwock. I am most honored to be here and look forward to touring the shipyard and learning more about your Navy."

David Wong then introduced me to the admiral, explaining that I worked for a news agency focusing solely on stories about Asia and the Pacific. The expression on the admiral's face taught me everything I'll ever need to know about the word inscrutable. Our entire party then boarded a big black Russian Zil limo and headed for the Navy base.

"I trust you had a pleasant journey?" queried the Chinese navyman. "I am only sorry we could not get you on one of our jet planes but on such short notice they were all committed. Everything will be first class for you now that you are my guests and on my base."

"No apologies necessary, Admiral. I'm thrilled to be here."

I knew what we'd hear and see at the shipyard would be limited to nothing more than window dressing and platitudes, so I wasn't surprised with what came next.

Hank said: "Admiral, I've been working on legislation millions of Americans hope will lead to far better co-operation between our country's navies, resulting in lasting world peace."

"My government is fully aware of your foresight and we commend you. Given more time your countrymen will recognize the wisdom of your resolution and you'll have the support needed for passage, I am sure."

I noticed Hank looking at me and suddenly he seemed to realize that I, the American journalist who wrote only about things affecting this part of the world, might just be the person who could get his message out better than he could. The look on his face said: I'd better get to know this guy a lot better.

The tour began with a contingent of Chinese Navy brass leading us along pier after pier of ships in various stages of readiness. We then drove into the main shipyard, and although new construction and ship repair could be seen the major yard activity hid behind 10 foot high chain link fences cloaked in black canvas.

The sheer size of their fleet impressed me even though I had yet to see a single submarine. That, I figured, was being saved for the end of our visit.

"Our Navy is no longer just a coastal defense force," Admiral Kwock boasted. "We have a firm and funded plan to make it a first class blue-water force equal to yours by the middle of the 21st Century, and we're on target to achieve that goal," he noted, with a bit too much confidence I thought.

As the admiral continued I turned on my pocket tape recorder and backed that up with my own style of shorthand notes in my little blue notebook. "For example," Admiral Kwock went on, "before us is one of our newest LUHU class destroyers. We have two in our fleet so far. This is the QINGDAO and we would like to have you go aboard and let the ship's captain show you around, in the non-classified spaces that is."

"I'd love that," Hank said eagerly. "How big is it?"

"The captain will tell you all those details," the Admiral replied.   Boarding the QINGDAO Hank said how impressed he was with the sharpness of the crew and the cleanliness of the ship. I didn't tell him they'd probably been cleaning and polishing non-stop for the last 48 hours.

The OOD saluted smartly while the crew on the quarter-deck stood at stiff attention.   Although the ship's speaker system blared in Chinese we could clearly understand the phrase "U.S. Senator." Hank knew he was getting the red-carpet treatment, and was quite pleased with the way this trip was turning out.

"I am Captain Fong," said the ship's 40-ish looking skipper. LT Wong stepped up quietly and started translating.

There was something about Wong's demeanor and his well-honed professionalism that were immediately apparent to me, and looking closer at him I knew he was older than most career Navy lieutenants.   I'd been around Asians for years and knew they didn't always show their age, but after giving Wong the once over I came to the conclusion he was more like 45 or 50, not 30.   He was around ship captains and even admirals, and seemed to be on an equal par with them, not just some escort assigned for a week's temporary duty.   I made a mental note to keep watching him.

"This ship joined our fleet last year, gentlemen," the QINGDAO skipper began, "and is the newest of our multi-role destroyers. We hope to add two more in the next few years. We recently bought two unfinished Russian SOVREMENNYY class destroyers to be completed here. The first, named HAIZHOU, is currently dry-docked and is scheduled to be commissioned late this year. We may also buy two more if they are still available and fit our needs at the time," added Captain Fong via LT Wong.

"Why is it you want so many of these old Soviet ships?" queried Hank.

"Very good question," Captain Fong replied, "and the answer is quite simple. Timing! The Russians have ships to

97

sell and they need money. We have money and this gives us the time needed to develop new Chinese designed and built warships."

I thought a moment and then asked Fong: "Why such a buildup, Captain?"

"I will answer your question, Mr. Lincoln," Admiral Kwock interrupted, a visible scowl appearing on his now sullen face. "It is a matter of keeping strong to guarantee peace. Without a strong Navy we cannot protect ourselves from our enemies. But with a large and new Navy we will be among the nations of the world who, like the U.S., will guarantee world peace. Does that make sense to you?"

"It does, Admiral. You'll be quoted exactly in my story so there is no mistaking what China's position is. By the way, sir, what are those countries you consider to be enemy forces of the PRC? "

Turning slightly to Captain Fong, Admiral Kwock uttered a few non-translated words and then moved swiftly to the quarter-deck. LT Wong took the senator's arm guiding him behind the admiral and the ship's captain. "Your visit to the QINGDAO is over," he said quietly. We both knew exactly what he meant.

"Thank you, Captain Fong. Your ship and crew are impressive and hopefully our countries will exchange port visits," Hank said to the Chinese four-striper, and walked down the brow to the pier below.

Via LT Wong, the admiral concluded the shipyard visit saying: "That's enough touring for today gentlemen. Perhaps you'd like to freshen up and then join me for dinner and more conversation?"

"An excellent idea, Admiral," Hank responded. "I want to be fresh and ready to see your submarines tomorrow."

The simply excellent dinner was at Admiral Kwock's quarters and table talk was aimed mostly at American life. The admiral, unlike earlier, was quite talkative. He told of two business visits to the States and stopping in Honolulu both trips. He was very keen on that tropical city.

He wondered aloud: "Why can't my country have hotels as perfect as the Royal Hawaiian and the Halekulani? With all our history and culture we ought to build a world-class Chinese themed resort hotel right there in Waikiki." He knew the Japanese and Koreans had invested billions of dollars in Hawaii tourism and said so with veiled umbrage.

Following dinner we adjourned to his study for cigars and brandy. The admiral handed me a snifter of the drink and I was surprised when he asked: "How does our brandy compare to what you're used to, Mr. Lincoln?"

I paused a moment not wanting to say anything offensive, especially before we got a chance to look at his submarines, and then said: "Like so many other things in China age makes them better. You're rich in history and your brandy mirrors that history; properly aged, delightful to the senses, and memorable."

What a crock! I'm beginning to sound like Anderson, I thought. It tasted like strained swamp water, but lying with grace was an acceptable Chinese tradition, and one I was getting good at very quickly. Kwock smiled, bowed and pointed toward the bottle indicating I should enjoy to the fullest. Not in this lifetime, buster! At 11 pm we extended our appreciation for the hospitality, and took the Zil back to our quarters.

Before hitting the sack I listened to some of the afternoon ship tour tape, and corrected some of my notes. Tomorrow, I thought, should be the highlight of the trip. I hoped we'd get to go on board a submarine so I could see for myself if there are any differences between their boats and ours.

For the eager senator it had been a busy and informative day. As he brushed his teeth and slipped into bed he wondered what May 5th would bring. It, like so many other things in China, would be a big surprise for him.

CHAPTER 25 - DIM SUM AND TEA FOR TWO

May 5, 1999 - Shanghai, China

A cool and cloudy morning greeted us as we left our quarters after breakfast, joining LT Wong. "Hope you slept well, gentlemen? There is a slight change to our schedule. Today, we will tour the city of Shanghai!"

We gaped at him with expressions of disbelief, but quickly regained our composure knowing that change was the name of the game with the Chinese. We hopped into the limo, ready to tackle today's challenges as tourists.

"We *will* visit the submarines, won't we Lieutenant Wong? It really is important to both of us as I had intended to do a feature story on the growth of the Chinese Navy, with emphasis on the new HAN boats and your plans for future Chinese submarines."

"Yes, Mr. Lincoln. You will see our HAN boats and many others, but not until tomorrow. I do not know all the details but I was advised very early this morning by Admiral Kwock's aide that we would have to move your visit back one day for security reasons. And you understand security, don't you?"

We nodded our acceptance of the change in plans, and sat back in the car ready to play tourist for what turned out to be quite an enjoyable eight hours.

Shanghai is one of Asia's fastest growing cities and long considered China's key financial and banking center. The Huangpu River divides it into two areas: Puxi is to the west and is the original city center. Pudong lies to the east and is the new business district. Arriving at the city's center LT Wong commanded the driver to start our tour in Pudong.

The first thing that came into my mind was how similar it is to Tokyo. "What's that tall tower over there?" I asked Wong.

"That's the Oriental Pearl office building and TV tower. It's one of our newer landmarks, but just one of many including hotels and office buildings, shopping centers, residential complexes and even a new subway."

LT Wong pointed out new hotels prominently displaying Occidental names like Sheraton and Hilton.

"I prefer to put visitors up at a more traditional Chinese hotel called the Shanghai Mansions, over in the older section of the city on Suzhou Bei Lu. If you can get past the 1930s-style exterior the hotel is very friendly and has exceptionally large rooms." We both chuckled, and said we'd stay at the Mansions on our next trip.

We cruised through the city, crossed the river into the old French Concessions section, and stopped at a small building that appeared to be a residence. We got out and headed into the former home of Chinese revolutionary war hero Sun Yat Sen. Now a museum filled with his memorabilia it made for an interesting stop before lunch.

The senator ate it all up, never dawning on him that we were being given the first class party line tour and were being shown only what Beijing's leaders wanted us to see. This day trip had been planned long before our arrival in Shanghai, and was just another scene in our indoctrination of today's world-class China. That was fine with me because I had already mentally filed away dozens of feature stories to be written over the next year.

Ready for lunch our driver skillfully navigated the streets of the old French section, and within minutes stopped in front of a dim sum restaurant named Fulin Xuan. It was small, local, and the aromas drifting from it smelled absolutely delicious.

We took our time dining and talked about life in China and the U.S. David Wong was rather reticent discussing his daily life, but most interested in hearing all about Washington D.C. Though he had a wife and daughter his job didn't allow him to spend much time with them, he told us.

"After lunch we will visit our Shanghai Art and History Museum, which is filled with classic displays of early Chinese scrolls, ceramics and bronze sculptures. Are you interested in such art treasures?" We nodded yes.

The Shanghai Museum visit proved to be tedious but illuminating. A bronze replica of the Chinese Heavenly Horse from the Eastern Han Dynasty was on display, and tapestries that would look good in any home adorned the walls. After two hours Hank said he was getting tired and suggested we return to our quarters.

"I really enjoyed myself today, Lieutenant Wong," I said, "and the tour was just what the doctor ordered. We're ready to see the submarines tomorrow. Thanks again."

"Agreed," added the senator. "We appreciate your time and the information you shared with us, and we'll see you in the morning, Lieutenant.

CHAPTER 26 - LOOK BUT DON'T TOUCH THE SUBS

May 6, 1999: Chinese Navy Base, Shanghai

Lieutenant Wong and the Zil arrived outside our quarters promptly at 9 am, and drove us a few blocks into senior officer housing and pulled up behind another limo. RADM Kwock came out of his house got into his vehicle and we departed for the submarine base.

More Navy brass and some civilians I had to assume were the Chinese version of the CIA joined us and soon there was a convoy of Zils. Armed guards halted us at the gate and waved us through only after all passengers, regardless of rank, showed their I.D. I was impressed with this tight security especially since the commander of the base was in the procession and might otherwise be admitted without any check. Not in Shanghai.

We drove straight to the submarine piers, finding the pride and joy of the Chinese fleet tied to the first one. Admiral Kwock proudly began telling his visitors about their hunter-killer HANs.

"We have five of these 4,500 ton nuclear powered vessels, the first totally Chinese-designed and Chinese-built submarines. Your Navy submarine commanders have become very familiar with them while conducting spy patrols off our coasts.   I can't tell you details about speed and diving limits but these boats have six 21-inch torpedo tubes and very good sonar," he added.

"You cannot go aboard, gentlemen, for obvious reasons," the Admiral joked, compliments of LT Wong's translation. "However you will see other subs in the fleet and receive a briefing about their capabilities.   A U.S. senator of your importance should know the full story about our fleet, don't you think Senator Anderson?"

"I do indeed, Admiral.   By the way, what about those KILO Class Russian subs you got from Moscow?"

"We have purchased two and are looking at buying two more with delivery in the next two years. Right across the pier there is one of the KILOs currently in the fleet."

Dispensing with all this bullshit diplomacy, I bluntly asked: "Is it true, Admiral Kwock, that you keep buying and building subs to go after our aircraft-carrier battle groups?"

The admiral braced, then coldly stated: "I reiterate from yesterday that our Navy exists solely to preserve world peace and defend our country, if provoked. Can you cite any instance of our submarines attacking any U.S. vessels?"

Testily I replied: "Not yet but you know our superior technology and training might blunt your fleet into scrap iron! Also, many of my countrymen believe your recent ambitious submarine and destroyer building campaigns do not speak of peace, but rather of sabre rattling."

Taking a deep breath, LT Wong explained my question and sabre rattling to the admiral, who politely but firmly replied: "Mr. Lincoln, we have opened our Navy base and shipyard to you and the senator on very short notice. We value your friendship and interest in our country. But if you can not see the difference between our serious effort to become a first class Navy playing a major role in world peace keeping, and what you call sabre rattling, then I am afraid our visit has just come to an end."

Shooting me a stare that would freeze a volcano, Hank interceded: "No sir, Admiral. I'm sure Mr. Lincoln wasn't questioning your sincerity or your motives, but only asking about the growing size of your submarine force. I'm sure it seems large to him, as it does to me, when compared to other navies of the world and to our own."

"I accept your concern, Senator. A majority of our fleet are old MING and ROMEO diesel boats, without missiles of any kind, used mostly for coastal patrol in the Yellow Sea. At least our MING boats are armed with your Harpoon-type missiles."

Although the tour lasted another two hours Kwock seemed uninterested in telling us more about his ships. The tour ended at 1 pm when a noticeably colder Admiral Kwock abruptly made excuses, wished the senator well, ignored me and returned to his office.

The ever smiling, but ever cautious LT Wong was now our only host and said we should head for the airport and our flight to Hong Kong. As our Zil neared the terminal Hank said to the lieutenant: "I am impressed with your Navy and sorry if we upset the admiral. Our two countries really aren't all that different, and I believe you want peace, just as we do. I'll resolve that GPS matter and advise the admiral directly. Maybe that will let him know China does have friends in high places in Washington?"

"Thank you, Senator. And perhaps we can also schedule a port visit at Pearl Harbor for one of our Navy ships to coincide with your Fourth of July celebrations?"

"Now that's an excellent idea, Lieutenant. I love it, and will work on it straight away."

I was about to throw up my blue collar lunch right on the China-loving senator's lap but my journalistic mentality prevailed. If Senator Anderson was really taken in by all this manipulation then he might become the most dangerous man in Washington.

At the airport Wong bade us farewell: "Have a pleasant flight and keep in touch. Perhaps I can help you more than you know, and look up my cousin at Ming & Ching Things, in Georgetown."

"I'll try to Lieutenant," Hank replied, remembering Lily and his plans for her involvement in his future. "Shay shay. Thanks again for everything."

We boarded the plane and took seats in First Class. A few minutes later the Boeing 737 lifted off, turned slightly southwest, and headed for the Middle Kingdom's newest star, Hong Kong.

I took out my laptop and started entering the words of my story about the Shanghai Naval Base and Shipyard tour I'd just completed. It didn't take long to relate the events of the day, and within minutes I'd pressed the 'send' button and the story was on the way to PANS headquarters in New York.

CHINESE NAVY SEEKS PARITY WITH U.S.
NEW SUBMARINES AND DESTROYERS SEEN AS
THREAT TO AMERICAN AIRCRAFT CARRIER
BATTLE GROUPS IN SOUTH CHINA
By: Dan Lincoln

Shanghai, China: May 4, 2000 (Pacific & Asia News Service):

During a just-completed two day tour of China's largest naval base near this city, base commander Rear Admiral K.J. Kwock said: "The Chinese Navy is no longer just a brown water coastal defense unit. We have a firm and funded plan, to make it a first class blue water force equal to that of the U.S. by the middle of the 21st Century, and we are on target to achieve that goal."

Headed by U.S. Senator Henry B. Anderson of Minnesota, second ranking minority member on the Senate Armed Services Committee, the tour included a group of about two dozen American politicians, educators, labor leaders, businessmen and several people working toward getting most favored nation status for China in its trading relations with the United States.

MFN countries enjoy lower tariffs on their goods imported by the U.S., preferential treatment when it comes to bid awards, and the benefit of already being a trading partner with America, thus having an advantage over other nations competing for the same trade and business with the U. S.

The group was invited by the government of the Peoples Republic of China to attend May Day ceremonies in Beijing, and then visit some of the country afterwards. This reporter was included in the Shanghai tour.

The PRC Navy has two relatively new Chinese designed and built LUHU class destroyers. They hope to build two more in the near future. These impressive ships carry surface-to-air and surface-to-surface missiles, plus two anti-submarine warfare helicopters and torpedo tubes. We visited the QINGDAO, a 5,700 ton warship with a crew of 230. It is 468 feet long, 51 feet at the beam, and can reach speeds in excess of 31 knots.

106

The Chinese have also purchased four HAIZHOU class destroyers from Russia. These ships are quite large at 8,500 tons, and carry a crew of about 370 men. They also have both types of missile capabilities, plus four 21-inch torpedo tubes.

After witnessing the growing modern surface ship fleet at the Shanghai base, Admiral Kwock was asked why China felt it needed such a major ship buildup at this time. He said: "Today it is a matter of keeping strong to guarantee the peace. If that sounds like something you've heard before it is nothing but basic American rhetoric for rationalizing your worldwide fleet of aircraft-carrier battle groups, dozens of nuclear submarines always snooping off the coasts of what you consider to be hostile or terrorist nations, and warships twice the size and even more sophisticated than what we have. With a large and newly built blue water Navy, which we will have in a few years, China will take her place among the nations of the world who, like the U.S., will be a guarantor of world peace."

The major attack capability of the Chinese Navy is their large and rapidly growing fleet of modern submarines. Published reports indicate they had 15 MING and ROMEO class diesel boats two years ago. One XIA class nuclear powered ballistic missile sub and four fairly new Russian KILO class attack submarines augment another dozen older SONG class diesel boats. The latter are diesel electric powered serving as an interim class until newer 21st Century SSN and SSBN submarines are delivered.

The current pride and joy of the Chinese Navy are their HAN class hunter-killer boats. These 400 foot long 5,500 ton nuclear powered subs are the first to be totally Chinese designed and built. Most of them are currently in their South Sea Fleet. Admiral Kwock declined to comment on speed and diving limits.

When asked if it was true the Chinese Navy kept buying and building new subs to be able to attack American aircraft carrier battle groups, Kwock said: "Our Navy exists solely to preserve world peace and defend our country, if provoked."

The American magazine Defense News recently reported that Russia was considering selling two of their latest AKULA class nuclear submarines to the Chinese. They are capable of attacking any carrier battle group before the surface ships get in range to fire missiles or launch aircraft to attack the Chinese Mainland. The Chinese government has refused comment on the alleged talks with the Russians.

Prior to leaving the Navy base yesterday, the senator told Chinese officials that he would work toward getting a U.S./Chinese Navy ship exchange program set up, and that he would like to see one of their ships visit Pearl Harbor on the next Fourth of July holiday.

-end-

CHAPTER 27 - ONE BOX FULL

May 11, 1999: Honolulu, Hawaii

The sun rising over Diamond Head greeted us as our jet settled gently on the reef runway at Honolulu International where our Chinese hosts bade us farewell.   Being a returning resident I breezed through U.S. Customs and Immigration.

That well-worn face hanging on Bruce Ferguson greeted me at the terminal curb. I had alerted him to my arrival via e-mail saying I wanted to re-investigate Simon's death, but I hadn't told him about that letter in the safe deposit box.

"Aloha, Dan," he said shaking my hand. "How was the tour?   I've read the two pieces you filed for PANS. Interesting. You make it sound like the PRC is committed to taking on the U.S. Navy in the not so distant future."

"You wouldn't believe the depth of their hate for us, Bruce, and they believe they can equal our Navy and become a fighting force that the world will have to accept.   But, so much for the PRC.   Let's get some breakfast and you can fill me in on Simon's murder."

We hit the Zippy's on Nimitz Highway and over Spam and eggs with two scoops rice he filled me in on what little had developed since HPD was called to that small Chinatown club.

"They discovered a body with a bullet in the head, but an ID was missing. When Simon didn't show up for work by 10 am, we called the police giving them his description. The officer said that from our ID he felt they had the body at the morgue."

"Were there any clues to his murder, or how he came to be at that club? Did he have anything on him, something that could lead to who killed him, or even a clue to where he had been before getting hit?"

"Just some loose change and a bus transfer.   Pearl Harbor to Waikiki.   Hell, he could have used it to get to his apartment there."

"Could it have been used to go the other direction, I mean to Pearl Harbor rather than to Waikiki?"

"I guess so. Are you thinking he was on his way to Pearl after visiting the nightclub?"

"You knew Simon was a workaholic, not a drinker. Why would he be patronizing a small-time club in Chinatown, especially after midnight on a working night? It doesn't figure."

Bruce had to get to work and I wanted to go through the newspapers from the last couple of weeks, call HPD and talk to the detectives assigned to the case.

The morning was consumed reviewing the stories on the murder, and talking with the reporters who wrote them. The most recent done just yesterday covered Simon's wake and said he carried a hefty half-million dollar insurance policy listing a son Ian Basil Cardigan of London, as the sole beneficiary.

I grabbed lunch at the Columbia Inn and was soon joined by a fellow wearing a KGMB-TV polo shirt. "Heard you were on that junket to China," the Channel 9 guy said. "How was it? We're planning a trip there next year if we can get some help from the airlines and the PRC government."

"It was interesting, but don't expect to get any real hard news stories. They have your every step planned, and you see and hear only what they want you to. Tell that to Tim Tindall if he's the one who'll be going. Also tell him the Chinese believe they're *just slightly ahead of their time!* He'll know what I mean."

After lunch and a couple hours of shopping, I drove to the Kahala Mall branch of First Hawaiian Bank and showed my key to the vault attendant. She quickly checked her records and my signature, and then led me to box #103. She smiled and stepped back to give me some privacy, and I quickly accessed the envelope I hoped held the answer to Simon Cardigan's demise.

"All through," I said sliding the box back into its puka and removing my key. "Thanks for your help. Aloha."

I jumped into my rental car and headed back to Waikiki. The contents of Simon's envelope would have to wait for the privacy of my room and the time to digest whatever clues it contained.

"Good afternoon, sir," said the smiling young desk clerk at the Royal Hawaiian Hotel.

Reading his ID badge I replied: "Aloha Kalani, I'm Mr. Lincoln and I have a reservation for the next three nights."

Checking his computer, Kalani smiled and said: "We're happy to have you back at the Royal. Please sign the registration form and a bellman will take care of your luggage."

Once inside my room I opened a cold beer from the mini-bar fridge, sat down in a very comfortable chair overlooking the garden and turned to the big manila envelope from the bank.

The letter and several note pages were definitely in Simon's handwriting. Dear Dan, it began. If you're reading this, I'm dead!

Jeez, why couldn't he have left that part out?

Simon continued: Your supposition that I was investigating Chinese spying into U.S. Navy activities and projects was spot on. I have been back-grounding my research via several good contacts that confirm my suspicions, but I don't have enough for a story.

It began five or six months after I'd arrived in Hawaii when I was invited to a Navy League banquet, honoring outstanding young officers and sailors. I recognized several local Navy officers and one Chinese man I'd met in London while on the Standard. He was then attached to the PRC Consulate as a trade envoy, but when I approached him he acted like he never knew me. Then, in a few minutes, he came over and we talked about London.

What I was reading was fascinating, and on the next page Simon went on: I could swear I saw this guy, known to me only as Chan, talking to a few officers from Pearl Harbor. Weeks later, while building my contacts in the Chinese community, I met an older man whose life may hinge on him remaining anonymous. He fled Mao and his Reds and arrived in Hawaii in 1949, becoming highly respected in the local Chinatown community. We shared a mutual disdain for communism and he quietly told me that America should be careful because PRC agents were collecting information on military bases from Norfolk to San Diego, and at Pearl Harbor.

I needed a lot more information than just his to produce a story with teeth in it and one that could be verified. So, I dug deeper into a small population of Chinese in Hawaii loyal to Beijing, not Washington. They were the new generation who felt the west had screwed China and that their homeland must be on par with the U.S. to balance world power.

By page four I still had nothing of substance, but the last page listed people who could help me expose the story that Simon would never be able to write.

His notes concluded: Luckily, I found two people who may be willing to help you, one in Honolulu the other in Washington. You'll discover the spies are well entrenched in their communities and even in our military forces. These people play hardball and are totally committed to overthrowing the American way of life. They'll stop at nothing to achieve their goals. Good luck, and be careful. Look what happened to me!

Simon had passed to me not the whole story, but the keys that would allow me to figure out this puzzle of international treason.

CHAPTER 28 - BAD NEWS ABOUNDS

May 12, 1999: Honolulu, Hawaii

Simon had handwritten the word Aloha at the bottom of the notes and signed them with his initials. I was going to follow through on the contacts he'd named starting the first thing tomorrow, but for now I allowed my eyelids to close looking forward to the first full night of sleep I'd had in a really long time.

I greeted the next morning knowing precisely the direction my investigative journalism would take for the next several months. The first step on a list of things to do was to call a phone number in Aiea Heights. I hoped to set up a meeting with Simon's main contact.

"Wei," was the short reply I got when the phone was answered.

"Is Mr.Yao there please?" I got an answer in some broken English which I believed to be 'He no longer here.' Pressing on I asked where I could find Yao, but the line clicked dead. With no address and no first name I added him to my list of needs from the Chinese Chamber of Commerce.

Next I called Commander Matson's office at SUBPAC, but he was heading to San Diego so that lead went on the back burner. My phone call to the Chinese Chamber was more productive. A very helpful secretary answered and after I identified myself and said I needed some help in looking for a couple of Chinese businessmen in town, she set an appointment for me with the Chamber's Executive Director for tomorrow morning.

My next best use of time would be to talk with the HPD officers who actually covered the murder call. I drove to the new police headquarters on Beretania Street. I went up to the second floor of the cop shop and the office that said Detectives. The civilian secretary recognized me from my Times days and offered to help. I said I wanted to talk with the officers involved in the Simon Cardigan case, so she motioned me to the cubicle of LT Andrew Kahanamoku.

I asked the officer the question he had undoubtedly heard thousands of times, but he was no relative of the late great swimmer and surfer Duke Kahanamoku.

He waved me into a seat across from his desk, and asked how he could help me. When I said it was about Simon Cardigan he sat back and shook his head. "I knew the guy, not well, but he was in and out of here, covering some of the police beat when he wasn't doing the legislature. Tragic his life ended in that sleazy club."

"What about the crime scene? I know there was no wallet or other ID, and that a bus transfer was about all he had on him. Did you find out anything more? What did the club staff have to say, that kind of thing?"

Lieutenant Kahanamoku began: "The manager and two waitresses say a guy walked into the bar, went back to the table where Cardigan was sitting, and shot him in the head. He then ran out of the club down to Hotel Street and disappeared into the crowd. By the time we got there the club was empty and nobody could give us a description of the shooter, except to say he was Chinese and about 5 feet 8, which fits just about every Chinese in our mug shot books."

Do you think Simon intended to use the bus transfer to get to Waikiki or to Pearl Harbor?"

"I doubt it. It looked like he was using it as a memo pad for some appointments." I perked up at this and asked him to explain.

"It was sort of crumpled up among the change in his front pants pocket. On the back was written: Set up Int with Gov re Hawn Home Lands and Ck out Mr Penole."

In my notebook I put down exactly what LT Kahanamoku said and then asked: "Do you have any motive?"

"For now, perhaps he may have owed money to some local Chinese gamblers, couldn't pay off and ended up paying with his life. That's about all we can figure."

Still frustrated, I thanked the detective and left the cop shop pleased with the new information. I understood about the interview with the Governor, but learning what role Mr. Penole played in this story would require more work.

Next stop, Chinatown itself.   Parking at the Chinese Cultural Plaza I decided to do Chinatown on foot.   That was the easiest and most fun way to get around this colorful section of downtown Honolulu which had been refurbished over the past ten years, and was now safe and exciting to visit. Mysterious herbal food stores, restaurants, fruit stands, art galleries, and some new bars made for a colorful walking tour.

I'd been to most of these places but never to the one where Simon met his fate. This afternoon I'm adding Club Lotus to my experiences.   From the moment I finished climbing stairs up to the second floor bar, I knew the only thing I'd get was the drink I ordered.   After calling for a Sing Tao beer I asked to speak to the manager and was told I already was.

At the mention of Simon's murder a bamboo curtain dropped between us. She knew nothing and told the HPD the same. Her girls also knew nothing. "Contact police if you want information," she snapped, eyes burning like coals in a hot grill. Spinning around she disappeared through a curtain in the rear of the bar.   I finished my Beijing beer, and figured I'd better make that exit too.

It was clear that nobody in the Chinese community would talk about Simon's death, so it looked like the guy at the Chamber was my last chance. I hoped he'd help me find the elusive Mr. Chan.

My Thursday appointment wasn't until 11 am, so I walked up the beach sidewalk to the Halekulani Hotel and leisurely partook of their great buffet breakfast.   I absolutely *love* the popovers they feature.

An affable Mr. K.K. Luke greeted me at the Chamber. His secretary had told him I was looking for a certain Chinese businessman so the executive got right to the point: "My staff has looked through all the data on local business people named Chan, and apparently none have ties with the PRC in London. I'm very sorry, Mr. Lincoln."   Oh well, another dead end.

Before leaving the Royal, I thought of calling Janice and telling her the story of Simon's death, but that wasn't something you did in the course of a quick five minute phone call. I'd fill her in when I got home and when the time was right.

Honolulu city lights are always haunting when you fly out over Diamond Head. That night I watched them fade away off to my left as our big Continental jet climbed to its cruising altitude.

I sat back in my seat and put on the headphones to listen to some Hawaiian music as I left that magic place. The pretty young flight attendant had been told I wanted no meals until breakfast and to not disturb me if I was asleep.

The music of Gabby Pahinui played on and once I was asleep the stewardess un-plugged the earphones that were now down around my neck. She put a blanket over my body leaving me comfortably in dreamland for the next eight hours, flying back to my Janice's welcoming arms. I hoped.

CHAPTER 29 - HOW'D THEY KNOW ABOUT THE GEL?

May 17, 1999: The Pentagon

Three days home and I was still plowing through piles of mail, e-mail and phone messages. Bureau chief Ben Huntley had greeted me with a slap on the back and glowing kudos for the stories I'd filed from China and the planned follow-ups. I didn't mention Simon's death or why I was a couple days late returning home, other than to say I needed some more beach time in Hawaii.

I called Janice's office a couple times on Monday but she wasn't in. That evening I finally caught her at home and we talked about my trip, what I liked most the food, and the least, being away from her. I still didn't tell her about Simon.

Ben came into my office, flopped his big frame into a chair and asked: "What's with that gel you reported in your May Day Parade story?"

"Beats the hell out of me, but I'm sure going to find out. I was about to return a call from that Pentagon admiral who's been such a great source for me."

"Admiral Sharpe, is it?"

"Yep, he's really got his shit together. Something like 30 years in submarines so if anyone knows about gels he will. Now, give me a little privacy and I'll find out if there's more to this story than Navy toothpaste."

Ben smiled and left my office. I knew he liked me a lot and was happy he'd given me the Pentagon beat. Ben's bosses knew he had gone around normal PANS and Washington hiring practices to land this Dan Lincoln guy.

I dialed the now familiar Pentagon line direct to Bernie Sharpe. "Admiral? Dan Lincoln returning your call. Sorry to be a bit late, but I've just returned from my May Day trip to China."

"I look forward to hearing all about Shanghai. Did the Chinese president actually say stealth gel?"

"He did indeed, Admiral, and it caught me by surprise. I still don't know what it's all about but if it's not too highly classified I'd very much like to know about stealth gel."

The admiral grumbled something about spies and friends of the PRC, and was apparently thumbing through an appointment book while keeping me on the line.

"See you late this Friday afternoon."

"At your office, say 3:30 pm?"

"Good. And Dan, don't start asking around about the gel. It's best you hear it straight from me only. Okay?"

"Yes sir," I replied, as the line clicked off. I smiled knowing that the gel story had raised a huge *red flag* at the Pentagon, no pun intended, and in the office of the CNO. I assumed it wasn't details of the stealth gel that bothered the top brass as much as how the Chinese had access to something classified top secret or higher. That would be as much a part of my story as how the gel works.

Getting out to the Pentagon via the Metrorail was becoming a habit, and I knew the schedules by heart. From the Gallery Place Chinatown Metro station I took the Yellow Line train to Pentagon Station, the first stop across the river and into Virginia. Friday afternoon found me on a Metroliner at 2:45 pm.

Anxious to see Janice, I was quite disappointed when an enlisted man met me. Shortly the admiral emerged from his private office, greeted me and signaled me to follow.

We walked down the passageway to a small conference room with a slide projector and a video playback unit. Taking seats, Admiral Sharpe quietly began: "Dan, your May Day parade story hit us right between the eyes."

Damn, I thought, what have I dug into? I figured this was big time stuff but I wasn't ready for what came next. I took out my recorder, held it up for the admiral's approval, and pushed record. My trusty hip-pocket note book was out, pen at the ready.

"Nothing we didn't expect," Sharpe began. "But for the Chinese president to say his Navy is the number one force in the Asia and Pacific area is just so much horseshit! This stealth gel business is another matter. Some of the details I give you will be classified and not for release anyway. I sense a professional spy or just stupid American civilian is giving or selling our top secret submarine developments to the Red Chinese."

Suddenly, everything I heard and learned in Honolulu began tumbling into place. The admiral hit the TV/Video remote clicker and a video image, with a top secret classification, appeared on the screen.

The video began at the Norfolk Navy Base with a group of LOS ANGELES class subs. It zoomed-in showing the bow of one of the boats with a skin layer laid over the steel panels of the hull that helps make the boat less magnetically detectable. It also showed a group of small jet-like sprayers mounted in an arched ring around the ship's foremost portions.

In the next scene the sub was at sea, on the surface, and a close-up of the bow showed nothing unusual. I assumed the jet sprayers were recessed into the hull.

We then saw the sub submerged and fully underway. The camera focused on the bow and we could see the jet sprayers rising from their hiding place in the boat's skin and taking aim in a 360 degree spread around the front of the ship.

"Now watch this," the admiral said, "and see how this gel stuff actually slides around the entire hull providing a new level of quietness to our submarines. Testing began last January, and there has been no public release about it whatsoever. The only people who know about the gel are on the test boats and on my staff here in N-771."

"So, that's what's led you to believe in spies?" I blurted out.

"Hell no! I don't think spies are to be believed," he replied with a chortle, "but somebody found out about our submarine toothpaste and gave it to someone with direct access to the President of China!"

"Who other than those working on this project and some of you here at the Pentagon know about it?" I asked.

"None other than twenty members of the Senate Armed

Services Committee. I conducted a *for senators eyes only* top secret briefing January 10th, shortly after our gel tests off Norfolk. Everyone there was told that this top secret information was not to leave the hearing room. They all nodded their acceptance of those rules before I gave my briefing. I know most of those Senators, and can't believe any of them would sell out his or her country by being a spy for China."

He paused a moment and then asked me: "Do you remember that hearing last summer when the House Armed Services Committee was grilling the SECNAV about the budget?"

"Certainly. That's when Congressman Anderson went after Secretary Wetzel about funding for his Chinese-American military friendship resolution. Made a great story for me!"

"And Senator Anderson is known as a big China supporter, isn't he?" the admiral asked, rhetorically. "Well, that same senator was one of the 20 who sat through my January 10th *eyes only* briefing, and I remember now I thought it strange that he was the only senator in the room taking copious notes."

"You think Henry Anderson is a spy?" I got no response from Admiral Sharpe. "He's a bit pompous and as a traveling partner he's a pain in the ass. I was his seatmate on the trip to Beijing and spent too much time with him during our visit to their Navy base at Shanghai. He pushes the envelope of obnoxiousness, yes, but a spy? I don't think so."

"Perhaps you're right, Dan, but I'm not so sure about the guy. You seem to know him better than I do. Maybe you could keep your eyes open when you see him or interview him for future stories; let me know if you think he's acting strangely. My gut feeling is he may be the source of our leak. The big question is did he leak it knowingly on purpose, or just blab to someone who was already interested in such info and knew how to best get it to the Chinese government?"

"I don't know, Admiral. I can't believe a U.S. senator, even though he supports many of China's causes, would deliberately sell out his own country. However, if I find anything that even looks strange when I'm talking to him I'll let you know."

"Fair enough, Dan. Thanks, and keep in touch."

He stood up ready to head back to his office, but I stopped him: "Admiral, there's something else I need to discuss with you, sir." He turned around and sat back down. "What you got?"

"Well sir, an old buddy I worked with on the Honolulu Times, named Simon Cardigan, has been murdered. I found out about it just as I left Hawaii for China, and spent a few days last week looking into the matter. The local police are passing the killing off as a probable pay-back for gambling debts. I don't see it that way."

"I'm very sorry to hear about your friend but what does it have to do with Senator Anderson or my concerns about spies infiltrating our bases and giving secrets to the PRC?"

"Could be everything, sir," I said to the admiral, now with a tell me all you know look on his face.

"Simon was a great investigative journalist; always working on stories during his off-duty hours. Shortly before I left Hawaii to come here I got the feeling he was close to a story that probably involved a Honolulu Chinese spy organization. He wouldn't confirm it but a few days later he gave me an envelope and a hundred bucks to rent a safe deposit box for the envelope. I was not to open the envelope unless something happened to him. He was killed April 29th and I retrieved the envelope as soon as I got back to Honolulu." Now the admiral was all ears.

"Some handwritten notes confirmed he had discovered a spy ring in Honolulu apparently getting information out of a Navy contact at Pearl. He gave me the name of one person he felt would talk with me but when I tried to contact the guy he was nowhere to be found. Simon said he had also run into another Chinese man he'd known in London. He was a trade mission envoy with the London PRC Consulate and apparently was now in business in Honolulu. I got nowhere trying to find him, even with the help of the Chinese Chamber of Commerce."

"The only thing found on Simon's corpse was a bus transfer with some sort of laundry list on it." I passed a Xerox copy of the bus transfer to the admiral who put it in his pocket.

"If Simon was into something as big as spies infiltrating Pearl Harbor, and he indicated that his contacts had said there were more PRC moles in Norfolk, San Diego, Seattle and D.C., it could very well be Senator Anderson has been targeted by one of them. I knew you should hear it from me as soon as the time was right, and today is as right as it gets!"

"I can't tell you how important what you've just told me is," the admiral said as he stood up and prepared to close our discussion. "I can say, however, it confirms my long-held beliefs that these SOBs are right next to us on a day-to-day working basis. Others must hear what you've told me and we'll step up our efforts to find these operatives. You may have overlooked that while the spies are working for Red China they may not all be Chinese. That makes our job tougher. But knowing they're spying, we can do some defensive things that may bring these bastards to the surface, or at least into radar range."

We shook hands as the meeting ended.

I still didn't see Janice so I took the Metro back to the city my mind reeling. The whole question of spies and how Hank Anderson fit into it weighed heavy on my mind. Was he a knowing participant or just a pawn in some bigger plot? Simon must have stumbled into something that was even more widespread than he thought. Spies trying to steal Navy secrets? Could it be a liberal U.S. senator? Jeez, which was it, or was it both?

Stealth gel was real. That meant my Navy friends must be getting pretty close to a major breakthrough. It also meant I'd have to do another balancing act deciding which would be an exclusive story and its importance to national security, and which would be follow-up pieces.

I got off the train at 9th and G Sts. and walked to the C-C. After ordering my favorite whiskey sour, blended and served in a bucket, I relaxed for the first time that day. The drink came, did its stuff, and I slipped out of my daily routine.

CHAPTER 30 - ANNAPOLIS GETAWAY

May 22, 1999: Annapolis, Maryland

This was the weekend I had thought about every day; to be alone with the very beguiling and hopefully hot Janice Cannon. I couldn't help myself from feeling like I was falling in love.

As we drove down to Annapolis Saturday afternoon the top was off my Mazda Miata, so the warm spring breeze blew through Janice's gorgeous hair. I was relating experiences from my trip and she seemed keenly interested in them, particularly the QINGDAO; after all, she was Navy. She knew about Sen. Anderson's invitation to bring that ship to Pearl Harbor for next year's 4th of July celebration. I grimaced and changed the topic to what she'd been doing since I saw her a month ago.

"Just more of the same old, same old. I'm helping Admiral Sharpe with the new VIRGINIA details and when you're not around I work out a few nights a week at the gym."

After checking into a cozy motel we drove to Chesapeake Bay and snooped into some neat shops where I bought a half dozen fish platters for my mom and dad. Janice said her father had everything he needed and that she wasn't much of a shopper anyway.

"What, a woman who doesn't like to shop? Is there anything else unique about you I should know?" Pausing a moment, Janice then said quite slyly: "Oh, you'll see, in due time!" Wow, I was now really intrigued.

Janice rubbed against me and purred: "Are you going to feed me anytime soon?"

"Of course. I know this great little place around the corner," I said, pulling her closer, her magnificent jugs rubbing against me. Thank God for thin summer clothes. "Hell with eating out, let's just grab something to go and head back to the room for some..."

"No sir," Janice interrupted. "You're not getting off that cheaply. Feed me now, and you'll get your dessert later."

With that I spirited us away to a restaurant called the Atlantic Trawler which, in my humble opinion, offered the absolutely best seafood in the state. I loved the steamed clams and broth followed by crunchy fish and chips. As I had hoped Janice went for a chilled bottle of chardonnay.

Her selection came from the fertile Finger Lakes wine region of upstate New York, not far from my old hometown. "Good," I muttered quietly, "barriers are falling already."

She followed it with a half dozen oysters on the half shell and then a complete salmon entree. As the waiter cleared the table, Janice cocked her head at me and cooed: "Ready for dessert?"

"Message received Commander, loud and clear," I stammered, my throat getting slightly dry. Quickly I paid the tab and escorted my long-legged delight to our motel. There was only one awkward moment when she asked, wide-eyed innocence on her beautiful face, "Ah, don't all journalists travel with a friend?"

"Covered," I saucily replied, reaching into my bag for one of the same brand that covered Helen of Troy. At that point I decided to tell her about Simon.

"You may recall I was a few days late getting back from Hawaii after my China trip," I began. Janice said nothing as if she hadn't really heard.

"I stopped in Honolulu because one of my friends from the   Times was murdered just before I left for Beijing. His name was Simon Cardigan, an Englishman. We worked together for about three years and while we weren't real close, I liked him and was very shocked to learn about his death."

"What did he die of? I can see you're most upset."

"He was shot in the head. Cold blooded murder." I continued to tell her all I knew of the killing: "The police say he owed gambling debts to the Chinatown mob, and they took him out for not paying off. As far as HPD is concerned the case is closed. I'm not sure I agree with them, but there's nothing I can do."

124

"It really shook me up and I guess I'm not over the fact a friend was actually murdered!" I said nothing about the Pearl spy ring or Simon's notes.

We changed the topic and went to bed for dessert. In the morning we drove to the Naval Academy which Janice had never seen, and then headed back to D.C.

CHAPTER 31 HAPPY 223rd BIRTHDAY

July 4, 1999: The Mall, Washington, D.C.

Another insufferably hot day in the Capitol and Senator Anderson and his wife Linda sat stuck in Pennsylvania Avenue traffic. Air temperature and humidity were both at the 98 level and Hank fumed as he feared they'd never make it in time for the Fourth of July festivities.

"God, I hate all the events and socializing we have to do," Linda groused. "This sucks. I wish I were back in Minnesota on a cool July morning watching the local VFW and American Legion on parade."

"Cool it, Linda. I've told you a hundred times this is the way it's going to be. So chill out," Hank barked.

Finally past the barricades they were directed to a reserved parking place and escorted to a huge reviewing stand, complete with covered awning.

After being seated, a tuxedoed waiter came over and asked if the couple would like a cold drink. "Gin and tonic for me and a glass of lemonade for Mrs. Anderson."

Linda hadn't taken a drink for over a year hoping that if she could see the Washington scene clearly maybe she'd like it more. Unfortunately that hadn't worked. Now she merely put up with her day-to-day life in political-ville.

The Andersons had not been lovers for a long time, other than an occasional quickie after the make up of another short-lived argument. She was resigned to her current life and spent as large a percentage of it as she could with her children. Without them, who knew what she would be inclined to do to herself. So, she took them to school, organized their extra curricular activities, set up their social contacts and generally buried herself in their daily lives.

Hank, in the meantime, hadn't become involved with any one other woman but he was not opposed to the occasional after-hours drink with a political colleague, an interesting lobbyist, or anyone who had a life that was even half exciting.

The parade passed and Linda was impatient to leave. Hank had spent most of the time away from his seat, chatting with other party leaders, some Congressional friends from his old House days, and keeping the waiters busy at the gin and tonic post. Luckily for Linda her longtime friend Mary Johnson, wife of a current Minnesota congressman, joined her for parade evaluations.

Linda hoped she could make it through another five hours of being seen and meeting the people, as Hank liked to depict such gatherings.

The real action on Independence Day was on the Mall with merchants and crafters selling their unique wares. You could find anything from native Indian carved jewelry and turquoise to hooked rugs and handmade sweaters from the Amish of Pennsylvania.

Midway down the Mall, at a tent with the name Ming & Ching Things, Madam Shin was meeting with someone who seemed to be doing most of the talking. They were recently introduced by Fred Tong. As a major player in the Washington Red Chinese intelligence network, Lily was told that whenever contacted she was to follow this person's instructions to the letter.

The contact ordered Lily to have Cheryl get Senator Anderson to meet with Lily, the ultimate goal being to garner as much information as possible about American subs. Madam Shin was given the PRC spy's codeword, Fortune Cookie, which must be used whenever contacting this person and before she accepted any future instructions.

July 4th was capped by the traditional National Concert at the Lincoln Memorial. The finest singers, entertainers, bands and storytellers in America filled a star-studded TV program that was shown to a grateful national audience.

"You know, when I've been in the Senate longer they may have me read a poem or the Preamble to the Constitution," Hank mumbled as they strolled along the jam-packed Mall

"Sure, Senator," Linda replied cryptically, with all the feeling of the moment. "And I hope Joe America sees you for the power hungry egoist you are, darling."

Making their way down the booths, Hank spied one that stood out from the rest. It was no hippie crafter's display, it was Asian art. The sign read: July 4th Branch - Ming & Ching Things. An Oriental woman was bowing to a couple that had apparently just bought something and was about to leave.

"I know you," Hank said excitedly to the woman. Linda shot him a stern look of stink-eye but Hank went on: "I mean, I know of this shop. That is, if you have a regular shop in Georgetown. Do you?"

"Yes, sir, I have been there for about a year but few people have heard about it. How do you know me and my shop, please?"

"Well, I was in China recently and my escort and translator was a Navy officer named Wong who said he had a cousin running a Chinese antique shop in Washington. You must be her?"

"Why, yes I am! What a coincidence you two should meet. How is he? I haven't heard from him in several months."

"He is, or at least he was fine when I saw him in Shanghai back in May. My apologies for not introducing ourselves. This is my wife Linda and I'm Senator Henry Anderson from Minnesota, a state near Canada."

"I am familiar with Minnesota, and most honored to meet you Senator, and you Mrs. Anderson. Welcome to Ming and Ching Things. I am Lily Shin, the owner. Please come to our main shop when you have more time. I have a very impressive collection of original Chinese art, sculpture and antiques."

"Thank you very much, Madam...ah...Shin, is it? Yes, we'd love to. I saw many beautiful examples of Chinese art during my visit to Beijing, and would like to have a piece or two for my office, and maybe for the house. What do you think, dear?"

"I'm not much of an authority on Chinese art, but I'm sure it would be lovely."

Madam Shin bowed politely and said: "Please, before you go, do accept this small token as a reminder that you will come in the very near future and spend some time shopping, and spending money." She handed each a small cloisonné key ring bearing a tiger. "On our Chinese calendar this is the year of the tiger, a good luck symbol. May it bring your lives much luck in the years ahead."

"Shay shay is what I learned in China to say thank you. We both thank you and will be expecting that good luck."

"Nice meeting you," Linda said shaking Madam Shin's hand. "I look forward to seeing more of your wares in the future," added Hank. Your wears, on and off, he smirked to himself.

Walking away, Hank visualized how fine Madam Shin looked next to him on her couch, and wondered if she had met any other important people in Washington. Poor girl, she probably doesn't have any friends in the city. He would have to remedy that!

Lily would need a lot of people with money, real money, to keep a shop like hers profitable. He made a mental note to call her in a few days and chat about his China visit, her Navy cousin and her current lifestyle in Georgetown. Knowing an upward bound young U.S. senator could help a new immigrant, perhaps a dinner to discuss the immigration process would set the path to the Asian pleasures Hank desired.

Not far from the Mall activities, I was spending the holiday in my apartment. I talked on the phone with Chuck Matson back in Honolulu, about news of a Chinese spy operation there. The only helpful info he had was that he could find no flat denial there was such an operation. He did say his Navy Intelligence buddies raised some eyebrows when he brought up the topic, leading him to believe Simon was probably on to something.

After that I couldn't help think about Simon's last warning to me in his notes: Be careful as you get into this.

These people play hardball, and they'll stop at nothing to achieve their goals. Good luck, and be careful. Look what happened to me!

"Thanks, Simon," I quipped. At that point I decided to get out of the apartment and take a walk, maybe even to the Lincoln Memorial for tonight's big outdoor concert.

It was a sunny late afternoon and I walked briskly down the hill toward the Reflecting Pool. About to cross the street and head toward the holiday music concert site, I waited for the traffic light to turn green. As it did I stepped off the curb and began walking.

Midway across the intersection I was startled to see a large dark sedan speeding toward me. I jumped and fell to the curb as it swerved, blew its horn and then disappeared down the hill.

People who saw the incident rushed to my assistance, asking if I was okay and if they should call the police. "Thank you, thank you all, but I'm fine," I quickly assured them, getting up briskly to prove it. Since nobody had been able to get a license plate number I knew my chances of ever finding that asshole driver were as remote as bringing Simon back to life.

Reflecting on that moment, I could swear the driver was an Asian. Suddenly a shiver as cold as a Mongolian winter crept down my back. Was this a forewarning? Was there really a spy ring that knew I was following up Simon's efforts to expose them? Were they, as he had said, well entrenched here in D.C. and elsewhere, not hesitant to kill anyone getting in their way? Holy shit, they really do play hard ball!

I couldn't get to Admiral Sharpe for a few days to tell him about my near miss, but his reaction was predictable: "Get the hell out of the game. Let the NIS and FBI take over. Today!"

"I've agreed to play the game by the rules, Admiral, and not duck out just because there's some incoming flak. I'll keep my ears and eyes open to concerns you and I have talked about, but I'm not going to chicken out, even if the enemy sends kamikaze drivers at me."

"I can't stop you Dan, but like Simon warned, look what they did to him! Remember these people won't hesitate to kill for what they believe in. Your job should be to keep one step ahead of them, including your timing when stepping off curbs."

CHAPTER 32- THERE'S A MOLE IN OUR BOWL

September 3, 1999: Washington, D.C.

Summer was quickly sizzling away. It would be goodbye stifling heat, welcome aboard cool autumn breezes and the palate of leaf colors that would suddenly turn Washington into a Van Gogh. It was just before Labor Day when I asked Janice if she wanted to do something out of the ordinary for a future weekend.

She thought for a moment and then said: "Doctor's orders. I think the prescription calls for a three day cruise to the Bahamas."

"I'll check out the schedules today," I said, trying not to sound too excited.

"No, let me. I know I can get us a better deal on tickets through MWR. I'll check over lunchtime."

"Perfect. I have a news conference at 2 pm in the SECDEF's conference room. Something to do with base closures."

It was 3:30 pm by the time SECDEF had outlined which bases were to be axed, how the realignment would affect military forces and their strengths, and questions had been answered about everything from replacing lost revenues and entire communities being stripped of their major economic base to the overall effect on the national defense budget and how we would be unprepared if a war should develop.

I slipped out a rear door and headed to Janice's nearby office. "Reporting as scheduled, Commander," I said giving the lovely lady officer a peck on the cheek. "What did you find out about our next sea duty?"

"We leave on the Friday after Thanksgiving, and return the next Monday at 6 am. Total per-person cost for the cruise is just $249, and I've got airfare for $199, round-trip, each. Not a bad deal I'd say."

"It's a great deal! Now we need to get the time off."

"Piece of cake. I've already gotten the admiral's okay, and hoping you'd approve, I made the reservations," she smiled at me.

A knock on the door was followed by Bernie Sharpe entering Janice's office. "Sorry to barge in, Commander, but I thought Dan might drop by here after the news conference. Got a sec, Dan?"

"You bet, Admiral. What's up?" He motioned for me to follow him, saying to Janice: "I'll be back after we finish. Please don't leave."

A naval museum is how I'd describe the admiral's corner office.   Its bulkheads were wall to wall photos, certificates and ship's plaques presented to him by dozens of allied navies and ships from London to Sydney.   Navy blue baseball caps with ship names and logos in golden thread rested on book shelves.   Pieces of spent ordnance commemorating the history of naval warfare overlooked a two by three foot color painting of Admiral Hyman Rickover, father of the nuclear Navy.

"This is the first time I've been in your private office, sir. It's a great workspace, if I do say so."

"It's definitely me, but I'd give it all up be back on a cramped submarine rather than processing the reams of paperwork that come across my desk daily. I see you were looking at old Admiral Rickover? He was a cold sonofabitch, and an impossible man to work for, but he taught me everything I know about surviving the bureaucratic wars. But, to the point of our meeting."

"It's about Simon Cardigan. No breaks are left for him, but perhaps his last words have given us the big break we've been looking for."

"Have you come up with something about one of those Chinese contacts Simon had made?"

"No, but intelligence says they've gotten something from that stuff written on the back of the bus transfer. They think Simon was definitely trying to send you a message. He counted on your finding that bus transfer and not taking it for a simple laundry list of things he needed to do the next day."

"But Admiral, it doesn't seem logical there's anything about Hawaiian Home Lands or setting up an interview with the governor that could have to do with stealing Navy secrets at Pearl. I tried to find Mr. Penole but he doesn't exist, at least not in the phone book."

"Right again, Dan. But did you stop to think that Mr. Penole could be a code word, not a person's name?"

"No sir, I didn't. Is that what your guys think?"

"Yes, a person and a place. They think Simon was telling you there is a mole in the Pentagon. P-E-N for the Pentagon, and O-L-E for the word mole. If they're right we've got ourselves a problem bigger than just Honolulu, and more than just another civilian spy ring. The PRC may have access to some of our biggest secrets in this very building!"

CHAPTER 33 - EIGHT RED

October 10, 1999: Washington, D.C.

"Knock, knock, are you awake in there?" It was Tom Carlson, Hank's chief of staff, in charge of researching info for resolutions and future bills. Actually Tom was the senator's confidant, handball partner and keeper of skeletons buried in the senator's closet. He too was pro-China and in favor of Hank's military friendship resolution. But his reasons for being pro-China were not exactly friendly.

Tom had lived for many years in China where his father was a United Nations Trade Mission delegate, remarried to a Chinese woman. Tom had cultivated friendships with Americans whose fathers were ex-patriot businessmen or officers at the U.S. Consulate. After a dozen years in Beijing the family moved to Hong Kong in the mid 80s where the senior Carlson took a position in the international trade department of Hong Kong and Shanghai Bank.

"Come in. I'm not sleeping, I'm just tired of the paperwork. What time is it, anyway?"

"Six thirty and time to call it a day. You're doing a great job, considering you've been in the Senate for less than a year."

"I can't understand why so many senators are set against improving our Chinese relationship," he said with a feeling of defeat. "I realize the Chinese themselves make it a tough sell, what with all their little tests like the war games off Taiwan a couple years ago, and buzzing our P-3 patrol flights. I know it, they're really spy flights, but to the American public acts like those certainly do test the image of China being our friend. And yet, we get away with the same stuff when our Pacific Fleet ships sail near Chinese land, and we simply call it patrolling off shore in international waters!"

"Tell you what, Senator; let's get out of here. My friend Tom Martz, number two staff guy on Ways and Means, is meeting me for a couple of drinks at that little bar next to my apartment building. My girlfriend will be there and it's usually filled with young staffers, all who look a lot better than me, if you get my drift.

"What the hell. I'll call Linda first. Going home after a few drinks is just a bit too late for dinner, so I'll say I'm working late and will see her in the morning. Grab my coat, will you. I'll lock up my desk and be with you in just a few minutes."

Tom Carlson was the quintessential political aide. Out for number one and the best way to get there was by keeping Henry Anderson in a favorable spotlight as much as possible. He disliked his boss's attitude and abrupt manner with most people who came to see him. But such was the game of politics and the benefits far outweighed the daily routine.

Tom returned to his desk and dialed a cell phone he kept in his desk drawer. The person who answered politely said: "Armed Services Committee Staff, may I help you?" Not identifying himself Tom replied: "Is Miss Leong there please?"

"Yes sir, just a moment." When Cheryl came on the line he said merely: "Call your mother and you two meet me at the usual place. Be there no later than 7 o'clock."

About a half hour later, the two men left the Senate parking garage. Following Tom's directions, the senator drove to The Honorable Gentleman, within shouting distance of the now infamous Watergate Apartment complex. As they walked into the bar Hank wondered if it was patronized by the likes of G. Gordon Liddy, Jeb McGrudder or any of the other Watergate notables. But why would they 25 years after the break-in and the subsequent downfall of RMN?

The place was filled with look-alike bureaucrats in their standard earth-tone tweeds and washed denims, talking about what Washingtonians talk about in these trendy gin mills: politics and who's sleeping with whom. It was a carbon copy of dozens of similar looking bars all over the District. Spotting Tom Martz, Carlson ushered Hank to a table at the back of the bar.

After pressing through the crowd of customers, Tom said: "Senator, you remember my girlfriend Patty Kagen?" Hank nodded.

"Hiya, Patty cake," he said giving her a kiss, "and this guy is Tom Martz, my buddy I told you about."

"Honored to meet you, Senator," said Tommy Terrific. "It's nice having some new blood in the Senate!   Please join us. We're up a couple on you, but Carlson catches up quickly, don't you?   This is Cheryl Leong, an intern from Georgetown University, working with our committee this semester, and her mother Lily Shin.   Madam Shin owns a great little Chinese antiques shop in Georgetown where we just purchased several authentic Ming vases and tapestries for our office."

Taking the younger woman's hand Hank said: "Thanks Tom. It's a pleasure meeting you. May I call you Cheryl? I had the pleasure of meeting your mother at last year's Fourth of July crafts festival on the Mall.   How nice to see you again, Madam Shin."

Tom Carlson maneuvered the senator to a chair between mother and daughter. "What's your major?" Hank asked Cheryl.

"I have a degree in political science and now I'm doing post-grad work in international relations, sir. I hope to get into a branch of government service, either the diplomatic corps or maybe even something up on the Hill."

"Very admirable goal," responded the Minnesota senator.

Hank soon found himself staring at the lady shop owner he hoped to spend many a night with.   She couldn't be older than her early 40s judging from Cheryl who he estimated to be about 23. As they drank and chatted he recalled that night after the Chinese New Year's party, and the near-disastrous meeting on the Mall with Linda at his side. Madam Shin had played it cool and for all Linda knew that truly was a chance meeting. Chemistry between east and west was, at this moment, instinctive.

"I visited your beautiful country this past spring, Cheryl. As I mentioned to your mother when we met at her

Fourth of July display, I was invited to attend the May Day parade in Beijing. Our interpreter was your mother's cousin, LT Wong. He and his Navy colleagues gave me and one other guest a special tour of the shipyard and base at Shanghai. It was most impressive."

"Shanghai was originally my home," Madam Shin replied, her pure velvet voice, modulated and assured. "Did you see anything more than the Navy base while there?"

"Only what I could see flying in and then during car rides to and from the airport." Struck by Madam Shin's beauty, Hank easily forgot to tell her about the day-tour of the city, the museum and the dim sum lunch. This was just so much small talk and his mind was entertaining other thoughts.

"Hong Kong is better known than Shanghai and draws the shopping crowds," she told the group. "I had a shop in Hong Kong before coming here. Not many foreigners get to visit Shanghai, but it is a wonderful city. You were fortunate to get there, Senator," she said, her black pearl eyes glistening.

At 8:30 pm Tom Carlson suggested the group leave the now smoke-enshrouded bar and drive about 20 minutes out of the District and up into Maryland, toward Rockville. He knew a guy there that ran small and very elite, if not illegal, gambling club.

"It's legit," Carlson told them, "but you had to be out of there by midnight." Apparently the guy had worked a deal with the local police so that everyone could do their thing, but not after midnight.

"I don't know," Hank chuckled. "I'm a U.S. Senator and if someone sees me there it could mean all sorts of bad press."

"Oh come on, Hank. No one's going to see you," said Carlson. "They have a special private entrance to the club. You'll be secure."

"And, don't forget you have me and that lucky tiger I gave you to look out for you," added a sultry voiced Madam Shin.

Tom Martz said he and Cheryl had previous plans for the evening so couldn't join them. Saying they'd see each other tomorrow the casino bound foursome exited The Honorable Gentleman from a little known back door, used by many not so honorable gentlemen in the past.

The gaming club was actually an eighth floor three bedroom unit in a condo. Two bedrooms had been converted into blackjack rooms. The dining area was home to the craps table, and the living room held the roulette table. A full bar occupied the kitchen where you could help yourself to anything liquid. The unit was decorated with comfortable furniture creating an air of respectability. The third bedroom appeared to be off limits to all but the owner.

They were greeted by a muscular young giant who looked like an escapee from the WWF, leaving no question who'd maintain the peace and enforce the midnight curfew. "Welcome. I am Stavros. Please make yourselves comfortable and help yourselves to a drink in the kitchen. The games are underway, and you'll be able to get in immediately. Call me if you need anything."

They checked the different games then sat down on a sofa, all except Hank. After seeing no one he knew or that knew him he went straight to the bar for a gin and tonic.

Rejoining the group he toasted them, saying: "I don't know about you guys, but it's roulette for me! Lily, come bring some of that good Chinese joss! See the rest of you at midnight, hopefully a lot richer than I am now."

There was room for two more at the roulette table so Hank and Lily slid onto padded stools. The senator smiled and passed two crisp one hundred dollar bills to the dealer calling, "Chips, please." The croupier pushed 20 blue five dollar and 10 rose colored ten dollar playing chips toward him saying, "Good luck, sir."

Hank was startled when the guy at the corner of the table said: "I know you, don't I? My name's Brogan, John Brogan."

"Sorry, but I don't know you."

"Hold on a second. Got it! You're that senator who loves the Chinese and wants their warships to visit Pearl Harbor next Fourth of July, aren't you?"

"Well yes I am, and I believe you and other Americans will come to see that our two great nations should not be fighting each other, but working together to better our futures." Hank said it like all the other rhetoric he'd rehearsed for TV.

Brogan wasn't having any of Hank's line, spitting out: "Hell, those commie bastards will never tell us the truth and you watch, they'll steal us blind and take all the secrets they can from our military. They're just no goddamned good!"

Knowing when to drop the topic, Hank put a $10 chip in the red zone and began to play. He started out conservatively, playing red or black, even or odd, getting the feel of the table and wheel. Shortly he hit a streak earning over $400, so he upped the ante. "A corner bet of $50 on 26-27-29 & 30," he said to the croupier. "Very good, sir, your luck appears to be running high tonight," smiled the man spinning the wheel of fortune. Madam Shin watched quietly. Lady Luck was with him now. Two plays and he was up another $800. He turned to his hoped for Asian prize, took the tiger coin from his pocket, and whispered in her ear: "You and your Chinese cat are bringing me very good joss, Lily. I hope it will hold all evening."

CHAPTER 34 - GOOD JOSS/BIG TROUBLE

October 10, 1999: Rockville, Maryland

Stavros appeared with Hank's fifth G&T of the evening since arriving at the Honorable Gentleman.

"Compliments on your fine club. I hope I'll be welcome in the future?"

"Your business is always welcome. Would you like me to open a line of credit for you, say $5,000?"

"Sure. Not that I 'spect I'll ever need it," slurred Hank. I'm doin' great, thanks to my friend Ms. Shin and her friend the tiger," Hank blubbered. "Here – hav' fun with few of my chips. Tell me, wha's your lucky number?"

"Eight. Eight is absolutely the luckiest number in China. People pay thousands of dollars to get eights on their license plates and buy apartments on the 8th floor of condo buildings. By the way, Hank, I wish you would call me Lily instead of Madam Shin. I'd like that better!"

"Lily it is," he said pushing a huge stack of chips her way, and putting $250 worth of his own on number eight. "Nothin' but good joss from now on!" Hank decried, as he momentarily returned his attention to the red and black number spots on the table.

Lily knew she had him right where she wanted him and decided she'd tease him now that his senatorial guard had left his post. She bent over, close to his ear, and whispered: "I'm sure there are many favors that will come to a famous and important senator like you. And your strong support for China gives us lots to talk about in the future."

Hank smiled and gave her a look that said: Me and my Johnson are ready whenever you are, my little Chinese chickadee.

Madam Shin knew more about roulette than she admitted; she won the next several spins of the wheel by betting on all odds, or all reds, or column bets. Hank felt his luck was high enough to bet on one single number, with a payoff of 35 to 1. That number was eight.

Hank began feeling very tired as his stack of chips shrank to zero. He signaled Stavros he wanted to use the newly granted line of credit. He continued to lose, they extended the credit further, and all of a sudden that last drink hit him really hard, and he felt like passing out. Stavros saw him slump and suggested he take a short nap, and with Lily's help they took Hank into the bedroom.

While sitting on the bed the senator said: "Thanks Stavros. I think Lily should stay with me while I take short nap. We'll rejoin the party before witching hour."

It wasn't long before clothes were shed and the two new friends were discovering that East can successfully meet West! She slipped into bed with Hank, immediately finding him hard and ready for something more than just another spin of the roulette wheel.

The sex lasted quite awhile, considering how much booze Hank had consumed, at one point with Lily riding him like a bucking bronco. After they'd had enough Hank said: "Let's grab a quick shower and now I really need a short nap. Make sure I'm up before their curfew, okay?"

A shower-for-two and Hank was off to dreamland. Bending over to give him a kiss on the cheek, Madam Shin spoke in a soft voice that was beyond the senator's current state of consciousness: "You are now mine, Mr. Senator Anderson, and you will give me everything I need about your precious submarines. Anything your Pentagon does in developing or improving subs will be headed straight to my husband in Shanghai, and when he is ready America and the world will feel the strength of the new China. Beijing will be where the new world looks for leadership in the 21st Century. China Forever!"

Groggily Hank stirred from a four-hour nap and discovered it was 3:15 am and Lily lay beside him. On the nightstand was an envelope bearing his name. His head was swimming but he managed to open the envelope and take out the single piece of paper. Focusing his eyes he read what appeared to be a promissory note, with his signature clearly in evidence. It said he owed $12,000 for his late night roulette efforts. "My God," he blurted, "what have I done?"

Slipping quietly out of the bed, he dressed quickly and was tiptoeing out of the room when Lily spoke up in a sleepy voice: "I had a wonderful time, Senator. Hope we can do this again, real soon. I learned much so from you. You won't forget to call me, will you Hank?"

The frazzled and confused senator ran out of the bedroom to the elevator. While slinking past the TV monitor-watching security guard in the condo lobby, a voice said: "Good night, Senator Anderson. There's a car waiting for you in the parking lot."

He got in and the driver headed south. Neither said a word. At this hour of the morning his trip to Georgetown was uneventful. He doubted his explanation to Linda would be the same.

CHAPTER 35 - LITTLE WHITE LIES

October 11, 1999: Washington, D.C.

"My office, right now," the senator commanded, storming into the office suite past a startled Tom Carlson. "Close the door, sit down and tell me what the hell you were thinking leaving me there with that Chinese nymphomaniac," he bellowed through clenched teeth. "You knew how tired I was. After all our years together I'd have thought you'd size up the situation and not let me be the last one to leave the place."

"I'm sorry, Hank. I thought you were in control when we all left about 11 pm, but you said you needed a couple more spins of the wheel to get your money back. You said you'd follow at midnight and would send Lily home in a cab. You did do that, didn't you?"

"Well, not exactly," mumbled Hank. "The booze made me drowsy and Stavros let me sleep it off in the bedroom. When I woke up, I had the headache of the century and Madam Shin in bed with me."

"I think we can handle that, Senator."

"There's more. Your private gaming club friends planted an IOU with my signature on it for $12,000. If this leaks out I'm through; marriage, career, everything. Just what the TV networks need. Another high profile politician porking a Senate intern's mother. Oh my God, what have I done?"

Hank slumped back in his chair head buried in his hands. Only the sound of Tom's pen rhythmically jotting down notes broke the long silence. Finally, Tom spoke up: "Don't worry, Senator. There will be no leaks. No bumps in the road ahead, I promise."

"Are you sure, Tom?"

"I'm sure Hank. Now, get some rest on the couch. I'll tell Mrs. Swanson to hold your calls for an hour."

Exhaustion finally overcame fear, and Senator Henry B. Anderson, Jr. fell sound asleep.

CHAPTER 36 - IDEA MAN COMES THROUGH

November 2, 1999: The Pentagon, Washington, D.C.

Thirty years spent seeking a stealth submarine. The search continued, but no longer headed by him. That didn't mean he wasn't still thinking every day of ideas that might produce that elusive new boat.

Admiral Sharpe didn't know it at the time but the next few months would change his life forever. All because right here and right now, at this very moment, one of his crazy ideas made good sense to him. Picking up the phone he dialed Buzz Russell's office in the Pentagon basement.

"Captain Russell speaking."

"Buzz, Bernie, and have I got something for you! Unless you're in a meeting with the CNO himself, sit where you are 'cuz I'm on my way down to your shop."

"I'm here, Admiral. Come ahead."

Bernie hadn't stopped talking since he'd arrived at the bargain basement. Buzz listened attentively to his mentor's basic ideas about enemy submarine sounds and emissions and agreed they were, in fact, one of the biggest problems currently facing our submarine crews.

The seasoned Navyman had come up with more than just basic concepts; he was ready to lay out a total stealth battle plan. But before letting the admiral explain his new ideas Buzz suggested including one other person.

"I'd like to have my best sonar engineer hear what you have to say if that's okay with you."

"Tell me a bit about him first."

That was easy since Buzz knew Chief Logan's background by heart. Logan had been with him at N-771 for over two years and there was none better on the team. "He's Senior Chief Sonarman Donald Logan. He's a retired submariner, one of the best computer geeks in the Navy and also has a sense of the unique, the unusual and the unreal."

Sharpe's right eyebrow rose with interest.

"Logan is an oceanographer by training. A 1978 honors graduate of the University of Massachusetts, and the Woods Hole Oceanographic Institution, he spent his first two Navy years in submarine schools. He became a qualified submariner during his maiden cruise as a junior petty officer on a Norfolk-based SSBN, and was then assigned duties as lead sonarman and ultimately as Communications CPO on three attack boats, one home ported there and two at Pearl. In my opinion, he's the most likely person to put meat on the bones of any idea you have that involves undersea sounds."

"Get him in here. I like people with off the wall ideas!"

Senior Chief Logan arrived and was introduced to the admiral. He was a thin man, just about six feet tall, and told them he was a proud fifth generation Californian. When he talked it was with great enthusiasm, but he did so quietly.

The admiral liked Logan immediately, and after a couple questions about deep ocean creatures and sound emissions he was sure the chief would be an asset to the team. The three of them moved over to an engineer's drafting table and for the next hour the man known to his peers as Hoosier from his Indiana school days laid out his own unique ideas.

"We submariners have been out in left field for the past dozen years, concentrating on things like hull designs and nuclear reactors. Not that they aren't important, because they are. Each boat we produce is quieter, but what we haven't been studying is the types of sounds they generate. I believe the key to stealth boats is not in the hardware or the weapons, it's in the *sounds they generate* and how the enemy perceives what they hear on their sonars. Does that make sense?"

"I guess so, sir," Buzz replied, "but we've experimented in everything from......"

"Forget the past. Let me outline for you how I see it. America's greatest threat is not from the air, it's from the sea. Actually, undersea. We face a far greater loss, in terms of trained professional lives and strategic property, from a few well placed Chinese torpedoes fired into one of our 7th Fleet Carrier Battle Groups than we ever will face from the air."

146

He checked to see that Buzz and Chief Logan were in agreement. They nodded heads suggesting he continue.

The admiral described something about underway sounds he had recently remembered from submarine school training. "It's the acoustic signature or footprint that every boat and every fish in the sea puts out. Each boat makes a totally different sound from any other. My conclusion is the greatest advantage a stealth submarine will achieve is to change the battle environment into which it enters so drastically it will trick the machines, sonar, radar and the observer's mind. It will also confuse those trained to be looking for a submarine with a known acoustic signature."

Sharpe paused for a second. "What they get is a one-eighty of reality. Here a second ago and now it's gone!"

Listening intently, Chief Logan twisted the ends of his handlebar mustache. Reaching across the slanted table he picked up a pad of yellow paper and some maneuvering boards. Soon, a rough drawing of a submarine showed squiggle lines coming from the boat simulating sound emissions. As he drew a typical battle scene on the maneuvering board, showing an enemy sub about six thousand yards away, he looked up:

"So, Admiral, if the worst thing we're doing is allowing an enemy to hear and record our acoustic signature for present or future identification of our whereabouts, then it goes to logic that if we change that footprint the enemy no longer hears our known ID so we must not be there anymore? Is that how you see it?"

"Spot on, Chief. Now, use even more of your vivid imagination. Try this. You're on patrol near one of the battle groups you're assigned to protect. All of a sudden, you hear an enemy nuke behind you and assume he's looking for the CVBG."

"You identify him, and have to assume he's got an ID on you. You know he wants to get past you to take a shot at the carrier, so you line up your torpedoes on him. If you're in battle conditions you fire and leave the area ASAP. If you're just playing cat and mouse, you save the fish and *then* you

147

broadcast a whole new set of sounds and emissions totally different from those your ship normally sends out, to confuse the enemy," Bernie said in lowered tones.

"The enemy sub's sonar operator will go nuts with what he's just heard and seen on his monitor. He'll swear it's either a Beluga whale or a giant squid escaping an unpopular location and a well lit periscope sweep of waters immediately around your last position will show the squid ink your stealth sub released. When the enemy skipper is faced with no more recognizable sound emissions from the American submarine, he's left to figure where you've disappeared and what the hell they actually viewed in the periscope and saw on their sonar."

The admiral contentedly smiled like the Cheshire cat in Alice in Wonderland. The room was eerily quiet. It now seemed all so logical and so simple. Why hadn't they thought of this before?

Taking a deep breath, Buzz Russell praised: "You know, Admiral, I think that's about the greatest naval tactic since the creation of the Thatch Weave.* Your concept is brilliant and I hope it will lead us to achieve total stealth for our attack boats."

Bernie stood up, thanked Chief Logan for his input, vigorously shook his hand and gave him a welcome to the inner circle pat on the back.

"Buzz, why don't you two take a day or so to digest this and then set up a meeting with your entire team so I can brief them and get them working on the computer chips we'll need. If they can turn this into a set of working designs in a few months, we'll need George Mason's help over at Milsoftel to put the whole thing together in a computer hardware system. Then on to sea trials, battle simulation exercises, torpedo firings and a ton of paperwork before this puppy gets to the Fleet."

"Aye aye, sir," Russell said, walking toward the old man. "It's a whole lot to work on, sir, but the crew will be thrilled to hear the specifics directly from you. How about 0900 Thursday? And Admiral, be prepared for dozens of questions from my gang."

"Thursday at oh-nine-hundred it is." Sharpe turned and walked into the labyrinth, but 30 seconds later the door re-opened and the admiral was back

"By the way, Buzz, I think you ought to cut Chief Logan a set of TAD orders. He'll need 90 days at Milsoftel starting next Monday. He understands what we need and I think he's the best person to get those computer types over in Virginia to understand what has to be done to build my stealth system. See you Thursday.

* **Thatch Weave: An aerial maneuvering tactic developed by Admiral Jimmy Thatch, USN, then a lieutenant commander and aviator during World War II, which allowed allied pilots to get behind or into a more favorable angle on enemy planes, providing them with an open shot at the enemy aircraft.**

CHAPTER 37 - THE ORIGINAL STEALTH

November 4, 1999: The Pentagon

Friday morning, 0858.   The N-771 staff sat in a horseshoe pattern in the main office area facing a slide screen, blackboard and podium. Each had notebooks or pads, and a document from Captain Russell outlining Admiral Sharpe's concept.

"Attention on deck!" barked the captain, as Bernie entered.

"At ease, ladies and gentlemen."

Everyone knew the admiral. A few had worked with him on a staff or sailed with him when he was a submarine skipper. Everyone thought he was a shoo-in to be CNO one day.

"I'm thrilled to be back here in the swamp my home for over four years in this damned basement!" he said to friendly head nods and honest laughter.

"You folks have done yeoman work over the years and many of your ideas are now standard equipment or systems on many of our boats. That toothpaste gel stuff is still being used by a few attack boats, and it led us to develop a new type of skin for the subs.   Of course, the Chinese don't seem to like our submarine toothpaste very much!"   The group chuckled, hearing that.

"Today, ladies and gentlemen, we're going to take a huge step into the Jules Verne world that really does exist. Our new boat is going to revolutionize undersea warfare. I've coded this top secret venture *Project Deep Ink*, and when you finally turn it over to the Fleet it just might put us in the position of being the only navy in the world with a truly genuine stealth submarine!"

"Here's the skinny," he began. "You have a primer with details about the audio sound emissions theory, and some basics on the transmission of new sounds. For years I've been carrying around the problem of the acoustic signature that boats and sea creatures emit into the ocean. It suddenly struck me that if an attack boat could confuse the enemy tracking its acoustic signature, our sub could exit the shooting encounter a la David Copperfield."

"Someone kill the lights over the screen." Sharpe continued: "Let me tell you a little about the giant squid, my newest and best sea creature friend. Only a few people have seen it because it lives between 900 and 18-thousand feet down in the ocean.

(Slide #1)   The largest giant squid ever found was over 57 feet long and weighed 6,000 pounds.

(Slide #2)   It has eight tentacles used for motion plus two extra long tentacle arms that can reach out to grab prey...

(Slide #3)   ...have powerful suckers that lock-on to whatever the squid has caught for dinner." The admiral looked up from his script and said: "This next part is very important. Here's where our new deep-ocean friend can be of great help to us.

(Slide #4)   Squid can change course with equal speed during motion forward or backward. Essentially, they swim by jet propulsion.

(Slide #5)   When the squid's muscles are relaxed water flows into the body cavity. When the muscles contract the water is forced out through a tube-like funnel, which can be moved in any direction. Now, to the ink trick." said the admiral.

(Slide #6)   "The giant squid discharges a brown colored ink-like substance when it's trying to avoid detection or escape from an enemy.

(Slide #7)   The cloud is cigar shaped and about the size of the squid itself. It coagulates and hangs in the water for up to ten minutes. It may also deaden a predator's sense of smell. Via our computer technology we're going to change the underwater sense of smell to the sense of hearing. Our new system will markedly deaden what enemy sonar operators hear in the battlefield waters. Please turn the lights back on."

Bernie continued his presentation. "The best thing about *Deep Ink* is that it's not a whole new submarine, it's a computer and sound system only, and a hell of a lot less expensive than making major modifications to existing boats.

I'd like this system to be operational by February. Yes, that's only four months away but if it can be done you will do it. First installations will be in the Seventh Fleet," Sharpe said to many quizzical faces.

The room suddenly looked like a field of waving corn stalks as hands shot into the air, the first from one of the spooks. "Admiral, John Fletcher, Naval Intelligence." Sharpe motioned for him to proceed.

"Sir, I leave all the technical details to my colleagues here. How certain are you it will remain our secret weapon? With all the civilians at Milsoftel who will be a part of the software programming, and the yardbirds who will have to physically install the hardware, how are we going to keep this secret?"

"That's a very good question, Mr. Fletcher, and I'll put my answer to you in the form of an assignment. Since you're assigned to the N-771 staff as its intelligence officer I'm sure there's no one better qualified to prepare such a strategy. By this time next month please have a workable plan for maintaining total security. Good luck and I look forward to reviewing it."

Chuckling throughout the room preceded the lowering of a number of hands. One, however, remained raised.

"Yes, Commander Stone, is it?"

"Yes sir, Admiral. Isn't it just a matter of time before a good sonarman can see through this ploy?"

"Under normal circumstances that would be the case, Commander. But the beauty of the new ploy as you call it, is that if it's designed properly and built to allow sounds of other ocean animals like whales and dolphins to be broadcast, the enemy is bound to be confused at best."

"Ladies and gentlemen I appreciate all your efforts because I know you're going to make this thing happen. Be as imaginative and creative as you can, and remember: we're now in a game of undersea show biz. You'll have to be part sailor, part computer geek and part magician; I have all the faith in the world you'll be all of them. Thank you."

CHAPTER 38 - SANTA DOESN'T CARRY A GUN

November and December, 1999: Washington, D.C.

A glorious Indian Summer painted the Capitol in Kandinsky colors but as Thanksgiving rushed upon us the trees literally threw their leaves to the ground. The weatherman showed his disdain as D.C. was slammed with the first blasts of winter. I was frozen to the bone. I hate winter!

I was still doing research on the new surface warfare ships. Bernie Sharpe had given me an overview several months ago, but now I was really intrigued with them. The guided missile destroyer, backbone of the Fleet, was designated DDX-21, obviously for the 21st Century. The cruiser was CGX-21 and a replacement for the 40 year old NIMITZ Class aircraft carriers was to be the CVNX.

They were square and squatty hulls with very little superstructure and virtually no masts or radar antenna aloft. The carrier was even neater with a whole new electrical aircraft launching system instead of the steam catapult.

It might be miserable weather in D.C. but Janice and I were jetting out of it, via Reagan National Thanksgiving morning for our holiday cruise. In less than two hours we were soaking up greatly needed sun on the beach fronting our Lauderdale motel. Friday morning we took a cab to the pier and boarded the MV CARIBBEAN ADVENTURE.

The ship was only three years old and convinced us we should be living on a ship instead of in an apartment. Seven dining areas, an entire deck of shopping opportunities, two swimming pools and a casino that opened once the ship was outside Florida's no-gambling limits.

Our stateroom had an outdoor balcony where we could sit with drinks at sunset, that is if we didn't want to patronize one of the dozen ship's bars. They even had one that served martinis only, 57 different kinds, complete with gins and vodkas from around the world. I decided not to encourage problems with my weekend partner, so I simply avoided the martini bar altogether!

We loved walking around Nassau, and our overall Caribbean adventure was just what the doctor ordered for two busy Washington professionals on their way up the career ladder.

December flew by as the politicians on the Hill adjourned their session well before Christmas and headed home for personal appearances and campaigning in the local districts. Y2K was just around the corner and no one knew what cataclysmic events January first would bring.

It was Thursday December 16th, as I recall, and I was returning from a news conference given by the Senate Armed Services Committee about the FY-'00 and '01 Defense budgets. Navy testified about their new ships and Army had some new fangled assault vehicle/mini-tank. It was interesting stuff and I would incorporate it into a special piece I was working on for the New Year's weekend Sunday editions.

Walking back down the hill to my office I had a creepy feeling I was being tailed. Turning my head slightly I spied a late model sedan behind me, with two men in the front. The episode last July when I was nearly run down flashed into my mind. No reason to panic yet, but the car kept pace with me. All of a sudden it speeded up easing into traffic. In seconds the car was beside me and staring me in the face was a huge pistol. I saw the first gun flashes at about the same time I dived for cover behind a car parked about five feet in front of me, crashing to the sidewalk right behind the Chevy's right rear side. Bullets splattered the car's trunk. I think there were at least four shots, maybe as many as six, but who's counting at a time like that.

The sedan skidded away like an Indy car, as a half-dozen pedestrians who were still in the area rushed toward me. A burning sensation filled my left leg, I felt weak and when I finally got to my knees I saw red blood running down my trousers. I ripped open the pant leg and saw the hole in me that was pumping all that good blood away from where it belonged. Someone must have called 911 since I could hear the siren of an ambulance getting louder. In a minute or so I was being loaded into an EMS vehicle and taken to a hospital near George Washington University.

Thirty minutes later the emergency ward crew had cleaned and dressed the wound, assured me that the bullet had gone straight through the fleshy portion of my calf and didn't hit anything vital. An intern suggested I be admitted and stay overnight for observation. I opted not to be a hospital guest and went home instead.

In the cab heading to my apartment I uttered something about the f-ing streets of D.C. not being safe even at midday. The cabby laughed: "And you're white! Doesn't usually happen to you folks."

Back in my place I said a little thank you to the man upstairs. Two near death incidents in less than six months. I must have known something that somebody didn't want me to know, or I was getting close to knowing information that would hurt or embarrass someone. My personal nine lives were now down to seven. As I lay on my sofa, with a stiff Scotch in my hand, I thought of Simon's warning: 'These guys play for keeps. Look what happened to me!'

If this was an example of the kind of presents I was going to get this Christmas, there would be no tree in the Dan Lincoln apartment and the month of December page would ripped off my 1999 calendar, never again to be recalled, thank you very much.

CHAPTER 39 – TRANSMISSIONS & TRANSGRESSIONS

January 23, 2000: Washington, D.C.

Senator Hank Anderson was not a wealthy man, and though the future looked bright he couldn't count on any big money until Henry the elder passed away. Consequently he and Linda lived conservatively. Hank drove a '92 Chevrolet Lumina and Linda a Buick station wagon.

Driving to his office on a typically dreary January morning the Lumina seemed to forget how to shift. Hank had to cajole it up to 30 mph before the automatic transmission shifted out of low gear and into something less noisy and more efficient.

Arriving on the Hill, he told Tom to get a repair estimate from a transmission shop. A few minutes later Tom knocked on Hank's door, entered and gave the senator the bad news: "A $1,100 repair bill plus one whole day in the shop, and it could go as high as $1,500."

Exasperated, Hank said: "Take the car in first thing in the morning." Pulling a check out of the center desk drawer he filled in $1,100 and gave it to Tom saying: "If the cost is any higher you tell them to keep the damned car."

"You've got it, Senator. You might think about getting a new one. Image and all, you know."

With the constant burden of paying down the $12,000 gambling debt Hank really didn't need any extra expense. God, what a night that little gambling encounter in the country was, he grimaced.

The next morning Hank tried reviewing some committee papers after Tom took the car for repairs. He looked forward to hearing what Alan Greenspan would have to say about the nation's current economy and the seemingly runaway stock markets. As soon as he got some extra money he'd put it into some of those high-flying Internet and computer stocks. What a killing people were making with them.

At that moment the intercom buzzed and the office manager said: "Senator Anderson, there's a call for you. The woman says its personal and to tell you her name is Lily Shin. Are you out or shall I take a message?"

"No, that's okay Mrs. Swanson, put her through."

A velvet voice murmured, "Hello Senator Anderson."

"Ms. Shin, how nice to hear from you. How're things at your shop?"

"Very fine, Senator."

"Good. What can I do for you? I've got a committee hearing coming up shortly and don't have much time right now."

"Actually Senator Anderson, Hank, I need to speak to you in person about a matter that involves both of us. You do remember our night in Maryland, don't you?"

Hank felt an immediate and huge ache in his stomach as it wasn't difficult to figure out what Madam Shin wanted to talk about. Since Tom Carlson had handled everything the day after the event, he hadn't heard a word since from anyone about that evening.

"Ms. Shin, Lily. I'm busy and I really don't know what we could discuss. That evening is history for me as it should be for you too." He spoke the words but knew they weren't really working.

"Hank, I think we had better meet as soon as possible," Lily stated firmly. "Six pm tonight at The Honorable Gentleman. You do remember how to get there?"

"I'd rather not go there. I'll meet you in the main bar at the Sheraton Wardman Park Hotel. I can't assure you I'll be there exactly at 6, but I'll try. And Lily, this better be important."

"It is." The line went dead.

The scenario was obvious. Hank knew it was a shakedown.

Mrs. Swanson moved his late afternoon appointments and Hank quietly walked out of his office at 5:30 pm. Without his car he had to wait a few minutes for a cab, so he didn't arrive at the Sheraton until shortly after 6 pm.

Peering through the crowded bar the nervous senator spied Madam Shin sitting alone. He took a seat opposite, his back to the crowd. Never know who may recognize you these days, he thought. He also waived off the waiter offering drinks.

"Good evening, Lily. Is this when you tell me how much it's going to cost me to guarantee you forget our evening at the casino?"

"I'll come straight to the point, Senator." She took a piece of paper out of her purse, handed it to him and said: "Read this and you'll know why we needed to meet."

On the note was written: You will provide me, upon my request, information of developments in the U.S. Navy submarine program; all improvements to ship propulsion systems and weapons; updates on the latest communications equipment including GPS tracking; plus efforts at achieving stealth capabilities to escape sonar detection during combat operations.

Hank folded the paper but before he could put it in his coat pocket Madam Shin snatched it from his fingers, placed it inside her blouse and laughed out loud quietly.

"You've got to be shitting me. I don't think you can disgrace my name or destroy my marriage, so the last thing I'll do for you is steal secrets."

"You will see it our way, Senator. This is not at all about money, or your reputation or marriage. You know I am from China and quite proud of my land. I know you as a powerful person with influence in your government," the wily woman simmered.

Hank actually felt the evil surrounding him, confirming his rising fears.

"We have a simple plan for giving you my silence. We appreciate all the help you will give us and if you're smart and work with me I will permanently forget our evening together, even though we had such a good time," she cooed, stroking Hank under the chin before he could pull his head away.

Here comes the real reason for the shakedown, thought Hank. He was right.

"My cousin David, the Chinese Navy officer, informs me that his superiors would look most favorably upon his career if he can obtain information about your Navy." Pausing for effect, the cool courtesan continued: "Nothing top secret or anything like that, but maybe just some of the things your Navy feels are important for the future. Do this for me and I promise you many more evenings equally as good as our first, but in private and far away from any snooping or public eyes," she said with a soft smile she knew would melt any resistance left in Hank.

"Just give me a few items to send to my cousin, something he terms of substance so he can impress his superiors. Now, isn't that simple?" Slightly dazed, the now perspiring senator muttered: "I don't know about this. I'm supportive of China but giving you American military information is not right. At least, not anything classified. You're really serious aren't you?"

Madam Shin sat motionless, maintaining eye contact with Hank. "We know you've sat through dozens of briefings that were not open to the general public and the news media, but perhaps there is something that is not a secret, and if known in Shanghai might put David a step up on the promotion ladder. Think about it, Hank, and get back to me next week."

She rose from her seat like a jungle cat on the prowl, and slowly insinuated herself out through the crowd. Ironic, he thought. What I hoped would be a fun evening with an exotic woman was now turning into a nightmarish coupling with an enemy of my nation.

Attempting to justify the situation in his own scrambled mind, Hank rationalized that China was truly a friend and we should be sharing some of our technology and naval developments with them. After all, they probably knew more about our Navy than they admitted.

Okay, so I slip Lily a few harmless tidbits to salvage my career, he thought. How can she know what's useful or not?

159

The failing politico's yearnings to taste more of this Asian delight easily swayed his better judgment. He began scheming how to have his moon cake and eat it too. Every couple of months, he'd pass along a few important sounding but harmless crumbs in exchange for more sexual favors from this woman. She'd pass the dry bread to her cousin, he to his bosses, and that would be that.

Still sitting motionless, Anderson made the decision; give the Chinese some innocuous information from past House committee briefings. He also had an idea how to get the info for the Chinese officer to Lily without being personally involved in the actual exchange. It was brilliant and could be done in total secrecy. This time next week it would all be over. The larcenous Lily Shin would be happy, and hopefully make him happy too.

CHAPTER 40 - NEW KID ON THE BLOCK

February 2, 2000: The C-C, Washington, D.C.

Ground Hog Day in the capitol, reminiscent of the one Phil spent in Punxatawney, PA, was beyond dreary which suited me fine as I suffered through the winter doldrums. There had been nothing but lousy weather for weeks and a dearth of real news stories on my beat. Half of that changed while I worked on my drink at the C-C. That pesky little Chinese reporter for New China News Service joined me at the Roundtable and promptly started a conversation.

"Since you've been in D.C. for only two years Dan, you probably haven't met many of my countrymen?" he asked. I shook my head that I hadn't.

"Too bad I only get to know you over last few months, or I would have tried to get you invitation to Kung Hee Fat Choy, last month Chinese New Year celebration at our Embassy in Georgetown. Several of your colleagues and many important American politicians were there, including the young senator from Minnesota. This was his second year in a row at the party."

Finishing my drink, I told Sung: "I am very much aware of the senator and his feelings for your country. I was at the hearing the day he and Navy Secretary Wetzel went at it, and you remember that he and I were on the same trip to Beijing you helped set up last May."

He ignored my reference to the SECNAV incident, did acknowledge the China trip, but then quickly turned his attention to the latest addition to the Roundtable, Bill Lake, a writer for one of the big Hong Kong metro papers. Which I wasn't exactly sure, but I thought it was the Standard. Lake nodded toward Sung. They had known each other for several years, and he was aware that Sung's press service was not only run by the PRC, but was also a front for their spy operations worldwide. Unfortunately he'd be hard pressed to prove it.

161

"See that you keep your Commie paws off our buddy here," Bill said to Sung in a friendly but meaningful tone. "Remember, when it comes to world power America is still number one and it's the U.S. Navy that rules the world's oceans."

Sung smiled and said he would promise not to corrupt me if Bill Lake would buy him a beer. Talk switched to the weather, next year's Redskins team, and what was what in today's political file. I couldn't help but think that while Mr. Sung Jiang was accepted as a part of the Roundtable, he was there only because of what he might be able to do for one of us in the future.

I doubted he really liked Americans, but he would be a good person to watch for any indication of major changes in Chinese policy or developments on their military front. Personally I rather liked the little guy so gave him the benefit of the doubt, at least until proven wrong.

Wrong would take several months longer.

CHAPTER 41 - ALL IN THE FAMILY

February 7, 2000: Georgetown

Hank spent the weekend at home with Linda and the children who were growing so shockingly fast he figured he'd better spend more time with them before they became young adults and left the family. His jobs on the Hill had prevented him from spending anything but minimum time at home, but he felt the children were happier with Linda in their daily lives than with him on the rare occasions he was home wanting to play father and family man.

His restless mind was obsessed about which piece of useless information he'd give Madam Shin, hoping to end this dirty mess. After Sunday breakfast he browsed through several pages of office notes from various briefings, finding one item that might be interesting enough for Lily's cousin and his comrades but not detrimental to our Navy's development projects.

It was back a year or more, while he was still in the House and before he left for his visit to China, that a Navy lieutenant commander briefed his committee about some of the things they were working on at that time.

Scanning his notes, there it was in a non-classified briefing given by a Pentagon Navy lieutenant commander two summers ago. It told about one project where the Navy was trying to make submarine drive shafts and propellers perfectly quiet. They designed an oil-filled tunnel to wrap around the shaft in the hopes that by floating it in the oil it would cease to be heard by enemy sonar. They tested it off Norfolk and while it did reduce shaft noise appreciably a reasonably good sonarman could still pick up the screw noises. "Yes, this is just right," Hank said under his breath, "let's give it to the conniving but lovely Madam Shin."

Monday morning Hank greeted his office staff, took his messages from Mrs. Swanson, and asked not to be disturbed while he returned important calls and reviewed a draft of the Navy's plans for the QINGDAO Pearl Harbor visit.

He'd been scheming how to slip his tidbit to Madam Shin. Now, to put it into action. He pushed the telephone intercom button for Tom Carlson's office: "Tom, my office, now please, and just you."

"What's up?" Tom asked as he sat in front of Hank's desk notebook in hand. "Something new on the legislative front?"

"I wish it was that simple. I met Lily Shin last week." Hank looked up, but Tom's only reaction was taking copious notes. "She's agreed not to ever say anything about that evening but *only* if I provide her with information on some Navy projects which she plans to send to her cousin. She thinks this info will help in his rise through the ranks."

Tom broke in: "What's she asking for, nuclear secrets or something less critical?"

"She wasn't specific other than to say something her cousin would believe has substance. I've reviewed my notes from House Armed Service Committee hearings and have found something. Remember that submarine shaft wrap-around tunnel with the oil? That should be good enough to get her off my back."

Tom's mind sped fast in reverse, trying to recall all the secrets they'd been privy to during dozens of Pentagon briefings. He recalled most of them, knowing full well their vital importance.

Tom knew his boss was once again asking him to clean up a dirty mess. Hank was just another of those hotshot Washington politicians who couldn't keep his johnson in his pants. It was always staff guys, like him, who saved the man's bacon. With some of them it was booze, others women and sex. Oh well, wouldn't be the first time a staffer had to save his boss' ass, and he assumed it would not be the last.

"Good idea Senator, let me handle this. As long as no one knows about it but you and me, it will be dealt with and you won't know how. You want to be clear of her, don't you?"

"Definitely. And I'll remember your help. I have an uneasy feeling this is just the first request she'll make. We have to be rid of her so we can look to the November elections, especially early Rhode Island returns. You get my drift?"

"Drift gotten, sir. Give me her number and I'll do the rest. I'll get back to you as things come together. And don't worry. The ball's in my court now."

"Before you leave look at this. Over the weekend I typed the info about the Navy drive shaft project on my old home typewriter because I don't want it traced here. Then I went to a local drug store and got a greeting card in a purple envelope. When this info is passed on it will look like someone getting a birthday card."

Tom took the unsealed envelope and returned to his office, unlocked a desk drawer, retrieved a private phone and made two calls. The first was to a number he knew by heart, and it was answered on the second ring. Skipping small talk he whispered: "The Weasel is making a worthless donation to the cause. We must insist on larger and more important ones." Tom listened a moment, said: "I concur," and hung up.

Then he called the number Hank gave him. It was answered: "Ming & Ching Things, may I help you?"

"Is this Lily Shin," he asked.

"Yes. May I please know your name?"

"Tom Carlson from Senator Anderson's office. We met at the Honorable Gentleman last fall."

"Ah, yes. What is it you wish?"

"Senator Anderson has asked me to deliver information you recently requested. He said you needed it for a paper your daughter is working on at Georgetown. Since I live in that area I thought it might be convenient to drop it off tonight?"

"That won't work for me, Mr. Carlson. I'm about to leave the shop for the day. Perhaps Cheryl could meet you. You know where Georgetown University is?"

"Yes, of course. I've been there many times."

"There's a little park just a block or so from the campus on what is called Volta Place, Northwest. I'll have Cheryl meet you there at 5 pm."

165

"I'm sure I can find it, but let's make it 5:30, okay?"

"That should be fine. I'll call her. Good bye, Mr. Carlson. And say hello to the senator for me." Hanging up the phone Lily smiled to herself. Things were going exactly as she planned.

Shortly before five Tom got his car from the basement garage and as he drove through traffic he rehearsed what he was going to tell Cheryl. Twenty minutes later he had no trouble finding both the little park and an open parking space on the street. He was locking the car when he saw a white van park next to a fire hydrant. There's a $300 fine, he thought. Cheryl waved from a park bench as Tom headed her way.

"Thanks for meeting me on my way home," Tom said, extending his hand to the girl who inquired: "Why didn't Hank come?"

"He's very busy, but he's willing to help your mother out this one time."

Tom handed Cheryl the purple envelope and said: "Our business here is concluded." Giving her a polite wave, he left the park and walked to his car. Again he noticed the white van and rightly assumed they had someone inside who photographed the transaction. Taking a final look around to satisfy his concern no one else was watching, he started his car, pulled into traffic and drove home.

Cheryl smiled all the way back to her dorm room, reviewed the document then dialed her mother.

"Mom, everything went perfectly. I have the *monthly sales report* and it's ready to be sent to Dad."

"Great. Any problems understanding the report?"

"No, everything went fine."

"Good. I'll meet you tonight at 8 pm at the *after-hours courier service* location, and we'll forward the report to Dad."

"I'll be there. See ya."

Two hours later mother and daughter entered the formal office of the Chinese Ambassador and greeted Fred Tong. Video and still photographers stood quietly at the side of the big room, and at Tong's signal, they began recording the scenario.

Cheryl entered the office, walked over to her mother seated on a bright red sofa, and gave her a big hug. She sat down, they chatted briefly, and then Cheryl opened her purse. She took out the purple envelope and made a big show of passing it to Madam Shin. Fred Tong entered the scene, took the envelope from Lily, and walked over to a large desk with a PRC flag behind it. He slipped the envelope into a desk drawer and locked it securely.

The camera lights went out and the photographers packed their gear. Alone in the office, Tong, Madam and Cheryl were joined by Ambassador Wu, who would never be publicly involved but had observed everything through a mirror-window in a secret room behind his office. The PRC's number one diplomat in the U.S. laughed before he said: "I think this calls for Chinese brandy all around!"

It did, they all partook, and the Chinese officials toasted Madam Shin and Cheryl: "To the first of many shipments of monthly sales reports from our very naive friend, Senator Henry Anderson." Lily and Cheryl bowed and then left the ambassador's office.

CHAPTER 42 - ONE PICTURE IS WORTH 1,000 WORDS

February 11, 2000: Capitol Hill & Georgetown

On Friday afternoon Hank received an unexpected but welcomed phone call from the antique shop owner. "This is Lily Shin, Senator. Thank you for the background material for Cheryl's university work, and may I ask when you and Mrs. Anderson might come see the fine Chinese art in our store?"

"I'm fully occupied on the Hill every day, but I might stop by around 6 pm one night after Linda leaves for some skiing in Minnesota. I'll look over your collection and perhaps become one of your valued local customers."

"Are you free next Monday night?"

"Oh, no," Hank stammered. "That's Valentine's Day and I promised my wife we'd dine out. She leaves on the 16th so maybe Friday?"

"Fine. Friday it shall be. Six o'clock? That will allow you and your checkbook plenty of time to shop for an hour."

The phone went dead and Hank thought to himself: She didn't mention the casino affair, so the oil shaft info must have worked. That takes care of her cousin, hopefully for a long time. I'm going to learn about Chinese antiques, vases, tapestries and artwork, and with any luck Madam Shin will show me some other things too.

The old Chevy's transmission purred as Hank drove to his date. Lily was helping a customer, but greeted him with a cheery: "Good evening, Senator, I'll be with you shortly. Please, browse around and see some of our newer items just in from Beijing."

He strolled cautiously through the narrow aisles of the shop, not wanting to tip over a Ming Dynasty vase or some other pricy object d'art.

"How have you been, Senator," Madam Shin said, gliding up next to him. I am delighted you have paid us a visit." As they moved through the shop she pointed out a variety of Asian objects, including all sorts of hand carved items, paintings, first class cloisonné, plates and trays, and vases, vases, vases.

Hank made an effort to pay attention, but his thoughts were running in another direction. He had decided there were only three items he wanted from this shop and one was not man made. "I like that large vase over in the corner and the hanging tapestry with the mountain stream and flower garden. How much?"

"For anyone else $3,000. But for an important U.S. senator who will also be my citizenship sponsor the price is half, just $1,500. How does that sound."

"Sold! Thank you very much," he replied and his thank you was genuinely appreciative.

"You are an astute shopper, Senator," playing to his obvious ego. "They will be delivered to your office Monday."

He actually did like most of the antiques and artwork and knew he would be acquiring more. With the $50,000 Christmas gift from Henry Senior he could afford some indulgences. The old man had said "Spend it on some fun." For Hank, that would be a snap. What he didn't realize at this moment was what it was going to cost him besides money.

"I think this concludes our business here," Madam Shin said. "Since you are free this evening, shall we have dinner?"

They drove to an intimate grille about ten blocks away, where Hank was certain he wouldn't be observed.

He enjoyed the anonymity because he didn't need to even think about being a U.S. senator. Throughout a dinner of fresh New Zealand prawns and broiled medallions of veal, conversation centered only on Chinese art and his new possessions. Why they had room for dessert was beyond him, but Lily ordered Black Forest cake and he opted for cheesecake topped with passion fruit, hoping to stimulate her imagination in a direction other than Chinese art!

Ten minutes after leaving the bistro they stood at her apartment door. "Great dinner, Hank. Come in and we'll have a brandy and a little soft music."

He was surprised by the invitation. She hung up her coat, put on some soft rock music, and filled two enormous snifters. Floating down gently next to Hank on the sofa and handing him his drink, she unexpectedly raised her arm in a toast: "To enduring friendship for our two countries and a long relationship between you and me."

Fourth of July sparklers crackled inside Hank's head. Was she referring to his friendship treaty or what? Shoving that problem aside, he enjoyed a big sip from the snifter in his hand. The warming effect took over immediately. As he relaxed and enjoyed the music, Lily curled up next to him. "Would you like to see some photos of me and my family back in China?"

"Sure, everyone's got family photos to show, why not you?"

The first showed her in front of her old shop on Hollywood Road in Hong Kong. The second one had her standing next to a Navy officer with warships in the background. Hank vaguely recognized the man, but put that off as having impossible odds. How would he know one man in a country of a billion and a half people having been there only once? Anyway, they all looked alike to him. Could it be her cousin?

With a sly side glance, Madam Shin reached into an envelope bearing the PRC flag, withdrawing more photos. Slowly spreading them on the coffee table, she leaned back awaiting the senator's reaction. It took exactly one second.

Now, large red lights flashed in his brain, bells rang in his ears and stars danced before his eyes. Involuntarily, his entire being shook. There, in living color, was Madam Shin hugging Cheryl; Cheryl giving the purple envelope to her mother; and then Tong from the Chinese Embassy locking it in a desk drawer. Hank was devastated when he saw the final snapshot: Tom Carlson handing the now-evil purple envelope to Cheryl.

Unable to speak, the now thoroughly flummoxed senator looked around and thought: Where am I? What's happening? And then he muttered: "What the hell have I done?   That Navy guy, he was my China escort. Lieutenant Wong, right?"

"Correct, my little panda.   But now you see he's a captain in charge of our naval intelligence gathering forces. Captain David Wong is not my cousin, he is my husband. We've been married for over 20 years and Cheryl is our daughter."

Hank ran to the bathroom and booted dinner, lunch and anything else that was still in his now wrenching gut.

CHAPTER 43 - THE FAMILY THAT SPIES TOGETHER

February 19, 2000: Russell U.S. Senate Office Building

Hank was still sick to his stomach when Tom knocking at his door: "Is everything all right in there, Senator?"

A feeble reply brought little assurance: "Yeah, yeah, everything's fine."

"Are you sure, sir?" Tom pressed.

"Jesus H. Christ, yes I'm sure. Leave me alone! I'll call you in awhile."

Tom backed off and returned to his paper work.

What can I do? Who can I turn to? Who can I trust?" he mumbled absentmindedly. "Linda. No; if I tell her she'll divorce me in a heartbeat. Tom? Yea, Tom. He saved my ass in that first Lily thing. He can do it again." The senator thought that might be the solution, but after some more time he wasn't totally convinced of that idea.

Even through his jumbled thinking, Hank knew they faced a daunting task keeping his good name out of a monstrous political scandal. I'll resign, he thought. I'd be free of those damned Chinese fiends. Say it's for health reasons. My constituents will still love me. But, in his heart, he knew the public devours politicians who stray from the American way. Rationalizing his transgression was small the senator declared: "Screw 'em! They trapped me and I'll fight 'em to the end!"

Things were back to square one at Ming & Ching Things, when Lily heard a familiar code-knock on the private office door. She moved swiftly to the door and flicked the lock open. Cheryl peeked in as her mother chirped: "We have a problem. Come on upstairs." Madam told her assistant to tend the shop and the pair hurried up to the apartment.

Cheryl busied herself brewing tea as Lily related the juiciest details of last night's episode.

"I thought he would throw up right here on my sofa. I wondered if he could make it home, physically. He certainly didn't make it, mentally. As if I care," she smirked.

"From now on we will not accept any little tidbits of information like the stuff he had us pass on to your father last week. That was ancient history of no real value to China. Now we demand detailed blueprints or computer discs of current top-secret projects," Madam Shin bluntly stated.

"Possessing those photos means that capitalist fool belongs to me, whether he likes it or not. We hold the top card in the deck when it comes to making demands."

"Hey mom, something really neat happened. A few days ago I met this second generation Chinese-American girl, but you can hardly tell she's Chinese. Her name is Samantha Wing. We call her Sam for short. Her grandfather has lived in Washington since the late '40s. He fought with Chairman Mao during the 30s and 40s and then Beijing sent him here to gather what information he could about the American government and its military."

Lily listened quietly, very interested in what she was hearing, and indicated for Cheryl to continue.

"I think the grandfather and Ambassador Wu are old friends. Mr. Wing's retired from Woodward & Lothrop's Department Store, where he was a men's tailor. Mrs. Wing died several years ago."

"Sam was raised in a liberal family in San Francisco, went to U-C Berkeley and has a post-graduate degree in computer programming from the University of Maryland. During those college days she had frequent talks with her grandfather about China and his role during the old days with Chairman Mao and Chow En Lai and the little red books. He convinced her that China is getting a bum rap in today's political world by western nations like Britain and the U.S."

"She learned from Grandpa Wing that patriotic Americans of Chinese ancestry were now helping the Middle Kingdom by passing along to Beijing things they heard or learned about America during the course of their jobs or at social functions. She believes that helping our motherland is

173

the right thing to do, so she wants to help him gather information."

"I'm sure she's a good overseas-Chinese, but do you think she can help us or your father?"

"Well, that's just the thing Mom. Right after grad school she worked for a year at the IRS, before she became bored and looked for another job. Then this hush-hush software company in Arlington took her on. It's called Milsoftel and has all kinds of contracts with the military. Have you heard of them?"

"No, but there are dozens of boutique computer shops around. You never know which one might be working on the kind of top-secret projects our country needs to know about," Madam Shin answered.

"I doubt our senator would fall for another evening at the casino," Cheryl chuckled, "but there must be other ways to get our hands on any classified secrets that Sam's likely to be exposed to."

"My daughter, we shall find ways; perhaps we should invite Miss Wing and her grandfather to the Embassy for tea. Mr. Tong and the ambassador could join us and show your friend Sam the importance of supplying information about her company projects to Beijing. Mr. Wing would be given some sort of honor for his years of loyal service to China, and Sam could be recruited to carry on his great work into the 21st Century."

The art dealer, cum Mata Hari, got up from the sofa and poured brandy into two glasses. Mother and daughter broke out laughing as they raised the glasses in a toast, knowing full well this was the same brandy the senator had consumed last night.

CHAPTER 44 - BET YOU CAN'T STEAL JUST ONE CHIP

March 13, 2000 - Milsoftel Labs, Virginia

"Doctor Mason? It's Don Logan. I've got some great news. We've made the breakthrough we've been shooting for. Could you come to conference room Bravo?"

George Mason beamed from ear to ear as he returned some calls requiring his immediate attention. One was to Captain Frank Russell, on his secure line at the Pentagon.

"Buzz, this is George Mason at Milsoftel. Looks like today may be our D-Day. Your retired Senior Chief Logan just called me to a briefing that he says will put the frosting on the stealth submarine cake. I hope so too. Okay, thanks. I'll call after I know more about this."

The scientist told his secretary he'd be in the Bravo conference room, not to be disturbed, and should be back in an hour. Grabbing a yellow pad, he walked at a brisk clip to the Laboratory main entrance. Pressing his palm against a blue electric reader-plate in the wall the door to the main laboratory area opened. Each division had its own meeting room for high-level conferences or private chats, away from other's eyes and ears, and free from electronic devices. That part was iron-clad policy for Dr. Mason and his teams.

Logan had an overhead projector pointed at a screen on the far wall. A VCR and TV monitor were also ready to roll. Basic submarine hull designs were posted on the two facing walls. The table in the center of the room had room for four people on each side with one chair at the foot so everyone had a direct view of the A-V offerings, and the wall charts as well. Mason entered, shook hands with Chief Logan and a couple senior team members, then sat at the foot of the table.

"We apologize for missing Admiral Sharpe's end of February goal, but we're way ahead of his final Independence Day deadline. We had to go over our findings before calling you into this briefing."

"Senior Chief, if you've really made the breakthrough, I doubt Bernie Sharpe will care if it's late. Let's see what you've come up with."

"Okay. First, let me say the info about typical submarine sounds from such things as propulsion noises, screws and prop shafts, periscopes going up or down, and other common hull emissions are well known by most submariners. Every good sonarman can pick up sounds and tell you they're from dolphins, the screws on a particular Russian built diesel sub, chatter from shrimp or singing from whales. It's their world and they get very good at knowing what they hear every day."

Everyone around the table listened intently, getting antsy waiting for Logan to get to the point.

"Sounds move best and farthest through the water in an area oceanographers refer to as the sound channel. It normally runs between 300 and 3,200 feet down, and starts when the decreasing water temperature line crosses the water pressure line. That seems to be the best transmission band. Sometimes sounds can be heard several thousand miles away from their source."

"Now, all navy sonar-types have precise knowledge about sounds and emissions from ships, submarines and other denizens of the deep. They identify them and pass them off as just what they are, sounds from ships or fish or other known sources. The operative words here are known sources. To give you an example listen to these sounds as they are heard and identified by a typical sonarman."

An aide started the tape playback unit and the identifiable sound of submarine screws came on first. Everyone knew that sound. Next was the sound of a surface fishing boat, then a destroyer and then another type of submarine. Each was distinctly different and even Dr. Mason could easily tell them apart.

"Okay," said Logan, "you passed that test. Now see if you can do as well identifying sea creatures." The audio guy played the second segment of sounds. First was the singing of humpback and blue whales, familiar to most everyone. Next were the sounds of about ten other fish, not generally identifiable to those without trained ears.

When a sonarman was asked to name what he heard he got only eight of the ten sounds correct. Granted, one was native to waters the technician had never sailed in and the other was from a sea creature rarely heard, although generally known to inhabit all oceans and make frequent visits to the water layers submarines fought in. Its very unique sound was known to the most senior submariners and those who sought to know the unusual sound pattern it made.

"We believe this very unique sound, which sounds somewhat like a Beluga whale, is a giant squid as it exits an attack it has just made on an enemy or as it flees from an encounter with some other creature it feels it cannot defeat, such as a sperm whale. No giant squid has ever been caught alive, but this sound cannot be confused with other whales or fish, and it sounds nothing at all like any other known submarine or surface ship emission."

Dr. Mason was dumbfounded. It *was* totally unique and different than anything he'd ever heard before. As he looked around the table he noticed all the team members smiling a smile that said: 'Gotcha! Here's our new stealth weapon...the giant squid!'

"There's more, sir," Logan said signaling for the VCR. "This video shows many aspects of that squid. We, ah, sort of borrowed a lot of this from Navy Department records and civilian oceanographic sources."

The video showed too much information about the giant squid, but before the highly-impressed Mason could interject his question, Logan asked: "I guess you're wondering just how the Navy can use all this giant squid material to fool enemy submarines?"

"Some scientists aren't the most creative types, so we took a rather unorthodox approach to this problem. We're dead certain we can combine many of these known underwater sounds, transmit them from our subs, and confuse the hell, pardon sir, out of enemy forces monitoring our ships. They'll think all they're hearing is a bunch of sea creatures."

Seeing nods all around he pressed on: "Under this cover our guys lock on the enemy ships and have a go at it as the Brits so colorfully describe a good kill."

The former chief, grinning from ear to ear, directed his attention to Dr. Mason, and went on: "There will be more occasions when we operate as usual, our boats making their sounds and prevailing where we control the waters and the general battle site, so this new ghost mode will be used only when absolutely necessary. Here's how a full battle situation would go down."

Logan picked up a piece of paper from the stack in front of him: "Imagine we're in a defensive position guarding one of our CVBGs in the South China Sea. We identify three or four Chinese nuclear and diesel submarines in the area and believe they're ready to attack. Our submarines screening the CVBG go into stealth condition, and transmit some typical dolphin, whale or other sea sounds that will be properly identified by the Chinese. Then we send them the giant squid sounds, load our torpedo tubes, set up firing programs and fire away. A minute or two later we release our version of squid ink, which is currently just weeks away from being ready for testing. The enemy are up to their asses avoiding the missiles and trying to navigate to safety, while our boats blow the ink and take off in a squid-like full-speed departure in the opposite direction from the just concluded battle."

Team members were all favorably nodding their heads and even Dr. Mason was now smiling.

"So, that's our story, and we're sticking with it. Any questions? Yes, Dr. Mason."

"Just one. Is that your final answer?"

Identifying with the Regis Philbin line on the popular TV show Who Wants To Be A Millionaire, Logan replied: "Yes and we hope it will also be the Navy's final answer to this long and very complex project. Let's go out and test some deep ink!"

CHAPTER 45 - SPRING FEVER

March 27, 2000: Washington, D.C.

I was shaken from daydreaming about my sweet Janice by Ben Huntley sticking a ream of papers in my face. "I need a feature piece, about two thousand words, on what Senator Anderson's resolution on world military friendship would mean to the U.S. and our allies, NATO and those in Asia."

"Hank Anderson has gone hog wild over this damn Chinese friendship business. You've been to China with him and seen their Navy close up and you certainly know a hell of a lot about ours. I want to know what does the average American feel about this friendship B.S. and what our allies would do if the Senate passes it. Can you have it ready for the Sunday editions a week before the vote?"

"Of course, but I think the more important question is what level of support is there in the full Senate and the Armed Services Committee where the first test vote will come? I'm not so sure Anderson has enough followers even in his own party to get the majority he needs. I'll do the piece from angles, the allies' reaction and what senators think. I bet the answers surprise us."

"Fine. Make sure I have it for the wire by April 20th the latest. Okay?"

"Get your butt out of here so I can start." Thoughts of Janice would have to wait. My first call was to an Admiralty contact at the British Embassy. As I suspected those blokes were no lovers of the Chinese and after having to give up Hong Kong in 1997 the British wanted as little to do with Beijing as possible.

That was off the record. However Commander Angus McDonnell, RN, did authorize a good quote: 'We have no plans for inviting Chinese Navy warships to visit our naval bases, nor do we feel the need for greater friendship with a country that continues to threaten free shipping and Naval passage in the South China Sea.'

The Australians and the Germans gave similar responses, while the Japanese, as usual, were a lot more formal. I was politely referred to their P.R. office at the Japanese Embassy, and after telling some deputy what I wanted, I was told they'd get back to me as soon as they could. Knowing that wouldn't happen before lunch, and probably for days, I dashed out for a quick meal at our local fast-food French restaurant, Jacques dans la boite.

Back at the office about 1 pm there were three phone calls on my message spike, plus the mail I hadn't gotten to before lunch. After throwing out the junk mail, going through the few letters and looking at each phone message, I dialed an unknown Virginia number.

"Admiral Sharpe speaking."

Startled, I said: "Dan Lincoln returning your call."

"I left my private number so I didn't have to use the main office line. There are some things I'd like to talk to you about. Are you open for dinner tonight?"

"Well, yes I am. I'm done here about 5 pm so where and when shall we meet?"

"The downstairs bar at Hogate's at 7 pm. Dinner's on me."

Any call from Admiral Sharpe always took my concentration off whatever assignment was currently on my plate. I decided to worry later about what he wanted, and turned my attention back to the Friendship Bill.

I called a few allied Navy contacts in Washington but didn't hear from the Japanese. What was more interesting were the responses I got from four Senators and Congressmen who were all against the friendship resolution. I'd have to concentrate on more liberal members tomorrow and see if there really was the strong support for his bill Senator Anderson led everyone to believe.

There was nothing more I could do today so I locked up, walked outside and hailed a cab.

"Where to, mon?"

"800 Water Street. A restaurant called Hogate's."

"Know it well. Go there about five times a night."

Fifteen minutes later I got out of the cab, fought my way around the ever-present reservations line and entered the bar. I had a feeling I was headed for a great dinner, and an even greater story.

Shouldering my way through the crowd, I was startled when a vice-like grip surrounded my arm. Before I could emit a few delicate phrases, Bernie began maneuvering me upstairs. That was the best move of the night, in what was to prove a most interesting evening of seafood and sea service talk.

"I hope you don't mind my taking you away from the ladies of Washington on a beautiful spring night," he said with a glint in his eyes. Did that mean he assumed I was always on the prowl for good looking women? We were quickly seated, drink orders taken, and offered menus for our review. I decided on lobster bisque and fresh Maryland crab cakes. The admiral went all the way with prawn cocktail and a full lobster, broiled.

"So that you'll be among the first to know, I'll be getting my second star April 1st," he said calmly. "Now I can add that other star and half inch stripe to my uniform. Unfortunately, it also means a lot more paperwork!"

"That's terrific, Admiral, and you certainly deserve it," I said as sincerely as I could. I knew this meant he'd be a shoe-in for more stars in the future.

Over drinks I told him about the story I was researching. I mentioned the interviews I'd done so far with other senators, and how there seemed to be a strong opposition to the legislation. After I told him I had yet to talk to the more liberal members of the Senate, the admiral admonished: "They may tell you it's a great idea but our sources say he won't have the votes. People back home are too much against it."

During dinner the admiral stopped eating and said: "I'll cut to the chase, Dan. You've done some stories about Senator Anderson lately. Have you noticed anything unusual about him since that China trip?" Shaking my head no I took out my trusty pocket notebook.

"I read your piece on his shafting the CNO's office for not giving the Chinese Navy the GPS satellite positioner we developed with General Motors. He then made some political hay by getting them direct from GM for the PRC's so-called off shore coastal patrol boats that don't have anything better than an old compass to tell where they are. Maybe that's why the fishing trawler sunk off Pearl a couple years ago was a bit off course!" He smiled a big smile and continued with what I now knew was currently bugging him.

"And, what about his end-run to get that damn Chinese destroyer QINGDAO a port visit next Fourth of July! It just had to be Independence Day when Anderson wanted the god-damned Chinese to have an open-house right in the middle of Pearl Harbor. If he'd been around in '41 he'd probably have invited the Japanese to do a fly-by over Pearl Harbor before breakfast on December 7th!"

"Admiral, you're being a bit rough on him, aren't you? Remember, he's only been a senator for two years and he could become the ranking minority member on the Armed Services Committee after the elections. You're going to be in contact with him for many years, so maybe you should cut him a little slack."

Grudgingly my host allowed: "If you haven't seen or felt anything about him that's out of the ordinary then maybe I'm all wet. But my old Indiana gut-feeling tells me there's more to this man than he shows. Yeah, he's pro-China trade, and has that idiotic friendship bill up for approval. But something about him has bothered the hell out of me for a long time now."

"This is the second time you've suggested I keep an extra open eye on Anderson, Admiral. Is there something more I should know about your interest in him? I mean, what exactly is it you're looking for?"

"Nothing I can put my finger on, and nothing I would confirm if I knew there was a problem. But, there are just too many loose ends that all seem to end up in his lap. It's probably nothing more than coincidence but he's just too palsy-walsy with the Chinese for my taste."

"I'm on Hank's calendar about the friendship resolution on April 13th. Ben's scheduled the story to run on the Sunday just prior to the bill coming up for a vote."

"When you talk to him, you might ask him about some of his off-duty interests. We hear he sometimes gets into roulette games at, shall we say, not always legal casinos. Work it into your conversation about casino destinations like Macao. See how he reacts to the word roulette."

The whole question of Admiral Sharpe's interest in him led me back to Beijing and Shanghai a year ago. He had been upset about President Jiang mentioning stealth gels in his May Day remarks. I knew it would be in my best interest to look closer at the senator's personal life and spend a little time observing his non-Senate activities.

CHAPTER 46 - BIG IDEAS HIDE IN SMALL PLACES

April 4, 2000: The Pentagon

Paperwork, paperwork! How does this man's Navy operate with all of the damned paperwork? Well, I guess that's one of the reasons I got my second star...to be an admiral you've got to put up with the paperwork!

Bernie Sharpe's bureaucracy frustrations were boiling over once again, keeping him from the important tasks. Oh, to be back on the bridge commanding a submarine, he thought. Hell, that's what I'm really trained to do. Give me the smell of salt air, or at least the ability to be a part of the submarine fleet, and my value to the Navy would triple.

The admiral's sweet daydreams were abruptly interrupted by the realities of his desk job. "Budgets," he muttered under his breath, yanking a thick manila folder off the growing stack in front of him. "Who wants how much, how soon, for what?" He was no newcomer to this process, having weaseled several of his own pet projects into various budgets over the years and had buried his current project with sea creature sounds somewhere in a budget where comptrollers would never find it.

Sharpe reviewed a dozen excellent projects deserving funding, signed off each and forwarded them up the chain of command for further review and possible ultimate approval.

A Navy-blue folder mixed in with the regulation manila ones caught Bernie's eye. Bright yellow-colored lettering on the cover proclaimed: Mescod, Inc. San Diego, California. A stylized anchor, submarine and some sort of sea creature formed a logo above a tag reading: Non-Nuclear Submarine Propulsion System. Project #99/838. Request for Extension and Modification.

Not recalling any company called Mescod or any new submarine propulsion system being worked on by the Navy, he decided to see what this was all about.

The narrative was short and to the point. They were a San Diego-based privately owned civilian laboratory, specializing in ship and submarine propulsion and support systems. Executive offices are in San Diego. Engineering lab, model center and boatyard are in Point Loma near the U.S. Navy submarine base, and research facilities are in La Jolla, supporting a working relationship with the Scripps Institution of Oceanography.

A Dr. Lloyd Davidson, listed as Vice President and Chief Engineer, was the author. Flipping to the bio section Bernie found that Davidson held degrees in both chemical and electrical engineering from MIT and Purdue, and had been with Mescod for five years. Prior to that he'd spent eight years working for Electric Boat Division of General Dynamics at their Groton, Connecticut submarine construction shipyard. Dr. Davidson had also been at the Newport News Shipbuilding and Dry-Dock Co. in Norfolk for about six years prior to moving to the San Diego area. Bernie's interest level increased when he saw the specialty was ship and submarine propulsion systems.

Returning to the basic presentation Bernie read the firm was awarded a 3-year $14 million contract in 1997 to develop new concepts in undersea propulsion. The request in Bernie's hand was for an additional $6 million and two more years to finalize the current work.

The document said: 'Mescod is nearing the point where a working model can be presented for evaluation of the benefits of our project to the future of the Submarine Service.'

The admiral's whistle had now been whet, and he dug deeper into the report. The narrative outlined efforts made in recent years by other governments and private shipbuilders to create non-nuclear powered drive systems. Bernie was aware of most of these projects, as well as several others, but got some vital up-dating from this report.

'The future of submarine propulsion lies not in bigger, better or even more secure nuclear reactors, but in fuel cell technology. Fuel cells are electrochemical devices that combine oxygen with hydrogen to produce electricity to drive generators that propel an undersea boat. Hydrogen makes up 75% of the earth's atmosphere but is very unstable in most situations.' Being familiar with fuel cells the admiral flipped to the next section.

Currently being developed, Dr. Davidson wrote, 'is a new breed of submarines that operate on what are called A-I-P or Air Independent Propulsion systems. Work on AIP subs has been ongoing since the end of World War II and in recent years Germany, France, Sweden and Italy have experimented with AIP. These boats are very quiet and less expensive to build than nuclear powered submarines. The cost for a German-built AIP sub range from 300 to 500 million U.S. dollars, compared to the one billion plus now being spent per nuclear attack submarine.

The Mescod brief continued: The most recent advances in AIP submarine technology include the use of PEM (Proton Exchange Membrane) fuel cells. They are popular because of low operating temperatures and resultant low amount of wasted heat to be detected by an enemy ship. One major problem that continues with PEM fuel cell use is the storage of the hydrogen.

Germany recently began construction of a new group of submarines known as the 212-A class, using a PEM fuel cell plant claimed to work flawlessly and without a detectable sound. However, these boats can stay underwater for only weeks not months like our nuclear subs.

Two private German shipyards, Thyssen Nordseewerke (TNSW) in Emden, and Howaldtswere Deutsche Werft (HDW) in Kiel, are building a new U-31 version of the 212-A class, which is expected to be the world's most modern non-nuclear boat. It will dive to depths of 400 meters, or 1,200 feet. The German Navy has four on order, and Italy is building a version of the same class. Other nations either ordering the HDW boats or their own fuel cell propelled ships include Greece and South Korea. The new German U-31 boat is to be launched in March 2002.

Admiral Sharpe put down the report and thought about what he had just read. He knew most of the fuel cell propulsion data, and recent German U-31 design work, but was startled with the approaching launch date. He turned ahead to the next section, and the headline immediately caught his eye: *A Fuel Cell That Doesn't Need Stored Oxygen and Hydrogen.*

Mescod has designed a modification to PEM fuel cells that will allow submarines to benefit from nuclear-free or diesel-free power, the ability to dive to far greater depths than ever explored, and be *totally undetectable, emitting no noise whatsoever.*

Bernie sat straight up in his chair, and launched into the final portion of the narrative. The past three years have been spent developing an operative fuel cell propulsion system that will meet all U.S. Navy goals for its next generation of submarines. We have working drawings now available and as of this writing we are on-budget for our initial contract.

This supplemental request for $6 million will allow us to progress to final stage of building a system not requiring oxygen or hydrogen storage aboard submarines. We estimate an additional two years, perhaps less depending on funding and current Navy needs.

Because this project is Ultra Top Secret, no further details can be discussed in this report. However welcome inquiries or visits to our facilities by appropriate senior U.S. Navy personnel. Please contact President A.J. Humphries to arrange such meetings.

Bernie knew he had just read the answer to his lifelong search for a bona fide stealth submarine. He didn't know just how Mescod engineers had worked it out, and frankly didn't care, but he sure as hell knew he'd put this funding request on the fastest track possible and find out everything he could about this dramatic new development. He pushed the talk button on his desktop intercom, saying:

"Chief, please call the CNO's office and request ten minutes with him before the end of the day. Tell him it has to do with state of the art submarine propulsion. And then, get me on a non-stop to San Diego anytime after 0900 tomorrow. And call Commodore Dick Partridge at the squadron headquarters there and ask him to book me for a couple nights at the Senior Officers Guest Quarters. Thanks Chief, and let me know ASAP."

Half an hour later Bernie's intercom buzzed. "Admiral, Chief Northcutt here. I got through to the CNO's office and Master Chief Johnson says his boss is chock-a-block today, including dinner. He will be in his office at 2100 to go over his briefing for a meeting with POTUS first thing in the morning. If you can be there he'll give you 15 minutes."

"That's great. Now, how you coming on the plane res and the guest quarters?"

"Both accomplished, sir. You're on an American non-stop departing Dulles at 0900 tomorrow. Your tickets are at passenger service. The commodore says he'd like you to stay with them at their quarters. He'll have a car meet you at San Diego airport."

CHAPTER 47 - FRESH OFF THE DRAWING BOARD

April 6, 2000: San Diego, California

With a sigh of contentment, Bernie sipped a Bloody Mary as the big American Airlines DC-10 sped toward San Diego.

During last night's meeting, the CNO was noticeably impressed with Bernie's outline of the new fuel cell propulsion system Mescod was working on. Sharpe had found out, prior to the meeting with Admiral Lynch, the La Jolla project belonged to ONR and was one of many they had on-going. When he'd called the project officer and asked him about Mescod he was told: "I'm sorry Admiral, the Director is the only person who can comment on this project. You'll have to speak personally with Vice Admiral Terwilliger but he's out of town today, sir."

Knowing the system Bernie decided to pass that response on to the CNO. After hearing the story Admiral Lynch indicated in no uncertain terms he would have the ONR Director brief him tomorrow, at the CNO's convenience. Bernie chuckled to himself, imagining VADM Terwilliger having to make a presentation to the Chief of Naval Operations on a project he probably knew little or nothing about.

Five hours later Sharpe exited the airport, walked to the curb and got into a Navy car and headed toward the submarine base at nearby Pt. Loma. The driver stopped in front of a building Bernie recognized and he walked into the squadron headquarters of Commodore Richard Partridge.

The two old shipmates greeted each other and Bernie thanked Dick for offering to host him at his quarters. "I'm looking forward to seeing Betty again, and I'll bet it feels empty not having young Richard at home any longer." Partridge nodded and replied: "You can't keep them in the nest forever, Admiral."

Wasting no time Bernie said: "Dick, I'm out here to look over some R&D being done by one of your local civilian contractors. Can't go into details but I can say what I've seen of their project could go a long way to giving boats like those you command a big edge over potential enemies."

Commodore Partridge acknowledged there were many things even he didn't know about, and asked: "Is there anything I can do for you other than make sure you have a car and driver while you're in town?"

"Actually there is, Dick. I need an office to make a few phone calls and copy some documents I expect to receive over the next couple of days."

"You have it. My Chief of Staff is at sea all this week so you can use his office. It's right next door."

Bernie settled into the COS' office and dialed Mescod's local number. After identifying himself the receptionist quickly transferred his call to the firm's CEO.

"Good afternoon, Admiral, this is Art Humphries. To what do I owe the honor of your call, sir?"

"You don't know me Mr. Humphries but I'm working on the future development of our submarines and I've recently learned about a project of yours that intrigues me. I want to meet with you and Dr. Davidson to learn more about the fuel cell project."

"Ah ha! Must be Lloyd's request for extra funding has hit your desk. We'd be most happy to meet with you and show you what we can. When top brass calls we know we're on the right track. How long will you be in San Diego, Admiral?"

"Through early Sunday. Can we meet tomorrow in your office and then tour the lab and boatyard facility on Friday?"

"I'll clear my calendar right now. Ten am at the office and then lunch. I'll set up the lab tour for Friday but, unfortunately, I'm leaving town that afternoon so won't be able to join you."

"Thank you very much, Mr. Humphries. I'll see you at 10."

"We'll be ready for all questions, Admiral, and please, call me Art."

Bernie and his hosts spent an enjoyable evening together at the commodore's quarters. Old times, mixed with news about families, and served with a typical California dinner. The difference in time zones caught up with Bernie, so he said goodnight at 10 pm and hit the sack.

He awoke to a brilliant purple California sunrise, quickly dressed and headed for a jog around the Navy housing area. "Oh how I wish I could do this every day back in Washington," he nearly shouted to no one in particular. "Lousy weather and meetings, meetings, more meetings."

By 0800 Dick had long ago left for his office. After a Sumo wrestler size breakfast Betty Partridge forced him to eat, Bernie excused himself and went out on their patio. He reviewed his notes about the project and also began a list of questions that had come to mind about this new non-PEM fuel cell idea the engineers and scientists had nearly ready to make into a working model.

His car and driver arrived at 0900 to take him to Mescod's downtown headquarters in the Wells Fargo Bank building, near the harbor just a couple blocks from the popular Gaslamp District of downtown. A pleasant young receptionist escorted the admiral into a nearby conference room, and as he was about to scan the photo-laden walls two men entered.

"Good morning, Admiral Sharpe. I'm Art Humphries," the suntanned CEO said. "And this is the man who makes it all come together, technically speaking, Lloyd Davidson."

"I've read your impressive bio, Doctor Davidson. We're thankful you're on our team!"

"Lloyd and I are pleased you came out here to see what we're doing for the future of U.S. Navy submarines," the young president said. "Please have a seat. Coffee?" Humphries pushed an under-table buzzer and Maria the receptionist appeared almost instantly. "Two coffees please and Lloyd will have his usual cup of tea with the bag left in."

Small talk until the drinks arrived and then Art bluntly asked: "Well, what nerve did we hit? Was it the extra $6 million, the extra two years, or the project itself that got your attention, Admiral?"

"Frankly, Art, all three. I've been involved with submarines for almost 30 years. I've sailed on them, I've skippered them, and commanded them as squadron leader. Now I'm saddled to a Pentagon desk attempting to motivate some of the brightest minds in the Navy to devise new ways to build better, quieter and yes, less expensive submarines. I've seen all the gadgets that were designed over the past three decades and have even come up with some off-the-wall ideas of my own. But until I read your project outline, I never believed a system like yours could possibly exist. I still don't know exactly what it is and what it will do.

"I'm here the entire weekend if need be to learn everything you can teach me about this project. If it does what you claim, not only will you get your extra $6 million and two year contract extension, you may end up building the next generation of U.S. Navy submarines. We're talking a design for the future that will free us from the vagaries of nuclear propulsion and more importantly, one that will allow our boats to achieve total stealth; a dream of mine since I tossed my cap in the air at Annapolis."

For the next two hours Davidson and Humphries laid out in plain English a graphic and clearly understandable presentation of their modified fuel cell system for submarine propulsion. It was absolutely fascinating; Bernie listened attentively taking notes but not asking any questions until the duo finished.

The basic concept centered around an integrated propulsion system that required the usual fuel cell elements, but took the oxygen and hydrogen directly from the very salt water the boat operated in; the ocean itself.

Mescod's design did away completely with the need to store the two gases, as is necessary with all conventional fuel cell systems. When he had first read the report, the main thing that caught Bernie's eye was the fact this design incorporates a turbine as part of the engine. He knew that was also a primary element of the Virginia class design. The turbine propels the boat through the water similar to the way a jet engine propels a plane through the air. The beauty of the

Mescod system is it's a generator and propulsion system all in one, plus extra oxygen can be removed directly from the generator for use as breathing air, and by reverse osmosis drinking water can be produced.

Lloyd and Art showed Bernie diagrams and chemical formulas, and a mini model showing how their system operated. After more than an hour of technical briefing Dr. Davidson turned to the admiral: "I know you're trained in nuclear propulsion, and you may have questions about our system, but let me put the whole concept into one paragraph."

"What we've designed is, in a sense, a reactor, but it's not nuclear it's molecular. It's much safer than a nuclear reactor plus it's a space saver, and on a submarine that can be critical. Today's boats, including the new VIRGINIAs, dedicate a major portion of their space to the power plant. Our system doesn't have to store fuel, since we take it from the ocean. There's no combustion in our system, it's heat-free. There's no exhaust to give us away, so it's quiet. And I mean q-u-i-e-t. *No other sub or surface ship will ever be able to hear us in the water.* And we're also capable of generating a horsepower rating of 30,000 plus, compared to today's nuclear boat power of about 20,000 horsepower."

When Lloyd paused, Bernie jumped in, asking a bunch of questions. Some were promptly answered but others were deferred until the scheduled laboratory and shipyard visit, now set for 0900 the next morning. Bernie agreed he would be able to understand better when actually looking at the specific parts of the propulsion system.

"Gentlemen, I am dumbfounded with what you've shown me and dying to see the real McCoy tomorrow. I'm also tremendously excited about seeing the new ship design."

"Thank you, Admiral. Can we assume we'll be getting the go-ahead to build one of these unique little Jessies?"

"That'll be my recommendation to the CNO, and if I know his thinking you'll get your funding and then some."

"Great! Now, what do you say to some good Mexican food and a pitcher of cold beer?

The vote was three to nothing, in favor.

CHAPTER 48 - NEED TO KNOW

April 7, 2000: San Diego, CA

After lunch Art gave directions to the La Jolla lab and he and Lloyd went back to work. Bernie called for his Navy driver and when he arrived the admiral said: "I haven't been here for several years, so could you give me a quick tour of the base?" Forty-five minutes later he was dropped off at Commodore Partridge's quarters, telling the driver he wanted to be picked up at 0800 the next morning.

Bernie played host that evening and took the Partridges to Rockin' Baja Lobster, a place he had enjoyed in Old Town, a section of San Diego known for its Mexican restaurants and entertainment. He said: "Rockin' Baja is far better than fighting the crowded border to eat coastal Mexican food and they make fantastic margaritas, big enough to swim in!"

Bernie's visit hit its apex the next morning when he arrived at the project's waterfront warehouse, a building surrounded by a 10 foot tall chain link fence with razor wire on top. The sign on the structure said: Mescod, Inc. Maritime Services. An overall-clad man swung open the gate and then quickly secured it after the sedan was inside the compound.

Lloyd Davidson walked up briskly as the admiral got out of the car. "Good morning, Admiral. Welcome to La Jolla."

"Morning, Lloyd. I don't think I slept a wink last night. I can't wait to see what you have to show me."

"Follow me. Jules Verne is just inside and ready to give you the key to his kingdom. If he can't explain it to your satisfaction, I'm sure I can."

The boatyard was a combination of indoor laboratories and outdoor water tanks, some nearly as long as a football field. The tank tops were cut off so the test vessels inside were easily visible. Bernie followed Lloyd into a lab where he was introduced to three people. He thought to himself: "God, how young these creative geniuses are. Was I ever that age?"

"Let me demonstrate the working model of our propulsion system," Kimberly Peters said. She looked too young to be handling such a serious operation, but Bernie was quickly assured she knew what she was doing. "I degreed in electrical engineering at Stanford University's School of Oceanography and joined the team three years ago." Smoothly, Kimberly gave an in-depth, but easily understood view of the molecular reactor.

The group then moved to an outdoor tank where another engineer, Tim Guardino, showed how a vehicle could be powered with the Mescod propulsion system. It was a cylinder-shaped vehicle resembling a small submarine. When Guardino pushed a couple of buttons it moved down the open tank, no plume of water exiting its stern.

Returning to the lab, the group went to a second floor office and laboratory. Every space was crammed with cad-cam computers and drawing tables, artist's renderings of submarines were on the walls, and clay models of future undersea boats were on work tables.

This was the domain of Ralph Winter, MIT, a maritime designer with expertise in structural engineering. Another Navy vet, he spent several years in Italy working with a major cruise ship design firm. What Bernie saw as he walked slowly around Ralph's office took his breath away. All the designs, models, and computer projections were of submarines. And all looked like sea creatures!

They were subs, to be sure, but nothing resembling today's nuclear attack boats, or even the brand new VIRGINIAs. No traditional tube-like hulls, no tall conning towers or permanent antennas sticking up, and the boat Winter showed him was tiny compared to what Bernie expected to see. It was a miniature version of what looked like a giant squid!

It looked exactly like the squids he showed the N-771 staff, but the stuff he was seeing now was science fiction turned to reality. One clay model caught the admiral's attention.

"Like that, Admiral?"   Winter told him: "This is my baby.   I'm installing Lloyd's propulsion system into this boat I call *Squidy*.   And because of the system compactness I won't need a traditional sized submarine hull.   Mine will be less than 4,000 tons, with a double hull, about 150 feel long, and will dive to 7,000 feet and stay there for an unlimited period of time.   Instead of 125 or 130 men we'll need only 60 officers and crew, total.   As Lloyd and Art explained to you yesterday, *Squidy* will operate by taking in seawater to make electricity for power, and additionally the system will produce drinking water plus oxygen for breathing as needed."

"Whew!   This is very difficult to believe," was about all Bernie could mutter.

Dr. Davidson brought the admiral back to earth: "You must be thinking there's a catch here somewhere, right? Wrong!   Perhaps we couldn't see the forest for the proverbial trees.   Or in our case, we couldn't see the infinite power in the water surrounding us.   Sea animals constantly run seawater through their systems to generate energy to keep them moving.   It if works for a whale, or a giant squid, why not for a whale-sized U-boat?"

"Why not, indeed," Sharpe heard himself saying.

"Your dream boat, completely stealth, is no longer a dream, Admiral.   The *Squidy* is a reality and it can be the backbone of your attack fleet for the next hundred years.   Just give us the funds to finish our preliminary work and then let us build a few for the Navy.   What do you say?"

"There are no words to express my extreme pleasure with what you've created.   Give me as much information as you can and I'll guarantee the CNO will have a full report from me on his desk within the next week.   We've spent a ton of money on hundreds of different submarine projects over the years, but I've never been more excited about anything than I am right now."

Bernie thanked everyone and walked back to his car with Lloyd Davidson at his side.   "Admiral Sharpe, thank you for your visit.   We're thrilled that you like what we've done and that you'll give us your support with the top decision makers at the Pentagon. Please keep in touch and if you need anything at all, day or night, just give Art or me a call. Have a safe trip home, Admiral."

The driver dropped Bernie back at the Submarine Squadron Headquarters and he scurried right to Dick Partridge's office. "Dick, sorry to barge in on you like this but I've finished my mission here and I'm going to try to catch the last flight to D.C. tonight. I appreciate your hospitality, and give my regards to Betty."

"Can't you stay the weekend? We love having you with us!"

"No, Dick, I need to get back and let the CNO know what I've discovered out here. Great things are ahead for us in the submarine service. You'll find out soon enough, but get to know Art Humphries at Mescod. He and his people are doing great work for the Navy. Aloha and I'll be seeing you again soon."

Bernie landed about 9 am D.C. time and went directly home. Knowing the CNO's office would be manned even on Saturdays he called and got Master Chief Johnson on the third ring.

"Admiral Sharpe calling, Master Chief. I've just returned from San Diego. Admiral Lynch wants a full report on what I found out there. Can we do it Monday morning?"

"He's with SECDEF and the other JCS heads right now, sir, but I'll try to fit you into his calendar for Monday. As soon as he's free I'll tell him what you want. If he can see you I'll leave word on your cell phone with the time of the meeting. Will that be okay, Admiral?"

The master chief called late Saturday and left a message that the CNO could see him Monday morning at 1000. Bernie worked on his report all day Sunday, and after a good night's sleep he was prepared to meet with the top U.S. Navy officer in the nation.

CHAPTER 49 - A GO FROM THE CNO

April 10, 2000: The Pentagon

Admiral Edgar R. Lynch welcomed his colleague into his plush corner office overlooking the Potomac. "Have a seat Bernie, and tell me all about your visit to the whiz kids at Mescod. That must have been some trip for you to ask for a meeting with me so shortly after your return from the Coast. Before you begin, Vice Admiral Terwilliger has briefed me about the San Diego operation but he wasn't too impressed with the importance of the whole concept."

"As far as I'm concerned, Admiral, what I saw out there is what we've been searching for since I left the Naval Academy. They may be young and play with model ships and football field sized testing tanks, but they've come up with what our submarine service needs, sir."

Showing project examples, including a clay model of *Squidy*, Sharpe's report gave the CNO everything he needed to make a decision on this pivotal change in submarine concept and design.

"This is absolutely the wave of the future, the turning point in submarine warfare," Bernie stated, hardly able to control his exuberance. "I can approve their request for the additional grant and time to finish their initial contract, but it's going to be up to you, the JCS and the SECDEF to modify our current submarine construction programs for the next decade to include at least a half dozen of these new attack boats. I'd like to suggest that if you like what you see in this report, you authorize us to begin a special *Need To Know Only* project to build and test the first of these boats."

"Well, I don't know, Bernie. We're committed to the VIRGINIAs and those will cost a bundle, even though they are cheaper than our current boats since we ordered four from the same contractor. What's the price tag for your boat?"

"Because of the smaller hull size and much less space

needed for the power plant, we're looking in the neighborhood of four to five hundred million dollars. Operating costs will also be less since the *Squidy* crew totals only 60. We're now paying over a billion each for LOS ANGELES modified subs,"

The CNO looked over a couple pages of Bernie's report and made a few observations. "We need ideas like this to keep our Fleet a few steps ahead of the enemy. Basically, I like the idea but it will take a lot of selling to convince some of the more conservative thinkers in this building. The cost is an advantage, as is the power system and its stealth capabilities. Those will help us, but getting another entirely new concept approved by our military colleagues and politicians on the Hill is a big dream. And since this would be a whole new stealth weapons delivery system, every navy on Earth will try to steal it, even while we're building the prototype. How will you prevent that?"

"I gave that a lot of thought flying home Friday night, and I have an idea. If this project gets your approval, at least for one experimental boat, why don't we build the *Squidy* on Midway Island?"

"Midway! As in the1942 Battle of Midway?"

"The very same island, sir, but not with the facilities they had in '42. Until 1993 we had a huge Naval Air Station out there and the basic infrastructure is still in place. Barracks, clubs, recreation areas, great beaches and plenty of old airplane hangers that we can convert into shipyard shops and labs. The modification to the old base could begin almost immediately and the cost included in some existing military construction budget."

"Go on. You're starting to make some sense now."

"Midway is only 1,200 miles northwest of Honolulu, and we could easily fly materials from the U.S. mainland through the Kaneohe Marine Corps Air Station away from snoopy eyes at Honolulu International, and then out to Midway. The project can be efficiently supervised by COMSUBPAC from his Pearl Harbor office, and done through NAVSEA Systems for the actual construction. Pearl Harbor shipyard can assist with technical and engineering support."

"Actually, I envision enlisting an entire crew of engineers and technicians from the active duty Fleet. It would be a one year, non-accompanied tour, and would need the highest security clearances possible. We'll have to run the island like we are at war, complete with a prohibition on personal phone calls and e-mails. The only things we won't have are ration stamps, fireside chats from FDR, and Bob Hope's USO show."

"Your imagination expanded in La Jolla. Let me think about this for a day or so. I do like the idea and if it's feasible I'll go to bat for you Bernie, but don't set your hopes too high. This is virgin territory. I'm going to have to be a super salesman, and may ask you to join me when I call in some favors from my colleagues. I'll get back to you."

Bernie stood, picked up his briefcase and cap and said: "Thank you, Admiral Lynch. I appreciate your support and we'll move ahead as you see fit. One step at a time, as they say, but with *Squidy* they won't be able to hear us coming!"

A week later Chief Northcutt buzzed, saying the CNO was on line two for Bernie. "Good morning, Admiral Lynch."

The four-star didn't even pause before happily saying: "Looks like we've won our battle. Proceed immediately with the prototype, exactly as you outlined in your report. Co-ordinate with the Mescod people, set up the Midway facility and work with the Pearl Harbor shipyard skipper and COMSUBPAC."

"Four hundred million is approved. Get the boat built and in the water by 30 June 2001. That will allow time to test her and get a crew trained and ready to join the Pacific Fleet by the end of next year.

"We're tentatively naming her USS JAMESTOWN. Just as the original American colonists chose Jamestown, Virginia as their first settlement, we've chosen that name to be the first submarine in a class that will take our modern day submarine pioneers well into this new century, almost 400 years after the establishment of the Jamestown colony. Good luck, Hoosier!"

Bernie thanked Admiral Lynch, hung up the phone, smiled broadly to himself and said: "USS JAMESTOWN. Hot Damn! *Squidy* now has a real name and is about to become my long sought after stealth submarine."

CHAPTER 50 - THE HONORABLE TRAITOR

April 13, 2000: Washington, D.C.

Morning rush hour traffic was thinning when I boarded the Metro for Capitol Hill and a meeting in Senator Anderson's office. Tom Carlson greeted me with a welcome cup of steaming java. Word on the Hill was Tom single handedly kept Hank's political underwear out of the dirty laundry pile during the man from Minnesota's rapid rise to power.

"Understand your boss has been chock-a-block lately. Rumor has it he's going to take over Senator Potter's minority leadership role if the old boy gets beat this fall. What else is he up to?"

"The senator has many balls in the air, Dan. You've got to keep your eye on the ball and your ear to the ground at all times, as they say. Don't know just who they are but it's good advice."

The senator appeared interrupting our banter. "Come on in and let's do this interview so I can make my floor call."

Our conversation was brief. I said I was doing a feature story on Spratly Islands. We exchanged a couple of anecdotes from our China trip and talked about the Pearl Harbor ship visit next July. He remembered I'd lived in Honolulu before moving to Washington.

Trying to keep everything friendly, Hank asked me to recommend a hotel in Waikiki but I suggested he get away from the crowds that would probably haunt his every moment and stay at Turtle Bay Resort on Oahu's North Shore. He thought that was a great idea. Of course he had no notion no one would see him way up there and that it would take him an hour to get to Pearl Harbor and at least half an hour more to Waikiki. I chuckled to myself knowing what a bad boy I was and loving every minute of it!

"I'm also doing a piece on your military friendship

agreement to run just before its introduction. Several of your colleagues tell me their constituents don't like it, so you probably won't get their support. Is that a fair assessment of the Senate's feeling?"

Storm clouds rising on his face, Hank slammed his hands on the desk, nearly shouting: "Hell no, it isn't. And I'm very upset you would even think such a thing. Have you talked to anyone other than conservative Republicans? Have you talked to my colleagues on the Armed Services Committee? I bet this is just so much smoke. What's with you, Dan, I thought you were quite impressed with the Chinese during our visit there last spring."

"Calm down, Senator. I'm not here to accuse you of anything anti-American. It's just that I get the feeling China is not as popular here as you think. And if there's shooting over the Spratlys or anything else between the U.S. and China, we're in for big trouble."

"You're absolutely right, Dan. There is a strong group of senators favoring my bill and several don't. You never know what the numbers will be until the roll is called. Here's a direct quote for you."

Hank dictated a typically one-sided statement I dutifully recorded. I cleared up a few details, thanked him for the interview, and just before leaving I remembered Admiral Sharpe's interest in the Senator's gambling.

"One nice thing about having better relations with China is that on trips out there we can probably get into the casinos at Macao real easily, don't you think?"

Hank looked up with no expression on his face and said softly: "I guess we could."

"Ever play roulette, Hank? I love the game."

"I've done it a couple times. Very interesting game as I recall."

"Some of the boys at the Roundtable found a great little place with roulette, craps and 21. It's outside the District in a nearby suburb. Ever hear about it?"

It looked like the senator might fall out of his chair. A quiver in his hands betrayed him, and after a beat he said: "I don't know anything about any gambling casino in Maryland. At any rate it would be illegal and lawmakers don't do things like that. Now, if you don't mind, I've got to find a couple documents for the session. Thanks for coming, and I hope your story includes all the things I've told you, not just dirt from the other side."

I had the feeling I just torched a house. Walking past Tom's desk I nodded my thanks. Just then the intercom sprang to life and I heard Hank calling for Tom Carlson to come to his office immediately. Had I stayed another 30 seconds I would have seen the beginnings of another Hank Anderson cover-up.

I may not be the world's greatest detective but I knew I had the senator when he located the casino in Maryland. I'll remember this little Capitol Hill lesson forever; never fill in the blanks.

Heading back to my office I pondered the senator's reaction to my probe. Okay, so it was illegal and he was a senator, but who was going to make a big case about a little off-hours roulette. I thought, is there more here than just gambling? Why is Admiral Sharpe so interested?

Suddenly it began looking like a very big story, not just suburban games. Was there someone or something being covered up? There was only one way I could move on this hunch; talk to Bernie Sharpe ASAP.

At my office I checked my puka for messages and the only one of any interest was from CDR Noburo Hyashi of the Japanese Military Self Defense Force. I called the embassy number on Hyashi's message and when the commander came on the line I explained that I desired a statement from him presenting Japan's reaction to Senator Anderson's China friendship bill.

"Very touchy matter. I must contact Tokyo before I can give you official position. I'll call you in a week."

"That's a shame. My deadline's tomorrow and it would look good in my international story to have a firm Japanese statement," I said slyly. He said he would make some immediate calls and try to get back to me. Hell, I had expected him to freeze me out all together so this was better than nothing. The Japanese are notorious for being very studied in all their business and political dealings.

Grabbing my private phone I dialed that special number in Virginia. The voice that answered said stoically: "Admiral Sharpe, this is not a secure line"

"Good afternoon to you from my just completed visit to the hallowed halls of Congress and one senator in particular."

"Hello, Dan. How'd the interview go?"

"Good, Admiral   As a matter of fact most of it went so well I need to share it with you, immediately."

"I'm jammed right now. Tomorrow night is my first opening.   Meet me here and we'll go to The Seven Seas, a neat little pub I like down in Alexandria."

"Deal. See you at 1700 tomorrow."

CHAPTER 51 - THE PLOT THICKENS

April 14, 2000: Washington, D.C.

Why does time seem to crawl when you're anxious about something? Feeling like a horse player I thought: Come on, five o'clock.

My arrival at the admiral's OpNav office was met with a kiss. Yes, from Janice. The year was speeding by so fast she and I had spent only three or four weekends together since New Year's Eve. "It's wonderful seeing you. How about dinner next Saturday?" I was taken aback when she responded: "I'll get back to you on that." Her answer sent a chill down my back. Not that we were much more than good friends and happy lovers, but I wanted to be with her and pay more attention to this special woman.

Bernie came out of his office shortly after five carrying a bulging brief case and a big smile on his face. "Dan, my favorite scribe. How goes the battle?"

"The good guys are still winning, Admiral. How 'bout you?"

"Let's get out of here and I'll tell you all about my week on the way to the pub, all I can without having to kill you!"

Despite heavy commuter traffic we made it to Alexandria in about 20 minutes. The admiral led us to a quiet booth, sat down and asked: "Okay, what did you get from our favorite Chinese-loving senator?"

"My gut says there's something here Admiral. Since you haven't told me why you're interested in him, I suppose it has to do with the Navy and some of your projects?" Bernie simply said: "Proceed."

"Well, I interviewed him at his office yesterday, ostensibly for my story on his bill that comes up for a vote on May 1st. He honestly thinks he has the votes to carry it. Our allies sure aren't in favor of it, I can tell you that."

"I don't doubt it."

"After we finished talking about China and politics I changed the topic to gambling opportunities in Macao, and roulette in particular. He said he'd played it once or twice, but was very non-communicative about gambling in general. When I told him about the suburban casino and asked if he'd ever heard about it his answer was: 'I don't know anything about any gambling casino in Maryland.'

"The point is I didn't say the casino was in Maryland, just that it was out of the District. After I mentioned that location he sunk into his chair and the color of his face was like a San Francisco mime in full makeup! What's this all about? What's a Maryland gambling den have to do with it and how's the senator involved in projects that push your hot buttons?"

"You've done me a great service, Dan. Granted I haven't brought you into the loop on my interest in the senator and who he sees in Washington. I can't tell you everything but I can tell you this. And Dan, respect what I tell you is still top secret. You *can not* use this in print until I give you my personal go ahead. You'll get it before anyone else in the news business but for now it's classified."

"Okay. I know how the system works, remember?"

"I do indeed. And I'd still like to see you get re-activated with the Navy Reserve and promoted to chief."

"Just an advance break on the story would be fine with me, Admiral."

"Very well. Now, listen up because here's what I can tell you about Senator Anderson. First of all, he's probably just a naive politician who thinks riding a liberal wave of support for China will bring him promotion and greater voter approval. But his ambition may have been responsible for some major information leaks to the Chinese about our most recent submarine developments."

I uttered some acknowledgment as I took notes and made sure my tape recorder was properly running.

"Remember when President Zemin told the world they already knew about our stealth gel? Most people passed that off but at the time it was top-secret and known by only a few at the Pentagon and its civilian providers. It was part of a briefing I gave the Senate Armed Services Committee in January, and all the attendees were sworn to secrecy. As I recall, Hank took lots of notes. So the questions are, did Zemin get his information from a D.C. spy ring, loose-lipped Navy personnel, a civilian employee or our senator? If it's the senator, whom did he tell? And, is whom he told connected with the PRC? Interesting questions, eh?"

"They are indeed, Admiral, and you have to ask why the Chinese president used the gel item in his speech. The only logical reason is to tell the U.S. the best of our secrets are getting into enemy hands."

"If our young senator wasn't involved in more than roulette he would get a wrist-slap from Senate leadership if he got caught," Bernie continued. "What if the visit involved a woman as well as gambling, and what if that woman claimed Hank was her wife-cheating lover and got her pregnant? Get my drift, Dan?"

"I do, but what does this woman have to do with stealth gel and Chinese communists?"

"I can't comment on that now but I can tell you whenever there are suspicions about the security of a major Navy project, other agencies are called upon to follow up and find the details beneath the surface. You know what I mean?"

"You've piqued my curiosity. I'll keep my ears and eyes open even wider than usual. You think the senator is just a Sinophobe, not a practicing spy, don't you?"

"I want to believe that, Dan. We're aware of his every move and if information develops to prove us wrong then appropriate steps will be taken. At this point we just have to wait and see. And that's exactly what I expect you to do as well. Don't try to be a hero. If this proves to be more than what I think it is, there could be some rough times ahead. And that's not the role I see you playing in this drama."

After two drinks the admiral excused himself saying he had dinner plans back in town. He drove me to the nearest Metro station and after one station change later and I was home before 8 pm.

I flopped down on the sofa and called Janice. She greeted me asking: "Everything go okay with the admiral?"

"Just fine, thanks. He said to tell you to relax this weekend as he's expecting a super busy week starting Monday." She laughed and said: "So, what else is new?"

"How about driving down to Williamsburg this Saturday? It's a great place to spend a weekend. We can walk around the old town, have drinks at Chowning's Tavern and make love like the Colonials did. If I'm a bad boy you can put me on display in the town's pillory!"

"You're always a bad boy but unfortunately I'm busy, shopping with a girlfriend. If you still want to do it the following weekend I'm yours."

Disappointed by having to wait another week, but still very much looking forward to the time together, I decided to work on my story. Why wait 'til the last deadline? In a matter of minutes it took form.

ANDERSON SEES CHINA-U.S. MILITARY FRIENDSHIP BILL PASSING SENATE BY 2 TO 1 WITH GENERAL PUBLIC A STRONG SUPPORTER POLLS SHOW OTHERWISE

By: Dan Lincoln

Washington, D.C., April 29, 2000 (Pacific & Asia News Service):

The sponsor of an upcoming Senate resolution establishing better military relations between the U.S. and Communist China said today he expected May Day Senate approval by a 2/3rds vote. Senator Henry B. Anderson, Jr. (D-MN) also said he believed the nation would be a strong supporter of the agreement, and he had thousands of pieces of e-mail and faxes to that effect.

The bill, officially named the Chinese American Navy Friendship Agreement, faces a vote after several weeks of speculation about whether Red China will attack and occupy The Spratly Islands, a chain of 100 small islands and coral reefs in the South China Sea. Occupation of these islands could lead to China proclaiming a 500-mile offshore Exclusive Economic Zone, and allow them to prevent shipping of any kind, commercial or military, through the South China Sea, without their specific permission, which it is expected they would not grant.

Many U.S. Senators say this is the wrong time for Anderson's friendship bill and predict it will die for lack of votes. A recent poll of registered voters showed 37% in favor of the bill, 51% against and 9% undecided. There is a margin of error of plus or minus 4% in the findings.

Senator Anderson has also set up another major headline generating event, a visit by a PRC Navy destroyer to Pearl Harbor on the upcoming Fourth of July holiday. American allies seem universally opposed to that event and any so-called friendship pacts. Speaking for the British Royal Navy, Commander Angus McDonnell said: "We have no plans of inviting Chinese Navy warships to visit our naval bases, nor do we feel the need for greater friendship with a country that continues to threaten our very right of free shipping and naval passage through the South China Sea."

Many U.S. military sources say that taking over the Spratlys would be the first step in even more serious actions to thwart Western powers. A full-blown attack on the island nation of Taiwan is seen as being a follow-up to a Spratly occupation.

-end-

CHAPTER 52 - YOU DESERVE A BREAK TODAY

April 29 & 30, 2000: Williamsburg & Norfolk, VA

Getting out of the D.C. political pressure cooker felt wonderful! We tried frantically to bring each other up to date as we sped through the Virginia countryside.

"The admiral monopolizes my time preparing him for briefings and completing his project research. Even when he's gone for days he checks in with me on his cell phone. And what has kept you off my radar screen lately, mister? I've really missed snuggling with you, but last weekend was planned for weeks. I promise, tonight will be enough to more than make-up for lost time. Think you can handle me?"

When Janice slipped her hand between my legs I nearly ran off the road! I didn't realize I could stand at attention so quickly. Taking a deep breath, I replied: "Some of our newshounds told me the Spratly Islands might be a Chinese target. Your beloved Admiral gave me a backgrounder so I could look into the situation and I'll have a story by late May."

"The Spratlys! Don't you know they're called the Nanshas? China does have a valid claim on them but it's doubtful they'll do something as rash as attacking them."

The last hour of our drive was mostly idle Capitol Hill gossip. I located our motel in Williamsburg, did a speed check-in, attempted to convince Janice a nooner would relax both of us, but she demurred saying: "Let's eat dinner before dessert. I think you can hold off until then, hmmm?" Seeing I wasn't getting anything but some lunch right now we walked over to Chowning's.

Our afternoon was spent touring the restored circa 1600 settlement, filling our heads with early American traditions. This worked up a hearty appetite, so we searched out a quaint seafood spot on the James River. Janice suggested a dozen oysters for my appetizer: "If what they say is true, you're going to need them tonight, buster."

Sunday greeted us too soon, and having seen all we wished of Williamsburg we decided to look elsewhere for some adventure. We checked out and drove to Norfolk since I wanted to see the Naval Base. "We can also take a lover's stroll on Virginia Beach." After stopping for a late breakfast at a Denny's near Jamestown, I picked up a copy of the Sunday Norfolk Virginian Pilot which routinely carried PANS stories. I turned to the OpEd section and spotted my Anderson story on the front page. Janice briefly scanned it and said: "You're kind of tough on the senator, aren't you?"

Sensing something in her tone I asked: "Not at all. I've merely reported what a lot of people told me, both for him and against him. What bothers you about my piece?"

Somewhat evasive, Janice shrugged: "Nothing in particular. It just seems he's trying to do something constructive in a destructive world and he gets pissed on for proposing a positive but different venue."

Not wanting to kill our good mood I told her: "I'll do another story on him if his bill passes next week."

Sunday was fun. The Naval Base was greatly changed since I spent a few weeks there back in my active duty days. There's a big amphibious base at nearby Little Creek and Janice's active duty ID card got us onto that base and its beach facility, where we spent a great afternoon in the late spring sunshine.

As the sun dipped in the sky we packed the car and headed north back to D.C. It was about a three hour drive up I-95, and shortly after 8 pm I dropped Janice off at her place. We kissed good night and vowed not to let so much time go by before our next date. "How about dinner a week from Tuesday? I'll cook this time. You'll see I'm more than just a pretty face," Janice cooed, slipping out of our embrace and into her apartment building.

CHAPTER 53 - AYE OR NAY...WHAT DO YOU SAY

May 1, 2001: The U.S. Senate, Washington, D.C.

Bam. Bam. Bam! The gavel shouted as Senator Donald M. Walther (R-AZ) pounded for order. For decades the walls of this storied room had reverberated with colorful opinions from equally colorful Senators, each representing the best interests of the nation in military matters. Some, such as the senior senator from Massachusetts, called for reducing the military to almost nothing, a gesture of peace to the world or as a great budget-saving scheme. The nearly 100 year-old senator from South Carolina vowed to maintain or increase our defense posture, for the long-term good of the nation. But, each realized nothing could better please foreign leaders than to have the U.S. caught with its fighting pants down when a real need arose.

Today, the chairman thought, the liberals pitching this bill would make a statement to the world, especially to the Chinese, that we are their ally, desiring only to work for peace in the Asian Pacific region.

How ludicrous. Today's bill was named The Chinese-American Navy Friendship Agreement. For more than a year its sponsor, Senator Henry Anderson, had been pushing public opinion toward its approval. But events in the last three weeks had noticeably dimmed its hopes. Polls now showed 62% opposition, reflecting the public's concern over getting in bed with a group of communists most people distrusted.

"The Chair recognizes the Junior Senator from the State of Minnesota, the Honorable Henry B. Anderson."

"Thank you, Mr. Chairman and fellow Senators. I rise today to solicit your support for Senate Resolution #25/2000, known as the Chinese-American Navy Friendship Agreement. The Chinese government representing nearly one and a half billion people, has taken an ever growing lead in world affairs and trade over the past few years, and has a plan to ensure

213

peace, beginning with a policy of military cooperation between our two navies. In a geographic area that has traditionally been both a hot spot and a vital area for American interests, such a policy seems like a most worthy goal for both nations."

"Let me remind you ladies and gentlemen, our country cannot afford to face the loss of billions of dollars in trade, needed oil shipments, and easy access to other nations in the region, which could be the consequence if we snub a government as big and powerful as that of The People's Republic of China."

Some boos were heard along with snickering from the visitor's gallery. Senator Walther gaveled for quiet.

Anderson continued: "The Chinese, like us, want a long-term agreement that will result in peace in the region, and a continued growth of friendly relations that have been fostered since the days of President Nixon. My fellow colleagues, I am sure you will ultimately see the merits of this resolution and vote your approval. Thank you, Mr. Chairman."

The response to Hank's speech was partisan; loud applause from many Democrats and liberal senators, cheers from China friends and left wingers in the gallery. Polite applause only from the Republicans who considered the measure an expression of support for an enemy.

The chairman hammered his gavel a few more times and then said: "It's time to call the question. All in favor of the Resolution 25/2000 say aye. Those opposed say nay."

The 15 members present all yelled out their votes at the same time, and it was difficult to tell who actually won. The senior senator from Virginia, a Republican, said: "Mr. Chairman, I request a roll call vote."

The committee clerk called each member's name and each answered for the record. The China friendship bill was defeated nine to six, as a dejected Senator Anderson slipped quietly out of the committee conference room.

CHAPTER 54 - NEW SHIPS WITH OLD LINES

May 8, 2000: Washington, D.C.

Today spring was in full bloom, seeming to celebrate Harry S. Truman's birthday. He was born with no middle initial but the Army, believing every soldier must have a first, middle and last name, gave him one during the First World War. I wondered what old Harry S for nothing would do if he was still president; surrounded by left-wing liberals, his own party senator pushing a love treaty with our Chinese enemy, and the stock market under pressure not seen since the Hoover Depression days. Give 'em Hell Harry would probably have knocked some Capitol Hill heads, called in a few IOUs and simply worked it out. The sign on his Oval Office desk said it all: The Buck Stops Here.

Winter had fled past like a missile. The Congress was still pontificating and we were headed into the Presidential election season, with several key Congressional seats up for grabs. All this plus my military beat kept me spinning faster than that infamous Maryland roulette wheel.

It seemed like yesterday Janice and I took our cruise holiday, but that was last Thanksgiving! Toss in the December holiday party whirlwind and I began 2000 not with Y2K problems but with an additional ten pounds on my already growing frame.

I labored until April to shed the extra pounds, and balanced dinners home cooked at Janice's helped. We were still sort of dating, but unsure about taking the relationship to a higher level. Mostly on her part, because I felt myself being captivated more and more by this tantalizing woman.

Regular checks with Admiral Sharpe failed to unearth anything new on Simon Cardigan's slaying, or that possible Pentagon mole. Come May Day I was working on background information about the Navy's new DD-21 ship design project, the prototype for an entirely new class of guided missile destroyers and cruisers. From artists' renderings the ships looked to me like the Union Navy's MONITOR and the Confederate ship MERRIMAC, those steel hulled combatants of Civil War fame.

The DD-21 ships were quite boxy, carried one deck gun and dozens of missiles, but had none of the distinctive superstructure common to warships of the past century. Since the Navy was about to celebrate the 100th anniversary of destroyers in the fleet during the year 2002, the Pentagon was pushing this concept.

My unofficial but always reliable sources indicated there was quite a bit of disagreement on what design the Navy would select; one from Northrop Grumman and Raytheon, designated The Gold Team, or another from General Dynamics and Lockheed Martin, dubbed The Blue Team. The eventual class would be named after the feisty former CNO Admiral Elmo Zumwalt. Construction was to supposed to begin in 2004 with the commissioning in 2007 or 2008.

When tummy-time arrived and my NAVSEA design department contact had not called, I pushed *save,* flipped off the computer and headed for the C-C. Walking past the reception desk I automatically checked my *puka* for mail, as was my daily custom. I smiled as I thought of how my time in Hawaii taught me several words and ideas typically Hawaiian, and how very useful they were in my daily routine. "What's up, Danny?" asked the New York Times as I slid onto my Roundtable stool. Lisa the bar waitress quickly placed a chilled mug in front of me. "Whatcha workin on these days?" chimed the Atlanta Journal.

"Just more of the same. A pinch of military mixed into a cupful of politicians, added to a taste of foreign involvement and all of a sudden I have a for-real feature story. Just what the editor wants."

Chuckles around the table acknowledged they had all been there, and the conversation turned to PS&S. Everybody was watching this week's PGA tour event, nobody wanted to talk shop, so I took the opportunity to head back to the office and continue working on the Navy's 21st century warship story.

CHAPTER 55 - A MEDAL FOR GRANDPA WING

May 11, 2000: Chinese Embassy, Georgetown

Hardly a morning his entire body didn't ache and protest when he got out of bed. Huang C.K. Wing was born in the Year of the Tiger 1914, but today he was too excited to feel any pains. He was going to a special luncheon at the Embassy to be honored for his many years of service to the Motherland, service always performed behind a cloak of secrecy.

Wing was a frequent Embassy guest sharing stories about fighting alongside Chairman Mao and doing his part for the Communist Party. This old man, the most senior member of the PRC spy cell in D.C., regularly delivered countless items of information about activities inside the Washington beltway. Now he was proud to be passing the mantle to his granddaughter Samantha.

Over the years Wing had accumulated a huge storehouse of information about his adopted country by keeping his eyes and ears open, whether at the store where he worked or in sojourns around the area. At Washington Senators baseball games in the 50s, Redskins NFL games, celebrations and holidays, even museums. Over a half century he'd learned people love to talk about their lives, what they do and how they help make America the number one country in the world. And Mr. Wing then quietly passed along, via his Embassy friends, anything that could be helpful to China.

"I always gave them good stuff," Wing said aloud, putting on his coat as Samantha arrived. Today could be his last formal contact with his beloved homeland. His granddaughter was prepared to fill his shoes, or so he planned.

She was 25, the daughter of his son and American wife. Samantha had spent the past five years in college and grad school in the D.C. area and the last year at Milsoftel, some kind of hush-hush government contract place in Northern Virginia. She lived in a small but convenient apartment in the suburban Quincy Park area of Arlington, an easy drive to her current job.

Sam, as she preferred to be called, had alluring long black hair, brown eyes and a figure to die for. In a sweater it was clear there was an atypical chest tantalizingly stretching the yarn. At five-ten, and the perfect mix of American and Chinese, Sam stood out in the D.C. social set like the Washington Monument. Men definitely desired being seen with her. She had no problem getting dates. To any man under 50, with any life left in him, this young beauty was something to envy or perhaps even to die for.

As the two arrived at the Embassy, Wing was greeted by the ambassador and Fred Tong as he was ceremoniously ushered into the formal office. Two men he had occasionally reported to stood silently aside.

Sam then introduced two women she thought he didn't know. "Grandfather, please meet Cheryl Leong who also goes to G-W and is a part-time Senate committee intern. This is her mother Lily Shin, owner of Ming & Ching Things, a Chinese art and antiques store not too far from here."

The ever courteous old man bowed politely but did not reveal he knew Madam Shin and her family, nor that he had met her several months ago and was quite familiar with her two businesses.

"It is indeed a pleasure to meet you. I must visit your shop and enjoy some of the best things China offers."

Ambassador Wu raised his hand motioning for Wing to come forward, and then read from a scroll in his hand:

"In recognition of lifelong devotion to the People's Republic of China, faithfulness to the Communist Party, and dedication to our cause for fifty four years, Huang C.K. Wing is hereby awarded the Sun Yat Sen Star for Outstanding Contributions to China, as an expression of gratitude from your country and your people."

"Signed at Beijing, on May 1, 2000, by Jiang Zemin, President of the People's Republic of China."

Affectionate applause cascaded from the small group, and all wanted to congratulate him. The old man proudly displayed his bronze medal award bearing the Chinese hero's profile and hanging from a bright red ribbon laced with small yellow stars. A ribbon bar, to be worn on a coat at special Chinese events, had the same red cloth with two narrow yellow bands at each end.

"All my work, over the years, has supported the cause of our Motherland, so I proudly accept this honor. My devotion will, hopefully, be carried forward by another in our family," Wing said looking directly at Sam.

"It is you who honor us, Comrade," Ambassador Wu said ushering everyone into the adjacent dining room. Eight people then enjoyed sweet and sour soup, Peking duck with plum sauce, cake noodle, and the rest of the meal capped by fortune cookies, each bearing the message: Great joss follows the person who fills the footsteps of Huang C.K. Wing.

Glasses clinked and Wing felt his life had definitely been worthwhile. Samantha beamed her admiration for her grandfather. The Embassy ceremony had stirred her patriotic juices for the Motherland. As the group finished their brandy, Ambassador Wu thanked them for coming, congratulated Mr. Wing again, and departed.

Walking to their cars Madam Shin said to Sam: "Please join me at my shop and I will show you some of my finest antiques, the ones I don't put out on the counters. Then we can go upstairs and get better acquainted. We Chinese have to stick together, don't we?"

"Sure, why not? It's Saturday afternoon, I don't have any plans for tonight, and I love Ming Dynasty art. So does grandfather, right?" Wing nodded politely and gave Lily a small side glance that went unnoticed by Sam.

Back at her shop Madam Shin said to her special guests: "These are the real thing," pointing to some tapestries that dated back to the early 1800s, as well as Ming Dynasty vases that had to be worth at least $10,000 each. Even though they were her guests, Lily held the date-established antique vases saying: "I show, you don't touch." No one objected

An enchanting 30 minutes sped by before Cheryl invited Sam and Mr. Wing up to the apartment for refreshments while her mother closed the shop. Everything was carefully orchestrated to cement relations with Samantha and to get her grandfather to convince her the mother and daughter were on the same team with him, and were working for China's best interests.

They sat in the living room, enjoying their drinks and finger food, listening as Wing told how he had helped the Motherland by simply passing along what he learned in the course of a typical work week.

"Over the years I developed good contacts that helped me maintain pace with American efforts." Looking sternly at Sam, Wing proclaimed: "You must continue my vital work. Take advantage of your job position to obtain important American plans. Deliver them to the Embassy as I have done for these many years."

Sam listened intently, nodding agreement, then turned to Cheryl; "What exactly is your role in this? You didn't know grandfather before today and you seem very well acquainted with Ambassador Hu, so why are we here?"

"Sam, I am just like you, born in China with parents working for our government. Mom was directed to move here a couple years ago, open this store as cover while she gathers information from people she encounters..."

Sam interrupted: "Your job at the Senate gives you access to American secrets, right?"

"Oh, no, no, no. All we're doing is keeping alert to information our Motherland finds useful. Hey, we're not doing any Watergate break-in stuff or sneaking peeks at top-secret materials. We're just being helpful and you can be helpful too. We want to make the international community aware there is a new China and the U.S. is not the only major world power."

"And that's all, just passing along some information? And you, Madam Shin, is this all you do also?"

"As Cheryl said I keep an open eye and ear and you'd be surprised what one can come up with. I'm limited to the people who visit my shop and those I meet socially, and I've met some pretty highly connected people. But Sam, you are employed by a company doing many important tasks for the U.S. government. Think how helpful to us you can be if you simply keep us informed about what they are working on."

Sam interrupted again: "But, isn't that spying?"

Madam Shin simmered: "We don't consider it spying as much as simply maintaining a level international playing field and helping our country grow against relentless American intervention in world events. Don't you see how valuable you can be?"

Cautiously Sam ventured forth: "I do want to understand this, and agree China must be competitive if there is to be a lasting peace. But how can I do even one small part of what my grandfather did? I don't have all those contacts."

Lily put the young woman at ease in a most motherly way. "We realize that, child. With a little work you will prove most beneficial. As the fortune cookies at lunch said: Great joss follows the person who fills the footsteps of Huang C. K. Wing. Samantha, you will become that person."

CHAPTER 56 - A WING AND NO PRAYER

May 25, 2000: Milsoftel Laboratories, Arlington

For three years Buzz Russell headed the N-771 team, testing all the latest and best stealth systems from gel-coated hulls to high powered propulsion units, however nothing achieved the ultimate goal. Russell knew his group, aided by Milsoftel, must create an absolutely unique computer system and to that end engineers, scientists and spooks had wholeheartedly bought into Bernie's undersea sounds and emissions concept and had involved several Pentagon whizzes.

A buzzer-like noise pierced his concentration; the secure-line phone. "This is Dr. Mason."

"How you doing, Doc? Your geeks have something that may finally work?"

"Actually we do, Captain. If you have some time today let us show you. We expanded one of Chief Logan's concepts and our crew thinks this could be *the* solution."

"Hot Damn! I knew it was possible. How's 1500 today?"

"That'll be fine and Buzz, don't you dare laugh when we show you what we've done with your ideas and some of our own."

At precisely 1500 hours Captain Russell, along with two trusted aides, got out of his car at a very ordinary looking building in a suburban Arlington business park. "Nice digs," he whistled. "These computer types have it all figured out. Find a nice quiet office setting in the burbs, and no one will suspect you're looking for better ways to blow up the world!"

The lobby directory of the office building listed Milsoftel on the third floor. When the elevator doors opened it was obvious the computer company occupied the entire floor. At the reception desk, Buzz said: "Captain Russell to see Dr. Mason." The vibrant receptionist chirped: "You're expected. Go to the blue door and Miss Frye will escort you to his office."

"Thank you very much," Buzz responded as the trio headed for the blue door. Once inside, a blonde cooed: "I'm Sally Frye, walk this way please." The Navymen all chuckled at that old line. She led them down a long corridor with several labs on each side, and finally ending in yet another reception area.

Mason's door flew open as he bounded out, grasping Buzz's hand. "The Navy has landed! Captain, you and your two assistants please come into my office. We have," he said teasingly as if with a group of children, "some new toys for you to play with!"

Inside the office Don Logan welcomed his mates with hand shakes and questions about his friends back in the Pentagon basement. Buzz got right to the point and asked Dr. Mason for a status report on all the projects.

"Well, gentlemen, you have invested a lot of money over many years seeking a true stealth submarine. There have been partial successes mixed with many failures. We are now where you need to be."

Turning to Logan, Mason said: "Don, the floor is all yours."

"Captain Russell, you can't believe this place. It's filled with people who think no idea is too crazy and who want to test anything new. After trying everything else that made any technological or scientific sense I proposed something so simple it just might work. It's so elementary and yet so far out I feel no enemy navy in the world will be able to subvert it for years to come. Follow me to the main sub lab and you'll see."

The five walked to the lab for a demonstration. With his entry card Dr. Mason opened a door marked Security Area - Need to Know Authorization Only.

Three officers were stunned by what they found; a fully-equipped, life-size SSN control room right down to the 1 MC, sonar and radar, even the diving horn. A dozen white coat wearing staff members occupied battle stations and PCs.

"Impressive, Doctor. Show us how it's designed and your truthful evaluation of whether it will work and do what we're hoping to achieve."

"Oh it'll work, Captain, but we still have much to do before it's perfected. You'll see how a Navy submarine will achieve the illusion of being there one minute, and then gone like magic, not traceable, not even in the same operating area."

"Our computer programmers have created new hardware systems, similar to those on submarines. They're modified to allow the boat to change how it emanates sounds and light. By modifying, the way light travels and is perceived, we can provide the element of surprise for your boats to fire and then safely escape. They will also permeate the water molecules with a substance similar to squid ink. We have created an offensive and defensive battle situation equivalent to the kind enjoyed by the giant squid."

No one spoke. They were too engrossed in imagining how this concept would work in actual combat.

"The real key is the lead computer chip of the three we're working on. Should be done by the Fourth of July. The most important thing is it cannot be duplicated, even if the original is stolen."

As the demonstration ended, Buzz turned to Dr. Mason: "This is magnificent, George. Great job. Proceed full speed ahead for tests this summer." Winking, he added: "That's an order!"

On the way back to the reception area Buzz glanced at an attractive Asian woman seated at a desk, gave her a smile and read her name badge: Samantha Wing.

CHAPTER 57 - MOVE OVER GOONEY BIRDS

June 1, 2000: Midway Island

The sleepy tropical island of Midway was about to be shaken from its decade-long slumber. Bernie Sharpe looked around, pleased with what he had organized in one short month. Toweling off after a refreshing morning swim in the ocean he marveled at the beauty of this atoll and said out loud: "Thank God the big hotel chains haven't discovered this paradise, because they'd put huge resorts all over these pristine beaches and ruin them within a year."

Two million Laysan albatross make Midway their home base, and years ago military personnel stationed there nicknamed them Gooney Birds because of their gooney behavior. Most recently Midway came under the protection of the National Fish and Wildlife Service, and 40 men and women from that agency spend several weeks on rotation from Hawaii. A short-lived sport fishing business was tried. Aloha Airlines offered a hit-or-miss non-scheduled service from Honolulu, and each arrival and departure was an adventure with the island fire truck hosing the ubiquitous birds off the runway and out of the jet engine intakes.

Bernie had spent a valuable week in Honolulu securing the cooperation of COMSUBPAC and the CO of the Pearl Harbor Naval Shipyard. A few strategic calls were made and a contingent of SEABEES were ordered to deploy to Midway. Their historic construction and reconstruction skills would prove valuable in refurbishing dilapidated hangers, potholed runways, and the building of new facilities required for *Project Squidy*, as Bernie now called the operation.   He'd even received an ultra top secret status from the DOD, meaning only those possessing need-to-know level clearances were aware of the project.

As the big C-130 cargo plane from Kaneohe MCAS settled onto the runway Bernie was the first to greet the

225

SEABEES, who had volunteered for this mission. No time was wasted as the shave tails from Hawaii started off-loading their valuable cargo: medium- sized Cat dozer, structural lumber, roofing materials and seemingly thousands of bags of cement. There were holdover pieces of rolling stock from earlier Navy days, including a few trucks, jeeps and a carry-all. The abandoned hangers contained many tools the Navy builders would need, including cement mixers.

The construction battalion leader, Lieutenant Commander Ian Hammond, had been thoroughly briefed at Pearl Harbor and at the Shipyard, and was prepared to jump into work. Amidst all the scurrying about, Hammond assured Bernie everything was under control. "Admiral, I have all the necessary plans, schematics and blueprints but I'm quite concerned about completing this job in only two months. However, rest assured that if anyone can do it, my group is the one. We can't let our reputation down."

"Commander, I know all about SEABEE pride and I trust you and the men will keep it alive. I will remind you, however, that you can not, I repeat *can not* go through normal channels while on Midway. Whatever you need, advise me and I'll personally handle it. Understood?"

"Completely, sir."

"Good. This job is ultra top secret. Period. Don't try tapping some usual pipelines for anything. Even your personal mail will be reviewed. This project could fail if anyone ventures beyond the strict regulations established as operational procedures here. Failure is not a word in my dictionary."

"So I've heard, Admiral." Hammond snapped off a quick salute.

CHAPTER 58 - SAMANTHA SINGS

June 6, 2000: Arlington, VA

"Madam Shin?   This is Samantha Wing. We haven't spoken since my grandfather's luncheon. Fine, thank you. I have been thinking about our conversation then and would like to.....yes, tomorrow at 7 pm at your shop is fine. Thank you."

Lily was ecstatic. Samantha would indeed now follow in her grandfather's footsteps.   She phoned her daughter and told her to be at the meeting.

When Cheryl arrived the next evening her mother closed the shop and they went upstairs. "Mom, I've been doing my part, double-dating some computer nerds Sam picked out. What a drag! Got something better for me to do? Please?"

"The fun, my daughter, is only beginning. Just wait until our newest helper arrives," she purred. The bell rang and Cheryl ushered Sam into the lair, brightly announcing: "Mom, she's here."

Madam Shin cooed: "Ah, my little one, welcome. May I offer you refreshments? A glass of wine, perhaps? We shall celebrate your coming successes." The three quickly finished the chilled Sauvignon Blanc and Cheryl got another bottle from the kitchen.

"I have done as you asked, but being at a very low level for information at my office has perhaps not given me everything you want. As grandfather did, I just kept my eyes and ears open."

Lily assured the raw recruit: "That's wonderful, Sam. See how easy everything is, just observing and learning about the Milsoftel projects?"

"Yes, it really is!   Several months ago our audio group was given a bunch of details about some kind of underwater

227

sounds submarines make. Last week our boss met with three Pentagon officers and now our top-secret Special Ops Group is working feverishly on something the Navy expects us to complete in weeks. It's a real hush-hush project."

Madam Shin pressed her: "Do you believe this has anything to do with their so-called stealth submarine project?"

"Absolutely I do. Is this what Beijing is looking for?"

"You can bank your fortune cookies on that, Sam," Cheryl chirped. "You've made a great start."

Emboldened by the praise and the sauvignon blanc, Sam effused: "Well then, you'll love this! Our big boss, Dr. Mason, has told my supervisor to assign me directly to the new stealth submarine research team."

Glancing quickly at her grinning daughter, Lily smiled broadly replied: "Yes. This is terrific. Samantha I have no doubt you'll become a most treasured asset in serving the Motherland. Your grandfather will be very proud. When might you have more info for us?"

"The Navy has given our team until the Fourth of July to come up with the hardware and software systems to be tested on U.S. submarines. Dr. Mason told the group he was sure he could meet that deadline."

"Samantha, it's patriots like you who allow us to maintain a balance of power between our two countries. When you have details contact Cheryl and suggest you meet for drinks one night after work."

"Well, they've put me right in the middle of their project so I guess I should have information for you soon."

"See if you can tease an invitation for dinner from one of your co-workers. No American male can resist a stunning Asian, particularly one with your superstructure."

The laughter and easy banter belied the deadly reality these three unassuming women had entered into a conspiracy that could ultimately destroy the U.S. With glasses raised, Samantha offered a toast.

"As my Navy colleagues would say: Full speed ahead! I'm proud to serve my country with you, Madam Shin."

"Please, just call me Lily."

CHAPTER 59 - I THINK WE'VE GOT IT!

June 14, 2000: Washington, D.C.

Keeping a secret is impossible, particularly something as huge as this Navy business. Samantha Wing would find her listening role easier than she imagined.

Proof came as some of her junior co-workers and several senior programmers decided to celebrate as work ended. One man asked her to join in. Without a pause Sam shut down her PC, grabbed her purse and merrily followed along.

Eight or ten young computer whizzes all in their late 20s or early 30s, piled into two SUVs and headed off for the pub which ironically turned out to be The Seven Seas, the same tavern where Admiral Sharpe and Dan had met to discuss suspected political leaks in the stealth submarine program.

Quickly the party divided into two groups; those actually working on the project and those on the fringe. Sam turned to Bobby Walden, a programmer she often spoke with. "Some doings, huh? Did we accomplish something really big? Like, invent a new gun?" she inquired. Everyone knew the company was working on something for submarines but not everyone, including Sam, had the clearance to know what the project was.

"It's nothing like that," Walden replied. "I really don't know too much about it, but whispers are it has to do with the submarine itself. There are different teams working on this project and my end makes sonar capable of transmitting audio sounds from their subs. Some other guys in the shop take my work and tie it into whatever they're working on. They're pretty tight on security here so I don't know the full story."

"I thought we only work on software and chips, like what I'm doing with the programming of new software for improved and harder to detect voice communications."

"Well, I guess it's something like that, but what I hear is the chips we've designed will make our submarines almost totally undetectable by other subs. At least, that's what I hear."

"I guess we should be proud of the success the company seems to have made for the Navy and our country. Maybe we'll even get a bonus!"

"Don't count on it, Samantha. I've been here for five years and haven't seen the first dime of a bonus yet! But then, maybe they'll give us hazardous duty pay for having to listen to all those fish noises the sonar types are always playing."

"Fish noises? What fish noises?"

"Well, it's probably not important but for the last few days one of our audio labs has done nothing but play the kind of fish sounds sonarmen hear when searching for sounds of other subs or surface ships. The ocean is alive with all kinds of sound, very distinctive sounds from dolphins, whales, schools of fish and shrimp to unique sounds of some less common fish and sea creatures. I guess they want to make sure our new chip can quickly and accurately detect and identify these sounds so the sonarmen can concentrate on listening for enemy subs and surface warships."

"Here's to fish noises," Sam said, raising her bogus scotch and soda look-alike drink of ginger ale to clink with his MGD. "May they all be clear and identifiable."

"To fish noises and to the success of Milsoftel. May the boss break old habits and cut us all bonus checks."

By 8 pm people began talking about getting something to eat or heading home. Sam claimed a seat in an SUV next to Bobby and asked to be dropped at a Metrorail station so she could go home. Throughout the short trip back to her apartment, her mind searched for clues as to what had occurred at work today.

How significant was it to the U.S. Navy? Was this important for the Chinese Navy? Has the U.S. actually created a stealth submarine? Fish sounds; important or just fantasy? She wondered: Can I get Bobby to open-up more, or is he too small a fish and should I go up the ladder to bigger prizes?

Sam decided she would opt for a compromise course, leaving her maneuvering room if Bobby Walden's info proved to be only so many fish noises of no strategic value. When she got home she dialed Cheryl's phone number. It answered on the second ring.

"Cheryl? Hi, it's Sam. Fine, thanks. I need to talk to you and your mother as soon as we can. Cool. I'll await your call. Bye."

Cheryl called back before Sam could get into her jammies. "How about joining Mom and me for dinner this Friday? We can chat and Mom will show you her latest imports. Make it at seven. See 'ya."

Just closing her shop as Sam entered, Lily smiled and called out: "Ne Ho Mah! How nice to see you again, my dear. Let me show you some pieces of history from the Middle Kingdom. Perhaps you will become a collector of the time honored art of the Motherland."

"This is a great shop, Lily. When I can afford it I sure do want to start collecting some of these pieces. Is Cheryl here yet?"

"She arrived about 30 minutes ago. She's cooking dinner tonight so I get to sit back and enjoy myself with my favorite young ladies of Washington. Shall we go upstairs?"

After a meal of gon lo mein with sweet and sour pork, the three women adjourned to the living room and the real reason for the dinner. Lily came right to the point: "Cheryl tells me you've come across something that might be of help to us."

"Well, yes and no. I don't know if it's really important to you and Ambassador Wu, but what I heard had to do with Navy submarines and you've said that was one of the areas for which I should be keeping my ears open."

Samantha related the evening of celebration and when finished Lily asked: "Are you certain there was nothing else you heard or that you may have overlooked? Perhaps they're aiming this new software at a certain type of submarine, could that be it?"

231

"No, I don't think I missed anything."

Like a good handler, Madam Shin highly praised Sam's report. "You're already doing your grandfather proud. I'll see that Ambassador Wu is told you were the source of this data."

Escorting Sam to the door Lily touched her shoulder gently and said: "You have performed a great service for your country. Be careful as you leave this area and remember to call Cheryl to let her know you arrived home safely, okay?"

"Yes, but don't worry. Bye and thanks for dinner."

Lily and Cheryl sat together, broad grins plastered across their faces. They didn't know exactly what all the fish noises meant but there would be plenty of experts in the Chinese Navy who would. Pouring another sherry Lily picked up the phone and dialed an unlisted number that rang less than a mile away.

"Wei. May I help you?

"Good Evening, Mr. Ambassador, it's Lily Shin. Yes, sir, business is fine. I received an excellent piece of Ming pottery today and knowing your interest in that dynasty I should like to drop by tomorrow, at a convenient time, and present this merchandise."

"Noon will be fine. Shay-shay."

She carefully placed the telephone in its cradle, staring at it for a few seconds and then quietly, almost inaudibly she said: "It has begun."

As a nearby clock struck noon, Madam Shin, carrying a brown-paper wrapped package was quickly escorted into the ambassador's office. Bowing from the waist she then sat in a chair offered by Ambassador Wu.

"Ah, that is the vase you spoke of?" he asked. "Tell me the story that comes with this very valuable piece of art you've uncovered for me."

"It's about Samantha Wing; she has come across something I believe is very important."

Wu listened attentively as Madam Shin related the whole business about fish noises and her opinion about what it could mean.

"I want to present this info to Senator Anderson and get him to check its authenticity and learn what it's all about. Do you concur?"

"Most certainly. Do it as soon as you can, as we need everything we can get about Navy progress, especially relating to submarines."

"Congress is about to take its summer break, Ambassador, but I will call on the Senator before he leaves for Minnesota. And I hope you enjoy the vase, sir. Consider it a contribution to the Embassy."

CHAPTER 60 - UP THE POLITICAL LADDER

June 30, 2000: Washington, D.C.

Muttering to himself: "Whoever thought of putting the capitol here should be shot. It's only June 30th and the temperature is over a hundred." Hank was really feeling the heat because he had been overwhelmingly defeated on his China friendship bill. But, he still rode the crest of a wave of public acceptance, and besides, tomorrow he was jetting to the gentler climes of Hawaii. At Pearl Harbor he would welcome the visiting Chinese destroyer QINGDAO with a speech reinforcing his contacts with the PRC.

He recalled his trip to China last year and promises to the PLA Navy to look into their Global Positioning Satellite request. The search at the Navy Department showed it had been aging in someone's in-box for over a year, and the attitude was: If it came from Beijing or Shanghai, screw it. Let them call GM for GPS help, but the U.S. Navy would not be their coolies. Hank leap-frogged bureaucracy, called GM directly and within a month the Chinese were installing GPSs on their boats for about what a Cadillac owner paid for his.

The China lobby loved him for it but the Navy was anything but pleased. They couldn't make much of a squawk because the senator was being touted for Minority Leader of the Senate Armed Services Committee. Flashing back to the GPS request Hank scowled recalling that he now knew Lieutenant Wong was really Captain Wong of Chinese Naval Intelligence, and husband of the vile Madam Shin and most likely behind her increasing demands for Navy submarine program details.

"She keeps pressing for more than a few non-classified documents," he moaned to himself. "Or else."

The or else part was what gave the senator shivers. Yet, he thought, he could still do a tightrope act by passing Madam Shin non-vital materials while continuing to seek her bed.

Simultaneously, he was learning how to twist the news media to suit his needs. Despite the fact his plan for the PRC Navy destroyer Pearl Harbor visit flopped last year, he'd pulled it off this year. So, before leaving town he called a news conference to promote the QINGDAO visit. As TV cameras rolled he told reporters:

"Just as our nation comes together every year to celebrate our successful break from Great Britain in 1776, there is no better time for America to extend its hand of freedom and peace to the people of China. We welcome them into the worldwide community of nations with our exchange of visits by Navy ships. It is my hope the visit of the Chinese destroyer QINGDAO to Pearl Harbor next week will openly demonstrate to everyone our two nations can live in harmony, sharing a mutual regard and friendship."

A largely liberal group of supporters had been rallied at the last moment, thanks to Charles Finkel the newly elected chairperson of CAFS, an American group seeking greater cultural ties with Beijing. Hank had met Charlie on one or two occasions a few years ago during various Capitol protests Finkel organized in support of the Peoples Republic. Signs and posters proclaimed U.S. Chinese Friendship, or captured some new math; Navy 2 Navy 4 Friendship. The TV crews loved it, and Hank's pitch got the results he sought.

"Who would have thought this would ever happen, especially on Independence Day," quipped Rush Limbaugh on his national radio talk show the day before the event.

CHAPTER 61 - THE VICE TIGHTENS

July 1, 2000: Washington, D.C.

The Senate is always face-to-face against new budgets and this year was in lock-step. Hank's Armed Services Committee must soon present their version of the proposed FY-2001 Military Budget. While majority Republicans beat the drums for ever more defense money and new weapons systems, the incumbent president held firm, placing so many riders on the legislation it never had a chance to see daylight. The diluted version from the Democrat White House did keep pace with ordinary cost increases but left no money for new ship construction or weapons systems.

Hank's 1999 visit to the Shanghai Naval Base had proved valuable in comprehending U.S. Navy requests for new hardware and ships to thwart what it perceived was an ever-growing Chinese Navy threat. At one briefing he was told about our trials in creating a stealth submarine. He was quite impressed but couldn't shake the feeling the Chinese could be doing exactly the same thing!

Remember what that admiral said about gel, he thought to himself. Hell, the Chinese president even spoke of stealth gel at the May Day Parade, didn't he? Another chilling thought slammed into his brain; what will I give that Chinese Mata Hari Shin the next time she demands more secret information?

Funny coincidence but at that moment, across town at the PRC Embassy, Lily was bragging to Ambassador Wu about how well her spy ring was operating. "I shall politely ask that wormy Senator Anderson to get us exact details about the fish noises Samantha spoke of. He is mine, and I have him positioned so he must tell me whatever I wish to know. I am exploiting his foolish ego and greed for money and power. I shall make him utilize his power on the Armed Services Committee to gather classified information from the

Pentagon. And, if he desires to spend more time with me every moment will cost him, in so many ways."

A sinister smirk crept clear across Wu's chubby cheeks. "His public demonstrations of support for American recognition of us as an MFN trading partner, and his silly Navy friendship agreement, are designed solely to get him favorable press and name recognition with voters. Foolish fellow. His burning desire to become committee minority leader will play nicely into your hands."

"He doesn't yet know the meaning of the phrase payback is a bitch." Dropping her voice she proclaimed: "And I am his bitch!"

"Wei. Keep after this weakling with the big ego. Play him as one would a fish, gently with bait until it is time to reel him in. Report to me again soon."

"As you wish, Honorable Ambassador. I'll show him more of my bait." Then, with a gracious bow, Madam Shin left the Embassy. Hmm, she thought. I think it is time for an expanded lesson in Asian romance. Oh, these Americans and their yearning for the exotic.

CHAPTER 62 - PEARL HARBOR WORLD PREMIER

July 4, 2000: Pearl Harbor, Hawaii

My Navy Base pass read: Dan Lincoln, Pacific & Asia News Service. Valid 4 July 2000 ONLY. It did its job, getting me inside the Nimitz Gate. It took some coaxing; some might call it begging, before my editor reluctantly assigned me to cover this historic Fourth of July visit by the PRC warship QINGDAO. Bruce Ferguson had scrounged me enough local credentials so I could go almost anywhere at Pearl to get gut reactions to the ship's visit.

I made my way toward Pier Mike 2 where the guided missile destroyer QINGDAO was tied-up, across the water from the U.S. Navy guided missile destroyers RUSSELL, O'KANE and HOPPER. The PAUL HAMILTON was deployed. The American cruisers LAKE ERIE and PORT ROYAL were just down the pier and I noticed all of the ships were within view of the famous World War II battleship USS MISSOURI, for the past year and a half tied to a pier on Ford Island as a floating museum of U.S. naval history.

I jotted down that hundreds of noisy demonstrators were just outside Nimitz Gate protesting everything from China's miserable human rights record to the recent threats to takeover the Spratlys. Other pickets, regularly seen at Hawaii peace gatherings, waved signs proclaiming: China is Our Treasured Friend.

For the moment Hank Anderson was winning. He had the giant photo-op he needed to hype his recently delayed resolution. I could tell the whole damn scene was staged because there was not a single Chinese American or any other Asian American in the ranks. In Hawaii the only place to mine protestors was to go to the local activists who need money for their agendas. I circled the word staged in my notes.

More show business. A small percentage of the guests being checked by the Marine Corps gate guards were locals of

Mainland Chinese ancestry which is not unusual since we do recognize Beijing diplomatically and exchange billions of dollars of commerce every year. What was unusual were the people not present; the U.S. military and their families stationed on Oahu, and local residents. If it had been an American carrier or even a British or Australian cruiser or destroyer open to the public the crowds would be huge.

Scheduled time for the official ceremony was 2 pm after traditional Independence Day events such as the Kailua parade and Punchbowl remembrance ceremonies had finished. Evening fireworks displays from Pearl Harbor, the Hilton Hawaiian Village in Waikiki and Ala Moana Beach Park would conclude the day.

We took advantage of a lull and grabbed a quick bite at the former Officers Club, now called The Banyans, open to all ranks and some select civilians. Bruce got us in on his Navy League membership card. I asked: "How often do you come onto the base?"

"Not as often as in the past," he sighed. "It's a whole new ballgame concerning civilian access ever since the World Trade Center was destroyed. There's the occasional press conference but we'll never go back to open base access any time we're in the mood. And frankly, the public has lost its appetite for military stories these days."

"Except when: Navy Ship Collides with Tuna Fishing Boat."

"Right, but with no real threat Pearl is a quiet place."

"Yeah, just like December 6th, 1941."

We finished lunch and walked about four blocks to the visiting warship. Its standout red flag with small yellow stars in the upper left corner flew from the pride of China's fleet.

Long lines formed at the ladder leading up to the ship's quarter-deck. Several people were already aboard, most on the helicopter flight deck at the aft end of the ship, where bleacher-type seating had been set up. There were also five rows of VIP chairs arranged in front of the bleachers, for the dignitaries who had been invited to Senator Anderson's big production.

At a special VIP table to the left of the brow we were politely welcomed by a PLA chief petty officer who examined our credentials, then had us escorted to a special section where two of the chairs had been reserved with our names neatly printed on them. We were given programs which had complete details of the day's ceremonies and stats* about the QINGDAO, the first modern warship entirely designed and built in China.

Stats: Commissioned in 1996. 468 feet long, 5,700 tons, top speed 31.5 knots. Equipped with radar and sonar, surface-launched missiles and two anti-submarine helicopters in aft hangar. Ship's personnel complement 230 officers and sailors.

Well, I thought, state-of-the-art for China, but I bet most American naval officers would consider her propulsion and electronic systems obsolete.

I had a hot deadline so I scribbled names of people I recognized and Bruce kindly added others he said I would need to know. The translator provided still more.

Hawaii's Governor; the powerful and longtime senior Hawaii U.S. Senator; the urban Honolulu Congressman who was also a member of the House Armed Services Committee; the president of the University of Hawaii; the Vice Chairman of one of the biggest local banks, himself a Chinese American citizen; the President of the Chinese Hawaii Friendship Society; union leaders; a few hotel chain heads; and dozens of local business people and residents filled at least two pages in my notebook.

Promptly at 2 pm, the ship's commanding officer Captain H.K.J. Fong welcomed the visitors, and through a translator acknowledged several VIP guests. He expressed the pleasure of the Beijing government and his crew to be the first Chinese Navy warship to visit Pearl Harbor, saying this was a special day in the development of Chinese American friendship. He added his crew looked forward to visiting Honolulu on liberty and meeting the local residents.

His remarks ended with an invitation for everyone to visit the ship today and tomorrow, and speak with his crew. "You will quickly see that like you, we are peace-loving and seek only to grow our role in world trade and some technological developments."

At Captain Fong's request the audience stood for the playing of the two nations' anthems. Recorded music flowed from the ship's P.A. system, sounding a bit like e-mail greeting card music. After the anthems Fong introduced "The Honorable J.C. Wu, Chinese Ambassador to the United States of America."

"Ladies and Gentlemen, welcome to the QINGDAO, one of the growing fleet of new ships and submarines of the People's Republic of China. It is a pleasure to be here today at the invitation of the U.S. Navy, and I thank your Chief of Naval Operations for his foresight in setting up this visit and open house. I also wish to thank Captain John Claiborne, head of the Naval Station here for all the courtesies shown me, Captain Fong and his crew."

"This visit is the beginning of what all China hopes will become a warm and long term relationship between our two navies. It is obvious that our two countries are now the two leading military powers, so it is logical that improved relations begin with our two navies. Therefore, I wholeheartedly support the initiative put forth by your outstanding legislator Senator Henry Anderson of Minnesota. His Chinese American Navy Friendship Agreement will open doors for both nations. Ladies and Gentlemen, with great pride and pleasure I introduce Senator Henry B. Anderson."

Striding to the podium, his chest nearly exploding with pride, Anderson was greeted with applause from the bleachers, polite clapping in the VIP section, and a corny rendition of Yankee Doodle Dandy from the P.A. system. Grinning uncontrollably from ear to ear, Hank preened for the TV cameras, waving his arms exuberantly as if he had just been nominated for the presidency.

"Geez," I muttered to Bruce, "what a jackass!"

The senator acknowledged the crowd and then dived headlong into his speech. "Thank you. Thank you very much everyone. It is an honor to be here at Pearl Harbor, surrounded by so many memories of our gallant Navy, past and present, blah, blah."

"I appreciate Ambassador Wu being here and welcome again to the men of QINGDAO. Aloha, and have a great Fourth of July!"

CHINA SHIP VISIT BRINGS MIXED CROWD
SENATOR ANDERSON CALLS FOR CHINA TO BE
INCLUDED IN FUTURE RIMPAC NAVY EXERCISES

By: Dan Lincoln

Honolulu, HI July 4, 2000 (Pacific & Asia News Service):

The first ever American visit of a Chinese warship today drew protesters to Pearl Harbor, Hawaii, with placards supporting and opposing the visit of the guided missile destroyer QINGDAO.

In a ship exchange visit that was set up over Pentagon protests, U.S. Senator Henry Anderson of Minnesota was able to pressure the American government into allowing the Independence Day open house on the QINGDAO as part of his continued call for better relations with the Peoples Republic of China. In on-board remarks Anderson predicted passage of his so-called China American Friendship Agreement, even though his first version was defeated in committee two months ago. He said he will re-introduce the measure in the next session of Congress.

Perhaps the most controversial proposal was his call to allow Chinese Navy participation in all future RimPac and other allied naval training exercises in central and western Pacific waters. The senator said: "We must bring China into our world if it is to be considered a full partner in the defense of this region."

Senator Anderson and this reporter visited China as guests of the Beijing government for May Day 1999 ceremonies. We also toured the Chinese Navy base and shipyard at Shanghai where, while aboard the QINGDAO, Anderson first expressed his desire to have that ship visit an American Navy base. Over the wishes of most senior Pentagon officers the ship visit was arranged.

Present at the shipboard open house were the Chinese Ambassador to the United States, the Honorable J.C. Wu; two senior members from Hawaii's U. S. Congressional delegation; and hundreds of Chinese American business people and China supporters. Visibly absent were most American military leaders stationed in Hawaii and average American residents of Honolulu.

Early reaction to Senator Anderson's call for China to participate in allied training exercises in the Pacific brought this comment from a senior U.S. Navy flag officer, who asked to be quoted off the record: "It will be a cold day in hell before any U.S. Navy ship that I have control over will allow participation in any training exercise or share operational details with any ship from Communist China. And you can quote me on that. My words, that is, not my name."

-end-

CHAPTER 63 - SEAFOOD INFO PLATTER

July 10, 2000: Washington, D.C.

The jangling phone in Hank's desk drawer sent chills down his yellow spine. Quickly unlocking the drawer he grabbed the phone and answered in a low voice: "Good afternoon."

"And a good afternoon to you to, Hank. It's Lily. How's life in the U.S. Senate today?" she asked in a childlike singsong.

Bitingly Hank said: "I really don't like you calling me here and I thought we concluded our business months ago. What do you want now?"

"Don't be mean to me. I thought we were good friends after our little casino adventure last fall and when you visited my shop recently. I'm calling to tell you I'd very much like to see you again. Can you come to the store Friday evening for a private showing?" whispered Madam Shin.

What a predicament. He realized this woman was after more military information. But damn, she was one hot little fortune cookie he wanted to break open again.

As he thought just how to respond, Lily interrupted saying: "I have a new shipment of painted screens from Beijing. We can look those over while we catch up on things."

The offer and the expectation were too much for the weak senator to pass up. Linda was back in Minnesota on summer vacation with the kids at her parent's farm, so with that coast clear he confirmed a Friday night meeting at the shop. "I'll be there, but just for a drink or two."

Replacing the phone in his desk and locking it, Horny Hank smiled, thinking of the Chinese delights awaiting him. Then he remembered he needed to talk with his aide. He pushed one-five on the intercom and said: "Tom, perhaps you'd better come in and we'll finish what you and I were going over before I had to take a private call."

As Friday business slowly ground to an end, Hank decided he needed to freshen up for his Chinese side dish adventure. As usual, the D.C. summer was sweltering and a lunch engagement had taken him out of his air conditioned offices. That meant a change of clothes before his big event in Georgetown. Looking into his closet he carefully selected a pair of casual slacks and co-ordinate sport coat, added an open collar shirt, looked into the mirror and wished himself good shopping tonight. He closed things up and left the Hill in his now very smooth running Chevrolet.

More aware of his position inside the Beltway these days, the esteemed senator parked several blocks from Ming & Ching Things, glanced around to make sure he wasn't being seen by anyone he knew, then walked briskly toward the shop.

Seeing the Closed sign he knocked and almost immediately Lily opened it, beckoning him to enter. "I am honored by your visit, Senator. I hope tonight you find a few treasures you seek. I shall do my best to please you."

The sparring duo went through some rudimentary pleasantries and then Madam Shin suggested they go upstairs for a drink. "It will be more comfortable to discuss Chinese art, the paperwork for my citizenship along with those other little things I had mentioned." It was those other things Hank was worried about. Once in the apartment and settled on the sofa, Lily poured the two of them snifters of brandy. Offering one to Hank, he said: "Thank you very much. This is a great way to start our evening together." She raised her drink: "To China and the success of your Friendship Bill."

"Greater friendship between our two great countries."

The Asian enchantress pressed against the anxious senator. She began stroking his neck and shoulders. Soon she poured another drink for him. But just as he was set to make his first foray into pleasure-land, Lily stood up and said: "My husband in Shanghai sends his warm greetings to you. He says our Navy is making huge advances in ship designs, especially submarines." Hank slumped into the sofa, the wind taken out of his sails. "He says our HAN boats will rival anything the Americans can produce."

245

"That's nice," Hank muttered between clenched teeth. "Give my best to Captain Wong. I remember him from the picture in your family photo album."

Lily staged a coy smile and said: "He also told me your Navy is working on some kind of new computer chips for submarines that will make them almost totally non-detectable. Some private contractor in Virginia called Milsoft, or something like that, and their sonar people have apparently come up with a concept that involves fish noises. I'd like you to find out if this information is valid and if so give it to me so I can pass it along to David and help maintain a level playing field for China."

"I told you last time, Lily, I can't get top secret information, if in fact there even is such a project, and if I could I wouldn't betray my country by giving it to you. Not even for level playing fields, which I support."

"I understand, Hank," the manipulator cooed. "I'm not asking for anything top secret, only that you find out if such a fish noise project is being worked on, and if it is then my husband and his team of scientists and engineers can work out how such noises may be helpful for our subs and their future safety."

Hank mumbled something about better Sino-American relations and emptied his glass for the third time. He sensed a pretty good buzz coming on, but maintained his control and decided that changing the discussion back to Lily's impending citizenship might put her in a more romantic mood.

Madam Shin realized she had gone as far as she could in getting Hank to check on the fish noises info that Samantha had uncovered. She started music on the stereo, slowly turned to the now apprehensive, but still horny Hank letting her silk dress slip slowly to the floor. He was literally dumbstruck by this vision of beauty. She slithered toward him. "Now it's your time to once again enjoy the fruits of an ancient culture. You will forever remember every moment." As orchestral strings filled the room he made his second venture into the world of lovemaking, Chinese style.

He wasn't disappointed. After a successful sofa-based foray with the lovely lady from Shanghai, they moved to a more comfortable setting in her bedroom. The next hour replicated and exceeded his memories, vague though they were, of that night at Stavros' hidden place in the suburbs. Hank and Lily did a repeat of the shower for two, and then slipped back under the sheets for six hours of air-conditioned sleep.

Lily had a cup of hot tea ready after Hank dressed. The senator gave her a peck on the cheek and thanked her for a most enjoyable evening. He promised to check on the status of her citizenship application, and as he headed for the door she blew him a kiss: "Thanks again, Hank and don't forget to check on those fish and chips for me. I know someone with your clout in government will have no trouble finding out about this Navy meal! I'll call you in a few days. Shay shay."

CHAPTER 64 – MULLET OR MOLE

July 17, 2000: Washington, D.C.

Campaigning for the November presidential and congress-ional elections was in high gear as the annual summer break approached. Politicians were departing the capitol for their party's conventions and then heading for their home districts to shake countless voters' hands. Henry Anderson though not facing an election, planned on doing a bit of politicking to keep his name and face before the constituents. He'd make sure he got the extra TV and newspaper exposure that would keep him in the forefront of fellow Democrats' consideration for the job as Armed Services Committee ranking minority member.

Before he could leave Washington, one ugly situation had to be dealt with; Madam Shin and her escalating demands for vital military information. I'll get some tidbits about these new computer chips and ocean sounds, he thought. Just enough that Captain Wong can keep his own Navy engineers busy for months trying to figure out if fish noises are just another stealth gel.

Hank again fell back on Tom Carlson to pull his chestnuts out of the sticky situations he seemed to always be getting into. This one would take more than a phone call or two. It would be a major effort for Tom to snoop deeply into those computer chips and fish noises to find out if they were legitimate attempts to achieve submarine stealth. He buzzed Tom on the intercom and asked his aide to join him.

"Grab a seat, Tom. How's your day going?" That uncommon friendliness from his boss quickly put Tom on notice he was about to be asked to clean up some more dirty senatorial laundry.

"Good so far, Senator. What's up?"

"I'm heading home shortly to press the flesh, get in front of the TV cameras and mikes, and let the voters know I care. With my plans to capture the committee leadership in January I think it will be a good strategy to tell the folks something about what the military is doing for the future. Sort of like rest easy, your military is on duty type of stuff. From my top-level briefings I have a good idea of major projects that can be discussed in general terms, but it might be cool to let them in on some inside dope they can hear only from their favorite senator!"

"Just good politics, if you ask me. Is there any one project in particular you'd like to leak?"

"As a matter of fact I hear corridor whispers at the Pentagon that the Navy Department is fooling around with new fangled computer chips that make funny fish noises, and might be part of their stealth submarine development efforts."

"Seems to me anything of that nature is going to be classified, and probably secret or even top secret," Tom responded as he wrote some notes on a pad.

"Well I don't know about that but my sources tell me some think tank called Milsoft, or something like that, is working on this project. It may be nothing at all, and that's fine. But if there is something I could at least allude to with some of my bigger donors and their friends I would gain lots of credibility and probably a ton of new campaign money to boot."

"I'm pretty current on DOD projects, Senator, but there are dozens of private geek factories and most of what they do is usually classified secret."

"Tom, if anyone can find this civilian shop, and determine if there really is a fish noises story, it's you."

Tom paused briefly before answering: "Thanks, I think. I'll do what I can, but be prepared for either a no-comment or maybe a we-cannot-confirm-nor-deny type of answer."

I was in my office concluding a telephone interview for an upcoming story when Rhonda the Receptionist flashed my intercom light three times. That was our signal that an important caller was on hold. Quickly ending the interview, I picked up the blinking line: "Dan Lincoln. May I help you?"

"It's Bernie Sharpe, Dan. How've you been?"

"Just fine thanks, Admiral. Sorry I haven't gotten back to you lately but it's been real busy here what with the new fiscal budget and elections this fall."

"Listen Dan, can you spare me a half hour sometime this week? There are some unclass developments on the VIRGINIA submarines and you're going to like them enough to do one of your stories."

"I'll make time, Admiral. When?"

"Lunch Friday? Meet me here at 1130 and we'll drive down to the Seven Seas in Alexandria."

"Can't wait. See you then."

"Is this really a legit feature," I asked myself, "or does the old man just want to jaw about submarines?" I'd know soon enough.

When I hit the C-C after work, the bar was rapidly filling so I grabbed a spot at the Roundtable where the Navy Times and a couple P.R. guys were killing a pitcher of beer. I had grown to like Ray Kinny a lot. He was a veteran and loved the Navy as much as his job. When I mentioned my call from Admiral Sharpe he looked right at me and directed:

"If you talk to him again, Dan, ask about the Spratly Islands. You're familiar with them, I know, but my sources say things are very dodgy out there these days. Seems the ChiComs are antsy to boot the Taiwanese off the airbase they set up on one of the islands."

We chatted awhile before Ray headed home. Suddenly he had me thinking about those damned little islands and coral reefs, so far from here and yet so important to international shipping and the U.S. Navy's 7th Fleet.

As the week ended on Capitol Hill, Hank was cleaning up his office in preparation for the summer vacation beginning August 1st. He had just finished a phone call completing arrangements to have a private security company watch his house while he was away, when Tom knocked on the doorframe.

"Tom, how goes it? What you got for me today?"

"Well, I talked with a lot of contacts about that computer chip item and no one has a clue." Hank's cheery looks dropped like a turd from a tall oxen.

"But I recalled that admiral over at the Pentagon who briefed us a couple of times about the latest developments in Navy submarines. Remember him, Rear Admiral Sharpe?"

"I do," said Hank. "Wasn't he the guy who told us about the stealth gel and the oil tunnel for propeller shafts?"

"The very same. I called his office, he's out of town, but his assistant, Lieutenant Commander Cannon spoke with me. After identifying myself I said I was calling at your request. I told her you're interested in a think tank called Milsoft and asked if there is any unique project going on there. Not that she was aware of, but she'd check into it and get back to me."

"And, did she? Is there such a project?"

"Yes, she called just a few minutes ago, and gave me the answer I told you we'd probably get: 'We cannot confirm nor deny the existence of any such project, whether it's being conducted by the Navy itself or any private civilian contractor like Milsoftel.'

"Shit. Now I don't have any inside dope to pass on Dad's cronies and those old coots who can lay a few hundred thousand bucks on my campaign."

"You may still have a tidbit for the old boys anyway."

"How you figure that if you got the Navy's wave-off?"

"Well, when the military says they cannot confirm nor deny anything that usually means what you asked about is actually being worked on. Secondly, I told Commander Cannon that you'd heard a private group called Milsoft, or something like that, is doing a project like this. When she issued her official Navy statement she said Milsoftel. That's different than the name you gave me, and I have found a company by that very name listed with an Arlington address and phone number."

"Great work, Tom. You're the best."

When everyone had left, Hank unlocked his desk drawer and took out his private phone. After two rings a lilting Asian voice answered: "Wei? Who is calling please?"

"Your friend with the new antique collection. Those fish you were looking for can't be found now, and the pet shop owner couldn't say whether or not they'd have any in the next month or so. His private contact was still raising that variety of fish, and maybe he'd have some this fall. That's all I can do for you at this point, other than to say thanks again for your help in picking out my new Chinese painted screen. I'll talk to you in a few weeks."

The wily Madam Shin smiled. She understood the Navy gave him a can't-confirm-nor-deny answer to his request, but they did in some manner confirm that the fish noise computer chip project was being conducted. That would be enough to pass along to David and he would know how to go about taking the next step. And, Lily thought, I'd better call that Cayman Islands phone number and let Fortune Cookie know there's something really big underway.

CHAPTER 65 - WHO WILL SPRING THE TRAP?

July 18, 2000: Washington and Alexandria

I'll admit it; my heart was pounding when I arrived at Admiral Sharpe's office. I had come early hoping to catch a few minutes with Janice but she was out. The tall lanky creature was really getting to me. We hadn't seen each other for several weeks and it seemed an eternity. I scribbled a note about seeing her soon and stuck it on her calendar.

The Admiral was ready for lunch. We literally flew down to the basement motor pool where Bernie and I got into a waiting Navy sedan and drove to The Seven Seas.

After ordering, I casually asked: "Admiral, could you update me on the Spratly Islands and what China's involvement in them might be in the near term?"

Sharpe smiled that I knew you wanted something smile. "Wondered when you journalists would wake up to that under-reported hot spot."

"I know about the five nations claiming rights to the islands and the possible oil and gas deposits, but what about this EEZ they talk about, the one where China could take control of the islands then cut off commercial shipping to most everyone, including warship passage through the Malacca Straits and China Sea to the U.S. and our allies?"

"Get out your damned notebook, write this down and get it to the letter. You're about to hear a scenario that could lead to the next shooting war, or at least a major confrontation between the Chinese and us."

Admiral Sharpe talked for nearly ten minutes. We in the press had been used to incidents for years, such as the harassing of American high level spy planes over China; the live ammunition training exercises off Taiwan; and the continued tracking of our warships during exercises in the South China Sea. But this was a recipe for imminent disaster, with pre-war warnings similar to those Germany sent out in

253

the 1930s; such as the take over of southeast European nations and the annexation of Prussia. My God, I thought, where are my colleagues on this story? Am I the only one who knows about this international tinderbox?

Half way through our second round of cold beers, and before the fish and chips, the admiral got to the point of our visit. "Dan, you now know everything I do about those Spratlys, and you don't need to know anything more about the VIRGINIA class, the alleged topic of this meeting. However our friend Senator Anderson is at it again and this time it may just be the straw that will break the senator's back.

My nose for a news story was twitching. "What's the straw?"

"I was out of town, working on a special project, and Janice took a call from Anderson's chief aide Tom Carlson."

"Yeah, he's a good guy. Well connected on the Hill and over here."

"That he is. At any rate, Carlson said the senator wanted to know if we had any current information on submarine development we hadn't briefed the Armed Services Committee about. He told her he was about to go home for the summer break and wanted to be up-to-date on defense and Navy projects, particularly future generations of ships and submarines. He mentioned a computer chip project the senator apparently heard about through the grapevine, as Carlson put it. *And,* he mentioned a civilian shop called Milsoft that was working on this project."

"So, is there any truth to his request or is Hank just fishing for something to blab to his supporters back home?"

"You don't know how close to the truth you come when you mention fish in relation to his request. You know we're continually looking at acoustic signatures made by ocean fish and sea creatures heard routinely by our sonarmen. Hell, you can probably still tell a grouper from a groupie. Anyway, Janice did the right thing. She told him we could not confirm nor deny any of the projects our subcontractors are working on that are classified, our stock answer. You've heard it a hundred times, I'm sure."

"I have indeed, but in this case did the senator and his savvy aide hit a nerve?"

"Several, but nothing I can talk about. However, you can see why I'm so concerned about what Senator Anderson is doing. Anyone asking those kinds of questions, even if it was purportedly for his personal knowledge, raises a red flag in my mind. This guy is in love with the Chinese and who knows what he'd do with some inside information about future Navy projects."

"Tell you what. I'll try to arrange another interview with him in the next few days. I've wanted to do follow-up on the defeat of his friendship treaty and whether or not he'll pursue the China relationship efforts. I'll ask what his committee knows about our latest submarine development projects and if he indicates anything about fish noises I'll tell him that when I used to be on the boats we were always trying to record and identify fish noises, so we'd be able to distinguish them from sounds the enemy was emitting.

If there's anything off about his answers, I'll let you know immediately. He may be a misguided patriot but don't expect I'll find another John Walker family, okay?"

"That's all I can ask for. Thanks."

I didn't tell Admiral Sharpe I hadn't heard squat from my street contacts about anything other than what I now knew about the PRC fleet. And he didn't tell me he had already placed a 24/7 tail on Anderson's every move.

As soon as I got back to PANS I called Hank's office. Mrs. Swanson answered; I identified myself and in a matter of seconds I was talking to the senator.

"Afternoon, Senator. Hope I'm not bothering you."

"No problem, Dan. What can I do for you?"

"Well sir, I wanted to meet with you and get updated about your China friendship agreement. I'd like to know if the failed committee vote was just a setback or if the issue is totally dead."

"It is *not* dead, no more than those one and a half *billion* Chinese are very much alive. I hope to get out of here early in August but I guess I could find 30 minutes for you

255

before I leave for Minneapolis on the 5th. I'll switch you back to Mrs. Swanson and you tell her to fit you in sometime that week, okay?"

"That's great, Senator, I appreciate it."

The line clicked and in a few seconds Hank's office manager answered and said: "How's 10 am, Thursday August 4th?"

"Just right, thanks," I told her, inking the date into my appointment book.

CHAPTER 66 - THE BABY IS BORN

July 28, 2000: Midway Island

It was only yesterday the admiral had jetted back from the Midway operation, but with all that was happening it felt like an entire week had zipped past. In a couple of days he had to deliver a comprehensive *Project Squidy* report to the CNO.

On Midway, Bernie found the SEABEES doing a bang-up job restoring the old base to a modern state-of-the-art mini-shipyard. Two old hangers were now first class computer, sonar and radar service shops. The construction crew had converted one of the old gun bunkers and it now served as a small dry dock where *Squidy* could actually be built.

Sharpe's Midway mission was twofold; check on the reconstruction progress and personally thank the SEABEE crew for the super job they were doing. While there he would also welcome his old shipmate and protégé, Buzz Russell. From his earliest days on submarines to relieving him as head of N-771 and the stealth search that was now in its final throes, Russell had been Bernie's only choice for overseeing building of the USS JAMESTOWN. When it was finished he would take command as the boat's first skipper.

With Buzz's input, Admiral Sharpe appointed three key members of his management team who would serve on the boat's initial crew. The Executive Officer, most recently aboard the USS BUFFALO, would be Commander Ellis Sherman. Buzz had suggested LT Bill Bemus from his N-771 staff as Weapons Officer. That left only one more major position to be filled.

Bernie knew there could be only one choice for Chief of the Boat; a crusty old boatswain's mate right out of a Hollywood war-flick. Harold B. Esterhaus, 30 years in subs, was currently on the staff at COMSUBPAC as Command Master Chief. On the way to Midway Bernie visited: "H.B. don't call me Harold," and from the first minute knew he had to have this old salt aboard *Squidy*. H.B. jumped at the invitation before it even cleared Bernie's lips.

Buzz was thrilled with the crew selection, and looked forward to those men joining him in a few weeks. In the meantime, the team of top security-cleared, all active-duty shipbuilders had arrived on island, anxious to begin their milestone ship construction project.

The day before Bernie wrapped up this Midway visit, the *Squidy* team was assembled in the mess hall so Sharpe could talk to them. "You men and women are all volunteers and part of a new era in Navy submarine history. What you will build here will become the backbone of our submarine fleet for the next century. When JAMESTOWN becomes a part of the Fleet, America will have a weapon so awesome and so unique no nation will attempt to aggressively challenge us or attack the free nations of this world."

"You'll be working on a project surrounded by the kind of security that is absolutely necessary to protect this important new weapons system. You won't be able to talk about this venture for many years to come, perhaps even in your lifetime. For that I thank you personally, and bring with me the appreciation of the CNO, the Secretary of Defense and the President himself.

"Granted, there are only a few in our Navy or the government who are aware of *Project Squidy*, and that must remain the case for the foreseeable future. But I can assure you a grateful nation will, for years to come, remember those who actually built this boat. Even though you won't be its crew, you will be officially designated as Plank Owners of the USS JAMESTOWN, and have that recognition recorded in your individual personnel records."

"I'll try to visit as often as I can, but you're in very capable hands with Captain Russell. Anything you need, within the bounds of security, just ask for and it will be done. Thanks again. I know you're all going to do a super job. All ahead full!"

Sharpe and Buzz spent the following day confirming modifications NAVSEA Systems had made to the boat's hull and discussing the new inner and outer skin materials. A half dozen engineers, under Mescod direction, were on hand to supervise hull construction, and only they knew just what would replace standard steel plating. The boat would be assembled in sections using a new method devised by Lloyd Davidson. Rather than welded seams, it employed fusing the sections together.

Whistling under his breath, the admiral thought: Man, this is some boat. No shapes like a regular submarine, no traditional conning tower. It's a fish was the best description he could come up with. Its fins were what would become the forward diving planes. Amazing! Both external and internal communications systems would employ fiber optics capable of contacting orbiting satellites, and when the arrays were fanned out the boat looked like a giant squid. Retract them and JAMESTOWN was a whale.

Feeling everything was well in hand, Sharpe returned his base CO's salute, and then hopped aboard the small Navy jet that would take him back to Kaneohe MCAS. A day later he'd be back at his Washington desk prepping for his presentation to the CNO, and setting in motion his scheme to trap the elusive Pentagon mole.

CHAPTER 67 - NOW, HERE'S THE PLAN

August 1, 2000: The Pentagon

Admiral Sharpe's impatience ended with Admiral Lynch's entrance into the conference room. "Take a chair, Bernie. That must be the all important report you're clutching so tightly."

Lynch held out his hand, asking: "Are you going to surrender it or just keep it warm?" Bernie handed it over to the four-star who put it in his IN box saying: "I'll get to it as soon as I can, probably during my ride home tonight."

Starting to get up Bernie said: "Admiral, there's one other matter I need to discuss with you. It concerns this project plus another I've been involved with since last fall." The CNO sat back motioning for Sharpe to continue.

"Well, sir, as you know I've been trying for 30 years to find a way to build a stealth submarine. Last October I came up with an idea about using sounds made by fish and other sea creatures to throw off enemy subs by making them think the sounds they hear are coming from actual sea animals, not an American sub.

"To make a long story short, a private lab called Milsoftel took the idea and created a computer chip containing these sea sounds. When our ships transmit those sounds they believe the acoustic footprints will confuse enemy boats. We're about to commit big bucks to installing this system in at least one LOS ANGELES class submarine and then spend several weeks at sea testing it."

Pausing for effect, Bernie said: "Sir, I believe we have a mole in the system who is snooping for classified info and then passing it straight to the Chinese."

"Interesting. And what proof do you have?"

"Remember that reference to stealth gel by China's president last May Day? That was the first tip-off and now it appears they have some knowledge about the sea sounds project and want to get it to Beijing. It's only a matter of time, in my opinion, before the mole learns about *Project Squidy*."

"Do you have any idea who the mole is?"

"I've talked to all possible sources, and all have convinced me there has been an active Chinese spy ring here in D.C. for many years. It began a decade ago in Hawaii with a small group dedicated China supporters stealing secrets from various commands at Pearl Harbor. I believe this ring is also operating in San Diego, Norfolk, perhaps Seattle, and right here in this building."

"So, what's your plan to find this ferret?"

"It's not firm yet, sir, but you realize we must protect the *Squidy* project at any cost. Once someone inevitably discovers my process, they can replicate it in months. Besides, if the mole thinks we're hanging our hat on that project he'll do anything to get more information."

"Basically what I'm proposing is that we make the Milsoftel project a decoy and let the Chinese commies think that's our latest and greatest innovation. I'd venture they'll pull every stop in the book to get it and install it in one of their boats. And when they do steal that info we'll be there to rub the mole's nose in a criminal charge of espionage, and perhaps even sedition if the bugger turns out to be an American citizen."

"Sounds like a plan to me, Bernie. I say go for it My neck is out on this venture so for God's sake don't let it get in harm's way. The lefties would love to know we're working on a boat like that one. As usual, keep me posted."

CHAPTER 68 - THE WORM SQUIRMS

August 4, 2000:   Capitol Hill

Grilling is my life, whether it's subjects for a story or steaks on the fire. Tonight was rib eyes and corn on the cob for Janice. Add good wine and dinner at my place beat the hell out of any pricey restaurant in D.C. Janice, she of those long, long lovely legs and ample hooters, would hopefully be dessert!

Shoptalk seemed to dominate the evening, and when I mentioned I was interviewing Senator Anderson the next morning Janice replied: "I could hardly believe it when his own committee shot his China measure down in flames and...."

"Well," I interjected, "he doesn't think it's dead. In fact today on the phone he indicated it was still alive and kicking as far as he's concerned."

Janice shot back: "As I've said all along, he's brave for trying to take us forward by recognizing the importance of the world's oldest civilization, which just happens to be the biggest country on the globe. What is it with us that we're so afraid of China?"

"Could it be their naval buildup, or the few million People's Liberation Army soldiers poised to stomp all over Korea, or that possible takeover of Taiwan?"

"Bull pippy!" the lady commander laughed. "They're pretty advanced in many areas but they definitely aren't getting ready to attack their neighbors."

The mediator in me kicked in and I changed our topic of conversation to what Janice had planned for the rest of the summer.

She brightened and said cheerily: "I'm going to Hong Kong to visit my father. I'll be gone a couple weeks until right after Labor Day. Think you can do without me that long?" she teased.

"Hell, it seems like we never see much of each other anymore," I replied.

"You're right," Janice said pecking me on the cheek. "I brought a little nightie that'll let you see as much of me as you want tonight. Now, scrub the galley while I unpack my overnight bag." It was amazing how quickly I followed an order like that one.

The overnight delight went very well although I would like to have slept in for another hour. We got up at 6 am, dressed and had breakfast. We shared a train into the city center, where I got off. She continued on to the Pentagon Metro station.

I strolled to the PANS offices seemingly in a cloud, revisiting some very explicit sexual scenes from the night before. Janice was definitely a dream come true for me. I had to see and have lots more of Janice Cannon, USN.

August 4th was another lazy summer day. After checking the morning news wire I popped into Ben's office and said I had a 10 o'clock interview with Senator Anderson. He snickered: "Still wasting your time on that China lover? With his bill in the dumper what's so interesting about him now?"

"He says the agreement is alive and well. Anything you want me to ask him?"

"Yeah. Ask him to comment on the brouhaha about those Spratly Islands; the word on the street is the Chinese are about to take them over."

"Good idea, Ben. I'll do that. I've already done research on the Spratlys; they'd make an excellent story for a Labor Day weekend release."

Senator Anderson welcomed me into his office promptly at 10, and in a rather too-friendly tone said: "How you been, Dan. Sit down. Sorry it's so hectic here but if you kept my schedule you'd be ready to leave for Minnesota too! Okay, what do you want to know about the friendship bill?"

"Why do you believe the bill is still alive?"

"You can quote me on this," he began: "There is no doubt in my mind that as the American people realize the importance of China to our international trade, our search to maintain world peace, and our overwhelming desire to avoid war, they will be the leaders of the move to initiate dialog such

263

as the Chinese American Navy Friendship Agreement. It will happen." Ah, I thought, spoken like a true politician.

"When will that be?" I queried.

"Perhaps next year when a new Democrat sits in the Oval Office, one who already supports what my bill stands for, and knows we cannot continue to ignore China."

I asked him several questions about the Spratlys and got very little information that I didn't already have. The business about the islands being the Nanshas was the basis of his reasoning as to why China should be allowed to annex them. He said there was no way they would put up a 500 mile territorial zone around the island chain.

Hank shifted papers on his desk, hinting the interview was over, but I laid one more question on him. "Senator, as one who's known for being up to date on what's happening in the military, particularly the Navy, are there any new developments you know of that could become a good story for me?"

He sat back in his chair and asked: "What sort of developments?"

"Some Pentagon sources and my colleagues say the Navy is working on developing a computer chip that has to do with ocean sounds. You know, fish noises. Apparently it has something to do with their on-going efforts to create a stealth submarine."

If I had thought Hank looked like a San Francisco mime when I'd mentioned the gambling casino several months ago, he now looked like warmed-over death! He then became flushed and stammered: "I don't know about any ocean sounds, and the only thing I know about stealth submarines is that gel business Admiral Sharpe briefed us about months ago, before we went to China. Sorry, Dan, but I can't help you with any story here."

I said I understood and would have to check my sources further. Thanking him for his time and wishing him a happy summer vacation, I got up shook his clammy hand and left. I was hard pressed to hold back a smile and couldn't help but wonder what he would be doing the minute I closed his door.

Back at my office I dialed Bernie and told him about my interview with Hank and his response to my question about fish noises. "The guy nearly slipped out of his chair, and it was all I could do to not laugh. It was the same reception I got when I laid the Maryland gambling trip on him."

"Good job, Dan. Let me take it from here. You do the story about the Spratlys and his belief the friendship bill will again see the light of day, and I'll do the rest."

CHAPTER 69 - ISLANDS OF DESTINY

September 3, 2000: Washington, D.C.

Lily busied herself doing paperwork in her store. She loved Sunday mornings; they were perfect because no one would disturb her.   Sipping her morning tea her eyes wandered to the Washington Post. A front page headline virtually shocked her:

TINY SOUTH CHINA SEA ISLANDS COULD LEAD TO U.S. - CHINESE WAR

By: Dan Lincoln

Washington, D.C., September 2, 2000 (Pacific & Asian News Service):

U.S. military experts are saying a little known group of about 100 tiny islands and coral reefs in the South China Sea is a possible site for the next shooting war in the Pacific. Ownership of the Spratly Islands is currently contested by five nations: China, Taiwan, Vietnam, Malaysia and the Philippines, however only Taiwan actually has a garrison on the main island. Other than some offshore fishing, the islands are devoid of an economy and unoccupied. China, however, wishes to claim them, saying they have possessed them for almost two thousand years.

Why the concern over these desolate atolls? By claiming and occupying the Spratlys a nation can control all ocean traffic from Singapore to Tokyo. To the rest of the world, that is totally unacceptable.

Forcing her mind to relax Lily digested the speculation about future events. She realized she must take action. This could severely impact her small but efficient clan of China supporters, and possibly weaken support for her captive senator's plans. Wondering if their new recruit was keen enough to comprehend all this and perhaps get cold feet, she immediately called the Embassy for help.

Reaching the switchboard, Madam Shin asked for Fred Tong, and blurted to him what she had read in the Post. Tong said he hadn't seen the article but would set a meeting for her with the ambassador later that afternoon.

Across town Henry Anderson sat in his den with the Post story on his lap and a strong cup of coffee in his hand. He was pissed the author had made what he felt was a case for multi-national control of the islands.

As for my comments about a potential invasion by China, Hank muttered to himself: "More right-wing speculation. The Chinese aren't going to close off the South China Sea or attack the Spratlys. That's just so much conservative bullshit." He took another swig of hot, black coffee and continued reading my story:

The prize to the nation that controls the Spratly Islands is control of the seas surrounding them. The Spratlys lie in the middle of the South China Sea, basically due south of Hong Kong, east of Vietnam, west of the Philippines and north of Singapore. Thousands of ships use this route to cut north from Singapore to Hong Kong, Taipei and Japan with container freight and tankers full of oil from the Middle East.
If China declared an Exclusive Economic Zone (EEZ) around the islands, it could proclaim its territorial waters extend 500 miles from their coasts. If enforced, that could mean the total cessation of any shipping through the South China Sea that China did not authorize, including freighters, oil tankers and warships.

It is expected the PRC would do just that, forcing shipping to avoid the quicker South China Sea route and require transit around the Philippines, thus adding thousands of miles to their voyages. If such a closing of these traditional ocean trading routes was implemented by China, it is believed a major shooting confrontation, if not an all-out war, would be declared by the U. S.

Currently two dozen troops from Taiwan are on the main island running an airstrip. China could easily effect a take-over within one single day with offshore bombardments, aerial attacks and by landing troops.

Recent rumors lead several U. S. military leaders at the Pentagon to believe such an attack could be imminent, and they see this as one more step toward control of the South China Sea and the retaking of Taiwan, considered by the PRC to be nothing more than their renegade off-shore province.

In his Falls Church home Bernie Sharpe laid down his Sunday paper and thought: Man, one dinner with Dan and he just may have opened some important eyes around the globe.

Bernie smiled to himself and thought: I hope this story has already reached high level people in Beijing, Shanghai and Taipei. He read the last words of the news feature then put the paper down with a look of satisfaction on his face.

There are known oil and gas basins around and under the islands, but so far no oil or gas development. The Sultanate of Brunei claims some fishing rights, as do other nations, but China says the islands are theirs. Their claim dates back nearly two thousand years to Han Dynasty naval expeditions to the islands in 110 A.D., and occupation by several Ming Dynasty groups in the early 1400s. China wants the Nansha Islands, as they call them, given back to them via historical acquisition.

Spokespersons at the PRC Embassy in Washington and the People's Liberation Army High Command in Beijing declined to comment for this story. Several Pentagon offices gave background information on the region and current situation, but would not be quoted on questions relating to PRC occupation of the Spratlys.

In a related matter, Sen. Henry B. Anderson (D-MN), a member of the Senate Armed Services Committee, told this reporter he fully expects his recently defeated Chinese America Navy Friendship Agreement to be revived after the first of the new year, and predicts its passage by the full Senate and signing by the new President.

For two days after my story broke I basked in lots of good on yas from colleagues at PANS and the Capitol Connection Roundtable. Ray Kinny gave me a grin that said: I gave you the idea, and then slapped me on the shoulder before demanding a cold pitcher of beer for the lead. Everyone was curious to know if I thought this could lead to actual shooting between China and America. "Hell, your guess is as good as mine. Who knows what those rice-eaters will do next?"

One journalist who wasn't at all happy about the discussion was Sung Jiang from NCNA. He laughed with the rest but stayed quiet when asked if he had been ordered to active duty with the PLA, or if he was planning a Spratly Island vacation this month.

When the China chatter died down, Sung told me: "You're playing with fire, Dan. That story may have a basis in truth, but now is not the time to be rattling sabers."

"I write what I find, and every time it involves the PRC my sources tell me bad things are going to happen. It's your people who are stirring up the waters. You can't say there aren't a lot of China supporters here in the States. As a matter of fact Senator Anderson believes he can still get his friendship agreement passed, and there was that ship visit to Pearl Harbor on the Fourth of July. That sounds and looks like some pretty good support for the PRC from my countrymen, wouldn't you say?"

"On the surface, maybe, but deep down I believe Beijing is furious at the impression the PRC is ready to attack the Nanshas and stop foreign shipping through the South China Sea. That story caused great loss of face for my government."

The so-called Chinese journalist, and undoubted spy, slipped quietly off his bar stool, nodded politely to me and the others who were too involved to even notice, and left the C-C. Ray, watching the entire exchange, said: "You can't win 'em all, Dan. The story was a good one. You should stick with it."

I finished my beer and said sayonara to the Roundtablers. It was home to bed for this tired camper. Little did I know my next foray into the China question would come sooner than even I had thought.

CHAPTER 70 - THE MOLE HOLE GETS DEEPER

September 6, 2000: Washington, D.C.

Wondering if he would ever get used to it, Hank was again startled by his office drawer ringing. He dreaded answering the phone sure it was none other than the malicious Madam Shin. He knew it was now time for him to fish or cut bait. Before he could speak, Lily purred: "Greetings my little helpmate. Will you meet me for cordial cordials tonight?"

The squirming senator stammered: "I'm quite busy and have to be out of the city all next week so I just don't have the time now."

She reminded him of the balance due her from their casino evening adding: "Tonight. Irongate Inn, six-thirty."

"Christ, what a nightmare," Hank muttered as he tried to concentrate on the mound of paperwork crowding his desk. Late for a floor vote, he did manage to get his position on the record but he couldn't keep his mind on business for the rest of the day. By the end of the afternoon Tom Carlson took one look at him and said: "You look like a cadaver. What's up?"

"Nothing, Tom." Hank then told the receptionist: "no calls." Hearing his staff leaving for the night, he opened his private filing cabinet, pulled out the bottom drawer and grabbed a small box which he took into the bathroom. Opening the box he removed a 3 by 6 inch mini tape recorder and clipped it to the rear of his belt. He attached a clip-on microphone to the back of his necktie after running the mike cable up the inside of his shirt. "Test one, two, three. This is a test, straight from the toilet," and he heard himself chuckle at the fact the dumper job he was about to embark on started right here in his own lavatory!

The recorder worked fine. He re-wound the tape, turned the light off, and returned to his office where he picked up his suit coat. Switching off all the other lights at the main door he headed for the elevator.

She's pushed me too far, Hank thought grimly. How did I let her maneuver me to this point? Is this my punishment for thinking below my belt? Gathering strength, he spoke out loud: "Sure, let them ruin my reputation, even my career. Kill my bill. But I'm an American first and always and I'm not going to allow some war-mongering communist spies to steal U.S. secrets."

The Irongate was a classic District watering hole and eatery. More political deals had been made there over a steak and martini, than most politicians cared to admit. Before entering the restaurant the nervous but determined senator reached under his coat and turned on the recorder. "You'd better work tonight," he told the little machine.

The maitre'd welcomed him warmly, calling him by name and title. "Just a quiet table for two, Bertrand. I have a brief appointment with a staff assistant from my Armed Services Committee."

"Yes sir, Senator, your appointment is already here. I have the perfect table. Please follow me."

Hank was not surprised to see his nemesis had arrived ahead of time. Maintaining his composure he said: "Good Evening, Lily. We won't be having cocktails tonight. This meeting won't take long."

Hank then demanded: "What is it this time? I've told you I am not giving you anymore help, regardless of what you think you're holding over me."

"Ah, my little paramour," Madam Shin cooed, "don't be so defensive. My country feels your efforts to get that friendship bill passed demonstrate you are one of our valuable friends and I am here to thank you for that, and those little ocean sounds, and to ask you one last favor."

"Ha! One last favor. Where have I heard *that* before! What do you want, blueprints for our new VIRGINIA class submarines?"

Lily said: "All we're asking is for you to please clarify that story you had Mr. Carlson check out with your Pentagon friend's office. We want confirmation the project does involve fish noises. Simple, you see?"

"No. I've done everything possible for you. It all stops here and now."

In very measured movement Lily slid forward in her seat: "If there is truth here we must know about it to maintain the balance of world power. We cannot have your Navy going off half-cocked with some new weapons system."

Hank laughed outright at the thought of the U.S. Navy going off half-cocked. "What exactly do you want?"

"We know your Navy is working closely with Milsoftel. They apparently have something to make submarines undetectable. So, Senator, what exactly do you know?"

Staring at Lily's steely black eyes Hank said: "You've got to be nuts. There's no secret that all the major powers have been attempting to make subs harder to track, but with fish noises? Sounds daffy to me."

"Perhaps, Senator, but our sources report your Navy has made a breakthrough into a new era of undersea stealth by using fish noises. With that in mind please check with your connections about Milsoftel for us. You," she said, pointing a finger at Hank, "and no one else. Understand? Just you."

The now smoldering foreign agent concluded her speech. "This is not a friendly request you can sweep aside. We want this information, and we want it now. You may not see jail because of your past indiscretions, but they could prove highly detrimental to your silly political ambitions. And don't think we won't hesitate to leak them to people who have taken a strong dislike to you and your continued support of our causes. You will do as I ask."

As she rose to leave Hank motioned her to sit back down. "What you're asking is traitorous. If there is anything like these so-called fish noises, it would be top secret and if it is true do you really think I'm dumb enough to share the information with you? Listen, I haven't heard anything about this stuff, and I'm in a position to know what's going on with the Navy. I think you're getting a load of bad gossip passed on to you."

"Check it out again anyway, Senator. I'll be in touch."

After Madam Shin slithered out of the room Hank sat quietly thinking, what did I ever see in that bitch? He then went to the men's room which was thankfully empty. Ducking into a stall he locked the door, pulled the tape recorder off his belt, hit the *stop* button and pushed *rewind*.

The tape babbled for a few seconds before Hank hit *play*: "....check with your Navy connections about Milsoftel..."

"Gotcha!" Now he needed to figure out just how he was going to keep himself off the gallows and put the noose around Ms. Shin's neck.

His car arrived at the Irongate curb in a matter of seconds. Hank tipped the doorman while wondering how they did that since he had never seen where his car was parked when he arrived, and he hadn't seen Bertrand order the Chevy be brought to the door. Oh well, that's why he gave them such generous tips.

A possible solution to his problem popped into Hank's head on his drive home. A strong Minnesota Vikings football fan, he knew a good defense was useless without a great offense. He would take the offensive and leave Madam Shin and her Chinese communist friends on the defense, having to prove they weren't committing espionage by stealing top-secret U.S. Navy information.

By the time he'd passed Rock Creek Park, he had his plan worked out. Hank beamed. "I'll find out if there was anything to this fish noises business," he said out loud, "but I'll do it via Mr. Dan Lincoln, Pentagon reporter extraordinaire. I'll let that journalistic hound dog sniff out the truth about those fish noises."

CHAPTER 71 - A WEASEL WITH A CONSCIENCE

September 25, 2000: Washington, D.C.

"I'm coming," I yelled, running dripping wet from the bathroom to the living room to catch the damn phone call. "Hello!"

At first I thought the caller had hung up, but as I caught my breath a smooth voice said: "Hi Dan, this is Hank Anderson. Haven't talked to you since before my summer vacation."

"Yeah, Senator, it's been awhile," was all I could think to say wondering, why is he calling me at home?

"Dan, I think you and I got off to a bad start with some of my answers to questions you've asked me over the last few months. I'm not happy with your journalistic interpretation of my connection with the PRC and what my friendship bill is all about."

He's got to have something up that crooked sleeve of his, I thought to myself.

"At any rate, Dan, maybe you could come to my office this week, sometime at your convenience, so we can clarify these things and look at new developments you will be interested in. We can speak with no holds barred."

"That's very kind of you, Senator, but I think I have all the quotable quotes I need on your feelings about the peace-loving Chinese Communists. However, new developments a newsman never turns his back on."

"Very good. Call Karen Swanson and tell her I asked you to come in. And Dan, one other thing. I'd appreciate it if you didn't tell your buddies at the Capitol Connection. I'm so busy these days that I don't want them banging on my door asking for their own interview times. You understand what I mean, don't you?"

"I can accept that, Senator. I'll get back to Mrs. Swanson."

I returned to the bathroom, shaved and got ready for the day, but couldn't stop thinking about the more conciliatory senator and his strange early morning request for an interview at my convenience. With politicians, words like at your convenience don't exist, and no holds barred is a term they universally abhor!

Monday mornings at PANS are usually pretty routine; check the wires for weekend developments that could lead me to a story. There was nothing that interested me today. Maybe I was still dwelling on the call from Hank and what he was up to. Reporters' suspicions are always on full alert. Was he for real this time?

I thumbed through my pocket calendar and picked Wednesday for my confrontation with Anderson. I called his office and got one hour beginning at 9 am. In my wildest dreams I could never have imagined what I was about to learn on Wednesday the 27th day of September.

When I knocked on Ben's door as I left on Tuesday, and told him what I had planned for the next morning, he raised one of his big bushy white eyebrows and said: "More battles with Senator Anderson or does he have something important to talk about this time?"

"Hey, Ben," I called over my shoulder heading for the office exit, "it's budget time on the Hill and anything I can get about Pentagon spending for the next fiscal year could make a good story. So whether it's Hank Anderson or that old conservative Senator Strom Thurmond from South Carolina who wants to order aircraft carriers like he does hush puppies, I'm listening! Capish?" I smiled back at him as the elevator doors closed on his obvious displeasure with my flippant answer.

I high-tailed it over to the C-C where the gang was already a round ahead of me. I signaled Lisa for a pitcher and quickly downed the first teeth-chilling glass of beer. Hell, the temperature had pushed 97 degrees a few hours earlier and was still hovering there, so I felt the beer was well deserved.

Table conversation centered around the new NFL season and the fate of the Redskins. Perennial Buffalo Bills

275

fan and optimist Rick Davis, was collecting fivers for a pool on this week's game with the Skins. Ray Kinny joked: "Even with Doug Flutie at QB, the Skins should be a two-touchdown favorite." I put my two cents in saying: "If the Bills don't get Marv Levy back as head coach, all they've got to look forward to is more bad weather!" On Buffalo weather I was an expert.

By 6:30 pm everyone was heading home and I joined the march. At my place a wonderful chicken cordon bleu awaited, and as it micro waved I flipped to the WRC-TV early news. Nothing new on China, the Spratlys or Southeast Asia. All's quiet on the eastern front, I thought. That's either very good or very bad.

A chilled bottle of chablis was a perfect complement to my dinner. After cleaning up the kitchen I tried reaching Janice, but no answer. Darn, when I wasn't with her it seemed she was all I could think about.

To take my mind off her I started digging back through all the pieces I'd written about Senator Anderson. In the beginning he seemed the typical self-absorbed politician, ready to respond to questions and willing to grant the occasional one-on-one interview with select reporters. However, digging deeper I detected a change in his responses. In an April interview he seemed decidedly jumpy. At Admiral Sharpe's request I kept an eye on Hank, but the only thing I found was his Maryland gambling fiasco.

Morning came and even the heat couldn't take the smartness out of my step as I climbed the broad granite steps of the U.S. Capitol's Russell Senate Office Building. Inside the air-conditioned executive office center the security guards put me through the routine. I emptied my pockets and showed my note pad and pocket tape recorder, while a guard swept my body with a metal-detecting wand. Don't get smart with these guys, I cautioned myself. I was waved through, and headed for the elevators.

Senator Anderson's office was on the 4th floor. I walked past a maze of open and closed doors, some marked and others with no identification whatsoever, until I came to suite 444.

I opened the door, stepped into the cool reception area and was greeted by Karen and Tom. It was spot-on 9 am and in the several times I'd been to Hank's office this was the first time the senator was also in the reception area.

"Danny!" Extending a hand, he boomed: "Great to see you again, and thank you for coming on such short notice." The senator was all smiles and said: "You remember Tom and you've met Karen Swanson."

"Good morning Senator, and yes I sure do know your key people. They've been most helpful to me over the years."

"Let's go into my inner sanctum. I have lots of information for you, and I bet you have questions for me, right?" He led the way, while his aides remained outside. Motioning to a comfortable looking overstuffed chair, he offered: "Make yourself at home."

"How about some of Karen's iced tea? She adds a touch of pineapple juice and it's sensational!" He didn't wait for my answer, but picked up the intercom and asked for two Swanson specials. He started to fiddle with things on his desk, but Karen soon delivered the drinks and then quietly left.

"The iced tea lives up to your praise."

Hank nodded and said: "Dan, what I'm going to tell you is a bit daunting, so take as much time as you need to completely comprehend all this, okay? I'm going to share things that have happened to me over the past several months that I never ever thought I'd be telling anyone, let alone a journalist."

"Do you mind if I turn on my tape recorder?" He gave me a half-hearted thumbs up and continued.

His unbelievable story began unfolding. "You know I'm very pro-China, and despite losing some support for the friendship treaty, I firmly believe our two countries should be closer. However, I am first and foremost an American and if push came to shove I'd stand with my fellow Americans."

"Does that mean if the Chinese take over the Spratlys, start shooting at Taiwan or fire torpedoes at our Navy ships, you'd deplore the PRC and stand tall with the administration?"

"Let's not go there, just yet. Hear me out first. Before I get into the details I want you to know that I've had a thorough background check made on you, including your Navy days and your journalism career from Honolulu to here. I've read and kept a copy of every piece you've done for PANS since coming to Washington. I know you're a patriot and a strong supporter of the military and particularly the Navy."

"You could've saved a lot of trouble if you'd just asked me for my biography."

"Probably," he replied, "but I had to be convinced that you can be trusted with a story of this magnitude."

"I hope you understand that being trusted with a story is not the same as reporting it."

"I do understand, and I want your word the government knows got this information from me. Certain foreign agents must be investigated, arrested and either tried and jailed, or deported."

Beads of sweat formed on his forehead as he agonized the retelling of his story. "I've plenty of tape, Senator, please take your time."

For the next half hour I sat transfixed as the senator spun his tale of sex, spies and fish noises. Looking like a huge burden had been lifted from his shoulders, Hank then slumped into his chair, staring at his hands.

"I've told you all this because I believe you are the only journalist who can properly write and release this. But there have to be a few ground rules before I authorize you to go public."

"I don't normally accept any conditions on stories, Senator. But before I say yes or no, why don't you spell out exactly what it is you're asking me to do."

"I want those damned communist spies exposed, arrested and prosecuted, and I want everyone to know I am the source for your story. Granted, I did give them bits of information but never anything top secret. I want to be seen as a dedicated politician who supported better relations between China and America, but would not sit still for blackmailers and spies."

"You've admitted you gave them classified Navy materials and other info from your *For Senators Only* briefings. True?"

"If Madam Shin or her daughter go public and claim I have provided them with information about Navy developmental plans," he said slowly, emphasizing every word, "I will deny their claims and leave it up to the public to decide who is right; a U.S. senator or communist Chinese here to conduct espionage against our country."

"You're taking a risk since I could simply say no to your demands about sourcing, and run with what would be a dynamite story. However, I believe you and see how it could have happened exactly as you've outlined it. So, here's my counter proposal."

Now relaxed, Hank said: "Go on."

"As far as giving away government secrets or classified information, you'll have to deal with the appropriate authorities. I can't help you with any crimes you may have committed. You're on your own there."

"I am going to check out this story about fish noises, then meet with one of my Navy contacts for his input. If it's just as you claim, I believe the authorities will be advising you how to proceed, and I'll tell you how I'm coming on the story. I promise you'll get to review the direction, but *not the exact content*, before we go to press. That's as much as I can promise."

I could feel his mind churning, and then he haltingly said: "Deal; but be as easy on me as possible."

What a weasel. Goes traitor and then asks a reporter for leniency! What a horse's patootie.

He took a card out of a desk drawer, scribbled something on the back and handed it to me. "Call at any hour. I look forward to hearing from you and soon."

Hank stood up came around the desk and shook my hand. I thanked him for his candor, said I'd call as soon as I had something concrete, and headed for the door. Saying something like "Have a nice day" to his staff, I left the offices of then Senator Henry B. Anderson, Jr.

Woodward and Bernstein had Deep Throat. I had Shallow Conscience. The results would be the same; a government shaken to its core, more public disgust with elected officials, and the world's greatest superpower again wallowing in the muck of another tawdry deceit.

Even the possibility of a Pulitzer Prize couldn't erase the sinking feeling in the pit of my stomach. The man from Minnesota had just put a very large nail in the coffin of what was left of America's moral compass, and I was holding the hammer.

CHAPTER 72 – FO' REAL OR JUST FAUX

September 27, 2000: Washington, D.C.

Dashing into PANS I checked my messages and grabbed my mail from the row of pukas, headed for my office and retrieved a small address book from my locked desk. My fingers skipped to the S section and Bernie Sharpe. The powder keg I had for him had to be delivered in person so I hoped he was free today.

"Hello. I'm unable to take your call now. Please leave your name and phone number and I'll return your call as soon as I can."

"Admiral, it's Dan Lincoln. Please call me at home tonight. I need to talk to you about that game we're playing." I left my number and hung up. Now the irritation of waiting for his call.

I pulled my tape recorder from my pocket, rewound the tape and then hit *play*. It was all there clear as crystal. A subarashi smile took over my face; I had just enjoyed the fruits of what definitely would become the biggest story of my career, and I had it all on tape. I added that valuable little SONY package to my drawer, locked it tightly, and sat back to open my mail.

"Knock, knock. May I come in?" Since it was my boss he marched in and took a chair in front of my desk.

"Well, how'd the interview with Senator Anderson go? Get anything we can print? We need something for the weekend file, maybe an Asian tie-in to this crazy old world of ours."

"I got a few good quotes and he's still keen on getting that damn friendship treaty passed. Even though he realizes there's a lot of opposition to it, he says he still wants to re-introduce the bill next session. He gave me a few things I need to check out first and then I'll get with you to see how best to run the story."

Ben raised a finger and started to ask a question, but I stopped him in mid air. "And yes, Ben, I can have something ready by the weekend." He smiled, got up and as he left my office said: "You're not holding anything back from me, are you Danny?"

"Oh no sir," I lied, convincingly.

It seemed like forever before the afternoon ended and I could head home. Without dinner plans, dinner was a bowl of cereal with peaches. Not too bad, really. I was suffering through TV rerun season while waiting for the admiral's call. Hank's story made me feel like what Woodward & Bernstein must have felt after uncovering Watergate: Is it our greatest story or the downfall of the nation?

The admiral phoned at 7:15 pm and greeted me by saying: "There's no better place to spend a day than at 300 feet under the surface of the ocean in a U.S. Navy submarine. That's where I was. What did you accomplish today?"

"And a good evening to you, sir. What I did today you *need* to know and we need to talk about, so I suggest we meet as soon as you can tomorrow."

"I have a short meeting with the CNO at 1000, so why don't we make it 1130?"

"Works for me. And Admiral, be ready to take a few notes, because this is no request for a backgrounder on submarines."

Sleep came fitfully, even with the help of my good friend Jack Daniels. First thing I did the next morning was to call Bernie's office. Janice answered and assured me I was on his calendar, adding: "I'm looking forward to seeing your smiling face again. Some of my friends and I are enjoying your latest stories, especially those about the Spratly Islands."

Good; that made me feel really good. Janice sounded very warm and approachable. Perhaps I can stir-up some maneuvers with her this weekend. She's one cannon who needs regular firing!

I began drafting my working outline of Hank's almost unbelievable tale. Everything had to be compartmentalized, all the way back to the growth of the People's Republic of

China Navy and its submarine program in particular, and to U.S. Navy efforts to upgrade our nuclear boats.

Once I had made those facts clear I could get into how certain pieces of information had been transmitted to the PRC, knowingly or not. From there I would introduce the initial contacts by spies Lily Shin and Cheryl Leong, leading up to the most recent demand for information about something called fish noises. Shortly after 10 am I downloaded the file to a zip disk, deleted the original file from my computer, and locked the disk into my top right-hand desk drawer. It was now in the company of some pretty important documents, including my taped interview with the senator and my little black book, which was actually blue.

The ride on the Metro to the Pentagon station was rapid, and I had no problem getting past security and up to Janice's office. Greeting me, sans kiss, and without small talk she said the admiral was currently on long distance. Shortly the intercom on her desk buzzed. She picked it up and waved me into his office.

"Morning, Dan. I know this is going to be important, not just because you don't call unless you really need to talk privately, but because I talked to the FBI a short time ago and my Hooverville buddies tell me dodgy things have been going on with our friend from Minnesota."

"You've got that right, Admiral. I'd like to know what the fibbies told you, but first let me relay, in depth, the details of a meeting I had with Senator Anderson just yesterday. And I have to tell you, sir, I really feel like I'm on the horns of a dilemma with this one. It's a terrific story but the ramifications for the country are mind-boggling. I've never been in such a position."

"We'll address that in a moment; first tell me what you've learned."

I proceeded to tell the two-star officer every detail of my meeting with Hank leaving out nothing, and telling him every word of the interview was on tape locked in my desk. I also said Hank had done a similar tape-job on his meeting with Lily Shin last week.

When I finished there was no response from Sharpe. In a few moments, however, he said: "This business about fish noises; do you know anything more about them?"

"No sir but I did check and there is a Milsoftel over in Arlington and they do have several Navy contracts."

"I'm very familiar with those contracts, Dan. Where there's smoke there's definitely fire. And if these flames are fanned by the wrong hands we could be giving away millions of hours of work our Navy has done, and perhaps even compromise the lives of submarine sailors for years to come. Believe me, I know how you must feel, but please don't do anything more right now other than work on your story draft. Let me check with some of my colleagues and I'll get back to you in a day or so."

CHAPTER 73 - YOU'RE IN THE NAVY NOW!

September 29, 2000: Washington, D.C.

Click, click, click sang the keys on my computer as I composed my story in the making. Only the view of the lazy Potomac offered an occasional respite from the task at hand. The biggest journalistic challenge since Nixon's downfall had landed in my lap, but I soon realized Senator Anderson's puny mea culpa was just one tiny piece in a giant jigsaw puzzle.

The task of checking, rechecking and then fitting together countless details was daunting. "Ugh; this will take me weeks, hell maybe months," I groused. "Was the manipulation of the senator an isolated occurrence? Just how big is Madam Shin's espionage ring?"

After the craziness of the last couple days I decided to set all this spy and espionage business aside for a couple hours with a wet lunch at the Capitol Connection. At noon I locked up everything, checked my mail puka and walked briskly to our pub. Archie's throbbing air-conditioner quickly remedied the outside weather drying my thoroughly soaked shirt and sweaty face.

All the other news hounds were ensconced on their usual Roundtable stools, drowning the day with their regular poisons. I climbed aboard the one remaining stool and greeted the Navy Times, Hong Kong Standard, WALX Radio and the little man from NCNA.

"Good Day, Mr. Lincoln," Jiang said. Perhaps since he was not guzzling down beer by the pitcher his ability to see a newcomer was sharper than the others.

"Hey, Danny, Howzit?" said WALX. "Any hot gossip on the street you want me to blab on my show?" Their slogan was: If it's WALX, it talks!

"Sorry, Rick," I responded, "but why don't you monitor Rush Limbaugh today. Maybe you'll get something to sustain your three hours tomorrow morning."

The Roundtablers gave a big round of applause and Ray Kinny added: "Perhaps, Rick, you might read my column in this week's Navy Times and get a few story ideas from it."

"What are you working on these days, Dan," asked the man from Beijing.

"Glad you asked, Jiang. I'm still writing in-depth pieces about what your country is planning to do in the South China Sea. After the PRC Navy's repeated harassing of our CVBGs, the next step will be to attack the Spratlys and then try to take back Taiwan. Am I on the right track?"

"You're 100 percent wrong, Mr. Lincoln. The Nansha Islands, which you erroneously call Spratlys, have belonged to us for nearly two thousand years, even though others falsely claim them. As for a Taiwan take-over, that is your fantasy. That would mean war, and we are a peaceful people."

Right, I thought, and you're probably one of Madam Shin's gang. Jiang's somber interjection turned the conversation back to more mundane topics, including the big three; PS&S About then a cheeseburger I had ordered arrived, so I just listened to the conversation while eating my lunch.

Remembering the huge task awaiting me, I reluctantly walked back to my office. Concentrating on my writing was difficult when questions about Admiral Sharpe and those fish noises kept intruding. Also, what did his FBI guys have on the senator? As Bernie said, I'd have to wait for those details, concentrate on work and not worry about what came next.

My final outline of the big story had been completed the previous afternoon, and I had now started writing the first part of the piece; background on the PRC Navy and our submarine force. That led to the speech by the Chinese president regarding our experiments with stealth gels, and that took me into some murky waters about U.S. Navy progress on building a stealth submarine.

Avoiding charges of speculation, I quoted Pentagon sources who had said publicly the U.S. Navy has an on-going program to develop such an undersea boat. By the end of the day I had 20% of my story written. I saved it to a zip disk, made a backup copy, deleted everything from the hard drive, put the zip into a drawer and locked my desk. Before I could grab my jacket to leave, the phone jangled: "Hello?"

"Dan, it's Janice. Admiral Sharpe would like to see you tomorrow at 1330."

"OK, can do. Umm, how about spending a weekend together again?" Almost whispering, she said: "Sounds good, but call tonight. I can't talk now, okay?"

"I'll do that. See you manana, Commander."

The ball was now gathering speed instead of moss on its downhill run. I was sure Sharpe and the Navy had Senator Anderson and his connection to the Shin/Leong spy team clearly on their radar scope.

The next morning Ben assigned me to do a quick research job and fact sheet on a story he wanted. "Are you okay, Danny? You seem unusually quiet and you've been keeping to your office a lot the past few days."

"I'm fine Ben. I've been doing research on my next China story, but no problem getting this assignment done by noon today."

Simple stuff, really. Comparative numbers of past Defense Department budgets in the area of contracts to outside purveyors. How many contracts and for how many billions of dollars to your typical small and medium sized private firms. The comptroller's office at DOD understood my request and said they'd get back to me in an hour, and by 10:30 am I had their numbers and began to write up a fact sheet for Ben.

When I dropped it on his desk I said my Navy contact had something on the Spratly situation and we were getting together at 1:30 pm at the Pentagon. Ben winked at me, as if to say sure, and I headed for the Metro.

The air was electric when I entered Sharpe's office. Foregoing our usual pleasantries he dug right in, and it was immediately apparent there had been lots of conversation with the top brass about what my role would be.

"What I'm about to tell you is top secret; the highest level. Presidential status. Understand?"

"Yes sir!"

"Dan, I have had you recalled to active duty by the Navy." A gale-sized breath rushed out of my mouth.

"Is that absolutely necessary, admiral?" I said quietly even though we were in total privacy.

"We believe it is, because there will be great fall-out, politically, when your story is published. You are now on special assignment, reporting to me alone. This is an order you will tell no one about. Official paperwork will be delivered to you at home tomorrow at 0700."

"You're now in a situation not totally unlike several of the major World War II correspondents. Ed Murrow, Eric Sevareid and even Ernie Pyle had to agree to certain censorship of their stories before filing them. They were patriots, like you, and agreed to the limitations because they understood their role in the overall war effort and national security. It's much like my favorite old poster said: Loose Lips Sink Ships. Unfortunately, most of today's journalists don't think like that, especially many of the network TV reporters and anchors."

He continued: "Our Chinese relations are on the brink of failing, so we must corroborate every element of your story. If you're correct, we'll arrest and probably deport everyone involved long before the actual story sees daylight. The timing is critical, especially when you break everything. That story is our keystone for the entire operation."

Swallowing what felt like a basketball, I quietly stated: "I do understand and you can count on me. By the way, can you tell me what you found out about those fish noises?"

"Not right now, it's too long, but perhaps next week we can squeeze it in." I nodded that would be fine with me.

"What I can tell you, however, is that information about those fish noises was definitely passed by a young woman at Milsoftel to Cheryl Leong and her mother, and they're pressing the senator now for confirmation before sending it to Beijing."

"Dan, within the next 24 hours you are to pass to Anderson information which we feel he'll give to Madam Shin. We have ways of knowing if it surfaces in Beijing, and we'll know where our information leak is here. Then, we'll move on everyone involved and close the web on their activities. Now, take this down exactly as I dictate it and get it to the senator immediately. Do you want to record it?"

"Yes sir," I smiled, knowing the crafty old submariner was about to spring a trap big enough to catch all sorts of vermin, be they noxious fish or foul humans.

"Okay," the admiral continued, "tell the senator your top-level Navy contact says that Milsoftel is indeed working on a sound emissions reduction program for submarines. It concerns torpedoes, traditionally called fish. That why the noises under study on fired torpedoes are loosely termed fish noises by Milsoftel."

"Then tell him the Navy has been working on a new propulsion system for destroyers and cruisers. It's called PMP; Permanent Magnetic Propulsion, and they hope to have it for their new 21st Century class of surface warships scheduled for the Fleet by 2008. They're also trying to adapt that PMP system for torpedoes, since it will be far quieter and more fuel efficient than anything now known.

"So you see, Dan, we'll have torpedoes; fish, with no fish noises. And that subcontractor will be testing these new torpedoes in a month or so."

"That's quite a story, admiral, and when I tell Anderson he'll blab to Lily Shin and she'll flash it to her husband, who will gain much face when this hits the Beijing Navy fan."

"That's it in a nutshell. Get this story to our playful senator, and then wait for the fireworks to begin."

"Consider it done, sir. He's expecting to hear from me, so I'll arrange a meeting. One other small matter, sir."

"And that is?"

"Well sir, I seem to recall that you once said if you ever recalled me back to active duty it would be as a chief petty officer, and with retirement and medical disability benefits."

"Well, perhaps something along those lines, but my recollection seems a bit fuzzy right now. Get through this assignment," he winked, "and I'm sure my memory won't be as blurred as it is now."

CHAPTER 74 - SETTING THE BAIT

September 29, 2000: Washington, D.C.

I arrived back at my office about 3:30 pm, closed the door and went straight to the locked desk drawer holding my little blue book and several special business cards. I dialed the handwritten number on the top one, and after only three rings a voice said: "This is Henry, who's calling?"

"It's Dan Lincoln. Can we talk?"

"I'm finishing some paperwork and getting ready for a weekend at home. Did you locate that special gift for my wife I asked you to find?"

"Yes. Fortune smiled on both of us. I have it with me right now. Can you meet me after you leave your office?"

"For this," Hank nearly panted, "I'll make time. Where?"

I paused a moment and then directed: "The lobby bar at the Hay Adams Hotel, just across Lafayette Park from the White House, at six o'clock."

"Yes, that's convenient and I'll bring a check for the present."

Before the senator arrived, I took a booth near the back not easily visible from the bar. Hank showed up promptly and spotted me only after a thorough scan of the tables. He sat down and we exchanged pleasantries.

The waitress who took our orders was no one either of us had ever seen. When she returned Hank made a point of complaining about the lousy traffic and the god damned heat in order that she would not distinguish him from the dozens of complainers she'd heard say the very same thing that day.

"Here's the whole story," I said, and then carefully relayed Admiral Sharpe's dummied information, without letting him know where I got it or under what circumstances it was being given to him. When I stopped, the now bug-eyed politician muttered: "Fine. Fine. That's exactly what I need to know. But remember, if you fall down on your end of the bargain, Lincoln, I'll deny everything."

Patronizingly I replied: "Don't you trust anyone anymore? For me to win, you have to win. Our deal here is a win-win situation from the get-go."

"I've got to go now. There's one important phone call I need to make before I head home."

Sliding out of the booth, Hank dropped a ten dollar bill on the table and disappeared. I sat there for awhile finishing my beer wondering what his conversation would contain.

Immediately after leaving the hotel, Hank drove to a secluded side street, parked, and dialed a Georgetown number.

"It's me," he said when Lily answered. "I have that Senate bill backgrounder you asked about. It's far too long to summarize on the phone. Meet me in 15 minutes at the park on Volta Place?"

"Good, I have a dinner date at 8 but I can be back here by then." If Hank had not known the date was most likely the Chinese Ambassador, he would have been jealous.

Ten minutes later the senator pulled into Volta Place Park. Lily opened the front door of his car and got in, expecting to be given an envelope with the info inside. He greeted her coolly. "What I have for you I did not want put in writing. Listen good because I'm only going to tell you this once."

Word for word Hank passed Dan Lincoln's story to Lily, exactly as given to the reporter by Bernie Sharpe. Emotionless and with no civil farewell, the beleaguered senator firmly stated: "That's it. What you wanted to know about those damned fish noises, and yes, it's all true, even the part about silent torpedoes. So, tell your husband and his Beijing handlers no more info. Not even scores from the Army-Navy football game. Period. We're finished. Do you Understand?"

Exiting the car, a slight smirk morphed her lips as she said: "Of course, my little toy. But, perhaps you will reconsider and share another evening of Chinese culture with me? Yes?"

"No way! I've got to go, right now. *Goodbye, Lily.*"

He would no longer be her toy, betraying his beloved homeland. Yes, he had made errors in judgment and let Lily manipulate him for the benefit of China. Even if he lost his Senate seat, he would stand as a loyal American and face the music. Perhaps, he pondered, this is how my love affair with China ends.

CHAPTER 75 - RAISE YOUR RIGHT HAND

September 30, 2000: Washington, D.C.

Sleep came easily after yesterday's excitement but it didn't last long enough. I was pouring my first good morning jug of Java when a sharp rap on the door reminded me of important papers coming from Admiral Sharpe. Clad only in a t-shirt and my T-Hilfigers, I padded to the front and casually opened the door.

To my pleasant surprise there stood Janice, a beautiful sunny smile. She stepped in, gave me a great big kiss smack on the lips and headed for the kitchen. "Hey, I didn't expect the Pentagon courier to be so pretty!"

"Why not? I'm a commissioned officer; I know exactly what the admiral wants so I'm here to swear you back into active duty." With that said she put a packet of sweetener into her coffee, took a taste and proclaimed: "Better than that deck polish at the cafeteria." I ducked into my bedroom and grabbed some street clothes, returned and asked: "Do I raise my right hand or what?"

Janice led me through the short swearing-in ceremony, and then proclaimed: "You are now elevated to the rank of chief petty officer. Thank Admiral Sharpe for the promotion." A moment of silence followed and I realized this oath-taking was a hell of a lot more important than my first. Janice then handed over my orders which placed me at the sole direction of Rear Admiral R. Bernard Sharpe for a two year period ending 30 September 2002.

Finishing her coffee, she gave me another kiss and said: "I wish you well on this assignment. You'll be very, very busy over the next few months and it may be against military regulations for an officer to fraternize with an enlisted man, so maybe we should plan another weekend soon."

"Would next weekend be too soon?" I swooned, returning her kiss. Janice's firm breasts shoved strongly against my chest as she wrapped a leg around my waist. Oh man, I thought, she's one number who could do it all while standing up!

Looking into my eyes, she enticed: "Well, it just happens I'm free then, but keep it simple. No driving all over the countryside. Just you and me around home and lots of sack time." She smiled, I swallowed hard and walked her out, starting to plan what would turn out to be our last weekend together for a long while.

Around 9 pm that evening the phone in Madam Shin's Georgetown lair rang and she quickly picked it up.

"This is Fortune Cookie. The message you gave us several days ago reached your friend and he says to say thank you. He adds that the photos you sent him were most welcome and that he will put them in his scrapbook just as soon as he gets the negatives to make detailed blowups."

"I may need some help on that, but please tell my friend I'll send him those negatives as soon as possible. And, thank you for the call."

The smirk on Lily's face said it all. "The bird has caught the worm." Then she poured herself a snifter of very fine old Chinese brandy.

CHAPTER 76 - WONG'S WAY TAKES SHAPE

October 7, 2000: Shanghai, China

The PRC submarine PEOPLE'S VICTORY lay quietly at a pier in the Shanghai Navy shipyard. One of the first of the HAN Class nuclear boats designed and built by the Chinese, she was under the command of veteran submariner and career naval officer Captain David K.Y. Wong. Nothing appeared unusual, but the fact that Captain Wong and his entire crew were rebels fully intending to take their boat and its complement of missiles out to sea not subject to PLA Navy orders, and hunt down an American aircraft carrier Battle Group, that was unusual!

Many years as an intelligence officer had served Wong well. He knew who in government and the PLA Navy were merely bureaucrats putting in their time, and who were the officers who thought like he did and would issue him orders simply on his personal request.

The radical captain also surrounded himself with navymen who didn't want to wait on Beijing's long term plans to gain international supremacy, either in diplomatic or military matters. They wanted to be kings of the mountain right now! And that's exactly what David Wong liked about his young followers. They saw the world as he did, a vast planet of have-nots being controlled by fat-cat Americans.

Wong got himself a set of orders cut making him skipper of the PEOPLE'S VICTORY. His choice for Executive Officer was his brother-in-law, Lieutenant Commander Hiram Leong. The submarine was an eight year old boat needing a major overhaul. He quickly convinced his bosses to let him take the ship through the shipyard period, do the work needed, and then train a new crew which would be assigned for the next two or three years. It was a logical request readily approved by the PLA brass. Now Captain Wong had the hardware he would need to take his message to the Americans.

The skipper smiled, thinking about his wife Lily and the job she was doing for China in Washington. Her most recent message confirmed the fish noises business she had uncovered was actually a major U.S. Navy development project that somehow involved producing a stealth submarine. He had some of the details but was awaiting the rest of them. Even if Lily couldn't get everything he needed from her pompous U.S. Senator, he knew there were others in the Pentagon with highest level access who were working on his behalf. Soon enough he would know what the American Navy was doing and would be able to incorporate that into plans for his submarine's future.

From the time PEOPLE'S VICTORY began its shipyard availability the old crew was quickly transferred. Many were due for rotation, others were given medals of commendation for their alleged good deeds on behalf of the Motherland and then sent packing to some other ship, always at a base well away from Shanghai. Captain Wong brought aboard his group of rebels, all active duty, all committed totally to him and his goal of world domination by obliteration of the U.S. Navy. That task would begin in the South China Sea.

The ship needed to be refueled. Its nuclear reactor would last for about 30 years but every 8 to 10 years a new fuel core had to be installed. This process had taken the better part of the last two months, and would take another six, at least. Then the renovation would center on interior upgrades to sonar and communications systems, and especially to the missiles and torpedoes, including those that would be loaded with nuclear payloads.

Wong and Leong spent long hours pouring over the ship modifications they wanted made. By this time next year the latest upgrades of satellite transmission and receiving gear would be installed, as well as a new sonar system built by the Germans. None of it was cheap, but David had figured out how he would bury those costs in the overall project. It would take a pretty smart accountant, or a good crook, to find that the monies spent for an air conditioning system upgrade also contained the total cost of new sonar and comm gear.

Twice a week the skipper gathered his crew at the CAFS Hall, at the far end of the shipyard complex, for training and on-going indoctrination into the way they were going to shock the world in general and the U.S. Seventh Fleet in particular. He and the XO devoted as much time as they could to teaching the crew everything they knew about the American Navy and what to expect from the Yanks when push came to shove.

Wong had accumulated excellent video footage on every type of warship the U.S. currently operated. His taped video on American submarines was so good several of the crew asked if he'd stolen it from training libraries! What the rebel skipper didn't tell his men was that he probably could have gotten access to such libraries, or anything else in the U.S. Navy he wanted, thanks to the well organized spy ring operating daily at the Pentagon, and in Norfolk, San Diego and at Pearl Harbor.

Captain Wong was privy to the well-organized PLA plan to attack and re-occupy the Spratly Islands. That would be basically an Air Force operation, with Army follow-up, but he had been consulted by some of his PLA comrades about the mission. He contributed a few ideas about how to pull off the attack without the U.S. Navy becoming involved, and was fully aware of the political impact the operation would have, coming as it would on May Day next.

Back aboard his ship David took out a ledger from his cabin desk and made a note on the page for the 7th of October: Training session successful. Reactor work going well but slowly; new sonar and comm gear currently ordered. Installation due next spring. Final modifications to missile and torpedo design should begin November 1st. Total project now 35% complete. Target date for sea trials set for fall 2001.

October 11, 2000: Washington, D.C.

It was just before lunch when Janice phoned saying Admiral Sharpe wanted me to have a scrambler phone installed so he could send me information for my stories. "This will save you having to trudge over here to the Pentagon all the time. I guess that means I won't see much of you. Will you miss me?"

"There's always dinner and our special weekends, you know."

"Y-e-s," Janice said slowly, "and that makes every moment juicier. Makes me warm just thinking of you, and your...damn, got a call coming in. I'll ring you tonight."

Late that afternoon a pair of technicians from some Navy shop installed the pfunny phone in one of my side desk drawers. I could hardly wait for the first call.

My story about the spy ring activities was now several thousand words long but I was still missing a few key aspects of the total picture. The material given me by Hank was an excellent start. I had already checked it out and confirmed the details of his initial visit to the roulette table up in Maryland, and his subsequent evening of sin with the lady spy. I made a note to see how I could work that phrase into the overall story: An evening of sin with Lily Shin. Badda bing!

The direct connection for top secret U.S. Navy documents supplied to Madam Shin and forwarded to her husband was clear. It all originated with our Senator Anderson.

But, I still couldn't put my Honolulu buddy Simon Cardigan into the equation. We all knew of the mole at the Pentagon, but not if that mole was in bed, so to speak, with Madam Shin or reporting directly to Ambassador Wu. Could Simon's Penole be working directly for the PRC or perhaps even the rebel Captain Wong?

Full to the gills with my story, I saved everything to a zip disk, locked it in my desk drawer and headed to the C-C for some relief with my news junkie buddies.

As I got comfortable on my Roundtable barstool, Navy Times sat down and threw a copy of his latest edition at me. "Your buddy Bernie has made some headlines. Story's on page seven."

SHARPE PROMOTED TO THREE STAR RANK
TAKES OVER AS COMSUBPAC IN JANUARY

Beneath a recent photo of the admiral, the story with Ray Kinny's by-line, read:

Rear Admiral R. Bernard Sharpe, currently assigned to the office of the CNO, and heading the Navy's submarine development program, has been selected for promotion to Vice Admiral and nominated to become Commander of Submarine Forces in the U.S. Pacific Fleet. Sharpe, a 1970 graduate of the Naval Academy, has been involved in submarines his entire Navy career.

The Flag Officer Selection Board made Sharpe's date of rank December 1st. He will take over as COMSUBPAC in ceremonies at Pearl Harbor on January 2, 2001.

The new three-star admiral has served tours in Norfolk and Pearl Harbor, and was Submarine Base Commander in Bangor, Washington. He has been commanding officer on the USS GEORGIA and USS CHEYENNE, was involved in early Navy work on future submarine development, and has been one of ADM E.R. Lynch's strongest supporters on the CNO's Staff since assuming his current duties in 1998.

Admiral Sharpe is a native of Indianapolis, Indiana and is married to the former Barbara Buchanan, also of that city. The couple has three grown and married daughters.

"Hot shit! Couldn't happen to a better guy," I said. "Pearl is a great assignment, but I wonder how this will affect my Pentagon source info?   Oh well, guess we'll just have to talk long distance."

"What a lot of bull shit," WRC-TV said. "The kind of information that admiral is giving you was probably issued by the Navy News Service a year ago. Next thing you'll be telling us is he wants you back on active duty, since the Navy can't do without brilliant journalists and former sonarmen like you. Rotsa ruck!"

I laughed to myself about the being recalled to active duty.   But then, what did this young, good looking, but dumber than a stone TV reporter know from anything? Responding I said: "Yeah, you're probably right, and I won't ask for a secret decoder phone either."

That I was happy for Bernie Sharpe was an understatement. As I re-read the Navy Times story all I could think of was, three stars and you're out, Bernie. Out of the Pentagon rat race and out to the Pacific where you'll be back with the submariners and boats you so love. Good on ya. You may even get me back to sea.

The other end of my private line finally answered. I'd been trying to get the admiral since I'd read the Navy Times piece. He picked up the phone with a crisp: "Admiral Sharpe." That was all he said, but then it was a private line and he didn't have to go through all the normal jazz about unsecured lines and how may I help you, sir or ma'am.

"It's Chief Lincoln, sir.   I've been trying to catch up with you since I read about your new job to offer my congratulations and to thank you for my promotion."

"You're welcome, Chief. The extra star is nice but it's going to take me awhile to get used to being back with the boats and out of this puzzle palace. Actually I'm thrilled to be going to Hawaii to take over SUBPAC. It's the top job for a bubblehead like me.   By the way, how you coming on your story?"

"Actually I've been working on it hot and heavy for the past week. Most of the pieces are coming together but there are still two big gaps. One is how Simon Cardigan's story fits into our spy ring, and secondly who is the Pentagon mole?

I'm sure I'll solve the first but it may take your team of NIS types, with the FBI and CIA, to find out who Mr. Penole is."

"We're working on those loose ends as well, Dan. And that underwater sounds business may be the bait that leads us to our mole. When can I see a draft of the story?"

"I've been giving that a lot of thought. It's now mid-October and I need probably another month to finalize all my background research and investigation into the principals. One problem I have is that I'm still doing my regular beat. Even with that taking a lot of my time I should be ready for you to come over and brief Ben by mid to late November. He'll probably throw a shit-fit at first, but once he sees what we've got and realizes it will be a PANS exclusive he'll flip out with support and, I hope, ignore that I've been stonewalling him about this project for months."

The reason you haven't been able to get me until today is that I've been in San Diego, and I'm just in town now to get updated on my regular assignments before I take off again on November 4th for Hawaii. I want to spend some time with my predecessor before we actually move there."

"That's several weeks away. I expect to have my story done and ready for your review by the time you get back from Honolulu. That'll give you time to brief Ben and chop the piece through Navy security before we release it. We could set the weekend of November 18th and 19th as our target, with the next weekend as fallback dates. How's that work for you?"

"Cutting it a bit thin, Chief, but it may be doable. Hear me clearly, Dan, I said *may be*. You've got to remember there are others involved in this story."

"Let's try for a release on Saturday the 25th, just in time to make all the Sunday papers. If Ben concurs we'll release it on our Asia-only wire that morning, so people in that part of the world will learn about the spy ring passing U.S. Navy secrets to the PRC."

"Okay, Dan. Just give me enough lead time to get the story pushed through this place. They're not known for fast processing of routine paperwork, let alone a hot potato. Keep in touch, my boy."

301

CHAPTER 78 - ONE FROM COLUMN A

October 19, 2000: Georgetown

Madam Shin and Cheryl had been summoned to the Embassy on short notice. At 8:45 pm they walked the few blocks and were greeted by Fred Tong, who led them to Ambassador Wu's chambers, where he was perched at his huge desk writing something in a ledger.

Closing the book, Wu looked up and said: "You have both accomplished your tasks by obtaining most useful information from our erstwhile friend and Wing's granddaughter." The women bowed slightly, trying to keep their expressions impassive.

"The fish noises data you related has proved to be genuine and our Beijing specialists are moving rapidly in response."

"Young Shin, I spoke with your father yesterday and he forwards his congratulations and pride on your execution of a difficult task."

"Your words bring me great joy, Ambassador."

"Our navy knew of American efforts to produce undetectable torpedoes but having their magnetic propulsion theory will enable us to remain even with them. You have been very successful but you must continue to pressure the senator, and anyone else you can, for new details about future plans involving submarines and their surface warships as well," the ambassador added, looking straight at Lily.

"It will be more difficult because my confidant has said he cannot continue to assist me. He even told me he would refuse to give me scores of Navy football games!"

"Remember, we are known for our patience and perseverance, so continue pressing for more details. Information I am receiving from Admiral Ho leads me to believe the U.S. may face a major combat decision soon. He indicates that when they have been militarily challenged in the past they usually send a small token force under the United Nations banner, or do not respond at all.   They desire to maintain political correctness at all costs."

"They have avoided contacts with our warships, and coupled with increasing hostilities in the Middle East and Arab world, they may be unable to mount a two-ocean operation making them vulnerable to attack."

Pausing to light another cigarette, Ambassador Wu took a long contemplative drag and spoke once again: "A major strike by PLA forces against Taiwan would appear to bring the U.S. into the battle, but we're not certain they will come to the aid of their ally if it would mean the loss of thousands of American lives.   The current White House resident doesn't have the reputation of shooting first and then worrying about the outcome. We are counting on him to go directly to the U.N. and let that bloated debating society talk about it for a few months."

"However, if we proceed with plans to attack Taiwan next year, our air and sea forces would be able to strike U.S. warships in the South China Sea. What I tell you must remain top secret. Understand?"

The two women pledged their silence and loyalty.

"The world will soon realize that China is a major player in the international community and that we now have a world-class blue-water navy to prove that point."

"We are honored to be a small part of what you have described, Excellency. You can count on my daughter and me, just as you count on my husband."

The ambassador nodded and said: "Remember, do not let Senator Anderson out of your control. He will be a good source of information for a long time to come." Getting up from his desk he smiled as Fred Tong escorted them out.

The Shins walked home and once inside Cheryl turned on the CD player, and then dropped contentedly onto the sofa. Lily popped the cork on a bottle of champagne and toasted her daughter: "It's Napa Valley not Chinese, but it will to do. Here's to China and to magnetic propulsion torpedoes whatever they may be!"

"Thanks Mom. This new CD, Eastern Energy by the TwelveGirlsBand, sounds terrific on your system; your speakers are much better than mine. Wanna swap?"

What the young spy didn't know was those speakers were also broadcasting their every word to the FBI, who had planted highly sensitive voice-activated microphones in them a few weeks ago. "You're now on Radio Free FBI," said the agent monitoring the Georgetown conversation he was now taping, including conversation about the events discussed in Ambassador's Wu's office just an hour ago.

CHAPTER 79 - SQUIDY GROWS UP

November 8, 2000: Midway Island

Bernie Sharpe looked like an unmade bed. Swollen blood-shot eyes, beard stubble and a uniform so wrinkled he'd be on KP for weeks if he were just a recruit. He was the sum of numberless trips from the Pentagon to Norfolk shipyards, the San Diego Sub base and the wearying 12,000 mile, four-day round trippers to this secluded paradise in the Pacific. Bernie was not a good in-flight sleeper and it showed.

Monday afternoon. He'd slept late at the guest officers quarters at Pearl Harbor then enjoyed brunch at the Club Marianna on Sand Island, with some old Navy mates. He slowly climbed the stairs to the offices of Commander, Submarine Force, U.S. Pacific Fleet, VADM Les Enderman, an Academy graduate two classes before Bernie. They had remained in contact since those days. For a good hour they talked about Bernie's pending take-over of COMSUBPAC and the fleet status currently under Enderman's command. When they finished Bernie asked the admiral's chief to contact CINCPAC headquarters at Camp Smith and arrange a meeting with POLAD Al Lewis, preferably December 29th, just before his change of command.

Tuesday, 0700. Bernie sat in the Kaneohe Bay MCAS air terminal, ready to board a Navy Lear jet for the 1,200 mile flight to Midway. He kept under wraps his excitement about progress in constructing USS JAMESTOWN, a squid look-alike capable of emitting a similar curtain of concealing ink. He had nominated all future *Project Squidy* boats to be of the DI Class, for Deep Ink.

The jet's flight path took them over the popular tourist island of Kauai and then on past Nihoa and Necker Islands; French Frigate Shoals, the native Hawaiian Monk Seal and Green Sea Turtle called home; Gardner Pinnacles; Laysan and Lisiansky Islands; and finally Pearl & Hermes Atoll, named for

305

two British whaling ships that sunk there during a violent storm in 1822. Minutes later the jet swept over the calm turquoise waters surrounding Midway's spectacular and wide beaches and settled on the main runway, to a welcoming entourage of the island fire unit and a Navy golf cart with Buzz Russell at the helm.

Stepping off the jet's ladder, Bernie quickly returned his friend's salute then pumped his hand repeatedly. They jumped into the cart and sped toward the island's north shore special guest quarters reserved for the admiral. Sped is probably not the right word, since they had to dodge dozens of the two million Gooney birds that make Midway their home. Bernie was pleased to see the cottage was new, not one of the hundred-year old plantation style houses built back in 1903 when the first Trans-Pacific underwater telegraph cable was laid and Midway was a major hub on that project. He quickly stowed his gear and they headed for lunch at the mess hall.

Several enlisted men approached him and Admiral Sharpe questioned them about their work and living conditions. "I know the conditions you're enduring and if there is anything you need, let us know, understood?"

"Everything is fine, sir" a first class electrician's mate told him. "The food is like being on a cruise liner and we get two days a week off to enjoy the beach. We could stand a few more hours in the day to make sure this boat gets done. But, don't worry Admiral, we'll make it on deadline. Count on us."

After lunch, Bernie and Buzz went to the office to review schedules and problems that had come up.

"You'll flip, Admiral, when you see how the Mescod pros are assembling this ship. The inner and outer shells are fused, not welded together. It's almost seamless, and that outer skin is unlike anything I've ever seen. Some type of plastic or laminate that gives and flexes when something sharp strikes it, like a mine. Unfortunately, their engineers can only show you a small section right now."

The admiral cocked his head and then said: "Sounds more than exotic. What about all the interior systems, the miles of wiring and piping that have to be installed?"

"Well now, that's different too.   Since there's no nuclear reactor, and the boat's smaller than what we're used to, there's no need for most of that stuff." Waving his hands about, Buzz went on: "With all the new off-the-shelf sonar and communication systems installed, the Comm Center on JAMESTOWN will look more like the inside of a kid's computer game store than our LOS ANGELES boats. They'll feel right at home!"

"What major problems have come up, assuming we still have problems to solve?"

"They aren't really major, sir; it's a pleasure working on this project.   Being isolated eliminates the usual snoops, even from NAVSEA Systems and the Pentagon. What did you and the CNO do to those normally nosy people back there?"

Bernie laughed out loud and replied: "We're stone-walling all their bitching. I dispose of it daily.   As long as you stay on course I'll keep everyone off your back. Funny, but up to now I haven't had one request for information or access. That's either very good, or something awful is about to happen!"

"I don't think anything's going to go haywire, Admiral. Got too good a crew. Hey, let's go look at the shops in the big hanger, then I'll show you the pride and joy of Commander Hammond and his SEABEES. Their dry dock even has new railroad tracks for launching *Squidy* when she's ready. Before they left, Hammond said to apologize to you for being a bit late in finishing their job, but there were a few minor snags."

The rest of the afternoon was filled visiting work places, and getting the latest scuttlebutt from the personnel assigned to the project. At the design loft, Bernie was amazed at the final artist's renderings of the new boat. Sea creature was the only apt description he could give to the boat's exterior design it looked so much like an ocean-going animal. He loved the smooth lines and the way the ship would be able to maneuver.

Compared to current boats, there were some radical changes; the conning tower was much lower, with just enough height for a periscope shaft. Smaller 180-degree visibility periscopes were in port and starboard positions where a giant squid's eyes would be. There was one less deck, but crew movement, even for tall people, would be easy. "You'll fit comfortably, Admiral," a Mescod engineer told the 6 foot 2 inch flag officer. "Good," Bernie replied, rubbing his mental hand over numerous bumps he had earned in older, cramped hulls.

The ship's drive and electricity would come from a revolutionary fuel cell scarcely larger than an officer's stateroom, about five by eight feet. Hull draft would be shallow enough to permit action well inside enemy waters and able to reconnoiter with Navy SEAL teams.

Flipping a steak over the backyard grill at his waterfront cottage that evening, Bernie told Buzz about the soon to be released revelations of the Chinese spies and Senator Henry Anderson. "I'm convinced they used him, playing on his wanting to aid Sino-American relations, and it will cost him plenty. My FBI friends tell me he faces prison time. I've been keeping close company with a young journalist who seems to have the best take on this sordid affair. Name's Dan Lincoln, maybe you've read some of his stuff."

"I've seen a few of his stories about Asia and the Spratlys and other articles he's written. You've given him some material on future Navy ships and submarines, haven't you?"

"I have indeed. He's a good guy, Buzz, and quite frankly I feel he can be of even greater help to us in the future. FYI only, I've recently had him recalled to active duty, under my direct command. I'm going to see if I can get him out to the Seventh Fleet to do some stories on our operations there and those of the PRC Navy. The world needs to know what those buggers are up to, and it wouldn't surprise me if their next act will be to take over the Spratly Islands."

Conversation throughout the evening covered other current Navy topics, Bernie's upcoming transfer to the top submarine job at Pearl, and finally the two called it a night. Buzz said he and his trusty golf cart would pick the admiral up at 0730 for breakfast and another day of observations at the world's most remote shipyard.

Indoctrination into *Squidy's* new torpedoes and other devices was Wednesday's highlight. The former would be carried aboard attack subs and DI class boats, and the latter used to lay mines or detonate enemy ones, photograph enemy installations, plus transport personnel, including SEALs, to and from difficult to reach locations.

The new high density integrated PMP vehicles were housed in a small shop away from the main project operation at the far end of the island. The engineers and torpedomen were building permanent magnetic torpedoes that would emit only a low acoustic signature, half as noisy as normal

Bernie loved what he saw, and was full of questions for the Mescod staff. Some they would answer and others they merely said were proprietary. By the end of the day the admiral had seen everything there was to view, and was ready to fly back to Oahu.

Because everyone was so engrossed in their tasks, and time was a key element, Bernie dropped plans for a farewell pep talk, but profusely thanked Buzz Russell for the team effort. At 1500 the admiral's bags were loaded aboard the Lear jet, he returned Captain Russell's departing salute, and climbed aboard as the stairs retracted and the door closed. With the base fire engine running point, spraying Gooney birds off the runway with its powerful water cannon, the sleek jet reached the end of the runway, executed a 180 and fled back down the strip. Lifting gracefully, the pilot turned southeast and headed back to Hawaii.

Thinking about what lay ahead for him the soon to be vice admiral sat back in his unusually comfortable seat and decided to write his report to Admiral Lynch during the flight. If he couldn't sleep he might as well do something constructive, and the report would be it.

Two and a half hours later, with 80% of the report drafted, the executive jet touched down at MCAS Kaneohe, ending the first leg of what would be the long trip back to D.C.

CHAPTER 80 - STILL WORKING ON IT

November 27, 2000: Washington, D.C.

"Oh no! One more bloody time this damn machine has crashed on me! I'm sick of this," I screamed, slamming my fists on the desk. Betrayed once again by my computer I grabbed the tech manual for guidance just as the phone rang. "Dan Lincoln," I barked.

It was Janice and she laughingly grumbled: "Well hello to you too, Mr. Sunshine. I was going to ask how things are going but prudence tells me to get to the point. The Admiral says anytime you can get away for a couple of hours, from Monday on, he'd like to meet with you. He'll call you at home Sunday night to work out the time and place." I thanked her and, since she was obviously too busy to make small talk, I hung up.

Another damned weekend without even seeing the woman I was pretty sure I loved.   It crawled along into Sunday, and during the last quarter of Washington's game with their now popular new rivals the Baltimore Ravens, the admiral called.

"Dan, meet me at noon tomorrow at the Navy Marine Club up near DuPont Circle."

"Yes sir, something special?"

"You could say that, plus I don't want to offend your boss by always calling you over to the Pentagon. Sooner or later we'll have to bring Mr. Huntley into the loop. He's still not certain what you're working on, is he?"

"Absolutely not, Admiral. I can't wait to release the big story, but I've told him the piece I've been working on has more details from you and others at the Pentagon about the PRC Navy and their next steps in the South China Sea.   I'm also planning on some reference to what many in the ROC government feel may be an imminent attack on their island of Taiwan. That story's slated to run next weekend."

"Sounds good, but even if we're not ready to break the big one yet I'll see that you have plenty of info for a real newsy piece and still meet Ben's deadline. Thanks again. See you at noon tomorrow. Carry on Chief."

The line waiting for tables at the Officer's Club was nothing compared to most D.C. restaurants. By 11:45 all the bar stools were occupied by dozens of service officers and civilian suits. A battle group of 30-ish looking guys hovered over a sprinkling of attractive junior female execs, offering them drinks in exchange for a few minutes of the corporate ladder-climbing babes' time. Desperate guys always make passes at gals holding glasses.

When the maitre'd asked whom I was meeting and I replied "Admiral Sharpe," several heads swiveled my way. Quietly I was ushered to a private dining room, but along the way I couldn't help but feel a half-dozen sets of eyes marking my path.

"May I get you something to drink?" the maitre'd asked as I sat down. "Yeah, gin and tonic bucket; on second thought better make it an iced tea," I replied, spotting the dark blue Navy sedan arriving.

In a minute Bernie was seated across from me and a waiter promptly appeared to take our orders. Fresh seafood and chilled Mendocino County California chardonnay was the order of the day. The admiral got right to the meat of the meeting.

"Hope what I'm about to tell you will be helpful for your story on the Red rogues from Beijing," he began. "Our best Pacific intelligence confirms a major deployment of PRC submarines, all at one time, from every one of their sub bases; up north near Vladivostok, the main base at Shanghai and their southern post at Hainan Island. Since Labor Day our carrier battle groups have been closer to the Chinese borders than ever before. We know they're out there daily tracking our ships and submarines. So far no actual engagements have been made but Seventh Fleet people tell us the sheer numbers of Chinese subs and surface warships say some kind of offensive is imminent."

Scribbling as fast as I could and every few minutes checking my tape recorder, I captured the admiral's message. Lunch was a brief interruption before he continued. "What we need to do next, Dan, is to provide you with a few more juicy facts about the PRC Navy and what they've been doing in the past few months. That should give you enough fodder for any further routine weekly stories. If we find out that the magnetic propulsion torpedo information you gave the senator actually got to their Navy, and perhaps even to Captain Wong, then we'll move ahead.

"The FBI and the Attorney General are deciding what to do with Senator Anderson. He spilled the beans to us, via you, but he still gave away national secrets and will have to face the music on whatever charges they bring against him. I'd say his Senate and political careers are at an end."

I nodded my agreement with that evaluation.

"When the FBI and State Department have decided how to proceed against the Shin/Leong family, and when they plan to make their arrests, then we'll go to Ben Huntley."

I tried to say something, but he waved me quiet.

"We'll live up to our part of the bargain. You'll get the story first and it will be yours and PANS to run as you see fit. As I suggested earlier, get a good draft of the story written so I can review it and make sure it passes Navy security clearance. When that's done, barring any shooting war, we'll let you release the biggest story since Navy Chief Robert Walker sold out his country."

CHAPTER 81 - CALM BEFORE THE STORM

December 18, 2000: Washington, D.C.

I was humming softly, working on the fourth draft of my expose, when the secure phone rang. Lifting the receiver I identified myself and the caller said: "It's Admiral Sharpe. How goes it?"

"Just great, Admiral, and I'm about done with the story. What's happening on your end?"

"Things are definitely heating up fast, Dan. I'm in Norfolk again today but I'll be home tomorrow. It's time to get your boss into the game. Commander Cannon will call you soon with the name of the Pentagon officer who will be interfacing with Ben. Then, you immediately arrange a meeting, via the commander, with my Navy team and the FBI."

"Understood, Admiral." The story will be ready late today, and I could courier it to your office if you like."

"Bad news Dan; I'm afraid you're going to have to sit on that story awhile longer. The feds aren't quite ready to make their arrests; it may take until after the holidays. Now that the current administration is in the out box, the White House is stalling action on just about everything other than processing last minute bonuses for key staffers and having the Justice Department draft pardons for a few hundred white-collar criminals."

I let him know how disappointed I was with the delay, but what was a month compared to the magnitude of the story I was about to release. We talked a bit more and then said our goodbyes. Turning to my computer I saved the file containing my masterpiece.

Although few of my colleagues were working between Christmas and New Years, I returned to PANS on December 26th and began organizing my desk for the months ahead. When Congress reconvened in January politics would be the

313

only news story for awhile, what with the new President's razor-thin election victory and the Democrats trying to have him ousted even before he was sworn in.

Lucky for me, my Armed Services Committee GOP contact was re-elected, and we chatted some about his expectations for the DOD budget.

On Thursday, just before I headed to lunch, my desk drawer chirped; I knew it must be a telephonic visit from VADM Sharpe, now at Pearl Harbor and ready to take over as COMSUBPAC next week.

"Happy Holidays, Admiral. How's the weather in paradise today?"

"Just like the other 364 days, simply perfect. I don't know why the Navy doesn't just pull up everything in Washington and move here to Honolulu. We'd be so far away from all the politicians that we'd get the job done in half the time and still have daylight left to go beaching."

"How's your takeover going?"

"Fantastic, Dan. The boats and skippers are all great, and they're trained and ready if the PRC keeps provoking our Fleet."

"We're seeing more stuff on the wire about the PRC and its Navy," I told him. "Ben has me spending most of my time on China and Southeast Asia. I still cover the Pentagon but with an emphasis on your part of the world."

"That's perfect," he chuckled, "because I'm ordering you to join the 7th Fleet Carrier Battle Group for two months, effective after the release of the spy story. By the way, that will be the middle of next week. Then, as soon as you can wrap up your current business and Ben will let you go, I'd like you out here, reporting directly to me at SUBPAC. You'll be a guest of the government and an accredited DOD correspondent. I'll call Ben and invite you to do a series of stories for PANS about our sailors and ships, direct from the front lines. Doubt he'll object after what you're about to release on the China spy ring."

I told him how pleased I was to finally have a date for the spy story and then asked: "Are you sure you want me back at sea? It's been 20 years since my last tour with the Fleet."

The admiral ended the conversation saying: "You'll do just fine. Real sailors can never stay away from ships. I'll call your boss in the next day or two so don't brief him ahead of time. Talk to you later, Chief Lincoln."

My chirping bird went back into its nest and I began dreaming about the spy story release next week and spending a couple months onboard the best of the Navy's warships, right where the action would be, if action was to happen.

I couldn't help but think about the greatest generation of correspondents, the print journalists and radio commentators who covered World War II from beach landings and foxholes on remote islands to bombing raids over Germany and ocean battles in the Atlantic and Pacific.

Here was another golden opportunity to be where the news was being made. I could almost hear the sound of naval gunfire with jet fighters overhead, and almost smell the salt air as I walked to the Capitol Connection for lunch and some more day dreaming.

When I was summoned to Ben's office the next morning I did my usual flop onto the sofa. "Dan, I got a call from Admiral Sharpe. He's requesting you take a two month leave of absence and go back to Hawaii and then to the Seventh Fleet to cover China, Taiwan, and our military forces in the Pacific." Trying to act somewhat surprised, I asked, "And?" Ben said he'd taken a look at our office needs and figured he could spring me by the end of February.

"Newswise," Ben said, "he told me he expects a shooting war in a matter of months and that he wanted you and PANS to be there to make sure the coverage 'came out right,' are the words I believe he used."

"Well, what did you tell him?" I asked sheepishly.

"I said of course you could go. Quite frankly, I don't believe there's a better place for you these days than right back in the thick of it. No reporter in this town knows China and the Navy better than you, so I'd be a fool not to accept his offer."

This happy camper thanked his boss and left to begin a list of story ideas that were already germinating in my fertile mind. The February departure from D.C. couldn't come soon enough.

Feeling guilty for not keeping in closer touch with Janice for several months, I felt she should know what I had accomplished and where I was headed. I called her direct line and she began the usual SOP identification litany, but I stopped her short.

"I sure miss you. Please, please, please; can we get together sometime real soon?"

"Why not, I've missed you too. So, how about dinner Friday night at my place, and we'll see what we can get into after that."

"Friday night at Chez Janice it is. I'll be at Mockingbird Lane at 6 pm and I'll supply enough bubbly to take a bath in, if you provide the tub."

Friday's last rays of daylight were fading as I rang Janice's doorbell. She opened the door to reveal she was wearing nothing more than a smile. She gave me a big hug but only a kiss on the cheek. I was horny already. "Just call me Minute Man," I said, returning the kiss. She headed into the kitchen and I followed, stowing the champagne in the fridge.

"A glass of chardonnay for me, Chief. And you know where the gin and tonic are. Ice cubes are in the bucket on the sideboard."

We relaxed over the drinks and then she served dinner. Actually she didn't cook it but brought in some of my favorite take-out from a great local Chinese restaurant. Even fortune cookies. I opened mine and it read: "Seasoned travelers make wise shoppers."

Is this prophetic or what, I wondered.

Our version of military maneuvers followed after green tea sorbet and a snifter of brandy. We soon escalated to a successful invasion of the lady's hidden treasures. I had nearly forgotten how wonderful being in bed with Janice is, but somehow she seemed quietly distant. It was as if she had stepped back from us and was performing by rote, rather than with passion from her heart. Afterward, lying in my arms, she laughingly asked: "Found any more spies hiding in the Pentagon or on Capitol Hill lately?"

"No, but that doesn't mean there aren't some there. And I still don't know who killed Simon Cardigan, or who tried to shoot me or who that oriental guy who wanted to run me over with his Bat-Mobile."

"Keep working on it and they will come to you!"

Nice version of the Field of Dreams line, I thought, telling Janice about my upcoming trip to the Pacific. She seemed unaffected in any way, not really happy for my chance to be a DOD correspondent and not very disappointed that I'd be away for awhile. I thought that a bit strange.

"Admiral Sharpe wants me to spend a couple months at sea with the Seventh Fleet doing stories I can get only by being out there with the sailors. Ben agreed to let me go and I leave at the end of February. I probably won't be back until sometime in May so I wanted to see if we could set up a couple of weekends together before my trip. What do you say?"

Quickly my now cool bedmate turned to ice. "I'm very happy for you. But as for weekends, I'm not sure. My new boss arrives next week and that probably means lots of overtime, even weekends." She paused, then continued: "I think I'd rather we hold off any plans until I see how this and another thing work out, okay?"

"What other thing? Are you okay? You're not sick, are you? Being transferred? Some other guy?"

"No, nothing so serious. I know it doesn't match your trip but I was on the list for promotion to commander that came out a week ago. I put on my third stripe January 2nd."

"Fantastic, Janice! I really mean that. You certainly deserve it after all your years in the Navy, and I'm sure Admiral Sharpe is very proud of you."

"Don't really know since I didn't have a chance to sit down and talk to him about it. What with his promotion and move to Hawaii, and some hush-hush project he's been working on for the CNO, I've rarely seen him lately. He might not even know about my promotion."

I reached over and gave her the most intense kiss I was capable of. I prayed she would take it in the degree of love with which it was given.

On Saturday, our joint day off, we did something that D.C. people think is only for tourists; spent the day touring the Smithsonian Museum. I absolutely *loved* it and Janice seemed to as well. We saw the space capsule, the old Lindbergh Spirit of St. Louis airplane and walked through rooms filled with displays of American history that even I'd forgotten about. It was a great way to spend our last day together.

CHAPTER 82 - YOU HAVE THE RIGHT TO....

January 2, 2001: Washington, D.C.

The morning of the first day of the new millennium was boring. About 2 pm the big call from Janice came in. She advised that Rear Admiral David Paulson from Navy Intelligence would be accompanied by a senior captain from CHINFO, and an FBI agent named Peters. They wanted to meet at 11 am Friday to lay out the background on what she called the Anderson story.

I made a bee-line to the boss and told him we had to talk right now. "What's wrong? Do you have a family crisis?"

"No sir, nothing like that. I need to spill the beans about what I've been working lately concerning the Chinese Navy and the situation out in the western Pacific. It also has to do with Senator Anderson. Ben, I've stumbled into something that might turn out to be the story of the decade for PANS. Because it involves national security I've been contacted by my friend Admiral Sharpe to set up a briefing for you."

"Well, I'll be damned! I knew you'd been giving me the run-around! Didn't I say: Dan, are you holding anything back from me? I said that, didn't I!"

"I believe you did, Ben. Anyway, they'll be here Friday morning to bring you up to speed on what has transpired so far. We can then work out how the story will be released to the world as a special news report exclusively from PANS."

"*I'll be damned*!   I just said that, didn't I?   Are you saying we've got another White House intern scandal on our hands?"

"Perhaps not as big but big enough to put Pacific and Asia News Service on any map we're not already on, and just the magnitude to ensure your job for the rest of your life. It may even have coat tails long enough to get me another nice raise."

"Can you tell me more about Anderson's role, and why the FBI involvement?" I shook my head and said: "So, is Friday okay with you? I need to let my Pentagon contacts know immediately."

"*Of course* it's okay. Do it. Go call them. And by the way, just what do you plan to do for a story?"

"Way ahead of you, Ben. It's been in the works for the past two months and it's all done. Admiral Sharpe says he and the Navy security guys need 24 hours to give it a final chop. You'll have the chance to review and approve the piece before we run it. Release this Saturday afternoon would get us the widest possible distribution. By Monday the TV networks and my fellow journalists on Capitol Hill will be frothing at the mouth because they didn't get the story before PANS beat them to the punch!"

Thursday evening, while she and Cheryl were dining in her Georgetown apartment, Lily said: "Fred Tong called Tuesday. That new info we supplied has been received with great pleasure in China."

Just then a knock came at the apartment door. Not expecting anyone and with the store closed Lily looked at her watch, saw that it was exactly 7 pm, and said: "Who is it, please?"

"Ms. Shin, I'm a friend of Senator Anderson's from Minnesota, and have been looking for some Ming vases. He told me your shop is the best. I'm sorry you're closed but wondered if you might let me look for just five minutes to find a vase I can take home when I leave tomorrow."

Not one to turn down what might be a big sale, she opened the door.

"FBI! I'm Special Agent Peters," he said showing his badge and ID card. "I have warrants for the arrest of you and your daughter Cheryl Leong on charges of spying against the United States on behalf of the government of the People's Republic of China. You have the right to remain silent..." and he went on with the rest of the Miranda rights, the standard opening dialog of all criminal arrests. Stunned, the spy gang leader hardly heard a word; her mind a frozen fog. All she could think was I have failed my country. I have disgraced my China.

Another agent handcuffed the speechless duo, helped them sit down, and then briefly searched the residence. A highly trained criminal investigation unit would go over the entire apartment with a fine tooth comb. The agents secured the premises and then led the suspects to waiting sedans.

A cadre of FBI agents would guard the area until the CIU arrived. As Agent Peters placed the women in separate cars, the first chapter of my story entered history. The suspects were transported to a government detainment center in Virginia for processing. Anxious FBI and Naval Investigative Service agents prepared for what would be many hours of interrogation.

State Department officials were advised both Asians were in the country on green cards only, and that Cheryl's student visa had expired seven months ago. The INS was requested to immediately process the paperwork for their deportation to China on charges of espionage and to advise the PRC Embassy in Washington that Madam Shin and daughter would fly to Beijing within 48 hours, under tight guard.

Action was about to begin at Hank's office. Shortly before 5 pm the Deputy U.S. Attorney for the District of Columbia, under direct orders from the Attorney General, asked to see Tom Carlson. After showing his ID he was escorted to the senator's office.

"Senator Anderson, I'm U.S. Attorney Peter Bowman. Before you speak please be advised you are under investigation on charges of giving classified United States government secrets to a foreign nation." The advice to not speak was unnecessary. For once in his life, Henry Anderson Jr. was dumbstruck. Continuing with the news that crashed into Hank's brain, Bowman said: "Such acts are punishable under federal law and carry with them a mandatory prison sentence and probable fines." Hank, who had not gotten up to greet the officer, was white as a sheet and seemed to slump even further into his chair.

"This paperwork contains all the charges against you and spells out details of initial arraignments and subsequent hearings. In the meantime, because of your position, you are free on your own recognizance but restricted from leaving the District. There will be further instructions from our office via the U.S. Marshals, in a day or so, but we suggest you make no comments to the media on this matter at least until you've checked with your attorney."

With that said, Bowman placed the large manila envelope on the desk turned, and left. Tom Carlson remained ready to again come to Hank's aid, but was waved off before he could say a word.

"Not now, Tom. I need time. There's more to this than what the Feds have said, and I'm not going down the tubes because of what some conniving Chinese bitch has said about me. Please leave me alone to think about it some more. I'll fill you in fully, but not until morning."

CHAPTER 83 - NAILING THE SPIES IN OUR PIES

January 5, 2001: Washington, D.C.

As Friday the 5th of January brought its sunny debut to my bedroom, I jumped out of the sack with more energy than I could recall since my high school days. That energy was inspired more by the weather in Buffalo and the fact that if you didn't get up and going quickly you'd freeze your ass off six months of the year! I expected this day would be like no other I'd ever experienced.

I grabbed some cereal and raced to the office. I actually had sweaty palms as I thought what reaction Ben would have when the Pentagon team laid out the story for him.

Good news? Hell, it was great news! Janice called about 9 am to say the admiral had chopped the story I'd sent him and the Navy approved the final draft. She'd bring it with her since she'd be accompanying Paulson and Edwards to our meeting.

The tension in the office as the Navy team entered was like that of a rubber band stretched almost to the snapping point. Ben and I stood quietly and then he stepped gingerly forward to shake hands with the admiral and captain. Special Agent Peters said only: "Brad Peters, FBI." Jack Webb couldn't have been more deadpan.

Silently we all moved into Ben's office and took chairs around the large coffee table he used for entertaining visiting VIPs. Janice introduced herself and gave the titles and office affiliation of the two Navy officers.

Rear Admiral Paulson spoke first: "Thank you, Mr. Huntley, for meeting on such short notice. We had to maintain the utmost secrecy until this very moment. Because of the nature of this matter, its impact on national security and the deep involvement and cooperation of Dan Lincoln, we're asking you to make public the story I assume he has already briefed you about."

"Dan has kept this really secret, even from me. I have learned it involves China, his close Navy contact Admiral Sharpe and Senator Anderson, the subject of several stories he wrote. Dan also says PANS has a world-wide exclusive. Is that still true?"

"It certainly is, Mr. Huntley, and keeping this story quiet for as many weeks as he has must be driving Dan up the wall." The admiral looked at me and said: "I understand your story is written, chopped by the Navy, and ready to go."

"It's ready for the presses as soon as Ben approves it, hopefully today, so it will make the Asian papers on Sunday."

"Okay," Paulson said, "let me start with a little background on what this is all about and how people like Senator Anderson and your own reporter," he looked over at me, "got involved in what has become a full-fledged international espionage case."

The admiral from OPNAV did a superb job of presenting the facts and explaining how Henry Anderson had been blackmailed into giving information about Navy operations and new submarine developments to the mother-daughter spy team. He briefly reviewed the Maryland casino story and subsequent meetings with Madam Shin, concluding with the false torpedo info the senator had been given, his passing it along to his Asian lover and its ultimate arrival in Beijing and Shanghai.

My involvement in the matter was explained by Captain Edwards. He covered everything from my initial stories about China and its Navy, my visit to Beijing for the May Day ceremonies, my features about Senator Anderson up to the visit of the PRC destroyer QINGDAO to Pearl Harbor last Fourth of July. He also told Ben about my relationship with Admiral Sharpe and the fact that at the special request of the Secretary of the Navy I was back on temporary active duty to get this spy story ready for worldwide news release.

Special Agent Peters finished the briefing with details about the Shin family, their relationship to Captain Wong, her Georgetown shop operations and their arrests last night. "Are we going to deport them back to China?" Ben interrupted.

"Yes. Probably within hours. The president is being briefed right now by Director Moran, who has also okayed your exclusive release of the story, via PANS."

"Any questions, Mr. Huntley?" asked Admiral Paulson.

"If Senator Anderson supplied the Chinese with secret information, even under threat of blackmail, doesn't that still make him a part of the spy operation?"

"Admiral Sharpe has questioned Senator Anderson's loyalty to this country for many months. When he found various secret Navy projects turning up in Chinese speeches and the press he asked Dan to look into it, strictly as an investigative reporter, keeping the government out of the matter. That's when Dan uncovered Anderson's role."

"Even with the senator's total cooperation he will be tried under federal law. Justice Department officials delivered charges to him this week. Anderson remains free on his own recognizance and is restricted to his home and the D.C. area."

I shuffled a moment and the admiral looked my way: "I think I know Hank Anderson and I don't believe he's really a bad guy. Granted, he made several stupid decisions that placed him in this situation, but he knew enough to try ending the mess. He called me because we had traveled to China together and he felt I was the only news person he could trust. He has my promise I will portray him as having been solicited by foreign nationals for classified information. However, once he became aware of the Shin's illegal intentions he contacted the FBI and revealed the entire scheme."

Peters nodded his agreement. "Since I had been doing extensive research on the senator at Admiral Sharpe's request, the Navy and FBI came up with this way of breaking the story after the spy ring was arrested."

Ben threw me a stink eye that only I caught, and then told the group: "We are thrilled to be involved and happy to help the U.S. government. Pacific & Asia News Service thanks you. And I can't wait to see the Sunday papers after I review Dan's story." The four visitors got up, thanked Ben and me, shook hands all around, and then headed back to their federal offices.

The moment they left the shit hit the fan! Ben was really steamed! "What the hell kind of a relationship do you think we have? Huh? A journalist spying for the government and returning to active duty without even telling me? I know you're a good writer, but this is not how we go about getting a great story. Shit, when the competition finds out how you had the inside track on this blockbuster piece they'll eat us alive with their criticism. Why'd you do it this way, Dan?"

"Look, Ben, I stumbled on the story in all the right ways. I smelled a rat then followed the scent and asked people a lot of questions. I happen to have the kind of background that got me some great answers from those in the know. As Admiral Sharpe told me when he swore me to secrecy and put me back on active duty, this is like wartime."

"I got the story as it developed but I didn't report all that I knew. Rather like Edward R. Murrow and Ernie Pyle. They knew more than they were allowed to report, and as patriotic Americans they waited for the time to come when they could tell the whole story. And when that happened, just like it will this weekend with our story, we will not be chided or accused, but rather we'll be praised for the story we've dug up. I did what I had to do, Ben."

"That's a tough speech to follow, and you are right. You did a great job and I'm proud of you. But in the future if you so much as step off the center line of journalistic ethics, I want to know about it so we can plan our next steps. Okay?"

"Deal, chief. Sorry. Deal, boss. I'm the Chief!"

Ben brought me back to reality. "You'll have access to more info than the average correspondent, since you're on active recall. But you'll have to maintain the identity of being just a wire service reporter whose request to be assigned to the battle group was approved by the Pentagon."

"One more thing. I assume you'll get your regular chief's pay, plus allowances, correct?" I nodded that it was and Ben continued: "Okay. Here's what I'm going to do for you. I'll make up any difference between your current salary and what the Navy will give you. And the PANS portion will include a nice 15% pay raise, retroactive to October 1st."

I could hardly resist hugging Ben, so I did.

At 1600 Pennsylvania Avenue, the director of the FBI was just about half way through telling the same story we'd just heard, but the emphasis was on the spies and their pending extradition. The President was concerned about what was going to be released about Madam Shin and her daughter, how the PRC embassy would react, and exactly what information the FBI had garnered from their interrogations of the two spies. He was also ready to expedite the political questions that were certain to come when Henry Anderson's role in the scheme became known.

FBI Director Moran assured him State Department officials would handle all the details, giving the president a briefing late Saturday afternoon so that if he needed to call a news conference after the PANS story broke he'd be up to speed. "Sec State and I will be standing by if you need us."

After being chewed out and then kissed with the raise, I handed Ben the manila envelope containing my final draft. "You'll get the fastest and most favorable chop I've ever done," Ben said, "and unless there's something in here that puts you and me and the news service in a legal bind we'll release it tomorrow. Let's go for 6 pm D.C. time. That's past the deadline for the local Saturday papers and the TV network newscasts, but just right for domestic Sunday papers."

"And if we run it on our Asia-only wire at about 6 am tomorrow morning it might even work for editors putting together their Sunday editions. We've got a winner here, Dan. Go get some lunch and when you come back we'll go over this piece and you can tell me your plans for follow-up stories."

It was already well after noon and I was bushed as I walked around the corner for some lunch and conversation with the boys. Knowing their input would be limited to PS&S, lunch came first. I ordered a Ruben sandwich and tried to keep my mind off the events of the last 48 hours.

Navy Times asked me: "Something wrong? You seem awfully quiet today." I passed it off with: "Nah. Just the end of a busy week. Ray would never know just how busy!

327

CHAPTER 84 - DAN'S DREAM STORY

January 7, 2001: Washington, D.C.

Nothing satisfies a newshound more than a well-researched story brought to publication. That's how I felt when I opened my Sunday Washington Post and saw this banner headline:

D.C. SPY RING BROKEN
CHINESE MOTHER-DAUGHTER
TEAM ARRESTED
SOUGHT NAVY SUBMARINE SECRETS

Immediately below, Henry Anderson was pictured at the July 4th Pearl Harbor ceremonies.

SENATOR ANDERSON GIVES AUTHORITIES
INITIAL LEAD TO SPY FAMILY

By: Dan Lincoln

Washington, D.C., January 7, 2001 (Pacific & Asia News Service):

Two illegal Chinese aliens were arrested late Thursday at a Georgetown art and antique shop, and accused of stealing classified materials about new U.S. Navy submarine projects.

FBI and U.S. Naval Investigative Service agents arrested the duo from the People's Republic of China who were in the U.S. on green cards.

A statement from the Navy Chief of Information identified the alleged spies as Lily Shin, 46, operator of the shop called Ming & Ching Things and her daughter Cheryl Leong, 23. Leong, a Georgetown University student on a now-expired student visa is also an intern on the U.S. Senate Armed Services Committee staff.

328

Shin and Leong were taken into custody at the Georgetown shop last Thursday evening and are being held for questioning, according to Bradley Peters, the FBI special agent in charge of this case. State Department officials say the suspects have been deported to China.

Informed sources at the Pentagon have confirmed the husband of Ms. Shin and father of Ms. Leong is a PRC Navy captain named David Wong, currently based in Shanghai as director of the Chinese Navy's U.S. intelligence gathering division.

Details of the alleged espionage operation began to surface after U.S. Senator Henry B. Anderson, Jr., Minnesota Democrat and minority leader of the Senate Armed Services Committee, contacted the FBI.

During a trip to attend May Day ceremonies in Beijing in 1999, at the invitation of the People's Republic of China government, the senator met Captain Wong, but the Chinese naval officer was then identified as LT Wong, an escort for the party of visiting American VIPs.

Senator Anderson met Ms. Leong and her mother at an after-work party of committee staffers and interns. A few weeks later Ms. Shin approached the senator requesting non-secret information about Navy projects.

Sen. Anderson said he was initially impressed with the woman's desire to become an American citizen, and since he was promoting passage of his Chinese American Navy Friendship Treaty at the time, he gave her some un-classified already-printed information about Navy efforts to make our submarines undetectable by enemy warships. It was when she re-contacted him demanding higher classified info, that he became concerned and contacted the FBI.

PANS has learned from the Justice Department that the senator will be indicted on charges of giving classified information to a foreign nation, which is punishable by prison time. There was no response from Senator Anderson or his office when queried by this reporter.

Navy officials at the Pentagon said Friday there has been no compromise of any projects on which they are currently working. They did say, however the revelation about the spy network in the Washington area was not unexpected. A senior officer told PANS: "We found out about this family over a year ago, and have been monitoring the situation."

It is expected that President Williams will hold a news conference this afternoon to address the espionage operation.

NOTE: This reporter was in that group of visitors to China in 1999 and got to know Senator Anderson quite well. I have written several news stories about his Navy friendship treaty, the historic visit of the Chinese warship QINGDAO to Pearl Harbor last July 4th, and feature stories about his feelings toward the Peoples Republic of China.

-end-

Feeling my oats, I said out loud: "Not a bad job of breaking the biggest story in decades even if I do say so myself!" I quickly re-read my story, put on a clean shirt and sport coat, and headed downtown to the Hay Adams Hotel to order the most expensive breakfast on their menu.

Monday morning even before I opened PANS' door, I could hear the incessant jangling of phones. Rhonda was frantically manning the switchboard and Ben was fielding as many calls as humanly possible. The whole place was jumping! We had really stirred a hornet's nest.

Most of the calls were of the atta boy nature primarily for me, but a lot of Ben's old buddies called to congratulate him and PANS on the humungous scoop. Radio and TV stations around the globe wanted interviews but those all went in the call back file. Ben was very much into the situation and decided we'd first handle requests from our paid subscribers from Tokyo to Tel Aviv.

We had elected to produce at least two follow-up stories to run on Tuesday and the following weekend. The TV networks were doing their best to find someone at the FBI and Pentagon to talk with, but after the President's news conference yesterday afternoon there weren't any details left that hadn't run in our story or been amplified by officials at the White House briefing.

"The two female spies were deported immediately," the State Department spokesman had told the press. "They are spies, as simple as that, and we've sent them packing back to their masters in Beijing."

The big story on FOX and CNN this morning was shared by follow-ups to the mother/daughter spies and what the future would hold for Hank Anderson. Reporters had caught him entering the Capitol garage where he made a fatal mistake; he gave the herd of TV and print journalists a comment. He barked out: "Nothing classified was ever given to Ms. Shin or Miss Leong, and I was more concerned about arresting and deporting those spies than some unimportant already printed Navy story that I may have told her."

That wasn't good enough for most of the news analysts who had already started comparing him to the Rosenbergs and even to Benedict Arnold. Meanwhile Hank's fellow senators, mainly the Republicans but even some Democrats, were demanding his resignation. Others, smelling real political blood, said the nation demanded jail time for the man they called a traitorous senator. From every angle the political future for the junior senator from Minnesota appeared to be nothing short of disastrous.

Tossing more gas on the raging fire, my story for Tuesday added another element to the spy ring saga, sending reporters to all kinds of government contractors seeking anything they could to expand the story. I knew they were barking up the wrong tree.

THIRD FEMALE INVOLVED IN CHINESE SPY RING EMPLOYED BY NAVY SUBCONTRACTOR

By: Dan Lincoln

Washington, D.C., January 9, 2001. Pacific & Asia News Service:

U.S. Government officials say a third female is allegedly involved in the Chinese spy ring broken up last week by the FBI and U.S. Navy authorities. The unnamed young woman, arrested over the weekend and currently being held for further questioning, is reportedly an American citizen of Chinese ancestry, now living in Arlington, Virginia.

This latest arrest comes after government officials exposed one of the biggest espionage operations against the U.S. Navy since the John Walker and son case, in Norfolk, Virginia a decade ago. Reportedly, the Arlington woman is employed by a Navy subcontractor. Officials would not identify the firm or the woman.

"As an American citizen she has several rights and until and if we charge her with anything, other than suspicion of aiding known foreign spies, nothing further will be released about her," said Brad Peters, the FBI special agent in charge of the case.

On Thursday Lily Shin, 46, and her daughter Cheryl Leong, 23, were arrested at Shin's Georgetown residence, located over her Chinese arts shop Ming & Ching Things at 35th and Prospect Sts., NW.

When queried by PANS, both State Department and White House sources had no further comment on what had already been said by the President and the Secretary of State at last Sunday's news conference.

-end-

Nearly every metropolitan paper in America ran my follow-up, including the Honolulu Advertiser. About noon my desk chirped at me, and for a moment I forgot it was my scrambler phone. Bernie Sharpe was on the line.

"Great story in the Sunday paper, Dan, and today's follow-up. The wait was worth the time and the Navy thanks you for doing such a thorough job of reporting."

"Thanks, admiral, but as you and Yogi Berra both know: 'It's not over till it's over.' Something tells me this spy ring is only part of something much, much bigger as it relates to China and us. Am I on target?"

"Right on. Since we failed to find anything positive about Pentagon moles, I have to conclude that we're about at the end of the spy portion of the story. For the next couple of months you might want to focus attention on what's happening out here in the Pacific. My trigger finger is itchy and I'm feeling more and more positive we might be in a shooting war soon."

"I'm on the same wave length Admiral, and Ben also wants me to concentrate on the South China Sea situation. Looks like I can head for Fleet duty in mid-February."

"Good timing. By the way Dan, that story about the girl working for the Virginia subcontractor, be careful; there's more to her story than you know."

"I remember us talking about Milsoftel but you didn't mention any names. Most of what I wrote today came from Brad Peters at the FBI, and he too has urged me to tread lightly on that portion of the overall story. I will."

"Okay, Dan. Thanks again for all your cooperation with our guys back there. See you soon."

My final spy piece was to run Friday and I wrote it as a re-hash of the major story with updated reactions by everyone from the British and Japanese to the Taiwanese and the PRC itself. Editorials in the Beijing papers during the week had vehemently denied any such female or family spy ring and said it was "just more sabre-rattling by the U.S. administration and its Taiwanese lackeys."

I was able to use one good quote from the admiral in charge of the CVBG on station with the Seventh Fleet:

"The ships and sailors of the U.S. 7th Fleet are here for one and only one purpose: to protect our allies and to ensure safe passage of world shipping in the region. If the PRC should take any further action against the Spratly Islands or U.S. Navy ships, our response will be both rapid and deadly in its force."

CHAPTER 85 - MELTING A COLD SHOULDER

January 12, 2001: Washington, D.C.

What a great boyfriend I am. I had let myself get all caught up in the hullabaloo surrounding my story and failed to call Janice for almost two weeks. I'll bet she's pissed at me. I dialed her office number.

She answered on the third ring: "Commander Cannon. This is not a secure line. May I help you?"

"Hi long, lean and luscious; how're things?"

"Who's this?" she asked.

My heart took a deep-six. "Dan," I replied meekly.

"Hmm, I used to know a Dan Lincoln. Nice guy, wrote for some newspaper or something."

I jumped right in. "That's me!"

"And you'll still talk to little Janice?" she giggled. "Big news star and all?"

"Star, schmar," I replied. "I'm still just Dan. I'm really sorry I've neglected calling but this entire thing has just run over me like a tidal wave. Look, can we still get together for a weekend before I report to the fleet? Please? I'm begging!"

With that same detached coolness she had during our last weekend together she answered: "I'm sure you'll love being at sea again, and digging up all sorts of stories. You've caught me at a really busy time. My new boss is instituting new programs, and since my promotion I'm too senior for this assistant job and will probably be transferred. But, we ought to be able to arrange at least one weekend between now and when you leave."

Even if Janice doesn't share the depth of my caring for her, she is the lady I truly care about and want to be with for ever. Perhaps she seems cold to me because of our two very different lifestyles. Okay, I'll work on that. But for the present moment if it's only one weekend we have for the foreseeable future, I'll make it the best time we've ever spent together.

"How about going up to New York City and we take in several Broadway shows and see all the sights of The Big Apple?"

"Now that turns me on!" she said, sounding almost excited. "I'm free the last weekend of this month. Can you make all the reservations?"

"Oh, you bet. Doin' the town with a commander. Sailor's delight! You betcha. We'll celebrate your promotion. I'll call you at home later."

Putting down the phone, I felt just like a large mouth bass that had been masterfully played by a fisherwoman and, I didn't give a damn!

Now feeling the urge to work, I tackled my mountain of messages, tossing most into the circular file because their requests were out of date. I did write about a dozen notes to special people I wanted to thank for their support. Before I knew it my tummy announced: "Lunchtime; now!"

Strolling into the C-C my newsman instinct sensed a heightened atmosphere of respect. Not everyone at the Roundtable knew the feeling of finally hitting the story of a lifetime, but their attitudes showed their pride for a fellow journalist.

A pitcher of MGD accompanied by a grilled ham and cheese sandwich, materialized before me and Lisa said: "Compliments of Archie the Manager, at the place where the elite meet to eat!"

RED SKY AT NIGHT

PART II

UNDERSEA FACE-OFF

CHAPTER 86 - OPERATION HEAVENLY HORSES

January 12, 2001: PLA War Room, Beijing

"Comrades, I offer a toast to our President, to our great Motherland, and to our resolve to create a battle plan that will culminate in reclaiming our rebellious offshore province for the Middle Kingdom."

The dozen senior military officers leaped to their feet, the taste of battle on each tongue. They were ready to show the world the sleeping giant was awakening with a vengeance.

Battle plans for taking Taiwan back under China's talons were drafted and underway. Admiral W.H.C. Ho, Commander-in-Chief of the People's Liberation Army, and Pacific Fleet, had been summoned to Beijing to finalize strategy. His daring plan already had the Chinese president's blessing; the diminutive architect of their modern Navy with his PLA counterparts faced the daunting task of completing a detailed plan for victory. His power lay in the 40 million members of his Army, Air Force and reserve forces.

"Comrades, over the past few years several interactions have taken place with the Americans that handed us major public relations victories. You'll recall one of our *fishing trawlers* was sunk off Hawaii in 1998; we've had to persuade several U.S. spy planes away from our territory; and our submarines routinely track U.S. warships to their great annoyance. World opinion is on our side and now is the time to make additional strikes against America and the decadent West."

Eyebrows rose as the general in charge of the Army grumbled about being ready to go now, so why wait? As an answer to the fact he did not intend to wait Admiral Ho marched to a giant map of the Pacific. "In 1996 our live-fire exercises off Taiwan raised little global attention, so I believe a take-over there will bring not only little attention but minor opposition."

The seasoned admiral calmly lit one of his yellow-tipped cigarettes and turned back to his audience: "The key, comrades, is to neutralize all opposition from America and her allies in the region." Battle tested as he was, Ho literally crushed any opposing opinions and then called for a coordinated campaign.

His thin, effeminate finger moved quickly and landed on the map location for the Island of Taiwan. "If the U.S. comes to the aid of Taiwan we must stop them. We shall convince the world that China is merely reclaiming an island that belongs to us." Heads nodded approval as his intensity filled the room with new resolve.

"All military branches will participate," Ho directed. "All countries will know China's army is the largest in the world, and our airmen the best. Those who think us a nation of rusting World War II surface ships and second-hand Russian submarines will be paralyzed by fear as were Emperor Wu-Ti's enemies after he obtained superior equine breeding stock from the Huns. Our new fleet of world-class submarines and guided missile destroyers are latter-day Heavenly Horses well-suited to challenge and surpass the Americans in this part of the world."

More applause but Admiral Ho raised his arms and the room fell silent immediately. "We will continue to harass U.S. Navy spy flights off our coasts, and we shall possess the Nanshas by May Day, declaring a 500 mile Exclusive Economic Zone of in all directions."

His shrill voice cracked with electricity as his pointer suddenly became a weapon, making wide sweeps around the Spratlys and mainland China. "We will control all shipping in the South China Sea from Hong Kong to Singapore. Our forces will deny any traffic to pass within our boundaries, including the U.S. Fleet and their feeble allies!" The room shook with applause.

"Now, we must create our battle plan and start the new dawn. We *will* control the air and seas in the region. We *will* have naval superiority over the U.S. World public opinion will allow us the first, and our spy network in the States will take care of the second. Then, while the American guard is down and at a time no one will expect, we will *strike* the greedy capitalist dogs of Taiwan!"

Shouting their "Power to the people!" approval, the officers knew the clock was now running. What were another few months to wait for final victory? And with that victory would come recognition as a major world power superior to the self-appointed police force of the world: America.

With a triumphant smile on his face, Admiral Ho lit his third cigarette of the hour.

CHAPTER 87 - HUMPTY HENRY HAS A GREAT FALL

January 19, 2001: Washington, D.C.

Janice phoned with the news her transfer was final and when we returned from Manhattan she would join the China team in the Intelligence Division (N-2) of the CNO's office. "I'll be moving up in responsibility but down in floors. Into the Pentagon basement or Lower Level as we call it. Here are my new phone numbers." After spewing a mile long list, she signed off with "Looks like I'm going to be jammed until the New York trip, so I doubt I'll see you before we leave. Can you wait that long? I'll make it worth every minute." While checking my e-mail up popped an address I recognized but never thought would contact me. I clicked on *read*: Looks like the end's in store for me. You should have all the details to cap your story. Call me ASAP. Hank.

Grabbing my phone I called Senator Anderson's office and asked Mrs. Swanson how soon I could meet with him.

"Can you come immediately?" she queried.

"How about half an hour?" I replied.

"The Senator will be waiting."

Within the hour I was sitting before Hank who looked like hell. "Not sleeping well lately?"

Grumbling, Hank spat out: "Would you if you were in my shoes? Look, I've made a deal with the Justice Department to serve a minimum prison sentence. I'll probably do a year, at best. And, I'm resigning from the Senate effective tomorrow, the day the new President is inaugurated."

As a newsperson I thought: Smart move. Get your bad news buried way, way behind the good news of the inauguration. Minimize the damages. Writing down all the details, I asked him his future plans, and if he had any regrets.

"Of course I regret what I did. It was stupid. I acted like some college kid who let his dick get in the way of his brain. That led to more and more involvement and pretty soon my desire to live a peaceful co-existence with China had me stealing secrets for a country which has no interest whatsoever in being an American ally.   I feel like Richard Nixon must have when he lost his 1960 presidential bid to Jack Kennedy, saying: Now you won't have Dick Nixon to kick around anymore. Well, like JFK, you and your media buddies won't have Hank Anderson to kick around anymore, either. China will have to survive without my help."

That capped our talk, so I thanked the soon to be ex-Senator and said I would handle his story as gently as possible. I headed back to PANS and composed a story even I hated to write.

SENATOR HENRY ANDERSON RESIGNS OVER INVOLVEMENT IN CHINESE SPY RING VOWS HE WAS NEVER A KNOWING PART OF ESPIONAGE SCHEME

By: Dan Lincoln

Washington, D.C., January 19, 2001 (Pacific & Asia News Service):

U.S. Senator Henry B. Anderson (D-MN) will resign his seat in the U.S. Senate effective tomorrow, telling reporters he believes it is the right thing to do for both the nation and his constituents.   He has served in Congress since being elected to the House in 1992 and then to the Senate in 1998.   Anderson would have become Armed Services Committee ranking minority member after last fall's election defeat of Sen. Randall Potter (D-RI).

Anderson became embroiled in the Chinese mother-daughter spy ring case, exposed early this month by PANS, after admitting he had given confidential information from closed-door Congressional hearings, to Lily Shin, a Georgetown Chinese arts dealer and her daughter Cheryl Leong, then known to him as a staff aide on his Senate Armed Services Committee.

Voluntarily surrendering to Justice Department officials, Anderson claimed he believes that what he gave the women was in the public domain and he had no knowledge the women were foreign agents.

When Ms. Shin pressed the senator for additional and classified information about Navy submarine developments, he claims he became alarmed and contacted the FBI and other officials with his story.

Both Ms. Shin and Ms. Leong were in the country on green card work and study permits only, and have since been deported to China. Another young woman, an American of Chinese descent, has not been identified by the FBI but is said to have also played a role in the espionage operation.

Senator Anderson made his announcement at his office today, after calls for his resignation had gained increased support in both parties. A national poll, taken a week after the spy story became public, showed nearly 70% of those sampled favored Anderson's resignation.

Since there are more than two years left on Anderson's Senate term, the Governor of Minnesota will appoint someone to fill the vacancy. State law says any such replacement must be of the same party as the former elected official, so there will be no change in the current 51 to 49 majority enjoyed by the Democrats.

The Attorney General's office said, shortly after Sen. Anderson's resignation announcement, charges are still pending against him and they expect a trial to be scheduled for sometime later in the year.

-end-

I took no glory in what had happened to Hank Anderson. He was involved, certainly, but not as a knowing participant in an organized treason plot. As I looked back on my relationship with him over the years, I kind of felt sorry for him; kind of. He was an ambitious politician, with an ego a mile high. He wanted to be on top, whatever it took, but greed finally did him in.

"Sorry I couldn't help you at the end, Hank," I said to the office walls. "But you made your bed and now you'll have to sleep in it. Unfortunately, it may be a very uncomfortable one at some place like Fort Leavenworth, Kansas."

CHAPTER 88 - KISS ME & YOU TEMPT DEATH

February 6, 2001: Washington, D.C.

If our Manhattan weekend was to be the final act for The Janice Cannon and Dan Lincoln Show, it was an over-the-top smash hit. On Broadway we enjoyed Cats and a rather funky new show, strolled through the Guggenheim and spent hours in MOMA as the locals refer to it. I could feel some of the coolness fading from Janice.

Our best personal performances were showcased in our hotel room on a king-sized stage. Janice showed me what a last name that means the same as heavy artillery really means! We dined in several charming restaurants and especially enjoyed Sunday Brunch at the spectacular Windows On The World, high atop the World Trade Center. Just nine months later what happened to thousands of people in that very building and its twin, brings me to tears today.

"Why do weekends have to end?" I muttered to no one in particular. "Especially on Monday." Putting it out of my mind I turned to the job at hand, a story due this Thursday about the ultimate fate of Samantha Wing. Ben walked into my office and tossed a few pink message slips on my desk as I pounded away at my computer. "These came in for you while you were in New York, and Commander Cannon from the Pentagon called you."

"I was expecting to hear from her, Ben. She should have details about the last loose string in my spy story, the Chinese-American girl who worked for that Virginia lab doing special projects for the Navy. Must be the Feds are ready to charge her with aiding an espionage operation or perhaps just slap her wrists. Any other crises for me?" Ben shook his head.

I looked at the names on the phone messages, threw most of them away and then phoned Janice.

"Commander Cannon speaking. May I help you?"

345

"Good Morning, pretty lady. I've missed you and it's been less than a day!"

Janice started talking as if she was reading from a script: "Admiral Sharpe called. Said he couldn't reach you but asks you to get together with the NIS and FBI people regarding Samantha Wing. They'll be here at my office tomorrow at 1500 to brief you on the matter in question."

"I'll be there," was as much as I could get in before she concluded the brief conversation by saying: "See ya."

Ben was pleased we'd have a feature for the weekend editions. Heading to Virginia and the Pentagon the next day I felt more than one story might come from this meeting.

When I got to Admiral Sharpe's old office a Yeoman Second Class sitting right where Janice used to sit greeted me: "Commander Cannon will be right with you, Mr. Lincoln." Before I could get seated Janice opened the inner-office door and motioned me to come in. "Good afternoon Commander," I said, giving her a big kiss. Gently pushing me away she reprimanded: "I've told you, no fraternizing between ranks, Chief. The FBI and NIS are waiting in Conference Room Two and Captain Bill Edwards from CHINFO will join us at 1530."

I recognized FBI Special Agent Brad Peters from our briefings on the spy ring case last fall. The other man, introducing himself as Harlow Washington from the Navy Investigative Service, got right to the details of the meeting.

"One element of this whole matter that we knew nothing of before looking into Ms. Wing's background, is that her elderly grandfather, who has lived here since the late 40s, was a fighter with Mao Tse Dung in the days when they were all young communists working hard to drive Chiang Kai Shek off the Chinese Mainland."

"Although Samantha Wing is an American citizen, she's obviously in sync with the communist ideology of Lily Shin and Cheryl Leong or she would not have fed them information they could use to their advantage. In America, with its freedoms of religion and philosophy, commie leanings are not a crime; but passing along any phase of classified info makes her just as guilty of espionage as Senator Anderson. We can't prove her guilty because Lily and Cheryl are not here to testify in any court action."

SA Peters added: "Ms. Wing is not subject to deportation and her involvement with Shin and Leong was enough to get her terminated from her job at Milsoftel. At this point we believe the best course of action is to release her pending further investigation. She'll be under surveillance 24/7, but hopefully she won't have a clue her every move is being observed and recorded."

"Ms. Wing may run to Grandpa Wing, she may not. He's never gotten into any trouble with the law, but we've learned that he was a frequent visitor to the Chinese Embassy for many years. We figure he's been passing anything he can find that relates to our government and our military on to Beijing, via his long time buddy Chinese Ambassador Wu, and probably to Mr. Wu's predecessors for the past half century."

When Peters finished I asked: "Is there anything specific he might have passed to the PRC?"

"We don't know, but you can pick up a lot of things just by keeping your eyes and ears open, especially if you're in regular contact with the movers and shakers in our government, military and business circles."

As the three of us talked more about Grandpa Wing, Captain Bill Edwards of the Navy Office of Information entered the conference room. We all greeted him and he said that he had a 1600 meeting with CHINFO, so he'd try to give us his story as quickly and clearly as possible.

"Captain, is this a follow-up on Senator Anderson?"

"I knew you'd want to get right to the point Mr. Lincoln, so here it is. The former senator's case is being handled in the U.S. Court system. He's been indicted by a Federal Grand Jury, his trial is set for March 13th and I would guess he'll be convicted, fined a tidy amount, and sent to prison for a couple years. After that he'll be released and allowed to return to Minnesota."

"That sounds about like what I expected," I said to the Navy PAO. "I understand his replacement is a straight shooter, a veteran, and not out to revive Hank's Chinese-American Navy Friendship Agreement."

The G-men went their separate ways, and I walked Janice back to her office. Agreeing we'd meet on Friday night at my place, I headed for the Metro connection back to my apartment.

Thursday morning when I arrived at the office it was pretty quiet. I told Ben I was doing the story about the Wing girl from the spy ring, and he laughingly told me to be sure I didn't refer to her as Spy Ring Wing.

The conclusion to the Samantha story would be short, but it was what Ben wanted for the weekend wire. I had it done in less than 30 minutes and left it on his desk. He was out of the office for the rest of the day, but when I got to work the next morning he'd obviously read and chopped the piece as it was on our main wire.

THIRD WOMAN IN CHINESE SPY RING RELEASED PENDING FURTHER INVESTIGATION MARCH TRIAL FOR FORMER SEN. ANDERSON

By: Dan Lincoln

Washington, D.C., February 9, 2001 (Pacific & Asia News Service):

A former Georgetown University student employed by a civilian subcontractor working for the Navy on various projects has been questioned by the Navy Department and FBI and released pending further investigation of her involvement with an alleged Chinese spy ring.

The 25 year old Arlington, Virginia woman purportedly passed on sensitive information to spy ring principals Lily Shin and Cheryl Leong. The unnamed woman will not be deported or extradited to a foreign nation because she was born in the U.S.

In a related item, the Justice Department has set March 13th as the trial date for former U.S. Senator Henry Anderson of Minnesota. He has been indicted on treason charges for his role in the Shin-Leong spy ring operation. Anderson maintains he knew nothing about the plot, and gave Ms. Shin information he believed to be unclassified. He said it was part of his long-term goal to create friendship between the U.S. and China.

-end-

With Janice coming for dinner, I left the office at 4:30 pm. Before I could get everything arranged in my apartment I heard a soft knocking and knew who it was.

I opened the door and Janice brushed me aside, her teeth chattering. She came in out of the cold and we hugged each other for a long time. Hanging her coat and hat on the coat tree, she shucked off her boots and said cheerily: "What can I do to help?"

"A kiss or six to start with, plus a body hug would be nice. But first, fix us some drinks if you would please. My usual G&T, there's some cold wine in the fridge and booze in the credenza."

Continuing her unexpected assault of passion, and pressing her body tightly against mine, she whispered in my ear: "Kissing me is tempting death."

I thought briefly about what she said but put it on the back burner when I heard the kitchen calling. Romping with my beautiful love partner would have to wait.

While I heated the red sauce and cooked the pasta for my favorite dinner Janice stood behind me running her hands inside my pants. I felt myself rising to the occasion and as the beer commercials say: 'It doesn't get much better than this.'

Janice chuckled: "Just checking to see if the torpedo is armed and dangerous. You are planning a harbor invasion later, aren't you? It seems like our New York weekend was months ago."

As we ate Janice asked me: "Have you and the admiral come up with anything more about that Chinese spy ring?"

"Only the Samantha Wing story I just did and what will be the final results of Senator Anderson's trial in March."

"That was one hell of a job, Dan, and certainly an important victory for the country. The admiral is very pleased with how you worked with him on it."

We finished our meal and sipped some very smooth Scotch while listening to a album by my most favorite singer, Andrea Bocelli. But the evening and my emotions took a quick 180 when I suggested retiring to the big brass bed. Janice said no. She had an early meeting the next day so wanted to spend the night at home. For some inexplicable reason I couldn't mount the energy to protest, and her lips were now cold as an Eskimo's igloo. One minute my towering lover is all over me like a hot blanket; the next gone with the wind. You cannot possibly know just how frustrating that was.

A week or so whizzed by; my trip to the Fleet was shaping up nicely. All that was left was a quick mop-up at PANS before I flew off to Hawaii and the western Pacific.

I was headed to the Metro when it happened. It was pitch dark, and most of this section of downtown D.C. was abandoned for the night. As I approached a darkened doorway, a large figure sprang at me and slashed my shoulder with a knife. Sliding behind me, he bent my suddenly throbbing arm against my back.

"You too nosy man now you gonna die!"

I could feel my blood gushing so I started screaming for help. His grip tightened and I saw the shadow of a knife but before it could pierce my body again, a cop appeared. This was a hardened beat cop yelling, "Police. Drop your weapon." The officer then fired at least two shots in the air.

My assailant knocked me to the ground and disappeared around the corner. Sirens seemed to scream from all directions as two patrol units screeched to a halt and officers leaped out of their squad cars. The next welcome sight was a paramedic.

A patrolwoman asked for identification, where I worked and if I knew who attacked me and why. I couldn't get my mind to function so I mumbled: "Big guy, too dark to see."

The EMS team got my bleeding arm under control and walked me to their ambulance. This time I went willingly to the hospital remembering clearly the bullets I took in my leg last year.

In the emergency room the medics quickly sized-up my injuries, did a thorough cleaning of the wound, and sutured the jagged hole in my shoulder. "Damn," I said through clenched teeth, "that hurts like a sonofabitch." They kept to their work, telling me to get a tetanus shot and keep the wound clean and dry. Before I knew it they had me signing release papers, tons of insurance forms, and probably the Declaration of Independence if I'd stood for it.

"Okay man," the intern said, "you're outta here. Stop by the pharmacy and they'll give you something for the pain."

There are always cabs around hospitals, so I grabbed one and headed for home and my own bed. I was suddenly exhausted, but now my mind couldn't rest. Who? Why? Am I too close to something big? Have I exposed something someone wants kept under cover? Do I need protection before I head for Asia? Finally sleep dropped mercifully on me and I didn't wake up until 10:45 am. Good; I had the day off anyway.

By Friday afternoon I figured I'd better let Ben know about my attack. Luckily I wasn't seriously hurt and I'd had a day to rest up. From now on I'd just have to do a better job covering my six as my Navy friends called it.

CHAPTER 89 - FROM D.C. TO AT SEA

February 24, 2001: Washington to Warships

My mind was at sea in the western Pacific, so I was startled when Ben grabbed my arm while I was seated at Gate 24-B at Reagan National about to board a non-stop flight to L.A. "You don't think you're going to leave for two months without me here to see you off, do you kiddo?"

"You're very kind, Ben, but I thought that going away party at the office last week was a great send off."

"That was nice but I wanted to give you something special. Here, it's a laptop computer."

"Ben, I don't know what to...."

"Wait. It's configured so all you have to do is plug and play, as the computer geeks say.

"This is really way too...

"You're connected directly to our office. Filing your stories from anywhere in the world will be a snap. I expect you to give this gizmo a real workout."

No use trying to get a word in edgewise, so I simply took the laptop with a grateful smile.

"Here's the best part, Dan. We're nominating you for a Pulitzer Prize. The president of Pacific & Asia News Service is submitting the formal papers nominating you for the prize in Investigative Journalism. And, the Washington Post's editor and the managing director of CNN are both endorsing you. We're all very proud of what you've accomplished."

Frankly, I didn't know whether to cry out, or just cry. Smiling until my cheeks ached, I shook Ben's hand and he gingerly patted my wounded shoulder, wishing me a safe voyage and good luck. Handing me a huge manila envelope my stern but loving boss turned and melted into the crowd.

I opened the heavy envelope which held my gift and a note which said: To Dan Lincoln. May you always have fair winds, following seas, and prize winning stories.

The passenger service agent announced: "American Airlines Flight One to Los Angeles and Honolulu is now ready for boarding."

Here we go, I though, another adventure.

I had three reasons to be thankful to Ben Huntley; first was the Pulitzer nomination. Second was my new toy, the Dell laptop. I must have spent four hours of the flight reading the instruction book and playing with the slim three pound computer. The third and final reason was that Ben had authorized first-class seating all the way to my final destination in the western Pacific!

I changed to the Honolulu flight at LAX. Westbound flights gain three hours on the clock so the Honolulu leg offered lunch and a movie. After nearly five hours the captain advised that those on the left side of the plane could see the twin volcanoes Mauna Kea and Mauna Loa on the Big Island of Hawaii. Not half an hour later a long graceful turn to the right brought up the island of Oahu. We passed over Diamond Head and Waikiki Beach, and soon the wheels touched down on the runway at Honolulu International.

Let me out of here, I thought. I need some warm sunshine and a dip in the ocean.

As I checked into the Royal Hawaiian, the general manager came up to the front desk and introduced himself. "Aloha, Mr. Lincoln. Your stories about that spy ring were great."

I guess I wasn't quite ready for celebrity status because I blushed. He went on: "My secretary, Jeri Bosnick, says you stayed with us in 1999 on your way to and from Beijing, I believe?"

"You have an excellent secretary." I then asked him: "Perhaps you remember some of my Honolulu TIMES stories?"

"No sir. I've only been out here for six months, from Boston."

I told him: "I wish I could stay at the Royal for more than just one night but my schedule is set and I fly to Tokyo tomorrow at noon."

"Enjoy yourself, Mr. Lincoln. And should your plans allow, I've asked Coronado to save two places for you at our Luau tonight."

My room overlooked the hotel's manicured gardens, and after settling in I grabbed the phone and called Admiral Sharpe. He knew my flight schedule and said: "Save the evening for me."

"I have freebies for the luau tonight," I teased. "Want to bring Barbara along?"

"'Fraid not, Dan. Tonight is strictly business. I'll pick you up at 1900."

I grabbed forty winks, enjoyed a long cool shower, then dressed in my favorite Aloha shirt. "Welcome home," I said to myself, and went down to the beachfront Mai Tai Bar for an island concoction.

Over dinner at Don Ho's at the Aloha Tower Marketplace, Bernie kept saying how happy he was being back in submarines and especially to be at Pearl Harbor. He also went into great depth with news of the PRC Navy which had positioned more ships off Taiwan. "We're keeping close watch, and two more of our subs are heading for the Seventh Fleet."

"Before I left D.C. my boss gave me a new laptop. I'm really connected now." The admiral nodded his understanding and gave me his private e-mail address, saying it was secure so I could send sensitive material.

We talked about a wide assortment of topics throughout dinner. On the way back to the Royal Bernie offered to have me driven to the airport the next day. When I said I was on Japan Airlines at 1300, he told me to be at the hotel's porte-cochere at 1030 and his Navy driver would take me to the airport.

Honolulu International Airport can be a mess at times, but the kind people of Japan Airlines made it all seem so easy. A passenger service agent named Nakamura escorted me to JAL's First Class passenger lounge, and with an hour to kill before boarding I called Bruce Ferguson, my former boss at the Honolulu Times. His first words were: "Wow, Danny, you really copped the prize this time! Why the hell didn't you pull something big like this when you were on my staff?"

"That's only part of the story," I interjected. "I'm off to Tokyo in an hour and then to a Navy warship in the South China Sea."

"Hoo-boy! You really know how to climb the ladder, don't you? What'd they do, recall you to active duty?" he queried.

"Sorta. I'm a DOD accredited correspondent for the next couple of months. I'll be with a carrier battle group."

I could feel his envy over the phone. I was sure he wanted to come out to the airport and get on the plane with me. We chatted for ten minutes and I promised him I'd try to do a couple of features just for the Times if I could.

The agent came and took me for priority boarding on the jumbo Boeing 747. Locating my seat, I looked about the spacious two-level cabin and thought: Now, this is the *only* way to fly!

CHAPTER 90 - SAILING WITH TEDDY

February & March 2001 - South China Sea

Eight hours, two movies with English subtitles and an endless banquet of Asian delicacies later, I hauled myself off the jet into Narita Airport. The clocks read 5 pm, Tokyo time, Monday. I'd lost a day crossing the International Date Line. I wondered will my screwed-up body and brain catch-up with me any time soon?

People bustled everywhere in an endless sea of color. Searching the Departure TV monitors I located my connection to Taipei 12 gates away. I'd have to hustle to make the 6:05 departure.

Less than three hours later I stepped on the ground in the capital of the Republic of China. The next leg of my journey was tomorrow morning, so I spent the night at a nearby airport motel. My first class treatment came to an abrupt halt on the COD flight from the Taiwan airbase to the USS THEODORE ROOSEVELT, a trip memorable for its forgetability. And I can only describe our landing on the carrier as a controlled crash!

Getting oriented to this giant ship took several days, and I made certain to stay out of the crew's way. I'd expected to be in the Chiefs' quarters since I was officially back on active duty, but Bernie Sharpe apparently didn't tell the Navy that I was anything but a VIP journalist, so I was bunked in a tiny stateroom with two of the ROOSEVELT's junior officers.

The wardroom was just a deck away and most every area I wanted to observe from was on the starboard side of the ship, either in the tower or immediately below. With a ship the size of the T.R. my transiting track involved 10 decks worth of going up and down ladders for my every evolution.

Life on a U.S. Navy aircraft carrier is like living in a small city of 5,000 people, jammed into an area slightly longer than the size of three footballs fields laid end to end. I enjoyed interviewing the average sailor and got some great human interest stuff for stories.

My free run of the ship got me into pilot ready rooms, the crew's galley, the officer's wardroom where I took my meals, and even down into the bowels of the ship. There I found everything from a barber shop to the post office, to medical and dental centers which were second to none I'd been in before.

My second day aboard I was summoned to the CO's cabin for lunch. He wanted to know more about my two-month assignment and how he could assist me. "I know some of your background," Captain Ballard said, "from Admiral Sharpe and seeing your stories about that Chinese spy ring."

The captain brought me up to speed on the CVBG's mission, the status of enemy and friendly ships in the area, and what I could and could not do while on-board.

The best thing was that I could talk to anyone on the ship, and had access to the Bridge, the Flight Bridge Flag Plot and CIC. The only place restricted to me was the main deck during flight ops. Nice guy, I thought, exiting his cabin and making my way down a passageway back to my quarters.

Meanwhile, in the command center of the PRC Navy guided missile destroyer QINGDAO, the weapons officer was counting off the seconds until launch of two of the ship's awesome surface-to-surface missiles. "Thirty seconds, Captain. Range steady at 6 miles. Target bearing 235 degrees. Twenty seconds."

"Fire when ready, Lieutenant Ching," the seasoned commanding officer told him.

"Ten seconds. Five. Missiles away, Captain."

Within seconds radar and sonar technicians recorded a huge explosion at a location about 5 miles from their ship and 100 miles off the coast of the Nansha Islands.

Captain H.K.J. Fong stated for all to hear: "I presume our message has been received."

Midway through my third week aboard the TR the first GQ alarm went off. "General Quarters. General Quarters. All hands man your battle stations. This is *not* a drill. I repeat, this is *not* a drill," blared the 1 MC speaker outside my cabin door.

As I stuck my head out of the stateroom sailors with helmets and life-preservers dashed up and down the passageway heading for their battle stations. The captain had assigned me a small space at the rear of the ship's bridge, out of the crew's way where I was able to witness all that was going on and perhaps learn the cause of the current situation.

Within minutes, two radar search planes and about half a dozen F/A-18 fighters scrambled from the flight deck. Before they were out of sight, Captain Ballard addressed the crew: "This is the Captain speaking. The Taiwanese Navy destroyer LAO YANG has sent us a flash signal that they've been attacked, purportedly by missiles from a PRC Navy DDG. Her skipper claims she's in designated international waters, approximately 100 miles off the Spratly Islands."

"She has sustained extensive damage to her power plant and controls and is shipping water. An S-O-S has been put out, and the ship's captain says they may abandon ship in the next several hours. Our aircraft will reconnoiter the scene and await further orders. As they occur, I'll keep you posted on developments. That is all."

U.S. jets reached the sinking ship in less than 30 minutes radioing that the damaged ship might sink in a matter of minutes. Squadron leader Buddy Rogers identified the attacking ship as the guided missile destroyer QINGDAO, five miles from the site. Lifeboats were seen around the LAO YANG, reported by pilots to look like an old U.S. tin can.

The 7th Fleet Staff radioed our ship: No offensive response and then directed the CVBG to deploy two ships to the attack site to assist in rescue operations. Our planes were ordered to attack only if fired upon first.

Captain Ballard signed for and read the message, shook his head, and again picked up the 1MC. "This is the Captain speaking. Stand down from General Quarters. I say again:

Stand down from General Quarters. Two CVBG ships have been directed to the Taiwanese destroyer to render all possible assistance and rescue survivors. Two F/A-18's will remain on station over the area until further orders. All other aircraft will return to the ship. More information as it becomes available to us. That is all."

I waited until details of the ROC ship became known and then slipped quietly off the bridge moving as quickly as I could to my stateroom. Once inside, and grateful that my two bunkmates were on duty, I took out the laptop, fired it up and proceeded to recount the LAO YANG attack.

I dialed Ben's private e-mail number to begin filing my story. "Hope I'm scooping everyone," I said out loud, "unless Beijing knew about this earlier and already hit the press with it." In a matter of minutes, the world would learn of the PRC's latest act of we dare you to respond aggression.

TAIWANESE DESTROYER HIT BY PRC NAVY MISSILES WHILE PASSING THROUGH STRAITS OF MALACCA 20 SAILORS BELIEVED DEAD AS SHIP SINKS NO IMMEDIATE RESPONSE FROM BEIJING

By: Dan Lincoln

On-board the U.S. Aircraft Carrier USS THEODORE ROOSEVELT in the South China Sea, March 21, 2001, (Pacific & Asia News Service):

A Taiwanese Navy destroyer was fired on today sustaining two deadly missile hits. The attack ship is thought to be a People's Republic of China guided missile warship. The LAO YANG (DDG-930) based in Kaoshung, Taiwan, is about to sink and the U.S. Navy has dispatched two ships from a nearby carrier battle group to assist in rescue operations. The ROC captain reports 20 known deaths and several casualties, and has ordered the crew to abandon ship. It is believed there are adequate numbers of life boats and rafts to accommodate the crew until help arrives.

The U.S. Seventh Fleet Command confirmed that the PRC ship purportedly initiating the attack was the QINGDAO, homeported at Shanghai. After its initial firing on the LAO YANG no further offensive action was reported. U.S. Navy jets scrambled from the carrier USS THEODORE ROOSEVELT and are on-station ready to respond to any further attacks. There has been no comment yet from the Chinese Navy or the PRC government.

The LAO YANG is a 390 foot long 3,500 ton ship that normally carries a crew of 255. It was formerly the American Navy destroyer USS SHELTON (DD-790), commissioned in 1946 and sold to the ROC in l983. It was transiting the Straits of Malacca and was about 100 miles off the coast of the Spratly Islands when attacked. The Taipei government, along with Vietnam, Malaysia, the Philippines and Singapore all claim the islands belong to them. Beijing says the islands are actually the Nanshas which they say is the proper Chinese name, and have been a part of mainland China for hundreds of years. They claim them by what they call 'historical acquisition.' This is the first time a ship making such a passage has been fired upon by PRC Navy units.

This reporter was part of a group of American VIPs who visited Beijing in May of 1999. We also toured the big Chinese Navy shipyard and base at Shanghai. There I went aboard the QINGDAO, the second ship in the all-Chinese designed and built LUHU class of guided missile destroyers. The QINGDAO is a 5,700 ton ship with a crew of about 230. It is 468 feet long, 51 feet at the beam, and can reach speeds in excess of 31 knots.

This vessel was the first Chinese Navy warship to visit Pearl Harbor this past Fourth of July. It was part of a Chinese-American ship exchange visit set up by former U.S. Senator Henry B. Anderson (D-MN). Today's attack could lead to weakened diplomatic relations between Beijing and Washington.

-end-

Knowing time restraints, I quickly re-read my story and then hit *send* on my laptop screen. My first story as a DOD accredited correspondent was on its way to Ben Huntley in Washington, D.C. and from there to newsrooms around the world.

Jet planes zoomed back from the sinking ship and plopped down on the USS ROOSEVELT's deck. Before I could leave my quarters a blinking light and computer voice on my laptop announced *You Have Mail.* It was from Ben. Fun, I thought. Write a story half a world away, hit a button and my story is instantly in place.

With hopeful anticipation I opened Ben's e-mail: Good reporting. That's why you're there. Story has been relayed to our subscriber news outlets. Responses are great. Sending you back to sea was my best move ever. Keep feeding details.

I felt a sublime kinship with generations of war correspondents. Being in the battle, but sort of out of harm's way. I was jolted back to reality by the jangling phone. Captain Ballard's aide asked me to come to the skipper's cabin with a copy of my story.

I packed my laptop and headed up to the tower. The door was opened before I had a chance to knock by another Navy captain. Captain Ballard sat at his desk, opposite a two-star admiral. Oh, oh, I thought, my palms beginning to sweat.

"Rear Admiral Frank Williams, this is Chief Petty Officer Dan Lincoln." Remembering Navy regs, I saluted my senior officer. "Admiral Williams is commander of our Battle Group, and Captain Doug Collins is the skipper of our air group. Please be seated."

I couldn't imagine what fate was in store for me but my fears were quickly put to rest by the ship's skipper.

"Dan, we're aware of why you're here. This situation we're suddenly in may get a lot worse. We believe your reports can go a long way toward helping gain public support for our mission. You can make people aware the real threats come from China. Today's attack is undoubtedly only the first probe. We think the PRC will see just how far they can push us before we take any action."

Admiral Williams continued: "The last administration basically forced our military to sit on its hands but the current Commander-in-Chief supports a strong defense, and believes in retaliation when attacked."

"If I might interrupt, Admiral," Captain Ballard said: "Were you able to file a story about the QINGDAO attack, Dan?"

"Yes sir. It's in my laptop but, unfortunately, I didn't bring a printer with me on this trip."

"I'm certain we can get you to a printer," Captain Ballard said. "We're not going to censor your stories but posting copies of them on the ship's television channel might help morale."

"Thank you, sir," I replied. "You'll see everything I write, just as soon as I've filed it with my editor. Is that okay with you?"

Everyone nodded affirmative and the CO said: "I'll ask our Chief Journalist, Senior Chief Bob Fudge, to set up a system of retrieving the stories from your laptop after they've been sent to PANS."

"By the way, sir," I asked Admiral Williams, "do you expect any retaliation from Taiwan for today's attack on their ship?"

"That would only be speculation on my part, Chief. The answer is we'll just have to wait and see. I *can* tell you that both Seventh Fleet and CINCPAC, along with many people in the Navy Department, have sent strong recommendations up to the Secretary of Defense. You can be assured that SECDEF, along with the CNO, will take their case straight to POTUS."

It was clear the meeting was now over so I expressed my thanks, and got up to leave the cabin. As I opened the door I turned my head and said: "I'm also following Admiral Sharpe's advice and covering my six." Of the three officers, only the air boss had a big smile on his face.

CHAPTER 91 - SOUTH CHINA SEA BOILS OVER

March & April 2001: South China Sea

The LAO YANG sank. Our two fighter jets quickly returned from the sinking to the ROOSEVELT. There will be some great stories from those pilots, I thought.

Needing a caffeine fix I headed for the wardroom. One of the fighter pilots who had identified the attacking ship was finishing a sandwich and a bowl of soup. His name-badge read Walther. I asked if I could throw a few questions at him. He nodded his approval.

"Did you get close enough to the QINGDAO to see any kind of reaction to their provocation?" LT Walther slowly turned to me and I saw a hunger in his eyes that had nothing to do with food. "Yeah, I saw some reaction. They all had big smiles on their faces and most of them flipped me Mr. Digit. They were proud of what they'd done and knew we weren't going to fire on them. It was almost like they were shouting: 'We'll do whatever we want and you Americans can buzz off!'"

Sensing LT Walther wanted to be left alone I thanked him and went back to my stateroom. I made brief notes in my little blue book, and then hit the sack.

The ROOSEVELT's bells and sound system came alive at 0600 and if you wanted a good breakfast you'd better be in the wardroom early or the number of officers waiting to be fed would force you out of the dining area. As I was scarfing down a huge portion of scrambled eggs, the 1MC came alive.

"This is the Captain speaking. We've been informed by COMSEVENTHFLT that a PRC Navy coastal patrol craft was sunk at 0615 today by a U.S. Navy submarine off the coast of Hainan Island. The Navy Department says the sinking was in retaliation for yesterday's unprovoked attack on the destroyer LAO YANG. The dispatch said that if further attacks are made on U.S. or allied ships, the U.S. Navy will take appropriate and rapid action. That is all."

A huge roar enveloped the wardroom with cries of Right on! About time! It's kick-ass time!

Because the announcement had originated in the Pentagon I knew all the other news sources had the story, but perhaps I can get more info from the ship's CIC.

"It's dark in here," I said to no one in particular, as my eyes adjusted. Then I recognized LT Bob Lindgren, the duty officer. He offered me a seat in front of a non-manned computer terminal.

"Any further details about the incident?" I asked.

"Nothing I can tell you, Mr. Lincoln, other than the shooter was one of our fast attack LOS ANGELES class boats. You know as much as we do about the PRC boat. I'm sure there's a copy of Jane's on board; you can look up the stuff about Chinese patrol craft."

"Great idea," I said, thanking him while opening the hatch and leaving him to his monitors maps and darkness.

Jane was easier to find than I expected. In the back of my mind I recalled a small library in the wardroom, so headed there first. I found that Jane came dressed in several different outfits: Fighting Ships; Fighting Aircraft; and on the top shelf in pristine condition, All The World's Fighting Ships.

I went straight to the section covering the PRC. Their newest DDGs and submarines were highlighted, but I flipped ahead to the section on patrol craft. After making a few notes I returned to my cabin, took out the laptop and wrote my follow-up story.

U.S.-CHINA RELATIONS ON BRINK
BEIJING WARNED ABOUT FURTHER PROVOCATIONS
7TH FLEET SINKS RED PATROL BOAT

By: Dan Lincoln

At sea aboard the U.S. Navy aircraft carrier THEODORE ROOSEVELT in the South China Sea, March 22, 2001 (Pacific & Asia News Service):

Diplomatic relations between the United States and Red China were pushed to the brink early today when an American submarine torpedoed and sank a People's Republic of China coastal patrol boat off the coast of Hainan Island in the South China Sea. Details remain sketchy at this writing, but a spokesman for the U.S. Navy's Seventh Fleet said the boat was sunk in retaliation for yesterday's guided missile attack on the Taiwanese Navy destroyer LAO YANG (DDG-930) by the Chinese warship QINGDAO.

The LAO YANG was hit as it sought to sail through the Straits of Malacca and past the Spratlys, a group of islands the government in Beijing maintains belong to China. Jet fighters from the carrier USS THEODORE ROOSEVELT were dispatched to the scene of the attack and observed the sinking. They also flew over the suspected attacking PRC destroyer. One pilot reported the ships' crew were celebrating their deed.

The New China News Agency in Beijing today released a terse statement: "The brutal unprovoked attack and sinking of our patrol craft by the United States took place in Chinese waters. The incident that resulted in the loss of the Taiwan destroyer LAO YANG was caused when that ship knowingly tried to transit Chinese waters around the Nanshas a recognized territory of the People's Republic of China. Further attempts to challenge our lands, waters around or skies above them, will be met with similar and appropriate response by our military forces."

-end-

For the next few days you could cut the on-board tension with a knife. We continued to patrol in the western Pacific with everyone wondering when, where and if the next incident would occur. I continued interviewing crew members for future stories, but even seasoned veterans from the Gulf War ten years ago didn't want to talk about their reaction to the Chinese moves.

The air wing flew constantly. Take off, patrol two hours, and return to ship. Carrier landings are harrowing in daylight but at night they're something else! One pilot described it as: "Like trying to find a moving dimly lit postage stamp in a dark auditorium."

Captain Doug Collins, the air wing CO, invited me up to Pri-Fly one evening to watch plane retrieval. It was a motionless night in early April, with a skirt of low-level fog and temperature in the mid-40s. When the 97,000 ton ship wheeled dead-on into the wind at 30 knots if felt much colder. Heading into the wind gives the planes more lift.

The landing jets were visible only on radar as small blips; the only sounds being the pilot's radioing in-bound altitude, heading and distance from the ship's heaving flight deck, or the Landing Control Officer directing them in: "Call the ball, you're right on it," or maybe: "Come left five degrees and hold your nose up."

And then, as if from out of nowhere, another of the big F/A-18s would be right over the stern of the ship headed for one of the four arresting wires that would bring it from a speed of about 200 miles per hour to a screeching halt, in less than five seconds!

I couldn't help but admire these jet jockeys, but for me I'd take a quiet submarine at 300 feet below the ocean surface.

CHAPTER 92 - RED AND BLUE PROGRESS

April 26, 2001: Shanghai and Midway Island

Captain David K.Y. Wong and his crew on PEOPLE'S VICTORY were busy with the renovation of their HAN boat. Nuclear refueling was nearly complete, so installation of new sonar and communications equipment could begin in early summer.

The brilliant and cunning Wong had another weapon up his sleeve unknown to any of the crew, even his XO. The top level secret his wife Madam Shin had wrangled from that senator proved to be totally bogus. A smoke screen he easily saw through because his Navy already knew about permanent magnetic propulsion.

Wong had not fallen for the fish noises business. Unknown to the American intelligence community, he knew all about the real fish noises project thanks to a mole operating in the Pentagon, code name Fortune Cookie.

The audio system is what now engrossed David Wong and several cohorts.   They were nearly duplicating the American efforts to create a program of sea sounds that would help hide a submarine from the enemy. His capable assistant and expert sonarman, Chief Petty Officer Hwang, knew they would conquer the new battle device before fall.

That night before retiring to bed, Wong took out his ledger and wrote: April 26. Project now approximately 60% complete. Comm and sonar gear to be added in June, new audio system still under development. CPO Hwang confident of total perfection by target date. Still plan to be ready for sea trials by this autumn.

On the remote central Pacific Island of Midway, Captain Buzz Russell was also making a report on the progress of his major project, the creation of the revolutionary new attack submarine USS JAMESTOWN.

His boss, Vice Admiral Bernie Sharpe, was now stationed in Russell's back yard. He was well settled into his new job at Pearl Harbor and was due to visit the Midway operation within the next 48 hours.

The last time out here, before taking over as COMSUBPAC, the admiral had only seen parts of the hull, pieces of the equipment that would go into the control of the boat, and artist's renderings and engineering designs showing the final hull exterior and interior operational spaces. When Bernie got here this time he'd see the real McCoy.

The inspection tour began in the main workshop hangar. Dr. Lloyd Davidson of Mescod had been invited to Midway by Sharpe so they could review *Squidy's* progress together.

On a giant dolly rested the submarine's last section, a portion of the bow containing the sonar gear. A large crane gently maneuvered the equipment into the forward portion of the hull. This whole thing still looks like some giant fish, Bernie thought to himself. Finally, the Navymen and their civilian engineering colleagues from LaJolla got the sections together and Dr. Davidson told the group to stand back and watch! "Now we'll see what submariners 20 years from now will be taking for granted."

Bernie was left speechless with what transpired in the next few minutes. A band of cotton-like material encircled the point where the remaining two sections would be joined, and on a signal from the chief engineer a brilliant flash of light exploded from the joint. When the accompanying cloud of smoke cleared, Bernie and the others saw only one hull section!

Unlike welding, there was no seam. The entire boat was one single sheet of steel, stem to stern; not a shred of evidence it had actually been built in nine different sections.

"That, gentlemen," proclaimed Dr. Davidson pridefully, "is what we call fusion. It will be the norm on all future U.S. submarines, and hopefully all new Navy warships over the next two decades."

As the shop workers began to clean up the area and

prepare *Squidy* to be moved into the new dry-dock facility, Lloyd walked Bernie and Buzz back to the office.

"That fusion exercise came off perfectly. I'm not at all surprised at the great job Captain Russell's people are doing; they seem to be loving their work."

"Very true, Lloyd. We have guys who give up their days off so they can keep working on the portion of the job they've been assigned. I'd say fully half our crew is taking only one of the two off-days they get every week. This is absolutely the best bunch of sailors I've ever commanded."

CHAPTER 93 - BACK TO SEA WITH MISTER V

April & May, 2001: The South China Sea

If memory serves me, it was in April when we got an up close look at some Chinese Air Force planes. Our CIC and airborne scout planes had been tracking them for several minutes so it was no surprise they were headed our way.

We didn't want them to fly over us, so several of our F/A-18s launched to let the PRC pilots know our feelings. They screamed in anyway off our port beam, immediately kicking in their afterburners and going into a steep climb. Moments later they reappeared, waggled wings in their version of screw you, then headed back to Hainan Island.

The ROOSEVELT CVBG was due for rotation in early May, relieved by another carrier battle group. My ship and two others were scheduled to visit Singapore before returning home. I requested permission to remain aboard and then take a COD flight to the new carrier with some other officers returning to the group staff. Captain Ballard approved my request, and a week later we sailed into one of the cleanest and most beautiful cities in Asia.

Shore leave for me wasn't just fun and games in an exotic port. I spent a few hours with the PANS stringer gathering information for future stories. I'd also scheduled a meeting with the Royal Navy Military Attaché. He looked like something out of a British history book: tall with ramrod stiff posture, classic English accent, imposing features with a magnificently bushy handlebar mustache.

CDR Nigel Colin Smythe-Billings, RN, and I had met on several occasions at Washington functions, so we were not strangers. A good portion of our conversation was devoted to the sinking of the LAO YANG. It was not for attribution, but the wide-ranging interview gave me a better feeling about what the Brits and their former Commonwealth members might do if a shooting war with China became a reality.

After asking all the questions I could think of, Nigel invited me to join him for a drink at the historic Raffles Hotel. The real old Raffles was now surrounded by a giant high-rise. Luckily the developers kept the original hotel and its grounds, and the great Long Bar so famous for its Singapore Sling. I ordered one just to say that I had done so at the original Raffles, and then returned to my regular poison, gin and tonic.

Nigel suggested we also walk a couple blocks to the cricket grounds where a match was always underway on weekends. The downtown club overlooks the harbor and was another of the great old Asian landmarks I could now claim to have visited in person. Who knows, I thought to myself, I might write a mystery that can only be solved by finding clues at the Long Bar at the Raffles and in the Singapore Cricket Club.

The ROOSEVELT got underway Monday morning April 30th and in several hours we were close enough to the CVBG to take the COD flight to USS CARL VINSON, my newest home at sea .

Life on MISTER V was a carbon copy of my days on TEDDY. A meeting with the ship's captain and the CVBG boss had been set up for me by the XO. At 1500 precisely I knocked on the skipper's cabin door and heard "Enter." Captain Robert Buck Henshaw greeted me and introduced Rear Admiral Theodore R. Davidson, head of the battle group. The admiral asked how I liked Singapore. I highlighted my visits to the Raffles, the Cricket Club and a Sunday jog around the delightful Botanical Gardens on Nassim Hill.

"Been there, done that!" Henshaw smiled. "Now, let's get to the reason for this meeting, Mr. Lincoln, or should I call you Chief Lincoln?"

I indicated either was fine with me. The skipper continued: "Since you left the ROOSEVELT we've identified a lot of increased message traffic out of the PRC's Shanghai Navy headquarters. Our satellites show several ships leaving that base, and the base on Hainan Island over the last 24 hours."

371

"We don't know as much about the PRC submarines as we'd like to, but all our surface ships and subs have been ordered to increase surveillance on the Chinese boats and if they make sonar contact with any of them to stick with them for as long as possible."

A quick update of known enemy ship positions and an overview of our military status in the region completed the briefing. Like Captain Ballard and Admiral Williams on ROOSEVELT, these two senior Navymen made me feel a part of their team. I told them I'd provide copies of my stories for use on the ship's TV newswire.

It had been over a month since filing my last major piece on the sinking of the PRC patrol craft. This would be my chance to do some more Ernie Pyle style of writing. Not that I thought I could ever equal his work but it was worth a try.

BEIJING ORDERS MORE NAVY SHIPS TO SEA
INCREASED CHINESE MILITARY MESSAGE TRAFFIC
SAILORS AND AIRMEN TAKE WAIT AND SEE ATTITUDE

By: Dan Lincoln

On board the Navy aircraft carrier USS CARL VINSON in the South China Sea: April 30, 2001 (Pacific & Asia News Service):

The head of the U.S. Navy's carrier battle group currently on duty in the South China Sea today reported that China has dispatched several warships from naval bases at Shanghai and Hainan Island. PANS has learned from reliable sources that U.S. Navy ships on station here have detected increased military message traffic from both Shanghai and Beijing. So far, there has been no return to actual shooting in the area. The last episode was March 22nd when a PRC patrol craft was sunk by a U.S. Navy submarine in retaliation for the attack and sinking of the Taiwan Navy guided missile destroyer LAO YANG on March 21st.

For the thousands of American sailors, pilots and air crews on-board this huge aircraft carrier, and for other thousands on cruisers, destroyers and submarines here in the waters off the People's Republic of China, it's time to fish or cut bait.

I spoke with one pilot who had been ordered to maintain a position over the sinking Taiwanese Navy destroyer attacked while attempting to pass through the Straits of Malacca. LT Eric Walther of Blairstown, New Jersey, said he was over the Chinese Navy guided missile destroyer QINGDAO shortly after it fired on the LAO YANG, and he flew close enough to the ship to see their reaction to the sinking they had just caused.

"I flew low and slow over that PRC bastard and about 30 sailors and officers came out on deck as I passed over the ship. They all had big grins on their faces and most of them flipped me the digit! They were proud of what they had done, and knew we weren't going to fire on them. It was as if they were saying: We'll do whatever we want to in our waters, and you Americans can just buzz off. If I'd been able to I'd have dropped all my bombs and fired the missiles I had on my plane right then and there. But the orders came: Do not fire unless fired upon. Frankly, it sucks, and you can print that."

Most of the men and women I talk to are ready to fight, if provoked, and more than one told me they couldn't understand why top military authorities were holding them back. If the current build-up of Chinese warships off Taiwan cruising near this carrier battle group continues, Navy sources told PANS that any future provocation would result in what was called: the covers coming off and all offensive weapons being readied to fire when ordered.

-end-

CHAPTER 94 - MODERN DAY PIRATES

May 1, 2001: Spratly Islands, South China Sea

"Heading two-zero-five degrees, airspeed two-seven-five knots, altitude ten thousand feet." Major Donald K.W. Tang slowly and deliberately directed his PLA Air Force squadron. "ETA to target, six minutes."

In his headphones he heard General Chung K.B. Fong, head of the PLA Air Force, who was in the co-pilot's seat: "This important mission, Major, is the first step toward regaining our world position. Much time and effort have been invested so it must be accomplished with perfection." Fong's agile mind quickly replayed the past year he spent planning every moment of this sortie. He knew that no foreign power would dare intervene.

"Sir," Tang said, "we are honored to have you aboard this flight to witness the return of the Nanshas to our country."

"Thank you, comrade. This *is* a most historic day, not just for the re-taking of the Nanshas and doing it on May Day, but for what this will allow us to do in the near future. These islands are but the overture to a bigger conquest: the return of Taiwan to the Motherland."

"Over the target now, General."

"Very well. Drop the bombs."

It was over in less than five minutes. The island's tiny runway and outbuildings were burning ruins and like small toys tossed recklessly about an entire force of aircraft and vehicles was smashed to smithereens. More than half the island's military population was wiped out. General Fong, wanting to put a very large exclamation point to the operation, continued the murderous onslaught calling for a bombardment from PRC destroyers and frigates lying off shore.

374

Fong gleefully exclaimed: "This is the best training our shipboard crews have had in years." About an hour after the bombing a thousand Red Army troops stormed ashore and began killing anything still alive.

Having re-read all the pre-attack speculation in the press, the Taiwanese Air Force detachment on the main Spratly Island expected the worst. They had to stay to make a show of face against their Mainland cousins, but they weren't stupid either.

When incoming Chinese aircraft began appearing on their radar screens the ROC pilots went airborne, vectoring their jet fighters and hoping for a chance to get in a few licks against the Red Air Force. A few good licks would be all they got as Hainan-based fighters trailed their bombers by just five minutes and soon were giving the Taiwanese defenders a real good fight.

When all the air-to-air shooting ceased the ROC claimed a slight victory, 6 losses against 9 for the PRC flyers. The remaining Taipei-based crews knew when to retire to fight another day, breaking off and speeding east toward the Philippines.

The attackers waged a vicious but thankfully short bombardment, thoroughly decimating the small airbase on the main island. Though some underground shelters gave protection they were quickly overrun by the swarming PLA army troops landing on nearby beaches. No prisoners were taken alive.

Before the sun set the Spratly Islands were truly in the hands of the Peoples Republic. It had been like declaring a war and no one came. General Fong was right. Nobody intervened and nobody attempted to help the Taiwanese, not even their American allies. This was especially disheartening to Rear Admiral Davidson the Battle Group Commander responsible for patrolling the area. He had been called to his Flag Plot early that morning and shown on air and surface radar scopes the progress of the PRC invasion force.

His requests for permission to launch retaliatory fighters were denied by every command level up the chain, ostensibly all the way to the White House. Orders were to maintain patrol course patterns, avoiding any contact with the attackers. It was hands-off. Not the kind of decision a seasoned Navy officer wants to hear in time of battle. However, it wasn't totally unexpected.

Admiral Davidson called a meeting of the Flag Staff, all ship's department heads, and squadron leaders for 0900. He strode to the podium and the assembly fell silent. He was ready to command his eager warriors into battle, but his hands were tied by the Capitol's political correctness.

"Ladies and gentlemen, you are aware that early this morning the Chinese Peoples Liberation Army attacked and brutally killed approximately 25 Taiwanese military pilots and ground crew on the Spratly Islands, several hundred miles south of our current position." He pointed to the Spratlys on the map.

"The airbase was destroyed. A landing force of about 1,000 Red Army soldiers now occupies the main island, and a statement from Beijing claims the entire island chain to be occupied by the PRC. Beijing says they've owned the islands since 110 A.D. and will now actively administer the Nanshas."

"We have been in contact with our allies on Taiwan but they have yet to determine a course of action. They've manned that airbase for over 20 years. Our flotilla has been ordered to Condition BRAVO. We will maintain position one day's sailing time from the Spratlys. The President will address the nation this evening. That is all I have for now."

The grumbling began before Admiral Davidson could exit the Wardroom. Everyone wanted action, now. But all they could do was remain on alert waiting to see what Washington, in its infinite wisdom, would or would not do.

I headed back to my quarters, opened my lap-top and began my story, including as many quotes from the admiral as possible. When it was finished I dialed Ben's unlisted home phone number and after quite a few rings he answered: "Ben, it's Dan. I have an emergency story. Can we make any papers?"

"Geeze, Dan, it's nine at night here. This had better be

hot."

"Ben we've got real shooting out here. It's a flash for the international wire. The Chinese attacked and overran the Spratly Islands today, about 5 pm your time. If you turn on your tape recorder I'll dictate highlights and you can get it on the wire before some of the other services and networks do."

"Stand by, Dan." After what seemed like an eternity he finally came back on the phone and said: "Okay, it's recording. Go for it." Five or six minutes later I finished and Ben said it was all on the tape and he was headed for the office. He obviously made it in record time because an hour later my laptop gave a signal that I had incoming mail. I opened it and saw my story.

CHINESE INVADE SPRATLY ISLANDS
25 TAIWANESE SLAIN
SHIPPING EMBARGO EXPECTED
IN SOUTH CHINA SEA

By: Dan Lincoln

Aboard the Navy aircraft carrier USS CARL VINSON, with the U.S. Seventh Fleet in the South China Sea, May 1, 2001 (Pacific & Asia News Service):

Chinese aircraft and naval units bombed the main South China Sea island of the Spratly Island group at dawn today, killing all on the island including approximately 25 Taiwanese Air Force ground crew, and pilots who had scrambled their planes to intercept the invaders. The government in Taipei has yet to announce what action it intends to take, if any.

Seventh Fleet Carrier Battle Group Commander Rear Admiral Theodore R. Davidson, USN, told a gathering of staff, pilots and ship's officers on the USS CARL VINSON that aircraft bombing and shelling, and missiles fired from off-shore PRC Navy frigates and destroyers, totally wiped out the Taiwanese airbase. A PLA landing force, estimated to be about 1,000 men, secured the base and declared the island chain to be occupied by The People's Republic of China.

The further occupation by PLA troops and claim of sole ownership of the more than 100 tiny islands and coral atolls brings the bigger question of whether the PRC will declare the former Spratlys to be an Exclusive Economic Zone, allowing them to declare a 500 mile offshore limit to all shipping in the region. Such a limit would preclude most commercial shipping and naval warship passage through the Straits of Malacca.

U.S. Secretary of Defense James A. Gaston, said discussions were being held with all allies in the region, and that Taiwan had not yet decided on its course of action.

Admiral Edgar R. Lynch, Chairman of the Joint Chiefs and Chief of Naval Operations, said the U.S. would not stand idly by while Beijing decided how and when it would control the sea lanes of this vital part of the Pacific.

When asked just what specific action America would take, the JCS Chairman said: "Our response is being planned at this very moment, and the leaders of the PRC must understand they will not be allowed to get away with this 21st Century piracy."

Ships of the U.S. Seventh Fleet have been advised to establish Condition BRAVO readiness, one step below battle conditions. Secretary Gaston said President Crane has been fully briefed on the situation and the Pentagon is in continuous contact with the White House. The President is expected to address the nation at 9 pm (EDT) tonight.

So far there have been no statements of further intent from the Chinese government in Beijing other than to say the Spratlys, which they claim have been Chinese since 110 A.D., are actually the Nanshas and have merely been liberated and returned to Chinese control.

-end-

Within hours, Ben gave me my marching orders: Come home! He had already spoken with Admiral Sharpe in Hawaii and said for me to standby for orders. They arrived early the next morning and I was to fly off the ship at 0900 the following day.

Admiral Davidson and Captain Henshaw came down to see me off and thank me for my stay on the CARL VINSON. They said they were pleased with the results of my journalistic efforts and that I'd be welcomed back whenever I wanted to return.

At last, I would be heading back to the arms of my sweet, sweet Janice, and did I have some tales for her.

I had no idea if I'd ever sail on a Navy ship again. I'd get my final answer, however, too soon.

CHAPTER 95 - SHOOTING FISH IN A BARREL

May 1, 2001: The Washington Embassy of the PRC

Ambassador Wu and Cultural Affairs Attaché Tong sat in the Ambassador's office watching the NBC Nightly News. The Spratly attack was every network's lead story. Some described it as: shooting fish in a barrel. The usual talking-head TV anchor experts spewed speculation, especially those on the alphabet-soup networks and cable news outlets. Would the U.S. retaliate or sit on its hands? What if China blockades the entire South China Sea?

Everyone referenced the CNO's statement about holding the PRC responsible and not allowing it to 'get away with this 21st Century piracy.' No further military action had occurred in the past 24 hours but there were calls for a U.N. debate, which was good news for Wu and Tong because they fully realized anything under discussion at the U.N. would go nowhere!

They postponed celebrating knowing what else would happen within a fortnight; something they knew would really arouse the U.S.

CHINA DROPS BAMBOO CURTAIN
OVER SOUTH CHINA SEA
WORLD SHIPPING TOLD: DO NOT PASS GO

By: Dan Lincoln

Washington, D.C., May 11, 2001 (Pacific & Asia News Service):

The Peoples Republic of China today invoked an Exclusive Economic Zone (EEZ) around the former Spratly Islands, totally forbidding shipping within 500 miles of the coasts of the more than 100 islands and coral atolls that make up what the PRC calls the Nanshas.

What impact this will have on trans-ocean shipping is yet to be determined, but not being able to sail through the Straits of Malacca will mean at least another 1,000 miles per transit from Singapore to ports such as Hong Kong, Taipei and Tokyo since ships will have to go around the Philippines. This will affect cargo container ships, oil and gas tankers, cruise liners and warships of the U.S. and allied nations.

It is not known what, if any, retaliation will be taken by the U.S. government for the May 1st attack on the Spratlys, and the killing of 25 Taiwanese military personnel stationed on the islands.

President John Paul Crane, who told the nation a week and a half ago that "retaliation would be taken if the Chinese insisted on armed force in the region," has been meeting with western allies and the Taiwanese, but no action has been announced.

The U.S. Ambassador to the United Nations will speak to the Security Council tomorrow morning, but observers say that since China is a member of that five nation Council, no action will be allowed thanks to its veto power.

In a related story, Lloyds of London, the huge maritime insurance company, has announced that effective today rates on policies for ships transiting the South China Sea or waters of the southwestern Pacific Ocean will be doubled.

-end-

CHAPTER 96 - JAIL TIME FOR HENRY

June 5, 2001: Washington, D.C.

Back home at the C-C, I collected kudos from my fellow newsies, but praise from your peers can be oh so fleeting. Like about a week, and then it was the regular gossip as summer arrived, washing spring away in a deluge of rainstorms. Cherry blossoms had long fled, and the capitol would soon be swarming with tourists.

Delightedly, a welcome thawing was happening between Janice and me pushed along by a few dinner dates and drives into the Virginia countryside. She was inundated at her new intel assignment, and I couldn't help wondering if we'd ever become an item. I doubted it but deep down I wished we would.

Another unresolved part of my spy story saga clarified when I opened the Washington Post and saw its front page story:

FORMER SENATOR ANDERSON
GETS JAIL TIME
TIP-OFF OF CHINESE SPY RING
MITIGATING CIRCUMSTANCES

The brief story carried a photo of Anderson leaving Federal Court. "Hank, the times are showing on you," I said to the wall. With a severe frown plastered on his face he looked like an old man. "Well, now I know why you haven't returned my calls," I said to the photo and then scanned the story.

Washington, D.C., June 5, 2001 (Associated Press):

Henry B. Anderson, former U.S. Senator from Minnesota and ranking minority member of the Senate Armed Services Committee, was sentenced to five years in federal prison by U.S. District Court Judge Miles

Bernstein yesterday. Anderson had been found guilty of treason for his role in the Red Chinese mother-daughter spy ring case last winter.

Anderson gave classified information about U.S. Navy submarine development projects to Georgetown art shop owner Lily Shin. The info was then transmitted to the Beijing government via the People's Republic of China Embassy in Washington.

Judge Bernstein suspended four of the five years of prison for what he called mitigating circumstances. He told the court at the time of sentencing that: 'Because Senator Anderson brought details of what he believed was a blackmailing scheme by Ms. Shin and her daughter Cheryl Leong to the government's attention, and because he did not knowingly participate in soliciting classified information for a foreign nation, the degree of punishment is adequate at one year followed by four years of probation.'

Anderson resigned his Senate seat on January 20th this year, and has been replaced in Congress by Sen. Dennis Magnuson, a former Minnesota state legislator from Duluth. Sen. Magnuson was appointed by Minnesota Governor Carl Malmquist shortly after the Anderson resignation.

I thought to myself, the fall is always harder when it comes from the top rung of the ladder. I wondered if we'd ever hear from Hank Anderson again.

CHAPTER 97 - REDS STIR UP THE KETTLE

July 2, 2001: Washington, D.C.

"The South China Sea is about to boil over," Admiral Sharpe told me during a phone call from Honolulu late Monday morning. "The PRC has ratcheted up the ante by increasing sea patrols around the Spratlys and harassing foreign vessels, including several of our Navy warships."

Additional costs for ships avoiding the Straits of Malacca were monumental. We and our allies were growing more and more pissed over the situation, and increased naval exercises by the Red Chinese led many insiders to speculate that a shooting war over the Spratlys was definitely in the cards.

"Do *you* think we're headed for a shoot-out?" I asked.

"Hell if I know, Dan. You've been there and seen it all close-up. What's your take?"

"I just report what I see, Admiral. Not my job to speculate. Let the idiots on TV do that." With a snicker he gave me an Aloha and signed off.

Ben Huntley's head popping in my door intruded on my concentration. "Deadline on your Independence Day piece is 3 pm today. No grace period."

"No problema, senor. Comprende?"

"Yea, I got it," Ben replied, but remember, 3 pm today. No tarde, comprende?"

"With Congress headed for summer vacation, how are you treating their hands-off on the proposed defense budget?"

"Boss man, you worry too much. Have I ever let you down...don't answer that. Yeah, I have plenty of materials. Since Senator Anderson went to the Gray Bar Hilton I've built-up a pretty good relationship with the head honcho on the Armed Services Committee. So, worry not, I'll have it on your desk by deadline."

"Okay, I'm headed to lunch. Want me to bring you

some-thing?" Ben asked. "Maybe a tuna sandwich with a side of MGD?"

I finished the last paragraph, saved my document to a disk and e-mailed it to composing. Actually I was quite proud of the piece and hoped it might open some eyes in capitals around the globe. Barring any major changes from Mr. Huntley it would be on the PANS wire that afternoon in plenty of time for TV broadcast commentaries and U.S. holiday, as well as weekend editions of newspapers worldwide.

BEIJING ORDERS INCREASED NAVAL EXERCISES WORLD SHIPPING INCENSED OVER SPRATLY ECONOMIC ZONE U.S. AND KEY ALLIES CALL ON PRC TO RETRACT SPRATLY EEZ

By: Dan Lincoln

Washington, D.C., July 3, 2001 (Pacific & Asia News Service):

Informed western military sources report increased naval exercises by the Peoples Republic of China off the island of Taiwan. The island has been home to the Republic of China government since 1949, but is still claimed by Beijing as a breakaway province of the Chinese Motherland.

Red Chinese Navy destroyers, frigates, patrol boats and submarines have been observed conducting training as close as five miles from the Taiwanese coast. U.S. Navy ships assigned to the Seventh Fleet in the South China Sea, and other allied warships, report tracking PRC ships and positively identifying their submarines for the past several weeks.

A May 1st attack by the PLA Navy and Air Forces on the Spratly Islands cost the lives of about 25 Taiwanese soldiers and pilots, and downed six of their aircraft that had scrambled to do battle with the incoming PRC forces. The island is now being occupied by about 1,000 PLA army troops.

In response to a worldwide outcry against the takeover, Beijing said the islands have been under the control of mainland China since about 110 A.D., and are called the Nanshas, not the Spratly Islands. The PRC government maintains the May action was merely one of retrieving what is rightly their property. Prior to takeover, the Spratlys were jointly claimed by Malaysia, Vietnam, the Philippines, China and Taiwan, but only the Taiwanese maintained any forces on the group of 100 small islands and coral atolls.

When Beijing advised the world in mid-May that it was declaring a 500-mile Exclusive Economic Zone around the Nanshas, shipping times and costs to deliver ocean freight and oil skyrocketed. Lloyds of London, the major insurance carrier used by shippers, doubled its policy rates for vessels transiting waters in and around southeast Asia. Taiwan and other allied nations have complained loudly to the world press, and yesterday they, along with Japan, Australia, Great Britain, India and the U.S., filed a petition with the United Nations calling on that body to place sanctions on Red Chinese exports and demand Beijing withdraw the Spratly EEZ.

When asked if America was prepared to go to war over Taiwan if that nation is attacked by the PRC, a State Department spokesman said: 'We have treaties in that part of the world, including a 1954 mutual defense pact with Taiwan. Any attempt to take over Taiwan by the PRC or anyone else would definitely not be in the best interests of the United States.' A Navy spokesman at the Pentagon was more to the point when he said: 'If China or any other country opens fire on our Taiwanese allies, or takes a shot at any U.S. or allied Navy warship, we will not hesitate to return the fire.'

The current standoff between China and Taiwan has put Beijing/ Washington diplomatic relations on a foreboding track. Unless the EEZ situation is resolved soon there could be navies of several other nations joining the U.S. Navy in tracking the PRC. Those numbers alone might lead to a shooting war, one not really desired by any of the parties currently involved.

-end-

CHAPTER 98 - AND THE WALLS
CAME TUMBLING DOWN

September 11, 2001: The World

The world changed forever when those two jet airliners were deliberately slammed into New York's World Trade Center. People will never forget exactly where they were at those moments.

Far out in the blue Pacific on quiet Midway Island, Buzz Russell and his dedicated team labored late into the night. Going over the final plans for *Squidy's* sea trials, they were interrupted by a phone ringing. Buzz grabbed it and heard his executive officer, CDR Ellis Sherman, shakily announce: "Captain, a passenger jet just flew into one of the World Trade Center towers in New York City. The TV networks have it on right now. They say the plane was a hijacked American Airlines jet."

With a calmness he had earned over many years of unpredictable events, Buzz said: "Thank you, Commander. Keep monitoring those news broadcasts and make sure our comm links are up for CINCPAC and CINCPACFLT."

Hanging up, Buzz moved swiftly into action, first calling the CO of the small detachment of Marines assigned to base security. "Have your men fully armed, rounds in their chambers; deploy two- man teams in jeeps on perimeter sweeps hourly. All other troops will report to the shops to provide protection for those working on the new boat."

"Aye aye, sir. May I ask what the situation is, sir? My men will want to know."

"Tell them a jet airliner is reported to have crashed into the World Trade Center in New York City. Authorities believe it was deliberate, and the jet was hijacked. That's all they need to know."

Buzz turned up his TV volume and joined the world as a witness to the horror of the moment. Before their eyes, a second jetliner rammed into the second tower, which erupted in acrid black smoke and fire. "Holy shit, what the hell is happening?" Buzz cried out.

Flames shot out of the towers and ashes fell as from a volcanic eruption on people running in the street. Dozens of fire and police units converged at the site trying to help people escape from the twin 110-story buildings.

As the Navy captain watched the scene in lower Manhattan, the XO came back into his office, handed Russell a clipboard full of messages, and then immediately left. The first, from CINCPACFLT, ordered all ships and naval stations to condition ALPHA, the highest defense posture preceding full-out war. Crew leaves were canceled and those already on leave were called back to the ship. No civilians were allowed on base without a Navy officer escort and base perimeter security was beefed up to include guard dogs and patrols by sailors and Marines with fully loaded weapons. Buzz said quietly: "Done that already."

By noon the twin towers had collapsed, 200 were dead at the Pentagon, and a fourth plane, believed to be targeted at the U.S. Capitol, crashed into a field south of Pittsburgh. Ultimately the civilian death toll would escalate to nearly 3,000.

Who are these people, the skipper wondered. Didn't the FBI and CIA know about them? What went wrong at Boston's Logan Airport where two of the death-plane flights originated? Didn't the guards check passengers and luggage for guns and other weapons? Americans quickly realized we had become weak and vulnerable to attack, even from within our own borders. We had let our guard down and the country had become a base for terrorists entering on student visas or by crossing the border at some unguarded point and staying as illegal residents. Who checked these people? No one. Who allowed them to stay? Everyone, as long as it didn't interfere in personal lives. The old acronym NIMBY quickly came to mind!

CHAPTER 99 - THE BUCK STOPS HERE

September 20, 2001: The White House

America was stunned. For the first time in its history the entire nation felt totally vulnerable. Were more terrorist attacks coming? Where? When?

The facts slowly emerged, showing how the attackers embedded themselves in the fabric of everyday American life. Sixteen of the 19 hijackers on the planes were Saudis. All were radical Islamic terrorists, most loyal to their long-time proclaimed leader Osama bin Laden. If America wasn't familiar with his name by now, he would soon become the number one subject on the FBI's most wanted list, and the cause of America's entrance into the worldwide war on terrorism.

Air travel was just beginning to return to some semblance of normalcy and people tried valiantly to live their lives in a familiar pattern. But in Washington things continued to tumble like clothes in a dryer. Someone or some group with their own agenda of hate began mailing the deadly anthrax virus to top political leaders. The Capitol and other buildings on the Hill were closed for a week.

We at PANS didn't escape the threat either. About a week after the first anthrax letter was found in Congress a letter arrived addressed only to PANS. Rhonda the receptionist, while routinely opening all our non-personally addressed mail, came across a plain #10 envelope, and upon taking out the paper inside a small cloud of powder fell on her and her desk.

Jack O'Neill, standing nearby, grabbed Rhonda by the arm and quickly led her to the ladies room, telling her to wash off as much as possible. Jack yelled for 911 and I placed the call. Within minutes a DCFD Hazmat truck and crew swarmed our offices. An expert with the team quickly determined it wasn't anthrax and that Rhonda was fine.

When they left some form of normalcy returned. As I had wondered after my July 4th hit-and-run, and the drive-by shooting that sent two bullets through my leg two Christmases ago, was really it me this powdery warning was aimed at?

That evening President Crane told the nation just what it needed to hear. He saluted the magnificent jobs done by New York City firemen, police and EMS personnel. And he made a strong call-to-arms for all Americans to stand tall against the terrorists, refusing to let them dictate how we would live our daily lives.

He continued by saying: "We are prepared to take the battle to these Islamic radicals and members of the al-Qaida network in their known hideouts in Afghanistan and Pakistan. We will soon do just that via Navy missile attacks from our ships in the Gulf of Arabia, bombing runs from aircraft off Navy carriers, and by special troops that will attack from the ground. We'll work with the anti-terrorists patriots in Afghanistan and go after the rebel Taliban forces loyal to bin Laden and his men."

It was the kind of address symbolic of John F. Kennedy's 1962 call to Nikita Khrushchev to withdraw his Soviet missiles and troops from Cuba. It was also akin to the old World War II fireside chats given by Franklin D. Roosevelt to pump up domestic spirits and renew America's dedication to fighting against those who would attack our country, for whatever reason or ideology the enemy practiced.

The realities of September 11th were now a part of day-to-day life in America. U.S. military bases were closed to all but active duty military and cleared civilians. Airlines had canceled hundreds of flights and airports were a nightmare for passengers trying to get through security. We'd have to adapt to a whole raft of new problems and new terrorist activities. Life as we knew it was now changed forever.

CHAPTER 100 - DONE AND ALMOST DONE

September 24, 2001: Midway Island

"I've got some good news and some bad news," Bernie said. "The bad news is this terrorist business has everyone on alert status around the clock. I scrambled two boats that weren't slated for another tour until next year and the entire fleet is basically on wartime alert."

"And the good news is?" Buzz asked.

"My flight to Midway is only two and a half hours now and I'm about to pay you a visit."

"Well, things are just about wrapped up here. We came in a bit late on the June 30th date for final completion but the boat is in the water and we've given her a few test dives. Frankly, Admiral, she's a dream! I can't wait to be on her every day and take her into the fray, if that comes."

"It will come, Buzz. You can count on it. I'm positive the PRC will make a move on Taiwan thinking this terrorist situation has us completely distracted. Back to my visit. I'll depart Honolulu tomorrow at 1400. We need to meet as soon as I arrive and then I want to see *Squidy* and make sure you've got everything you need to have her ready to join the Fleet right after Christmas. Is Lloyd Davidson still there?"

"No sir, he left around Labor Day, once he was sure the boat was seaworthy and it could do what Mescod designed it to do. Also, Lloyd said he and Art Humphries would like to come back out for the ship's commissioning so we need to set that date as well."

The runway was clear of albatross when the admiral's jet touched down. "Good to see you again, Buzz. I'm sure it's a lot quieter here than it is at Pearl."

"That's a fact. Your cottage is all set and we can talk there after dinner. My mess guys will bring over all the fixins at 1830. Come tomorrow you're going to be even more

391

impressed with what you'll see than you were last time."

The evening was spent going over everything from budget numbers to weapons systems and from initial sea trial reports to the winding down of *Project Squidy*. All elements passed muster with flying colors, including being on budget.

The civilian team of engineers, contractors and shipyard workers had finished their jobs the first of the month. A small corps of maritime engineers from NAVSEA Systems and the Pearl Harbor Naval Shipyard remained. The XO, WEPS and COB had arrived on island along with a skeleton crew.

The balance of the 60-man crew was due to arrive during October so that training, final sea trials and dive tests could be made before December first. Based on that schedule Buzz suggested the commissioning ceremony should be December 7th, the anniversary of the Japanese attack on Pearl in 1941.

"I like that idea a lot, Buzz. I'll work on it as soon as I get back. We're only inviting the SECDEF, SECNAV and CNO from D.C. I'm sure we can get them to Oahu for the annual memorial ceremony on USS ARIZONA and then fly them out here for an afternoon commissioning. Is that okay for you and the crew?"

"Sounds excellent, sir. You're up to date now. I'll pick you up at 0730, we'll join the crew for chow and then review the boat."

To say that Bernie was pleased with what he saw that next day would be the understatement of the year. The JAMESTOWN was the most unlikely looking submarine he'd seen in his lifetime. *Squidy* looked more like a dead whale than a sub. Compared to conventional boats she was short and stubby with almost no conning tower, and sat in shallow water drawing almost no draft. She was painted traditional flat black, and just like the inner hull he'd witnessed on his last trip here, there were no exterior seams to be seen on the entire ship.

"Beauty in motion is all I can say," he commented after looking over the new 400 million dollar boy toy.   Captain Russell and the three engineers accompanying the party merely smiled. It was more than a boat, it was their personal creation.   It was their newest and best friend.   No other experience they could have in a lifetime would equal their love for *Squidy*.

The admiral spent the rest of the day on board going into every compartment, every control space, the crew's quarters and dining facilities. Even scale drawings had given no hint of the amazing roominess without a nuclear reactor or huge engineering spaces. The new propulsion system was so simple he wondered why minds greater than his hadn't thought of it in the last 30 years.

With less crew there was more space for creature comforts: two sets of clothes washers and dryers double the number in today's L.A. class boats, and space up forward by the torpedo tubes that held a mini-gym complete with two exercise machines and weights. The feature he liked best was found in the berthing compartments. They still had racks but these were far larger in size, with several more inches of room above the bed, and twice the locker capacity.

The veteran submariner checked out the control room, looked through the periscopes and had the COB show him the radar and sonar capabilities. He even asked to see the galleys and food storage spaces; huge compared to other boats.

By late afternoon the admiral was more than convinced that USS JAMESTOWN would be the revolutionary force in the submarine Navy he envisioned.

September 27, 2001: Shanghai, China

Two submarine skippers on parallel courses were having decidedly different days. Buzz Russell had completed construction of a new concept in submarines, and his boss was enjoying the ride of his life, describing it as like Disneyland but a helluva lot more exciting.

PLA Captain David K.Y. Wong's ride was filled with bumps and twists. Hardly able to control his mounting anger he sat scribbling in his diary. The renovations on his submarine were running far behind schedule. The reactor re-fueling was completed three months late and now the installation of interior systems was way past the date for his targeted sea trials, originally set for early autumn.

Wong had wasted the entire morning arguing with his Navy superiors. Two weeks ago the XO had told him several pieces of the new equipment being installed on PEOPLE'S VICTORY were faulty including sonar and radar systems. They were made in Germany and Russia and cost a high dollar, but they didn't work on his boat.

The captain wished he had gone to the Fen Shui Master who could have used bagua to show him when and where those systems should have been built instead of buying them from the Russians and Germans.

LCDR Leong's techs had tried everything, even re-wiring some of the gear, but nothing seemed compatible with the boat's electrical system.

Pissed off big time Captain Wong yelled at the shipyard's head accountant: "I want to see the invoices for this equipment. You tell me it's all brand new, and yet it doesn't work! Why is that? Do you suppose those damned Ruskies and Krauts sent us re-conditioned sets? Show me the paperwork and I'll get those thieves to come down here and personally install the systems."

The special equipment installation on which Wong's most trusted CPO was working was on target, based on the information and specifications Fortune Cookie got from Pentagon sources. Wong was pleased with that project, but he noted in his diary: I must be ready to challenge the American submarines, but it appears that will not likely happen before the new year. This is not good.

CHAPTER 101 - RETURN TO THE CRIME SCENE

October 1, 2001: Washington, D.C.

With the world now topsy turvy, I decided I needed to be back at the front with the Seventh Fleet in case my sources were correct and China opted to make a sneak attack on Taiwan or our CVBG. I absolutely had to be writing stories exposing the Red Chinese as bullies who can *never* be trusted.

I also needed to be in Honolulu, looking again into Simon's murder. I wanted that loose thread in my story tied-up soon. Now ready to sell Ben on the idea I headed to his office. He waved me in and said: "Well, what is it this time?"

"Ben, you may not like this but I think the most productive place for me over the next few weeks might be back in that Seventh Fleet Carrier Battle Group. Something in my gut says China isn't finished with her aggressiveness."

"You may be right, but why can't you do the stories from here, not 12,000 miles away?"

"I could do that, but I wouldn't have access to all the people and first-hand knowledge of events. I need to write top-notch stories, and there's nothing that can replace being on the firing line. Do you remember the Spratly mess?"

I looked at Ben as he asked me: "What would you write about that you can't get here or from the Pentagon?"

"Mostly feature stories with the rank and file in the fleet and the pilots that fly training missions every day so they'll be ready if the PRC starts a shooting match. Also, I hope to get the admiral's approval to ride one of his attack submarines."

"I'll tell you what. *If* you get Admiral Sharpe to order you back there as a DOD accredited correspondent, and *if* he'll pay for your round-trip airfare, and *if* he'll try to get you on a nuclear sub, and *if* he agrees to have you back here no later than right after the holidays, *then* I'll approve the trip. What do you say to that Chief?"

"I say you got a deal Mr. Huntley!"

CHAPTER 102 - TIP OF THE ICEBERG

October 9, 2001: Washington & Honolulu

After grabbing a sandwich at the corner convenience store I noticed the headline on a check-out stand tabloid: WAR ON HORIZON!   Bloody amateur, I thought. What the hell do you know? If you haven't been out there you don't have a clue.   That headline made me ache even more to be back on the waves.   Returning to the office, I took the scrambler phone out of the desk and dialed a very special number.   Immediately I heard that gruff but lovable growl of the commander of all submarine forces in the U.S. Pacific Fleet. "Good morning."

"Greetings sir, from your old D.C. home base."

"Dan! Nice to hear from you. Everything under control back there?"

"Things are super, Admiral, and thanks again for all the help setting me up with the CVBG skippers."

"Well what new tales of intrigue and excitement are you working on these days?" he asked.   "More spy rings in the shops of Georgetown or the halls of Congress?"

"Nothing quite so juicy, sir, but what I'm calling about might just put me in contact with some of those tales of excitement."

I proceeded to lay out my desire to return to the Fleet, in search of follow-up stories that highlight what goes on 24/7 with the men and women involved on our ships, and stories that would put the pressure on Red China. He muttered some positive grunts during my presentation and then I got to the deal I'd made with Ben.

"How can I refuse to have you back telling our story from the inside? Tell Ben we have a deal. My aide will cut you tickets for MAC and COD flights, and I'll visit with Commander Gruenwald, skipper of the USS BUFFALO, about your sailing on his boat."

"Thank you, sir. Please alert me to your timeline and I'll get a release from Ben."

"You're still on TAD so there may be some stories you won't be able to write about. I'll get back to you in a few days."

"Thanks, Admiral Sharpe. I'm really looking forward to coming back to the Pacific. Could I spend a couple days in Honolulu getting updated on everything out there?"

"Consider it done, Chief." The phone clicked off and I put it back in its hidey hole.

A virtual Simon Cardigan popped into my head. The Pentagon denied the existence of any mole or spy ring there, and the hunt for Simon's killer had ceased. Was he wishing for a big story, but never knew he was right in the middle of it? I'm sure it was a can't see the forest for the trees type of situation.

With several days built into my Honolulu layover I vowed to do more snooping on my own. Maybe now, two years after the murder, there would be someone who saw something that night in Chinatown or someone willing to talk with me about the people Simon believed were working on getting Navy secrets out of Pearl Harbor. I'd make one more effort and if I came up with nothing, that would be that.

Two days later I had my orders, if you could call them that. My base would be the USS CARL VINSON, anchor of the CVBG in the South China Sea, and I could spend a few days each on a DDG and a cruiser to get the feel of life on those smaller warships. Around Christmas I'd transfer to the BUFFALO while she made a port visit in Hong Kong, and stay on patrol with the sub for a week. In all cases, I reported directly and only to VADM Sharpe.

I hadn't spoken with Janice in weeks, so I called her office. No answer, so I tried her apartment and got her answering machine. I left a brief message: It's Dan and I'm heading west again on Tuesday. I didn't want you to think I've been avoiding you, although it sure looks like it. I'll be gone 'til January. If you're in D.C. please call, but if you're on TAD, sorry we'll miss each other. We'll hook-up when I get home. Love you. Bye.

"Boy," I spoke out loud, "what I wouldn't give for one more night enjoying that elusive but heavenly body."

What would become the adventure of my young lifetime began with a snappy salute from an Air Force sergeant as I started up the ladder of the MAC jet bound for Travis Air Force Base outside Sacramento.

Five hours later after lunch and about 150 pages of a James Patterson novel under my belt, we landed in the Golden State. A buddy of mine in San Diego calls it the Granola State because it's full of fruits and nuts, and a bunch of flakes. I deplaned and headed for the service desk to check my next hop. Showing my ID, they pointed me to a KC-135 tanker bound for Hickam AFB in Honolulu.

Half an hour later the P.A. system called out: "Lincoln, Navy Chief Dan Lincoln, meet your ground transportation curbside, gate three."

A KC-135 is a modification of the Boeing 707 and it moved along at over 500 miles per hour. The seating was not too great but more than adequate for the ten passengers on board. With my Alex Cross novel and the thought of a few days in Hawaii, who was I to complain?

Five hours after takeoff, we flew over East Oahu and Waikiki and then swung out to Campbell Industrial Park before doing a 180 and coming back over Ewa Beach and the Pearl Harbor channel entrance to land.

When I stepped off the plane an Air Force van was waiting to take us to our accommodations. We took the pilots to Base Ops, dropped several officers at the BOQ, then the driver said he would take me to the Hale Koa Hotel where room reservations had been set up for me. It's a military recreation center right on Waikiki beach next door to the Hilton Hawaiian Village Resort. It's for military and DOD personnel only, and the rates are half or less what the other hotels on the beach charge. Room rates are based on your rank so colonels pay a lot more than do privates or even Navy chief petty officers.

My room overlooked the ocean facing Diamond Head. As soon as I got settled in I noticed the light on my room telephone blinking. I pushed the *Messages* button and immediately heard the voice of Admiral Sharpe welcoming me to Hawaii and asking me to call him. It was already well past dinner so I opted to ring him in the morning.

I was still wide enough awake to want a nightcap before going to bed. The hotel's Warrior's Lounge proved to be the perfect place, and a double scotch on the rocks was in front of me before I could say humuhumunukunukuapuaa. For those of you I just lost, that's the name of the Hawaii State fish, a very small yellow fellow with a very long name.

Bernie Sharpe's routine placed him at his Sub Base office at 0700 every day except Sunday, so I knew he'd be there at five minutes after.

"Good morning, Dan," he said before I uttered a word. "I knew your body clock would still be on D.C. time."

"Well, it is me and I'm thrilled with the billet you set up for me at the Hale Koa. Great place, great beach."

"You can beach it later. I want you to plan on spending some time with me. I've got my regular 0900 staff meeting but meet me at my office at 1100."

"Admiral, can you get my rental car on the base?"

"Done. Go through Makalapa Gate, you know the one closest to the Sub Base."

Getting on base was no snap these days, but the Marine guards checked their list, my driver's license and TAD orders, and then smartly waved me aboard Naval Base Pearl Harbor.

Arriving at COMSUBPAC Headquarters I climbed the stairs and was greeted by the Admiral's administrative CPO. "Morning, Chief Lincoln. The admiral's expecting you."

VADM Sharpe came out of his office, grabbed my arm and literally dragged me inside, smiling all the while. It felt like old home week. "Sit here," he said, motioning for me to sit on a small sofa adjacent to his big desk.

"It's good to have you back here, Dan. I know you want to do some more human-interest features, but your timing is absolutely perfect on a different front."

"How so? Something brewing we don't know about back east?"

"You'll know in due time. Right now I'll give you a brief overview of the situation then my top intelligence people will give you all the little details you always hunt out. Okay?"

"I'm listening. Will I need my tape recorder?"

"Relax and let everything roll-out. If you need notes and all that we'll go back over things."

"Well placed sources tell us that shooting between Taiwan and the PRC could erupt at any moment. It's a tinderbox, but we've got a lull in the storm right now. We have learned that there's a group of dissident PRC Navy officers and agitated civilians, who may try to commandeer one of their own HAN class submarines."

"Geeze, Bernie...I mean, Admiral. Steal one of your own ships? Are these guys nuts? And, if they did, what in hell would they do with it?"

"We think they plan to load it with enough weapons and nuclear tipped missiles to sink an entire CVBG."

I whistled softly as my mind started evaluating the scene the admiral was laying before me.

"If that weren't enough," he continued, "we believe this group somehow has all the details on our new stealth computer chip system. You remember the fish noises business from last fall? They've apparently been able to duplicate everything Milsoftel designed. What makes it worse is the only way they could know is from a leak in our security system. Do you know what that means?"

Numbly I stammered: "That cryptic message Simon held when he was murdered was true. There *is* a mole in the Pentagon! This is obviously very top secret, nothing you'd ever allow in anything I'd write?"

"True. Dan, I need you to get back into your investigative journalist role and see what you can dig-up here in the local Chinese community. See if there's any word on a clandestine operation at Pearl. Bernie paused, and then quietly asked: "Are you up to this? Remember, Dan, this is a deadly game someone's playing. You've already been a target twice back in D.C. If Simon was correct, we may uncover a connection to the Pentagon. My guys in the five-sided building found no evidence of a mole, but I'd bet my stars that furry little fellow still lives there."

"I'll see what I can come up with Admiral, but Simon's trail is pretty cold by now. Maybe I can find that elderly Chinese man who helped Simon; the one he wouldn't name for fear of the old man losing his life."

"Do what you can and we'll meet here again late Friday morning. In the meantime I've got you scheduled for a lunch here in my conference room with the intel types. Sandwiches and cold drinks are on me. Talk to you later."

Over lunch I gathered additional information about the dissident Red Navy gang. Two commanders briefed me; Jason Westfield and Chuck Falconer. CDR Westfield said: "Let me first tell you that the leader of the red rat pack is PLA Navy Captain David K.Y. Wong." I couldn't help but let out a whistle.

"I know Captain Wong personally." The two officers were dumbfounded as I told them about my experiences with the PRC rebel. I began with the 1999 May Day ceremony trip, the subsequent visit to the Shanghai Navy Base and Shipyard and the discovery that my LT Wong was actually CAPT Wong, the husband of spy ring momma Lily Shin, father of her daughter Cheryl and head of Chinese Navy Intelligence, specializing in getting information about U.S. Navy subs.

We reviewed the entire espionage story, Wong's role in obtaining info from Senator Anderson via Madam Shin, and the business of the fish noises torpedo story covering up the real discovery of the squid computer chip stealth system. "Do you suppose that the stealth chip information was passed to Captain Wong *before* the spy ring was exposed and the principals arrested?"

"At this point in time," said CDR Falconer, "it looks to us like it was sent to Wong sometime last fall perhaps as early as the middle of September, way before your story ran. If that timeframe is correct all of the parties to the espionage plot were under very close governmental scrutiny. That means any transmission of secret info had to come from some currently unknown source possibly at Milsoftel but probably in the Pentagon. We believe it's the mole your friend Simon Cardigan alluded to. But the problem is we haven't a clue who that mole is."

CHAPTER 103 - CALLING CHARLIE CHAN

October 11, 2001: Honolulu

I spent every waking hour of the next two days in Honolulu's colorful Chinatown, searching for any clue to Simon's murder. It was door-to-door, walking the streets and talking with shop-keepers, asking if anyone recalled the Englishman reporter for the Times and it was always the same: a blank stare and quiet no. Were they telling the truth or had word spread it was not safe to speak with me?

Thursday I hit pay dirt. During the morning I visited herbal shops, grocery stores and even an acupuncture center. After lunch came the jackpot. In a small art gallery on Smith Street there was an area where elderly Chinese gathered every day for tea and conversation. Call it their social club.

Figuring I had nothing to lose I decided to put on a little act for the shop owner and the assembled seniors. In a voice that could be heard throughout the gallery I said: "This is a very beautiful vase, what dynasty is it from?"

"Ming, sir," the very polite lady owner replied. "Do you collect fine Chinese art?"

"Well, not really. That's why I asked about the dynasty. I used to work here, on the morning paper, but I moved to the mainland U.S. four years ago. While I was here one of my colleagues on the paper, an Englishman named Simon Cardigan, took me to several galleries looking for vases and Chinese art for his collection. He knew about the dynasties and what pieces of art were legitimate and what were, shall we say, of lesser quality. Simon said 'never buy anything that doesn't cost more than you think it should.' So if this vase is truly Ming, and I now see from the price tag that it must be, I'll buy it. The late Mr. Cardigan would have approved."

"Very wise choice, sir. Since you no longer live in Honolulu would you like us to pack and ship the vase to your Mainland home?"

"Yes, that would be very kind of you. Just add the cost to the price of the vase."

I handed her one of my VISA cards and said: "May I sit while you finish?"

"Certainly sir. Would you like a cup of tea?" I told her I would. She clapped her hands twice, softly, and a young girl came from the rear of the store and went directly to the tea stand. She poured a cup, placed a small spoon and some milk and sugar in cloisonné containers onto a tray and brought them to me. Bowing slightly she asked if I would like some li hing mui or other crackseed, but I thanked her saying no.

The strong Chinese tea hit the spot and my acting had been clearly heard by everyone seated in the gallery. After finishing the tea the owner/manager brought my charge card and receipt, thanking me for the purchase. "Shay shay. And please come back when you're in town again." She held open the shop door as I left, closing it behind me.

My stroll through Chinatown continued but I only browsed at shop windows. Less than two blocks from the art shop I heard someone saying: "Hey mister, hey Ming vase man." I turned and saw one of the men from the gallery tea-drinking group walking three or four paces behind me.

We were near the historic old Hawaii Theater on Bethel Street, now resplendent in its recent renovations. A cozy little park had been created on the makai side of the theater where the man said: "You like sit down? We talk more Chinese art?" This was just what I had hoped would happen. Finally I might have found a link to the community Simon knew so well.

We sat and I waited for the elderly man to begin the conversation. He looked around for a few seconds and when he felt we were not being watched said: "I knew your friend Simon. He very good to me and like Chinese people. He love Chinese art. Collect only the best pieces. No junk, he could tell difference quickly!"

"Do you know how he died?" I asked. He nodded raising his right hand, making a gun with his thumb and forefinger. "Did you also know he found something very wrong at Pearl Harbor?" He nodded yes.

"He on right track for story, but too eager. Talk to wrong people. Ask questions he shouldn't. I told him I help get to right people, but would take time. He said he on deadline, need to know right now."

"Police say he was killed for his gambling debts. Is that right?"

The venerable old Chinese man shook his head saying: "Good cover-up. Simon never gamble. He figure out too many things. Young men from PRC run things now, order him killed. Very sad."

He rose to leave as I asked one final question: "Please, can you tell me if you know any Navy people who may have worked with the PRC?"

"Saw very tall American haole once or twice with PRC men. Never know name." Appearing to see someone across the street who frightened him he jumped up, bowed quickly then ran around the corner into Pauahi Street. I sat in the park a few minutes more checking to see if anyone was watching me or took off in the direction the old man went. Nobody did.

After being more successful in Chinatown than I could have ever hoped, my last night in Hawaii would begin with another dip in the ocean, a quick shower and a stroll along Kalakaua Avenue before dinner. Watching the sun set at the Moana Banyan Court, I thought of what to say to Admiral Sharpe the next day. I had a lead, but where would it take us? Simon was murdered because he knew too much about some ruthless communists hell bent on stealing our American secrets. Who was that tall American?

Next morning I drove out to the Navy base in uncharacteristically light traffic. Just before 1100 I went to the admiral's conference room where the N-2 commanders sat with the Chief of Staff. "Dan, you've met Captain Mike Buck?"

"Yes sir," I replied.

"Well, Chief Lincoln, what have you been able to dig up around Chinatown?"

"Surprisingly, sir, I found the old man that Simon Cardigan trusted. I spent a few very productive minutes with him yesterday afternoon. He told me Simon was onto a spy ring, being run by Communist party members, and was shot for what he had stumbled onto, not for any gambling debts. My man said Simon talked to too many of the wrong people and that was what ultimately cost him his life."

"That's a huge step forward, Dan. Anything else?"

"Just one other thing, but it may be the key to this whole problem of Navy secrets flying into Chinese hands."

The three other Navy officers were taking notes as fast as they could write them down when the admiral said: "Anything concrete about who our mole might be?"

"Not exactly, sir. But, the Chinaman told me he had seen the local PRC men talking to a person he believed was their contact inside the base. He didn't know names but he did give me a description that could be a good starting point."

All four men were looking straight at me, waiting for my next few words. "The Navy contact was a tall American."

The first thing they asked was: Man or woman? And then: How old? We thrashed my info around for a few more minutes, my not knowing answers to their questions about the contact, and then Admiral Sharpe terminated the meeting. "Thank you, gentlemen. I'll get back to you on this later. Chief, please join me in my office before you head to Hickam."

In his private office Bernie turned to me and said: "You've knocked the bottom off the iceberg that's been in our way for four years now. We'll carry the ball from this end but keep your eyes and ears open when you're with the Fleet. Find out everything you can about what's going on in the PRC and with Captain Wong. We've *got* to find these spies before they really do sink our ships."

"I'll give it my best, Admiral."

"I know you will." I stood at attention and as I turned to leave, the admiral added: "Here's what my boat skippers say brings them luck at sea." He handed me one of his personal coins. It had the COMSUBPAC logo on one side and his name and three-star flag on the other side. "I hope it will work for you too. Aloha, and good luck, Dan.

CHAPTER 104 - BACK TO THE ACTION

November 15, 2001: The South China Sea

I still couldn't grasp the minuscule size of an aircraft carrier in the middle of a giant sea, but my pilot came in right on the red ball, plopping us firmly on the CARL VINSON's flight deck.

Once you're aboard, a flattop is a whole lot larger than a postage stamp and finding my quarters was no easy trick. The moment I ducked into the small roomlet a petty officer knocked on the door and handed me a message. RADM Davidson wanted to meet with me to go over my itinerary and some new details that had developed since I left Pearl. I asked the messenger to tell the admiral I'd be there at once.

It was like I had never left the VINSON. CAPT Henshaw shook my hand and the Battle Group commander's welcome was friendly and genuine. The admiral motioned me to sit saying they were glad to have me back, especially in light of what had happened during my recent stopover in Honolulu.

"Very frankly, Admiral, Captain, I got lucky but what I learned from the intel people at SUBPAC has thrown an even bigger monkey wrench into the situation out here."

Admiral Davidson looked very concerned, saying: "We're well aware of the renegade Captain Wong and what his goals are regarding the CVBG, but the biggest thing you can do for us right now is what you do best every day of your life: report on the world around you."

"Talk to as many sailors and pilots as you like here on CARL VINSON and, per Admiral Sharpe's request, we'll try to get you around the fleet to ride on some DDGs and cruisers. You'll transfer to USS BUFFALO after we pull into Hong Kong for our port visit December 21st. So, welcome back to the Seventh Fleet, Chief. By the way, Captain Gruenwald says to tell you he's eagerly awaiting your visit."

Getting back into the routine of life at sea took a few days but soon I was all over the ship looking for stories. The morning I sat in on pilot briefing, I was pleasantly surprised to see everyone was in higher spirits than the pilots on TEDDY ROOSEVELT back when their wings were clipped; not permitted to retaliate for PRC harassment of our flotilla.

Since President Crane had ordered immediate response to overt action it was a new ball game; I could almost see their trigger fingers twitching. Man, I want to be here when this becomes the OK Corral, I thought.

I made friends with several chiefs and officers who manned the CIC. Captain Henshaw had okayed my spending time there as long as I didn't ask about anything classified. That was fine because all I wanted was to get the feel of this critical room and what went on there. This is the heart and brains of the whole shooting match, I thought, gazing at all the equipment necessary for instant handling of everything transpiring in the CVBG's area of responsibility. Information from the CIC enabled the top command to make all the decisions for the Battle Group.

Like the waves of the Pacific Ocean a month slipped by. My stockpile of interviews and human interest stories would keep Ben in weekend features for six months.

While visiting Flag Plot one Sunday morning, I overheard a sailor tell Admiral Davidson: "There's a call for you on the scrambler phone from the USS BUFFALO." The admiral took the phone and said: "Good Morning, and what's new with your family?"

The scrambler sounded a bit crackly but he and I clearly heard: "Good Morning, Uncle. My sons send their thanks for the game you sent last month. They've been playing it with several new kids on the block and so far none of them has understood how it works. Twice as many other kids have come to the playground over the last three days, some not so nice. They're staying near their naughty cousins. If I were a betting man I'd put a few bucks on someone's mother punishing those kids pretty soon."

"Glad the boys like their gift. I'll pass your comments along to some family members. Good luck and see you soon."

What the admiral heard was a report on the most recent evaluation of PRC submarine activity in the CVBG area. It was in a loose code but he understood exactly what the submarine captain aboard BUFFALO was passing on to him:

Tracking Chinese submarines in immediate area. No radar or sonar hits from them. They appear unaware of our presence. Further, PRC sub fleet in the area doubled in past three days, most off Taiwan. Odds indicate Beijing preparing to commence shooting war soon.

Davidson quickly relayed the message to his Chief of Staff, but added: "Keep this information secret until we can assess it further. We don't want to tip off the enemy if, in fact, they're ready to start attacking Taiwan. Assemble the entire staff and all ship skippers for a meeting tomorrow at 0900 here on VINSON. We'll finalize our plans so that we're ready for anything the PRC is about to hand out."

I was playing with a new radio that afternoon in the Chief's mess. I had bought it in Singapore and it was touted to pick up nearly every radio station on the planet, but all I wanted were broadcasts from Beijing. The Chinese president was due to address the public gathered in Tiananmen Square, a speech I assumed would be filled with hateful rhetoric toward the cowardly Western imperialists. Slowly tuning the short-wave band, I hit on the correct station. The sound of band music in the background and a narrator speaking Mandarin confirmed I was in the right place at the right time. I don't speak Mandarin but that didn't matter. I'd tape the speech and one of the on-board translators would give me the English version.

Seaman Joe Chang had a printed translation delivered less than 60 minutes after the president finished haranguing the West. Overall, it was the usual boring B.S., however I did pick-out a few quotes. I included them in the story I was writing, which should run in Sunday's papers back home. This is pretty damn newsworthy, I thought. I hope Ben beats the competition to press.

CHINESE PRESIDENT PROCLAIMS
SOUTH CHINA SEA OUR OCEAN
VOWS TO SHOOT DOWN AMERICAN
RECONNAISSANCE FLIGHTS

By: Dan Lincoln

Aboard the aircraft carrier USS CARL VINSON in the South China Sea, November 25, 2001 (Pacific & Asia News Service):

In a nationally broadcast and televised address to his country, Chinese President Jiang Zemin told a crowd of thousands in Tiananmen Square today that the People's Republic of China would not hesitate to shoot down any American military aircraft if they ventured even one mile into Chinese territory. Calling them spy flights the Chinese leader indicated that such territory included the Nanshas. The PRC Navy sank the Taiwanese Navy destroyer LAO YANG on March 21ˢᵗ and took over the islands on May1st after bombing and killing the Taiwanese garrison there.

The president's address included a reference to his country's current navy. "We are rapidly achieving equal strength with the U.S. Navy. With the completion of surface ships and submarines that are already under construction in our shipyards, we will soon be able to keep all navies out of our ocean, the South China Sea."

Western news sources in Taipei, Hong Kong and Tokyo have all reported increased numbers of PRC warships on the move this weekend. U.S. Navy officials of the Seventh Fleet had no comments on the news reports.

-end-

Sunday was quiet if you can call the constant roar of jet take-offs and landings pretty quiet. All aboard would tell you a carrier never sleeps. We remained at condition BRAVO but you could taste the anticipation and alertness in the entire crew.

The admiral stopped me on his way to lunch in the ship's Wardroom. "Good story on Zemin's speech. I caught it on the ship's TV wire. You do a nice job covering us. I enjoy your stories about the crew. Helps me to get to know them better, even if it is second-hand. It's likely you'll be receiving more material very soon. There's increased activity in the PRC fleet around Taiwan, and with so much movement above and below the water the CNO has briefed the President about the current situation. The President has made an important decision to..." he trailed off as he waited for two petty officers to pass. "Orders are for all ships and planes to fire at will on any PRC warship or aircraft attacking." I couldn't suppress a grin when he added: "The President has put Harry Truman's old plaque on the Oval Office desk. Remember what it says?" In unison, we both chimed: "The Buck Stops Here!"

CHAPTER 105 - SQUIDY GETS A LIFE

December 7, 2001: Midway Island

The Secretary of the Navy spoke movingly at the 0755 ceremony on the USS ARIZONA Memorial, comparing that attack 60 years ago with the acts of cowardice done by the radical Islamic terrorists on September 11th. At The National Memorial Cemetery of the Pacific Admiral E. R. Lynch delivered his keynote address at the annual service honoring those men and women who made the ultimate sacrifice at Pearl Harbor.

The media thought it was a great coup for the Navy to have both the CNO and the SECNAV in Honolulu for the day's ceremonies. If they had checked, they'd have found that Secretary of Defense Gaston was on the island, enjoying the early part of the day in a suite at the Hilton. They would not know he was in town with the other dignitaries for an additional ceremony, still on December 7th but being held some 1,200 miles to the northwest.

Sharpe's party of six buckled into the Lear jet at 1300 and sped off for Midway Island, arriving there three hours later. The day had been busy for the Mainland guests, but stepping onto historic Midway Island, with its memories of that June 1942 battle, renewed their patriotic spirits. To a person they were eager to participate in the traditional Navy ceremony at the beach.

A fleet of golf carts was positioned on the tarmac, and as the dignitaries deplaned Buzz Russell greeted each one individually and then a full-dress Marine escorted them to the carts. Immediately they were whisked to the commissioning site.

It seemed like every person on Midway was assembled on the pier and a loudspeaker played John Philip Sousa marches. "No Navy band," someone muttered. "There's a first!"

The guests were seated under a canopy, protecting them from the sun. Bernie made a few remarks about the new boat, being especially complimentary of Buzz, his military engineers and shipyard workers, and the creative Mescod geniuses who conceived this new submarine.

Adhering to protocol he turned the program over to Admiral Lynch and it was immediately apparent the CNO was impressed with this weird looking addition to the Navy. He alluded to the changing face of today's submarine design, and his remarks were seconded by both the SECNAV and SECDEF, the latter making a connection with the 9-11 events saying: "Never again will our nation be caught off guard by terrorists or other enemies of democracy. These new defense systems and ships will guarantee that the United States will remain the world's most potent and dominant force."

The JAMESTOWN's XO, CDR Ellis Sherman, read the Navy Department message officially naming CAPT Frank B. Russell, USN, as the ship's commanding officer, and in less than 30 minutes *Project Squidy* was officially finished and the boat was commissioned a warship of the line.

The official party adjourned to the oceanfront club on the north shore for a fresh fish dinner. Bernie couldn't resist making a champagne toast, and doing it in true Hawaiian style: "Okole Maluna! Here's to the little boat that can and will leave its mark on the world forever."

CHAPTER 106 - CHOP TO SEVENTH FLEET

Mid-December, 2001: Pearl Harbor and Midway

The JAMESTOWN was ready for action. Sea trials complete, Russell and his key crewmembers were summoned to Honolulu for briefings at COMSUBPAC on the 12th. Arriving at Admiral Sharpe's headquarters, everyone but the skipper went with the Chief of Staff to his conference room for an orientation briefing. Buzz went to the admiral's office.

"Sit down, Buzz. How about an iced tea?" He nodded in the affirmative and the admiral pushed a small button on his desk. A petty officer immediately entered the office from a side door. "Two iced teas please Liddle, and perhaps some of those great chocolate chip cookies you get from KEY WEST."

After the tea and cookies were served Bernie turned his attention back to the submarine captain. "You, your crew and I are going up to CINCPACFLT at 0830 tomorrow to meet with the commodore of the squadron you'll be assigned to in the CVBG. Then you have a political briefing at CINCPAC in the afternoon. Looks like you'll be working with either the ABE LINCOLN or TEDDY ROOSEVELT groups."

It was pretty much a one-way briefing so Buzz sat there and listened. "I believe the Red Chinese see a golden opportunity to begin a limited war in the coming months," Bernie solemnly proclaimed, "and will try to reclaim Taiwan. That's why your new boat is so vital to coming operations.

"I know you have a lot on your schedule while you're here and if I can provide any direct assistance, come see me. If you have no plans for tonight, I'd like you to come to my quarters for dinner."

"Admiral, I'd change any plans to dine with you."

"My driver will meet you at the BOQ at 1730. I'm in a great old house on Ford Island with a view of both the ARIZONA Memorial and the battleship MISSOURI. I know you'll appreciate its significance."

As Buzz got up to leave the admiral added one more comment: "Be careful when you get out there, Buzz. Those Chinese are no dummies and they've developed a pretty fine Navy over the last few years. No question that we have the advantage but I have reason to believe the PRC Navy may have been getting info about submarine projects we've been working on for years. There have been several leaks that we know about and they may even have gotten access to the fish noises project you're so familiar with."

Promptly at 1730 the Navy sedan pulled up and Admiral Sharpe's driver got out to hold the door open for Buzz. It was only a five minute ride, via a new ferry-replacing bridge named after former COMSUBPAC and World War II Navy submarine hero Admiral Bernard 'Chick' Clarey.

The Admiral's quarters, old but in excellent shape, nestled in a quiet park-like setting. The view was spectacular: sweeping panoramas of the main base, and the Koolau Mountains back-dropping Aiea and Pearl City.

"Welcome to Ford Island," the admiral greeted his guest. "Come on in. Barbara's waiting to greet you and has some pupu and margaritas for us."

"Buzz," Barbara smiled, "it's wonderful to see you again. I'm looking forward to hearing some of your very interesting stories over dinner."

"Only the unclassified ones," the admiral chided. "Both of you know the rules."

Bernie walked out to the lanai deck, motioning Buzz to follow. Barbara headed back to the galley, as she called it, to finish preparing dinner.

The two old shipmates chatted about recent Navy activities, and where people they had worked with were now. Bernie told the skipper about some of the changes made since he took over SUBPAC and gave him a brief background about the two admirals he'd meet with tomorrow.

"The Fleet Commander, Admiral Tom Darcy, is one of our biggest supporters. He's a black shoe sailor but understands our boats and their importance to the fleet. He'll give you total support. You'll get a detailed briefing about the military situation in the western Pacific and Admiral Darcy's China experts, two civilians who know how the PRC thinks and works, will bring you up to speed on what to expect from Beijing."

"In the afternoon CINCPAC will give you their latest skinny. They're in command of all the forces out here. You'll probably get the most information from their POLAD on PRC fleet activities and where they are currently deployed." The admiral popped a tasty tidbit into his mouth, and then proceeded: "At the end of the day you'll know exactly what's going on and where, and most importantly, where you and your boat fit into the operation."

Half an hour later Barbara joined them, saying: "Dinner is served!"

The lamb and all the trimmings were perfect. And when dinner was finished Barbara offered snifters of brandy. Buzz was enjoying himself so much he nearly lost track of the time. At 2150 he called for his return to the BOQ. It had been a perfect evening and after thanks and good nights, he got in the car for the short return trip to the Sub Base.

CINCPACFLT headquarters at Makalapa overlooked the naval station below, with a view of Pearl Harbor and the battleship USS ARIZONA Memorial. Russell and his team of three sat through the regular daily briefing and got a basic overview of the U.S. Pacific Fleet program.

By 0945 the briefing shifted to a smaller room to receive specifically tailored plans just for JAMESTOWN. The walls were covered with huge maps of the Pacific and sliding panels displayed detailed map sections. Navy Captain Dennis Sullivan motioned the group to seats around the table. "I'm in the Staff Operations Division; I'll review current status and plans for our assigned area," he began. As his presentation unfolded it confirmed what Admiral Sharpe felt about PRC activities and possible motives.

Commander Julius Goldman from Intelligence spoke next, updating everyone on PRC vessels and ending his portion by warning: "We detect immense activity in the

Shanghai area where they base many of their submarines." Looking straight at Buzz he continued: "We'll try to get you info as quickly as our operative sends it to us."

Last to speak was Navy oceanographer and meteorologist, CDR Dave Donaldson. His data was most interesting and quite different from everything that had been shown before. Commander Donaldson dealt with the difficulty of finding subs hiding in cooler water depths.

"By operating at levels below the favorable thermoclines, flowing under warmer water, you will definitely avoid pings from surface ships and even airborne sonar devices." He unfolded several maps saying: "These charts indicate the areas where you will most likely operate, with the ideal depths of thermoclines."

The XO and WEPS wore big smiles after getting copies of Donaldson's charts. Buzz thanked everyone involved: "You have each taken a huge burden off my crew and me."

As it was now time for lunch, Captain Sullivan escorted the four men from JAMESTOWN to the ground level where the flag mess and the admiral's offices were located. Before entering the dining room, they were taken to the admiral's outer office where materials about the command were displayed including Chester Nimitz' 5-star Fleet Admiral shoulder boards and his ceremonial sword.

Admiral Darcy stepped from his office and Captain Sullivan introduced Buzz and his team.

"Welcome aboard gentlemen. My staff has you fully briefed, I presume?"

"Yes, sir; very, very valuable information."

Darcy asked the group, "Okay if I join you for lunch?" Buzz replied: "We would be honored, sir."

There was absolutely no doubt who was in command, but Admiral Darcy spoke with every member of Buzz' team, asking them about their families and hometowns, their Navy experiences and career goals. Turning to Master Chief Esterhaus, he said: "You were a third class boatswain's mate 20 years ago serving with me on the ARTHUR RADFORD. Remember that old destroyer?"

Flattered by the admiral's attention, Esterhaus spoke right up saying: "Yes sir. I remember you, but I sure didn't think you'd remember me! Probably my shy, quiet nature!" At that, his fellow shipmates broke out laughing.

When the dessert dishes had been cleared, the admiral wished his visitors well and told Buzz: "Captain, I know you and Vice Admiral Sharpe are working closely these days. That unique boat of yours can be the key factor in any shooting war that we get into out there and I'm counting on you and your crew to show your stuff. If you need anything that you can't get from the 7th Fleet or from Bernie you send a message to me and I'll go to bat for you. Good luck and God speed."

After lunch the JAMESTOWN team headed to CINCPAC, halfway up one of the Aiea hills behind Pearl Harbor. A new office building tentatively to be called the Nimitz MacArthur Center, was under construction on the ocean side of the property, and slated for completion by late 2003 with occupancy in March or April of 2004.

A guard at the gate directed them to the compound. Entering from a side door they were met by a ramrod-stiff Marine officer. "Major Woods, sir," he said, smartly snapping off a manual-perfect salute. "Captain Russell, please follow me. Colonel Porter and his staff are in the briefing room."

. "Good afternoon. I'm Colonel Ned Porter the Ops Deputy at CINCPAC. Contributing to your briefing are Commander Oliver Phillips, head of our PRC Navy intelligence team and Mr. Al Lewis, our POLAD." Buzz, his key officers and COB took seats facing a wall of sliding map panels with a video screen in the middle.

Colonel Porter slid the panels to the left and pulled out one showing southeast Asia. A panel on the right showed Malaysia, Indonesia, Singapore, and the island of Borneo, plus hundreds of islands in the Philippines and then up to Taiwan and Japan.

"This is the area you're going to operate in for the next six months, under water but within range of any of these countries. Your main responsibilities will first be to help provide protection for the carrier battle groups, especially the carriers themselves." Glancing around the room Porter continued: "Second, to locate and identify PRC ships. Scuttlebutt here is your sub can do some pretty unusual things."

"Well, we're pretty confident the JAMESTOWN will live up to her expectations."

As Colonel Porter finished, Commander Oliver Phillips took over. "I'm going to share information with you that you'll soon know first hand. My team concentrates on what the PRC Navy is doing, where their ships are, and anything else that could be useful." Then he revealed charts pinpointing the last known positions of their ships, and when he mentioned increased activity in the Shanghai region, Buzz' mind sprang to attention.

Phillips then introduced the POLAD: "This is Al Lewis, Naval Academy grad, and intelligence officer for six years prior to joining the CIA." Buzz rated this briefing the main event of the day.

Printed notes showed Lewis had served at Langley and other locations for over 20 years, and the past four as CINCPAC's POLAD. After speaking his first words the JAMESTOWN team recognized he was a real heavyweight in the spook department.

"Gentlemen, welcome to CINCPAC and soon to the hottest area in the world, the waters off Red China. What do we know about this unique country other than the fact that most of our radios, cameras and other electronic gear and shoes come from there? China, where more people are in active-duty or home-defense-force military uniforms than there are people in the U.S. China, where they still look at Taiwan as nothing more than a renegade province to be returned to the PRC, come hell or high water or any type of military intervention from the U.S. Navy or her allies."

For the next 30 minutes Al Lewis delivered a masters degree course on Chinese politics and history that you could never have received in four years at Stanford, Yale or Princeton. When he finished, everyone had questions.

"Who runs the Chinese Navy?"

"What role does the Chinese Premier play in everyday military decisions?"

"How many nuclear subs do they have, and where are they located right now?"

"Can we take out their Navy ships without them sending in waves of planes and ground troops against Taiwan?"

Al Lewis was up to all questions and even went beyond some of them to suggest how to handle different situations if and when they came up

Colonel Porter interrupted: "Gentlemen, I have another meeting in less than half an hour and must get some papers from my office before going to that appointment. I trust you've learned some helpful information, and feel free to chat with Commander Phillips and Mr. Lewis awhile longer."

After Porter left Buzz turned to see his key officers still asking questions, some directed at CDR Phillips and even more for Al Lewis. At 1555 he said: "That's all for this trip, guys." To Phillips and Lewis he added: "We really appreciate this, and what you've shown us today will definitely help us in any and all of our critical decisions. Thank you."

Back at their quarters Buzz warned: "For security reasons, what we learned today must stay with only us. When we're underway and on station I'll tell the others only what they need know. See you in the morning."

Before the group departed their Lockwood Hall quarters for the return flight to Midway, Bernie Sharpe addressed them: "One of your biggest tasks in the coming months is to keep out of sight and not let anyone see your boat. It will be tough duty but when you need a break return to Midway, your official homeport." Bernie didn't know from the men's faces if this was good or bad news. "Maintenance is under a volunteer group of active personnel who are pledged to absolute secrecy."

"That's great news, Admiral. I know the men will be pleased to learn they'll be back with their friends the Gooney birds in the foreseeable future."

The admiral reminded Buzz to call or e-mail if he needed absolutely anything, and then quipped: "You're about to take a huge step in Navy submarine warfare history and I know *Squidy* will come through with flying colors and waving tentacles."

Captain Russell's crew spent the rest of the week back on Midway, cleaning up loose ends, provisioning the ship and preparing for deployment.

USS JAMESTOWN sailed at dawn on December 20th, arrived in the western Pacific on the 23rd and chopped to the 7th Fleet two days before Christmas.

CHAPTER 107 - UNDERSEA WITH BUFFALO

December 26, 2000: South China Sea

Having visited Hong Kong several times previously I decided to forego all the shore leave partying on this trip and spend most of my time transferring to the USS BUFFALO (SSN-715). I wanted to be ready when she departed early Wednesday morning.

My Saturday, however, was spent doing one of the things I really enjoyed most in this port, browsing through the antique shops in Hollywood Road on Hong Kong Island. As I got out of the cab and started my slow walk up the street I couldn't help but recall that Lily Shin once had a shop in this very district. I did find a few little baubles for Janice to remind her of her times in China.

By Sunday I began adjusting to the submarine and my life for the next few days. Captain Bob Gruenwald introduced me to his COB, Master Chief Terry Adams who got me squared away in the Goat Locker. It was great being on a U.S. Navy submarine again. By Tuesday night the entire crew was back aboard the boat and we were ready to sail at first light.

The skipper invited me to join him and the OOD on the conning tower bridge as we maneuvered out of the harbor. Huge freighters loaded with hundreds of containers were headed to the main dock areas near Kowloon, and dozens of small sampans scurried about in front of us.

After we'd passed Hong Kong Island and headed into open seas I went below. CAPT Gruenwald ordered the boat dived and we cruised at 300 feet for several hours on our way back to the CVBG.

I was bunked in with the COB and after five minutes with him I knew I was going to like the most senior enlisted man on the boat. He was a bit older than the skipper, but used his maturity to work with the young men in the crew. We chatted about the upcoming patrol as the master chief cut into the stack of paperwork he said was always waiting to be done. Since I was there to do a story on a day in the life of a submariner I got some very good background from him, and found that life on an SSN today was about the same as it was when I rode them.

"One thing for sure Chief, we're very likely to make contact with PRC Navy ships at least once while you're aboard. They're pissed at us for hounding them all over the South China Sea; I doubt we've seen the last of them."

"Agreed," I said. Knowing Chief Adams was privy to what I'd learned about David Wong and his rebels I asked him: "Anything new on that group of dissident Red Chinese and their Shanghai submarine?"

"Nothing yet, but it's only 0945 and we're barely away from the smell of Hong Kong Harbor."

Not wanting to waste any time I spent the morning exploring the sub, except for the nuclear reactor and several engineering spaces. I was pleased how quickly the layout came back to me 20 years after my sea duty.

Meals were in the chiefs' mess and by lunch that first day I had met most of the E-7s and E-8s. They impressed me in two ways: their youth and their professional and technological skills. Math, physics and electronics were all talents most of these men brought to the BUFFALO.

Captain Gruenwald called me to his cabin the next morning. "We have a message from CVBG command that may affect us. Intelligence reports that Captain Wong is close to completing the modifications to his HAN class submarine, called the PEOPLE'S VICTORY, and could be at sea as early as next week."

"Does the battle group commander think Wong might try a direct attack?"

"Can't say, but everyone knows that when you're employing nuclear weapons close is good enough."

"I read you loud and clear Captain. What's your plan now that you know Wong may be underway soon?"

"He'll come looking for us, but we still hold the advantage." I opened my mouth to speak and he stopped me:

"I know Admiral Sharpe says the stealth system may have been compromised and the Reds could have the information needed to duplicate it. But until we know for certain, we'll operate under normal procedures."

That night after the movie I got the master chief talking about how sophisticated, accurate and reliable today's U.S. subs are. I took notes about the acoustic footprints emitted by submarines and how a good sonar operator can tell a Russian AKULA from a Chinese HAN. Lead Sonar Chief Bill Morton who was involved in tracking and sinking three enemy subs in a paper drill, gave me more details on sonar developments.

In my quarters alone with my thoughts, I pictured my Janice; the best hull in the fleet, gorgeous face, the whole package to complete my life. If only she wasn't off-keel so often. I was definitely trapped in her web of mystery. Is love a screwy proposition, or what? To top it all off, I missed celebrating Christmas with my elf, if you could call her that. Today it's yesterday back home, so it's Christmas Day. That International Dateline crossing stuff...go west gain a day, go east lose Christmas with your lady.

The next day was spent observing Chief Morton and learning more about the sounds PRC submarines make. I planned on using as much information as the Navy would allow, adding it to my growing notes from interviews with the ship's crew. I knew my series was going to be good reading. Saturday I sequestered myself in my cabin, began pounding my laptop's keys and watched as my story unfolded on the screen. Even if I hadn't written this, I thought, I'd buy and read it!

That weekend my time riding BUFFALO was up and I was off to the CARL VINSON at 1400. I thanked Bob Gruenwald and COB Adams, but little did I realize that just around the corner was a story that would far surpass my big spy story. I was about to sail smack dab into the middle of a real shooting war!

CHAPTER 108 - THIS IS NOT A DRILL

December 31, 2001: Aboard USS JAMESTOWN

The JAMESTOWN proved a very elusive quarry throughout the first week of fleet shakedown maneuvers. Seemed sonar trackers just couldn't get a lock on the new boat. The skipper reported they were experimenting with prototype anti-detection devices and not to expect his boat to make any appearances on CVBG sonar screens anytime in the near future. He laughed to himself, knowing little *Squidy* was passing her final exams with flying colors. But the tests quickly turned much more difficult.

"Conn, Sonar. Two new PRC contacts, bearing zero-seven-zero, range 20 thousand yards, speed 15 knots."

"Very well, Sonar. Continue tracking and advise me of any changes. Begin audio emissions at 10 thousand yards," said LT Bill Bemus, WEPS officer and currently OOD.

"Sonar, aye. The four existing surface contacts we're tracking have also come to course zero-seven-zero. Keeping a watch on them as well."

LT Bemus picked up the phone and rang Captain Russell's cabin. "This is the Captain."

"Skipper, it's WEPS. Sonar has picked up what they believe are two new PRC submarine contacts, range 20 thousand yards and heading zero-seven-zero toward Taiwan. Four surface contacts have assumed the identical course."

Within a minute Buzz entered the control room, heading straight to the lead sonarman CPO Jack Smart, asking: "You're sure the new contacts are PRC?"

"Yes sir. I've been studying their acoustic signatures for months. I believe they're the two AKULA class boats China bought a couple-three years ago. They're nuclear powered but carry no ICBMs. They're basically a poor version of our LOS ANGELES attack submarines."

"Good job Chief," the skipper replied. "Stay with them and run tapes of their signatures for our library." **Aboard USS**

Aboard USS CARL VINSON

1300 Monday, New Year's Eve. I was in the chiefs' quarters reviewing some notes when our boat heeled slightly to starboard. I thought: Change of course. Where to now? We'd been executing slow circles to port, so this could be a major course adjustment. My snoopy journalistic side came out so I scaled up the passageway ladder two decks. Peering out an open hatch I could see we had begun heading due north.

What's this all about? Something big about to happen? The ship had been unusually quiet and tense all day, as if everyone on board could smell trouble brewing. Returning to my bunk, I grabbed a note pad and began jotting down thoughts about what might be a coming skirmish in the next 48 hours. My inside knowledge reminded me that POTUS had authorized retaliatory action if any U.S. or allied ships were attacked.

On Board the QINGDAO

Above the quiet sea, Captain Fong moved restlessly in his starboard bridge-wing chair on the Chinese Navy guided missile destroyer QINGDAO. She was the flagship of China's planned attack on Taiwan. In charge of the operation was Admiral W.H.C. Ho, eager to prove his military mettle to the world.

Captain Fong sprang from his chair as the Admiral entered the bridge, assuming a position of stiff attention; he saluted the four-star. "What is the news, Admiral?"

"It has been decided that in eight hours we shall send Taiwan a special New Year's greeting. It will be colorful and devastating. We do not expect any opposition from anyone including the Americans."

Admiral Ho continued smiling broadly: "The Taiwanese are not capable of defending against our missiles, bombs and aerial attacks. We expect them to be completely off guard celebrating. Are our ships positioned for tonight's action, Captain?"

"Yes, sir. The flotilla includes three LUHU-class destroyers and four HAIZHOU destroyers that we commissioned last year. There are several other DDs, a frigate and three submarines leading us. Trailing support craft include six patrol ships. Admiral, we are ready to commence this glorious task for the Motherland."

"Excellent, Captain Fong. You will join me for dinner in my quarters at 1900 hours and we will review all battle plans."

"Aye, aye, Admiral. I look forward to this evening."

As China's Pacific Fleet boss left the bridge the QINGDAO skipper sat back in his chair, looked over a chart showing the locations of all PRC ships and subs, and waited for sunset.

Aboard USS CARL VINSON

"Party Time!" echoed throughout the passages of the aircraft carrier, as several impromptu New Year's Eve celebrations broke out in the crew's mess. Alcohol was forbidden while underway, but large quantities of beer miraculously began emerging from bunks, footlockers and other hideaways. American sailors are truly ingenious where beer is concerned. However, the beer began disappearing just as quickly as word spread that Marine Master-At-Arms teams were sweeping every deck. "Damned party poopers!" could be heard throughout the ship.

Walking along an outside passageway I stopped to enjoy the setting sun. A few minutes after it sank the sky turned to beautiful shades of rapidly changing oranges, reds and dark red-browns. Flashing back 20 years, I recalled the old mariners' rhyme: Red sky at night, sailors delight. Red sky in the morning, sailors take warning. Tonight's sky was definitely a sailor's delight but I wondered which Navy it was meant for, them or us?

With no news of any imminent attack I headed for chow and then ducked in on the nightly flick. Feeling jolly I endured two virgin eggnogs. It was about 2200 hours when I wished everyone another Happy New Year and headed off to my quarters, looking forward to the year 2002.

It arrived with a *bang*!!

At 2330 hours Captain Henshaw's phone rang. He quickly came awake saying: "Captain."

"Skipper this is Lieutenant Commander Alvarado, the OOD. CIC reports radars are showing the presence of many aircraft coming on screen from mainland China. We've also been tracking several surface contacts that have been heading in a general northerly direction all day, but now they've increased speed to an average of 25 knots and appear headed directly toward Taiwan."

"What's your ETA for those planes over Taiwan?"

"Midnight, Captain, precisely at midnight."

"Very well. Sound General Quarters. Notify the Air Boss and Admiral Davidson. I'll be there in a minute."

I actually smacked my head on the upper bunk when the GQ sirens erupted. As I sprang out of my rack the loudspeakers screamed: "General quarters. General quarters. All hands man your battle stations. This is *not* a drill. Repeat, this is *not* a drill."

Sailors of every rank filled the passageways strapping on life jackets and battle helmets, while sprinting for their assigned stations. One thought raced through every mind: Is this the big one?

"All pilots report to your ready rooms. Repeat, all pilots report to your ready rooms."

For something as huge as a skyscraper on its side, the nimble CARL VINSON quickly swung bow-first into the wind, and the deck crews were already preparing their fighter jets for take-off. Knowing my assigned spot, I retreated to the little space on the bridge and prepared to record this event.

I began scribbling notes. It could be *the* story of the year, and the biggest story of my life.

On Board the QINGDAO

"Little Red Book, this is Red Leader. We are within missile range and have the targets locked on our fire-control radar. Request permission to launch missiles."

Quiet but steady, a voice replied: "Red Leader, this is Little Red Book. Permission granted."

CHAPTER 109 - A GAME OF UNDERWATER CHINESE CHECKERS

January 1, 2002: Aboard USS JAMESTOWN

Buzz liked to prowl his boat late at night. "Hell, you can always grab 40 winks during the day when normal people are handling all the jobs," he liked to say. Besides, in a sub day is night and vice versa since you don't have windows. At 2345 he slid into a control room chair and scanned all the latest incoming sonar info.

"Captain," Chief Sonarman Smart called out. "Can you come take a look at this?"

Looking at the sonar screen, Buzz counted five surface contact blips. "They've all picked up speed in the past 15 minutes." Smart said quietly, "and changed courses right toward Taiwan's shipyards in Kaoshung."

As he was showing the skipper what was going on above he stopped in mid-sentence: "Oh, shit. Those AKULAs we're tracking are coming about and heading straight for us. There's no mistaking that sound."

"What's ahead, Chief?"

"Just the Chinese surface ships we've been following, but a couple of hundred miles astern is our CVBG and a bunch of our boats down here with us."

With his pulse quickening, Buzz calmly ordered: "Officer of the Deck, sound General Quarters and man battle stations. It looks like we're going to have a chance to prove ourselves in battle conditions. Chief Smart, what are the AKULA's range, course and speed?"

"Steady on course zero-eight-five, doing about 20 knots and probably 30,000 yards from us, sir."

"Very well. WEPS join me at the fire control panel with your key. Let's get it open for business."

Aboard USS CARL VINSON

The huge carrier was a giant floating hive, with worker bees moving methodically, readying the stinger-jets for combat against an advancing enemy. Admiral Davidson watched from the Flag Bridge as everything moved toward the initial launch.

The admiral's CVBG had arrived at this destination not by accident. Top Secret messages from Pentagon officers told him they expected some sort of hostile Chinese action near Taiwan on New Year's Eve. He could launch fighters immediately, giving them a head start, but prudently awaited aggressive action from the on-coming Chinese fleet.

What he wanted arrived at 0005, when the Taiwan Air Force Base reported that Chang Kai Shek Airport at Taipei was under missile attack from PRC aircraft. Dozens of planes on the tarmac were destroyed, and pilots were scrambling to get airborne in anything that could fly.

A minute later another radio signal came in, this time from the ROC Navy Base at Kaoshung. They too were under attack from PRC Navy-launched surface-to-surface missiles and PLA Air Force bombs. Immediate help was requested. The admiral ordered the attack and the 1 MC blared: "Launch aircraft. Launch aircraft."

Aboard USS JAMESTOWN

"Twenty thousand yards, Captain. I've still got them locked on, but they haven't found us yet."

"All stop. All crew members remain as silent as you are able." The boat rapidly came to a halt in about half the time it would have taken for an LA Class nuke.

"Aye, aye, skipper. Distance 18 thousand yards," the chief sonarman said in a hushed voice. "Still heading our way, but one AKULA is turning left 90 degrees and seems to be looking for other subs or surface ships. His sister-ship remains on course 17 thousand yards out."

"Captain, we've received a message from the CVBG over the tentacle," said the communications officer, entering the control room. "Taiwan is under attack by PRC planes and ships hitting the air force base at Taipei and the navy base and shipyard at Kaoshung. We have orders authorizing us to shoot at any PRC target we can acquire."

Captain Russell read the message, initialed it, and picked up the 1 MC. In the brightest but quietest voice he could muster he told the crew: "Gentlemen, this is the Captain. We have been advised that Taiwan is currently under attack by Navy and Air Force units of the People's Republic of China. The Taiwanese are an American ally and we have a treaty obligation to come to their aid, if asked. They have asked. We have authority from the President to return the favor so it looks like we'll do so in the very near future. Stand-by, keep alert and good luck."

"Skipper, the other AKULA has turned again and is high-tailing it back toward our position," Chief Smart said as quietly as he could. "We have her and her sister on our sonar about 12 thousand yards out. She still doesn't seem to know we're here."

"Of course. What did you think? After all we are totally stealth aren't we?" Smart smiled his acknowledgment and Buzz said: "Good. Let's keep it that way. OOD, make torpedo tubes one through four ready in all respects, and open outer doors on all tubes. WEPS get me a final firing plan and stand by to launch."

On Board the QINGDAO

The QINGDAO was close enough to Kaoshung to see the red in the sky from the direct hits on her Taiwanese cousins. Admiral Ho and Captain Fong stood outside on the wings of the bridge bundled in warm jackets, looking at empty skies behind them and returning PRC planes ahead and to their left. An officer came out and told them they could watch, on an air-search radar screen, a couple of dog fights between their pilots and the few ROC Air Force planes that managed to get off the ground. The two senior naval officers went into the pilot house to see the aerial encounter. It was over in less than a minute.

Aboard USS CUSHING

One of our destroyers that had been ordered to search for enemy submarines in the CVBG area was the Yokosuka-based USS CUSHING (DD-985). She was employing sonar buoys dropped by our tracking planes and listening to what those extra ears were hearing. Just before 0100 hours she locked on a KILO boat about 10 miles distant on a converging course at 20 knots. If both continued there would be action in less than 15 minutes.

"Captain, CIC reports target now 14 thousand yards away with range closing fast," the OOD called out.

"Very well," replied the skipper Commander Don Pickens. "Prepare a fire-control solution for our torpedoes. Come left 40 degrees and steady up on new course three-five-zero. Sonar, let me know if the KILO makes any course changes. WEPS, advise me when you have that firing solution ready."

Within seconds the OOD on the bridge yelled: "Enemy torpedoes in the water. Range less than five thousand yards. Coming from enemy position at zero-four-zero."

The destroyer skipper ordered: "Come right to course zero-four-zero, all engines ahead full. Stand by to fire torpedo tubes one and three."

The OOD had no time to acknowledge the captain's orders; while calling out the course change the whole ship shuddered. A huge fountain of water erupted on the starboard side just forward of the superstructure. It was clear that at least one of the KILO's fish had made its mark. We were now officially at war with China.

The ship was already at General Quarters so it didn't take long for the damage control teams to reach the area where the torpedo had hit. As the damage control officer was assessing the situation and about to report to Captain Pickens, a high-pitched sound was heard passing down the port side of the ship. DC Chief Chuck Wilson smiled to himself and called out: "There goes the other fish. Looks like the old man dodged that bullet. Now, let's get this hole plugged!"

Luckily for CUSHING the torpedo hit in berthing and office spaces, not in critical engine, control or missile areas. Sailors in the damage control party were able to lay timbers across the huge hole, jam mattresses and tarpaulins in, and secure the temporary patch. Larger timbers could be pounded into a secure position between overhead beams and steel footers quickly welded to the deck. Their patch was temporary but slowed the sea water to a trickle and would allow the ship to head for a shipyard at either Subic Bay or Singapore.

Captain Pickens radioed CUSHING's position to higher command along with all the details of the attack he knew at the moment. Within five minutes he got a signal from the CVBG staff to leave his current position and head for the Philippines. The frigate USS THATCH (FFG-43) would escort him for at least 24 hours. Both ships were ordered to continue searching for enemy submarines while headed south, with an okay to fire torpedoes, depth charges and all other weapons if they located and identified any PRC subs.

Aboard USS CARL VINSON

Air-Boss Captain Tom Brady grabbed a moment to relax. Two squadrons had been launched and a third sat anxiously on-deck awaiting his orders to take off. The first squadron headed north to Taiwan to intercept the unsuspecting PRC pilots. They wouldn't be disappointed.

The second group of F/A-18s was ordered to attack the Chinese base on Hainan Island. These were the folks who jailed one of our reconnaissance planes and its crew for a couple weeks last April. Tonight's bombs did a nice job of saying thank you to that base for hosting our crew!

Brady launched the third squadron to look for an opportunity to fire at PLA Navy surface warships. By 0115 they had two DD's locked on and commenced firing. The missiles did their job. As our pilots headed away from what return fire the Chinese could muster, they radioed the positions of several other DDs and frigates, and two even larger contacts they believed to be newer DDGs of the LUHU Class. Those positions would be passed along to all surface ships and submarines of our battle group that had now been dispatched to the forward area.

Aboard USS JAMESTOWN

With his ship stopped and maintaining silence, Captain Russell reviewed a message containing the latest known positions of PRC surface ships. His own sonar, along with sonar buoys dropped into the ocean by P-3 search aircraft, showed five or six enemy subs in the region to his stern, but they were clearly identified as older KILO diesel-electric boats. He figured he had plenty of time to worry about them after his team dealt with the enemy subs on which he was now closing range.

"Conn, Sonar. Range to the first AKULA now 18 thousand yards. He's holding his course and we show no indication he's spotted us."

"Conn, aye. Continue relaying position every two thousand yards. WEPS, Conn. Prepare tubes one and two for launching."

"WEPS, aye." All four torpedo tubes had been loaded several hours earlier and the torpedo room crew was ready for the orders now coming their way.

"Conn, Sonar. Range now 16 thousand yards to the first AKULA and about 30 thousand to the second one."

"Conn, Aye. WEPS, we'll launch when they're in the box."

LT Bemus and the captain had figured out their firing plans for both enemy subs and the weapons officer tingled with anticipation as he put his firing key in the panel. It showed green lights across the board.

"Conn, Sonar. Range, 12 thousand yards and closing. Range to second AKULA, 24 thousand yards."

"Conn, aye. Fire tubes one and two. Re-load when clear."

The sleek torpedoes left the tubes under 2,000 pounds of water pressure and started their programmed course. Their internal power supply kicked in and they sped through the water at 75 miles per hour. Two miles from the target the torpedoes engaged homing mode, definitely determining the enemy's fate. The target would never be able to survive the direct hits, now just seconds away.

On Board the GREAT WALL

Nearly a dozen officers were shouting commands, a sonarman told his captain he was certain an American submarine was in the vicinity but all he could confirm was a bunch of fish noises. Most puzzling was the image of a huge squid. He had no way of knowing USS BUFFALO was the boat transmitting the fish noises or that the tentacles were a trailed array from USS JAMESTOWN. The PRC sonar operators were certain no submarine was within ten miles but in battle, things tend to change rapidly.

"Captain, torpedoes inbound! Range five thousand yards." "Come left 90 degrees! All engines ahead full! Rig for torpedo attack," the skipper yelled over the intercom.

"*BOOM!*" The first torpedo slammed into the aft section. Men screamed. Darkness. Water gushed in. Two emergency lights flickered, briefly. Chaos.

"Damage Control," hollered the captain, "report your status immediately!" No reports came back. Now, only five injured men struggled valiantly to resume their duty positions.

"*BOOM!*" The second torpedo struck amidships, slicing the GREAT WALL in half. *Squidy* claimed its first victory.

On Board the QINGDAO

As they watched the red glow over southern Taiwan, a junior officer with a clip-board full of messages interrupted Admiral Ho and Captain Fong. "We have several signals from our ships and aircraft that the Americans have joined the battle. Here, sir, is the latest."

Ho fought to catch his breath, a sudden chill down his back. Glancing at the messages he uttered: "This is not good. You said they would not respond under any circumstances."

"I was sure that would be the case, Admiral. What do the reports say?"

"Dozens of planes have departed the carrier CARL VINSON, with most directed at us, a few at the Nanshas. One of our newest AKULA submarines is reported missing, and her sister ship, supplying the information, says they have tracked an enemy sub but cannot definitely pinpoint it." Glancing at another message, Ho slowly went on: "This is puzzling. GREAT WALL reports routine sea sounds and one unknown, possibly from a large Beluga whale."

"Aerial reconnaissance says the Americans are directing a cruiser and two guided missile destroyers in our direction, and sonar buoys are identifying four or five U.S. submarines." Pausing for effect and staring coldly at Captain Fong, Ho inquired: "Is this the enemy who would sit on its hands while their politicians debated whether to let us proceed, or attempt to stop us?"

"Sir, Admiral Ho. This may be the worst of what we can expect from the Americans. They normally order action only when they have been fired upon. Perhaps this is all bluster and a show for the Taiwanese."

"I'm not so sure, Fong. I am not sure at all. You'll excuse me while I go to make contact with Beijing and."

Entering the Communications Center the admiral was handed a message: "KILO fires on U.S. destroyer CUSHING. Damage unknown."

Bracing himself, Admiral Ho realized China was now officially at war with the greatest military power on the globe.

CHAPTER 110 - NO FORTUNE COOKIES
WITH THIS MEAL

January 1, 2002: On Board the QINGDAO

The ship's radio was silent save for the voice of President Zemin belching from overhead speakers: *"PLA Forces of the Peoples Republic of China have tonight fired missiles at and bombed military air bases, shipyards and Navy stations in the province of Taiwan. Rebel forces were unable to muster any significant response. Submarines and surface warships of the PLA Navy are massed off the Taiwanese coast and other locations at sea to prevent any response from the government in Taipei. Tonight's attack is but a warning to the leaders of the Taipei regime that the PRC will take back its break-away province at any cost."*

Zemin then said something his military leaders would live to regret. *"We have sent the rebels a message with tonight's attack, and used only conventional weapons to do it. We are willing to give them 24 hours to surrender. If that surrender is not offered, we will launch a second strike, and this time we will use tactical nuclear weapons."*

The Chinese president continued: *"Upon peaceful turnover of Taiwan we will assist the Taiwanese people, establish new local political leaders, and aid them in re-joining the Motherland as full and equal members of the Peoples Republic of China. Then the people of Taiwan will realize that the threat of military action no longer hangs over their heads. Long live China!"*

Aboard USS JAMESTOWN

"Conn, Sonar. That second AKULA turned in the direction of her partner. After the concussions we saw when the torpedoes hit the first sub there's no way that boat isn't on the ocean floor by now."

"Conn, aye. I concur, Chief Smart, but we can't wait for the remaining sub to go crazy and start firing everything it has. What's the distance to the enemy ship now?"

"Eighteen thousand yards and changing course often. Look! She's turning again headed right for us. Speed 20 knots, range 17 thousand yards."

"Lieutenant Bemus, is our firing plan ready for contact number two?"

The weapons officer nodded affirmative and moved over to the torpedo firing panel. He put his key in the lock and the panel went green again.

Buzz said: "Very well. WEPS, prepare to launch two more fish."

"WEPS, Aye sir."

"Conn, Sonar. We still have no pings from the AKULA. Current range just over 9 thousand yards and closing fast."

"Conn, Aye. Stand bye to fire tubes three and four."

"Conn, Sonar. Range 8 thousand yards."

"Very Well. Fire tubes three and four. OOD, come to course 180 and let's do a squid departure right now!"

Aboard USS CARL VINSON

A welcome blanket of darkness lay over the CARL VINSON's decks and crews were standing by ready for recovery of returning fighters from the first squadron. Arresting wires anticipated tail-hooks, and as the huge ship came into the wind the first wave of the F/A-18s and their re-fueling planes were spotted on the ship's radar, about 10 miles out and ready to grab the first wires they could find.

One by one the tiny specs in the night sky grew larger and larger until the loud *swoosh* of jets coming to a dead stop from over 200 miles per hour became the sweetest sound on the ship.

On Board the YALU RIVER

"Captain, I'm getting some very strange sounds on sonar." The young PLA petty officer from Shanghai continued: "I can identify most but I can't get any ping on a submarine.

"Do you see any American submarines in front of us, or not?" the captain yelled.

"No sir, I can't say we have a solid contact."

"*BOOM!*" The Chinese sub shivered from stem to stern as the enemy torpedo plunged into the forward portion of the boat. Sailors not holding on to anything were thrown to the deck as icy-cold seawater gushed in through huge cracks in the hull's seams.

"*BOOM!*" The second American torpedo plowed into the mortally wounded submarine, sending the twisted boat and everyone aboard to the seafloor. Exit Peoples Republic of China submarine YALU RIVER (SSN-32).

Aboard USS JAMESTOWN

"Conn, Sonar. Two direct hits and no further contact with the second AKULA, sir."

"Conn, Aye. Stop what you're doing but remember how you did it!"

Over the 1 MC Buzz informed his crew: "Score two probable sub kills for JAMESTOWN. You have..."

"Wow! We did it!" and other jubilant shouts interrupted the captain. Crewmembers were high-fiving everywhere.

"As I was saying...oh, the hell with it! Great job, guys. I

think there will be some special commendations coming for this, but we're still in combat so settle down and get back to your stations."

Buzz smiled at his control room team and ordered: "Re-load all tubes, come to course one-eight-zero, and proceed at 20 knots."

He asked the XO to join him in the wardroom. Once seated with fresh cups of coffee, Ellis Sherman said: "Well, skipper, the little sub that could, did. We've got ourselves a winner here."

"So far so good, Ellis, but let's not get too cocky. The PRC must have something else up their Red sleeves, and I want to be prepared for whatever they're planning. I'm sure that will include a visit from Captain David Wong."

With that said, USS JAMESTOWN triumphantly slipped away from its first field of battle.

Aboard USS CARL VINSON

Reports were flying furiously throughout the CVBG, some substantiated others still speculation. I was on the VINSON's bridge at 0300 as Admiral Davidson reviewed the status of the CUSHING, now limping toward the Philippines for repair. It appeared the remainder of the fleet was unscathed. Several F/A-18s mixed it up with their Red Chinese counterparts, but the invaders tucked tail and sped back to safety.

The Chinese ceased firing. At everything. Perhaps Beijing was hoping the Taiwanese and Americans would hold fire for 24 hours and rethink what had just occurred. Perhaps the threat of nuclear action would cause the Taiwan government to capitulate, returning their island to the PRC. From my perspective it wasn't bloody likely that any form of fallback, much less surrender, was in the cards.

China bit off a lot more than she could chew, I grinned, and found out quickly there ain't no fortune cookies with this meal.

I needed to get a story written and filed, *like now.* Thanking the admiral for letting me be in the thick of the action, I headed to my quarters. I had a hunch this was but the first of many pieces I'd be sending PANS on what was now a full-fledged war, and I knew my story would be on the front pages of most every major newspaper on New Year's Day.

CHAPTER 111 - THIS REALLY IS WAR

January 1, 2002: South China Sea

US-CHINA AT WAR
PRC AIR FORCE ATTACKS TAIWAN AIR BASE
ROC SHIPYARD AT KAOSHUNG BOMBED
ZEMIN PRAISES NEW YEAR'S EVE RAIDS
GIVES TAIPEI SURRENDER DEADLINE
PRESIDENT CRANE AUTHORIZES
U.S. FORCES TO SUPPORT TAIWAN

By: Dan Lincoln

Aboard the aircraft-carrier USS CARL VINSON in the South China Sea, Tuesday, January 1, 2002 (Pacific and Asia News Service):

Military forces of the People's Republic of China fired missiles at and bombed a key Taiwanese Navy base and shipyard at Kaoshung, in the extreme south of Taiwan in a surprise New Year's Eve raid. PRC Air Force jets fired missiles and shells, destroying dozens of Republic of China military aircraft at Taipei's Chang Kai Shek International Airport.

The lightning attacks were part of a coordinated effort to bring the Taiwan government to its knees and force the return of their island to the control of mainland China. Beijing has long considered Taiwan to be a breakaway province since the 1949 revolution that established what is called The Republic of China.

In a related and very unusual incident, PRC President Jiang Zemin, speaking from Beijing, emphatically stated this military action was the final warning to the rebels of Taiwan. He stated: "We are willing to give them 24 hours to surrender. If that surrender is not offered, we will launch a second strike, and this time we will use tactical nuclear weapons."

443

U.S. naval forces in the immediate area responded to the Chinese attacks, repelling the mainland invaders with jet fighters and submarines. An American Navy spokesperson said the biggest victory came with the sinking of two enemy submarines by U.S. Navy subs. Sources say they were of the AKULA class, purchased from Russia just a few years ago. The allies' response was in accordance with a 1954 Mutual Defense Treaty between Taiwan and the U.S., and was approved by President Crane two hours prior to the PRC action.

The advance approval was based on information obtained by the FBI revealing a planned New Year's Eve attack on Taiwan by the PLA and saying the PRC did not expect any interference by allied forces. When Navy sources detected large movements of Chinese ships toward Taiwan shortly before midnight December 31st, Rear Admiral Donald T. Davidson, the on-scene Carrier Battle Group commander, placed his air and sea units on combat alert and prepared to intercept and repulse any invading units.

Early reports indicate no major damage to any U.S. ship or aircraft. The destroyer USS CUSHING did take a direct hit from a PRC Navy submarine, but was able to make adequate repairs enabling it to proceed to a repair facility in the Philippines.

All fighting seems to have stopped, perhaps awaiting diplomatic discussions between Taipei, Beijing and Washington. The official word from RADM Davidson is that: "We are still at General Quarters and will remain so for the foreseeable future. We are actively seeking enemy targets both on and below the ocean surface and if more fighting is initiated by the Chinese Communists we will have no compunctions taking the battle straight to their homeland, including missile strikes at Beijing, Shanghai and other major Chinese cities."

Morale here on the carrier USS CARL VINSON is the highest I have seen in my two months as a DOD correspondent. A day ago sailors and air crews were anxious to have something happen. Today it's happening and they're ready to jump in with all they have.

-end-

I checked the piece for spelling and grammar, connected the modem, pasted my story to an e-mail and hit the *send* button. It went to Ben at his home address. As a back-up I sent copy to Jack O'Neill at the PANS office, and to make sure they would actually get the story I placed a very long-distance call to Ben, hoping to get him before he left for a New Year's Eve party.

"Ben, it's Dan, and all hell's broken out over here. I just filed a story via e-mail to you. Did you get it?" I asked.

"I'm in the living room watching some dumb movie. Let me go to my den and check the computer," leaving me hanging for about two minutes. He finally came back on line: "From what I read real quickly, you make it sound like World War Three has started. This isn't another of your little pranks is it?"

"Damn," I sighed, "I wish it was but those dumb commies couldn't leave well-enough alone."

Excitedly, Ben began shouting: "The networks haven't mentioned any of this. Looks like we're gonna kick some ass, again!"

Within an hour Ben had my story on PANS' newswires around the world. In the U.S., television was doing the usual New Year's Eve hoopla, and newspaper editors were deciding whether to lead with Pope John Paul blessing the Vatican crowds or photos of Baby New Year 2002.

And the mob in Times Square was growing when the huge flashing overhead ticker began running:

CHINA ATTACKS TAIWAN IN STUNNING NEW YEAR'S EVE RAID. AMERICAN SHIPS AND AIRCRAFT COME TO TAIWANESE AID. TWO PRC NUCLEAR SUBMARINES SUNK

For a brief moment the crowd was stunned into silence. As the news sunk in, murmurs built to a throbbing crescendo and people shouted: "Damn straight! Time to kick some Commie ass!"

My story made as much, if not more, impact on the world press than it did at home. I went to bed totally exhausted from the events of the past five hours but looked forward to what would follow when dawn arrived on the morning of January 1, 2002.

CHAPTER 112 - SHOOT FIRST THEN TALK

January 1, 2002: Washington, D.C.

Secretary of State Louis R. Bass spoke bluntly to Chinese Ambassador Wu: "Sir, we are each aware of what has just occurred near Taiwan. Please present yourself at my offices at nine o'clock tonight. Ambassador Donald Chang from the Taiwanese Embassy will also be here. Understand me, Ambassador, this is not a courtesy call."

Feeling the best chances of preventing a nuclear holocaust were via diplomatic solutions, Secretary Bass spoke deliberately to the two Chinas' ambassadors when they arrived. "Misters Ambassador, provocative action toward Taiwan has shoved our three nations to the brink of an unthinkable action. The United States is committed to supporting Taiwan, and is fully prepared to do so with whatever force is required."

Leveling his stern gaze at the ambassador from Beijing, Secretary Bass said: "If your nation continues hostile action toward Taiwan the U.S. can, and will, strike military bases and possibly civilian targets in your major cities."

Ambassador Wu blinked several times and attempted to clear his throat, but all that came forth was a croak. Bass remained stoic until Wu said: "Mr. Secretary, China's actions are in no way directed at the U.S. and..."

Breaking with protocol, Secretary Bass brought Wu to a standstill: "Sir, we consider your actions not just against our trusted ally, but also against the United States of America. You might as well have bombed San Francisco. My President has instructed me to inform you that any further aggressive actions will lead him to declare a formal state of war between our two countries. You do not have any 24-hour warning period. The President has sent this identical message to Beijing. Thank you for coming. We must now meet with the press."

447

Unruly representatives of the world media overflowed the U.S. State Department Press Room, and many were yelling questions as the three diplomats entered. Quickly moving to the podium before SECSTATE could react, Ambassador Wu struck a defiant pose and shouted: "We were not able to arrive at a meeting of minds regarding the situation in Taiwan. The Peoples Republic of China will stand by its demands to the rebels, and give them sufficient time to return the territory to us, the rightful owners."

He then bolted from the room, yelling: "Happy New Year to you all," leaving the U.S. diplomats to fend off the pack of reporters.

PRC STANDS BY ORIGINAL DEMANDS
MIDNIGHT DEADLINE SET FOR NEXT ATTACK
U.S. SAYS IT WILL SUPPORT TAIWAN
THREE NATIONS PREPARE FOR SHOWDOWN

By: Jack O'Neill

Washington D.C., January 1, 2002 (Pacific and Asia News Service):

Efforts at resolving the nearly day-old shooting war over ownership of Taiwan concluded unsuccessfully today at the U.S. State Department. In talks that lasted less than two hours, ambassadors from Taiwan and China stood firm in defending their governments' decisions regarding the return of Taiwan to the mainland Chinese.

Since declaring independence from Red China in 1949 Taiwan has sought to ally itself with western powers and go its own way economically. It has developed one of the strongest economies in the world, and its government has vowed not to surrender to mainland China. The Republic of China and the U.S. are allies under a Mutual Defense Treaty signed in December of 1954, and ratified by the U.S. Senate on February 9, 1955.

The U.S. Secretary of State, Mr. Louis R. Bass, told reporters he deeply regretted the no-give positions of the two ambassadors. He said President Crane had been advised of the talks' failure and that both nations had been warned about possible repercussions if fighting between them resumed.

-end-

CHAPTER 113 - ROUND TWO EVEN WORSE

January 2, 2002: Aboard USS CARL VINSON

The 24 hour pause in fighting zoomed past but allied forces wasted none of it, feverishly preparing all possible firepower. I found myself back on the CARL VINSON Bridge, while the Air-Boss prepared one squadron of jet fighters for a 2200 launch. If Red China resumed action at midnight, as promised, Brady's men would be on station near Taiwan ready for action and fully prepared for even a nuclear threat. This was getting to be good, and as the only journalist in the area I wanted to be as close to the front as possible.

Aboard USS JAMESTOWN

The telling and re-telling of battle stories continued much like locker room talk after a big football game. Everything had been executed just like training during their many shakedowns off Midway. The two Chinese subs were unable to ping on *Squidy* as a target, instead becoming targets themselves. Buzz's boys busied themselves, readying the boat for any further action. All of the torpedo tubes were reloaded and ready, as were their yet-to-be-used Tomahawk missiles.

On Board the QINGDAO

Rubbing his tired eyes, Admiral Ho impatiently paced the bridge. To no one in particular he muttered: "Those damned fool Taiwanese just don't understand the seriousness of yesterday's warning."

"They will when we fire nuclear weapons tonight, don't you think?" Captain Fong asked. "Certainly they can't be foolish enough to take this as a mere threat. We're alerting the entire world that we mean what we say."

"I trust you are correct, captain," the four-star admiral said quietly, "at least more correct than your earlier belief that our attack on Taiwan would be ignored by the Americans."

Aboard Ships and Aircraft of The CVBG

Round two. At 1145 the battle began anew. Twenty miles off the coast of Taiwan the QINGDAO prepared to lay siege to that island, while F/A-18 fighters from the VINSON screamed to the scene at 550 mph. Pilots locked-on the QINGDAO and another destroyer, trigger fingers itchily awaiting the signal to attack.

Six F/A-18s paced near PRC air and naval locations, their bombs, heat-seeking missiles and cannon armed. Squad leader Bob Holden radioed the ship they might want to launch a back-up squadron in case things heated up at midnight.

Bristling with an array of Star Trek style missiles and the AEGIS radar system, the guided missile cruiser USS PORT ROYAL and two DDGs positioned themselves about 50 miles off Taiwan. That radar system was so good it could select almost any target within 5,000 miles via GPS satellites circling above. Pinpointing a target for tonight's battle would be a piece of cake for this ship.

A senior radar intercept officer reported: "Enemy aircraft leaving mainland bases. All surface vessels maintaining last reported positions." Sonarmen on the DDGs were also tracking the PRC surface ships, and five submarines off Taiwan.

On Board the QINGDAO

Precisely at midnight, Captain Fong commanded: "Launch missiles." He watched as the two tactical nuclear WMDs blazed from the deck, rose into the murky sky and sped toward Taipei and Kaoshung. "Now, everyone will know we mean business," he said to Admiral Ho as they witnessed the missiles' fiery paths. "Kung Hee Fat Choy!"

At that very moment the OOD yelled to his skipper: "Captain, Sonar has detected a lot of sea noises and they believe there could be an American submarine about nine miles astern."

"Very well. Keep tracking and inform me if anything changes or if a positive ID can be made. How many minutes to missile arrival at targets?"

"I'll find out for you, sir," a junior officer replied. The impatient admiral was not happy with such an unacceptable answer. The first stages of combat had not favored his forces and now he expected everything would be executed in a precise, deadly manner.

In-Flight with CVBG Aircraft

China's big sky rockets were tracked from the time of their launch by American forces, and reaction was swift as F/A-18 fighter pilots clicked on-board computer arming systems from *ready* to *fire*. Air-to-air missiles then sped from under wing pods to seek and destroy the Chinese nukes before they arrived at their targets.

Aboard USS JAMESTOWN

Action was heating-up a few hundred feet down in the South China Sea. "Conn, Sonar. Contact DDG now 20 thousand yards, and no pinging by the Chinese tin-can."

"Conn, Aye."

"OOD, open outer doors on torpedo tubes one and two." JAMESTOWN was ready to launch its fifth and sixth torpedoes in two days.

"Navigator, Conn. What's the distance to the LUHU?"

"Conn, NAV. Fourteen thousand yards, sir."

"Very well. OOD, stand by to fire tubes one and two."

In another minute, Buzz said: "OOD, Conn. Fire tubes one and two."

"OOD, Aye. Firing tubes one and two."

"Conn, Sonar. Both torpedoes running smooth and straight for target."

"Conn, Aye. OOD, come left to two-seven-zero degrees. Reload tubes one and two. Maintain your current speed and make preparations to come up to periscope depth."

On Board the QINGDAO

"Captain Fong!" the Officer of the Deck squeaked in a cracking voice, "Sonar reports two torpedoes in-coming fast. Range 11 thousand yards, speed 75 knots."

"Reverse your course by 180 degrees," Fong shouted, "and increase speed to all-ahead full. New course one-nine-zero degrees."

Before the ship could complete the course change the first visitor from *Squidy* arrived.

"*WHAM!*" The torpedo caused the destroyer to shudder violently. Torpedo number two finished the job. Admiral Ho, Captain Fong and sailors of every rank found themselves tossed unceremoniously into the heaving sea. Within two minutes QINGDAO gasped a last breath and plunged to the bottom of the ocean.

In-Flight with CVBG Aircraft

With their own eyes F/A-18 pilots saw the red-orange glow of the PRC guided missiles flying toward their targets. Within two minutes of the QINGDAO launch an armada of U.S. anti-missile missiles left American jet aircraft and streaked off into the night sky toward their targets.

The few serviceable Taiwanese Air Force planes that managed to get airborne joined the U.S. F/A-18s. The two Chinese missiles were taken down, one over the ocean and the other over uninhabited countryside, possibly averting a nuclear horror.

With new spirit the American pilots bravely began searching for enemy aircraft to fight. They would also address bombing assignments worked out earlier that would take out two mainland Chinese PLA air bases.

The backup squadron from the CARL VINSON swept over the new PRC air base and coastal gunnery facility on the Nansha Islands, soon again to be called the Spratlys.

A third squadron of Navy jets scrambled when U.S. radar reported a flight of PRC planes heading in the direction of the CVBG.   They joined U.S. planes already airborne and downed seven enemy aircraft before six others tucked tail and fled back to their mainland bases.

Aboard USS JAMESTOWN

As mortally wounded Chinese jets plunged into the ocean, Captain Russell peered through the periscope at his surface foe exploding and sinking.   He could plainly see the QINGDAO crew in lifeboats and lifejackets bobbing in the oil-soaked water.   When he was sure the survivors had enough life rafts and could fend for themselves, he ordered JAMESTOWN submerged to 300 feet, and headed southwest where his crew had reported hearing what they believed to be KILO and HAN submarines off Taiwan.

The newer HAN boats, Chinese designed and built, were the pride of the PRC Navy. Buzz wondered if this boat might be the one stolen by the rebel Captain David Wong and if *Squidy* would get a chance to go head to head with that cunning American-hater.

"Conn, Sonar. Getting screw sounds from at least two, possibly three enemy boats. One is definitely a HAN; distance to her 30 thousand yards."

"Conn, Aye. WEPS, plot a torpedo firing solution for the HAN. OOD, come right to course zero nine zero. Open doors on torpedo tubes three and four."

"Conn, WEPS. Plotting solution now."

"Conn, OOD. Coming right to new course zero nine zero. Opening outer doors on tubes three and four."

"Conn, very well. Advise when ready to fire."

Buzz ordered the JAMESTOWN up fifty feet where water temperature would aid in avoiding being pinged by enemy sonar. The charts that CINCPACFLT meteorologist had given them proved to be invaluable in finding the best depths to elude the hunters.

"Conn, Sonar. Range now 20 thousand yards and closing fast."

"Conn, WEPS. We have a torpedo firing solution. Suggest course zero-seven-five at two-zero knots."

"Conn, Aye. OOD, bring the boat to new course zero-seven-five and make your speed two-zero knots.

"LT Bemus," Buzz called. "Stand-by to launch three and four at range 12 thousand yards."

"Conn, WEPS. At range now, skipper. Two fish away. Standing-by tubes one and two."

"Conn, Sonar. We can now positively identify the other two enemy boats as KILOs and like the other PRC subs they haven't identified us either. Torpedoes three and four running smooth and on target."

"Conn, Aye. Fire tubes one and two when 8,000 yards from the KILOs."

Captain Russell had no more than gotten the firing orders out of his mouth when his boat felt a low rumbling sound, and Jack Smart reported: "Direct hit on the HAN with torpedo number three. Secondary hit aft of target, perhaps exploding in enemy-released magnetic attraction. Sonar indicates breakup and sinking of the boat."

The two fish aimed at the KILOs were launched; after their course and steadiness had been confirmed by Sonar, Buzz directed *Squidy* to leave the area and look for some rear-echelon PRC diesel boats.

"OOD, come right to new course one-eight-zero, and maintain your current speed."

"Conn, OOD. Coming right to new course one-eight-zero, maintaining speed, sir."

The skipper then headed to the sonar area where Chief Smart was still on his console, and looked up as the skipper approached: "I got a clear indication that we hit one of the KILOs, Captain. Unfortunately, the second torpedo seems to have missed its target. I'm not showing its track anymore and I didn't see anything that would have meant a hit or the fish being blown up."

Buzz didn't say it to anyone, but still wondered if the HAN they sank could have been the PEOPLE'S VICTORY.

CHAPTER 114 – JUST YOU WAIT

January 2, 2002: On Board the PEOPLE'S VICTORY

Stinging reports of continuous PRC defeats poured in as Captain Wong sat sullenly aboard his submarine in the Shanghai Navy Shipyard, damning the disaster Beijing was bringing down on China. "If anyone had listened to me I could have warned them it would happen." To his XO brother-in-law he sternly vowed: "Even if we lose this battle, the war is not ended. We will get PEOPLE'S VICTORY out of dry dock and sink American aircraft carriers. That is my order!"

Aboard Ships of the Carrier Battle Group

USS RUSSELL radar spotted a PRC destroyer making her run and immediately launched a pair of Harpoon missiles at the fleeing vessel; within minutes they slammed into the enemy ship, most probably sinking it.

Putting a final exclamation point on the operation, PORT ROYAL, RUSSELL and HOPPER lobbed Tomahawk missiles at military targets in Shanghai and Beijing, and one right into the heart of Tiananmen Square.

Within the hour Radio China crackled with the message that the PRC was recalling all troops and withdrawing demands for Taiwan's surrender.

Aboard USS CARL VINSON

Game-set-match. Checkmate, USA! Time of battle, three hours and 27 minutes. Casualties: US zero, China more than could be immediately counted. But most of all, great loss of face for the PRC before the entire world. For Admiral

Davidson the victory meant remaining on station, and continuing to sweep the region for any sore losers who might want to continue the fighting.

I knew I'd been in a front-row seat for one of the all-time news stories of my generation. I needed to tell the world. Scurrying to my quarters, I lit my laptop and began typing:

CHINESE PICK NUCLEAR FIGHT WITH U.S. NAVY
AMERICANS BLUNT ATTACKS AGAINST TAIWAN
U.S. RESPONDS WITH NON-NUKE MISSILE
ATTACKS ON BEIJING & SHANGHAI
PRC ENDS ACTION AND DROPS DEMANDS
FOR TAIWAN SURRENDER

By: Dan Lincoln

Aboard the Aircraft Carrier USS CARL VINSON in the South China Sea, January 2, 2002 (Pacific and Asia News Service):

Two nuclear missiles were fired tonight at the Republic of China. Jet fighter pilots from the Taiwanese Air Force and the U.S. Navy aircraft carrier CARL VINSON, successfully shot down the missiles. One landed harmlessly in the ocean, another hit an uninhabited area. The missiles were launched exactly at midnight from the Chinese Navy guided missile destroyer QINGDAO, the first nuclear weapons fired in anger since the U.S. dropped atomic bombs on Japan in August of 1945.

Reports from the Commander of the American Carrier Battle Group say that shortly after QINGDAO fired the missiles she was hit and sunk by torpedoes from a U.S. Navy submarine.

China made air and surface attacks on Taiwan 24 hours earlier, in a surprise New Year's Eve raid. Attack plans were discovered prior to the raid by FBI agents from court-approved listening devices planted in the Washington, D.C. apartment of Madam Lily Shin, alleged leader of a Chinese spy team caught committing espionage against the U.S. Navy.

FBI and Navy officials were tipped-off about Shin by former Senator Henry B. Anderson (D-MN). Employing audio bugs and telephone taps, authorities learned of the plan from conversations between Shin and officials at the Chinese Embassy in Washington.

With this information American and ROC planes and ships were prepared. After deflecting the PRC missiles and downing numerous enemy jet fighters, the U.S. Navy launched a savage attack on PRC Navy vessels, sinking an estimated three destroyers and three submarines.

A group of American planes also bombed Chinese facilities on the Spratly Islands. The final blow came when American Navy cruisers and guided missile destroyers launched a series of Tomahawk missiles at military sites in Beijing, Shanghai and two coastal bases.

Within an hour Beijing radio announced a recall of all PRC ships and aircraft to their home bases, and withdrawal of demands for Taiwan's government to surrender to the PRC.

One senior U.S. Navy officer, who declined to be named, told PANS: "Why the Chinese didn't pour at least a few thousand Army troops into Taiwan is surprising. Given 10 or 20 thousand PLA soldiers, the battle equation could have been different."

The U.S. Navy remains on full alert with aircraft providing 24-hour reconnaissance in the skies over the region. Warships of the 7th Fleet continue patrolling the South China Sea.

It is expected the United States will call for a special session of the United Nations to vote on sanctions against the Peoples Republic. The Spratly Islands are expected to be placed in a trust territory status, to be administered jointly by the U.S. and Taiwan plus other Asian nations who had formerly laid claim to the islands between Singapore and the Philippines.

Chinese President Jiang Zemin has yet to make a formal statement.

-end-

CHAPTER 115 - THE STORIES OF WAR

January 2 to 6, 2002:   Asia, Hawaii & The World

Asian newspapers splattered my exclusive story across their front pages, shocking Far East nations and frightening many others. Would Red China take-out its humiliation on them? I missed some of the jubilation aboard the CARL VINSON, sleeping away exhaustion earned from working over my story until 5 am body time. For once, breakfast wasn't on my daily agenda.

I woke up about noon and flipped on my mini-TV, and clicked to CNN. Their Tokyo camera crew flew to Taipei and comprehensively covered the Taiwan government responses to the attacks, but Hong Kong reporters were barred from Shanghai, Beijing or other military bases hit by the Tomahawk missiles. A terse PRC statement said coverage was being arranged for the next day, but everyone knew they were stalling for time until they could get a fabricated story straight; one minimizing the devastation visited on them by the U.S.

The headline in Hong Kong's South China Morning Post read:

TAIWAN TARGET OF NUCLEAR ATTACKS
PLA AIR FORCE REPELLED BY AMERICANS
U.S. FORCES RETALIATE WITH MISSILE
STRIKES ON CHINESE MAINLAND
PRC WARSHIPS AND PLANES DESTROYED
BEIJING WITHDRAWS SURRENDER DEMANDS

The Japanese were good to their tradition of not offending anyone, even during a war condition. The morning headline in the popular Asahi Shinbun read:

YANKS AND TAIWANESE REPEL NUCLEAR ATTACK
BEIJING WITHDRAWS DEMANDS ON TAIPEI
CALLS FOR PRC FORCES TO RETURN HOME

After-battle reports from the CVBG showed casualties and damage were less than might have been expected with no loss of fighter pilots, although three jets were downed. Twelve PRC planes were shot down, five observed hit with no pilot ejections seen, and dozens left the battle and scurried home before it was their turn to receive an allied missile.

Late on the afternoon of January 4th two important messages were waiting for me. Ben congratulated me on my reporting about the Chopsticks War, as he called it, and then firmly reminded me my tour of duty was supposed to last only two months. Oh well, I thought; time to get back to being a desk jockey.

The other message was from Admiral Sharpe. I had to go to the COMM office to have it decoded. Superb coverage of the action. Best wartime writing since Edward R. Murrow's stories from London in World War II. Congratulations.

One other paragraph in the admiral's message caught my attention. The USS JAMESTOWN proved that it could work wonders. I may have another ship visit I'd like you to consider. Once your schedule is firmed call me on a scrambler phone and we'll talk about it. Unless I was wrong, I'd never heard of the USS JAMESTOWN.

My journalist's curiosity aroused, I e-mailed Ben: Admiral Sharpe has requested I remain on post for a month. He has some-thing special he wants me to cover. If there's nothing pressing I want to stay with the fleet.

Battle action was at all stop, so I was just hanging around the flag bridge watching flight ops when Admiral Davidson motioned me to his chair. I waited for him to complete an out-going message.

"Chief, you're going to the RUSSELL for a few days to see how life is aboard a much smaller and less opulent ship. Take enough uniforms for three days."

"Yes, sir!" I replied, excited at this new opportunity. "When?"

"You chopper over at 1530. Get packing."

The chopper ride to RUSSELL gave me a good look at my next temporary home. The first impression is that a guided missile destroyer is much, much smaller than a carrier. Duh. That impression was enforced once on board because I felt like I had to carefully plot every move or I would slam into a bulkhead or fall down a ladder.

Locating the skipper Commander Ken Keating was easy, and protocol was somewhat less formal than on VINSON. After leading me to an empty rack in the Chief's berthing area, he asked me to join him in the wardroom for a briefing. Over coffee the commander described his ship's role in the CVBG and her capabilities as a vessel of war.

"Very impressive."

"Yes, we're considered the latest in the Navy's armament. You'll get a fuller picture in the next three days."

"If you don't mind my asking you have a very familiar name. Growing up in New York State I remember my grandfather talking about a former U.S. Senator from Rochester named Ken Keating."

"He was my grandfather. You have a good memory, Chief."

For the next three days I had countless opportunities to listen to personal stories from crewmembers of all ranks. Their impressions of the situation here, coupled with battle experience, would make for good reading on the home front. Each had a unique story about the Chopsticks War. I now felt like a 21st Century Ernie Pyle on duty in the hostile waters of Asia.

U.S. SEVENTH FLEET STILL AT THE READY
CHINESE NAVY QUIET, BUT NOT GONE
U.S. SAILORS RECALL BATTLES

By: Dan Lincoln

At sea aboard the Guided Missile Destroyer USS RUSSELL (DDG-59) in the South China Sea, Sunday, January 6, 2002 (Pacific and Asia News Service):

Fighting ended a week ago between the People's Republic of China and Taiwan. U.S. Navy personnel have dubbed the action the Chopsticks War. Severely defeated, the PRC has suspended its demands for the surrender of the Republic of China. While the U.N. debates placing special sanctions on China, the U.S. Navy continues its constant area patrols.

In the past week aboard the Navy's Carrier Battle Group, this reporter talked to dozens of officers, pilots, and ship crew members, and for them morale has never been higher. The success of both New Year's Eve and New Year's Day battles brought smiles to the faces of these American military personnel.

Navy LT Sarah Hunter from Mill Valley, California, flying her F/A-18 jet that first night, recalls coming up on a Chinese Mig fighter: "He was loaded with missiles ready to fire when I came up fast behind him. He turned his head around, saw me right on his six, and the look on his face was nothing short of a guy tied to a guillotine watching the blade dropping toward his neck. My missile went straight up his tail pipe. He was still looking at me as I peeled off and went looking for more easy kills like him."

Carrier pilots don't get all the glory. Gunners Mate 2nd Class Anthony Scarpetti from Revere, Massachusetts, assigned to the USS RUSSELL, told me: "The ship was not far off southern Taiwan when the PRC jets started coming overhead. We'd been tracking them for several minutes on our radars, and as they got close to us they fired at least two missiles at our position. We have this great gun up on the O-2 level that is basically a 21st Century version of the old Gatling gun. Well, this little Jessie which looks like an R2-D2 robot, can fire a hundred rounds of bullets in one second! That's right, I said one second, not minute."

"Well, the missiles from the Chinese plane were headed toward us and we fired our R2 a few times and that was the end of their incoming. God, what a night that was. I'll never forget it."

Today all is quiet. However, sources believed to be reliable to us have confirmed that after clean up from allied bomb attacks on Chinese naval and air bases, the PLA Navy appears to be back in training. They're missing several ships but still have five relatively new

HAN Class submarines intact, as well as several older Russian built boats and hundreds of surface warfare and coastal defense ships in their Fleet.

It would appear the current status in the region is an update of the old Mexican standoff. America continues to maintain a large and vocal presence in the region, while China quietly goes about business as usual.

-end-

CHAPTER 116 - NEW TOY FOR BIG BOYS

January 6, 2002: South China Sea

The war continued for Captain David Wong and his band of rebels as they labored feverishly to free PEOPLE'S VICTORY from dry dock while formulating their scheme of revenge. Wong was plainly frustrated with endless delays, placing him four months behind schedule. He itched to hunt enemy ships and destroy them all.

The captain and his crew pledged not to return to China until every missile and torpedo had been fired at the Americans. They fumed waiting for orders from Admiral Ho which would never come. The admiral and his executive staff now lay the bottom of the ocean, victims of the New Year's Day battle.

With stolen details of America's new stealth audio transmission system in his hands, Wong had endlessly drilled his crew for six months. His sub had been fitted with new hardware and software and new engineering systems he planned to use in a surprise attack on the U.S. Navy off Taiwan. PEOPLE'S VICTORY was manned solely with dedicated young communists who would follow their skipper to hell.

Madam Shin's husband had decided to steal his sub, then proceed into action without official permission. All that mattered in his warped mind was revenge at any cost.

He hatched a plan: at 1900 Sunday night, January 6th, he dispatched a small group of followers disguised as electricians to fix a shipboard power outage, created when one of his gang disconnected a main power line at the pier. The phony electricians had no trouble boarding the submarine and quickly overcame the skeleton crew of six. Ground power was reconnected and the Red Dragon rebels swarmed aboard in small groups every ten minutes and got the boat underway.

At 2100 PEOPLE'S VICTORY moved slowly toward the harbor, attracting little attention in all the chaos of damaged warships trying to enter the shipyard. At 2115 China's most deadly submarine ever entered open ocean under a clouded sky. The captain gave the first command: "Prepare to dive!"

Turning to Lieutenant Commander Leong on the bridge, Wong's face took on an almost evil grimace. "Those Americans have carried their big stick too long, hiding their soft bellies. Now, China will reclaim the respect we deserve. We will deliver the telling blows. And to you, U.S. Navy submariners, stand by. You will be the first to feel the might and wrath of the new China."

As Wong and Leong slid down the ladder into the control room PEOPLE'S VICTORY picked up speed and slipped under the dark surface of the South China Sea.

A somewhat somber side note to the Chopsticks War was that the JAMESTOWN crew, like their boat, could celebrate only in silence. No publicity about their *Squidy*, what she looked like or how she performed. And definitely nothing indicating that she had truly achieved total submarine stealth levels.

Admiral Davidson ordered the submarine on active patrol status, to begin operational tests again and allow the crew to hone their search-and-destroy skills. Buzz's peace of mind was jolted when he received a message from VADM Sharpe: 11 Jan: Intel reports PRC submarine PEOPLE'S VICTORY departed Shanghai on 6 Jan. Info indicates unauthorized operation. Proceed with caution, but intercept. Take action only on my command or if fired upon.

Buzz paused a moment, then exclaimed: "It's that damned Wong! Has to be." Quickly he connected all the salient points from the Washington spy ring to information Madam Shin forwarded to her husband. That bastard's got one goal; sink our ships any way he can, even if it means using nukes. He wants revenge because he knows China has lost the battle. Buzz knew that he and Wong would face-off in an undersea duel to the death.

CHAPTER 117 - SHIP HOPPING FOR STORIES

January 14, 2002: South China Sea

Obviously Ben liked my story about life aboard the USS RUSSELL, because he e-mailed and advised me to remain on watch in the South China Sea. Perhaps you can land another big one, he wrote. Keep the folksy flair going readers are eating it up, and have something ready for next Sunday's editions.

My ego was interrupted by a message from Captain Keating. I was wanted in his quarters. It took just a few minutes to get there on the compact ship compared to the jumbo carrier I just left.

"Morning, Chief Lincoln. Great story you did on Gunner Scarpetti." I nodded my appreciation.

"Chief, you are transferring to the LAKE ERIE this afternoon to see what it's like on a cruiser. Because you don't have a full complement of uniforms, you can pick-up something over there. They have a much larger uniform shop than we do."

I had to scurry to make my 1500 flight, say goodbye to people I'd met and interviewed, get an e-mail off to Ben and pack my few belongings. Lifting off the destroyer's helo deck, I marveled; three entirely different ships in just two weeks.

Stepping on to LAKE ERIE's deck the XO greeted me and said: "You're wanted on the bridge. Follow me." I quickly discovered my fame preceded me. From officers to enlisted, it seemed everyone had read my stories.

On the bridge I was presented to a Jimmy Stewart look-alike, Captain John Richard Kennedy. As I saluted he said: "Welcome aboard, Chief. We wanted to make certain you paid us a visit. Maybe you'll uncover some interesting people to write about. Oh, and unlike Captain Keating, I don't have any famous relatives." Turning to the XO, Kennedy directed: "Get him squared away in the Goat Locker and turn him loose."

Shipboard routine is pretty much the same on every vessel: it's the people that give her a personality. My job was to make it come to life for readers around the globe. Operating Systems are another matter. It didn't take me long to learn that the Aegis system was very different. Radar is the heart and it's connected to global positioning satellites that can tell within 30 feet exactly where on the globe the ship is. Some heart!

LAKE ERIE was participating in CVBG gunnery exercises and Captain Kennedy sent me to CIC to see exactly what was happening. As my eyes adjusted to the green radar screens in the inky blackness, I saw little blips everywhere. The weapons officer, LT Jon Lindeman, said the drill was to down an incoming missile launched from another U.S. ship hundreds of miles away.

"Here, look right here," he said pointing to a new blip. "They just launched and there's our covering signal. We're locked on."

There was a lot of noise from the foredeck and immediately our own interceptor missile blasted skyward, streaking smack into the invader. Seeing it all unfold so quickly I thought I had a pretty good take on the value of the Aegis system. What a story this will make!

The balance of my visit to the cruiser was spent in a stem to stern tour, conversations with several sailors and a couple of games of cribbage with a chief who had been playing the game for nearly 30 years. Good thing we were playing for only a penny a point. I hadn't played for that long but did consider myself a very good crib player. Unfortunately, my performance palled before that old boy.

My stay on LAKE ERIE ended at 1700 on Thursday when I hitched a chopper ride back to CARL VINSON. "Back to the lap of luxury," I announced. All the specialty shops and services; medical, dental, barber shop, post office, computer room, recreation rooms, gyms and health centers, and movie theaters. I made a mental note to do a feature on the luxury aspect of life at sea.

A quiet three weeks had slipped by since the Chopsticks War; you could hardly tell it occurred. Sure, the Spratly Islands were returned to Taiwan but the United Nations gave the PRC a cursory slap on the wrist and the world community seemed to have forgotten there had almost been a World War Three.

The whole sordid mess remained forefront in my mind. I knew it influenced every line I wrote. Life on the VINSON appeared normal as we steamed to liberty port in Singapore but normal for me was about to take a big shift. Chief Glover in communications called to say they had a message for me they were currently decoding. "I'm on my way," I answered.

The message was from Bernie Sharpe, and having known him for four years I knew it had to be something special. This time Bernie topped himself. He was offering me a chance to be a part of U.S. Navy submarine history. I sat down and read the following: Your stories are just what the doctor ordered. Keep them coming. The biggest dividends came because you were on the front lines with the CVBG and scooped everyone else. I feel there may be more action coming.

First the praise, then the request. Knowing Bernie I read on: I am offering you a special assignment which you may decline. It involves a radically new submarine known only to the Navy and select civilians. However, it must be understood that *you will not be able to report what you find.* The ship is currently attached to your group, and I can arrange your transfer immediately if you accept the above terms.

My excitement grew as I wondered what this sub looked like and what she could do that traditional boats couldn't. Bernie continued: The submarine is the USS JAMESTOWN, commanded by my friend Captain Buzz Russell. I can authorize a four day tour of duty aboard, if you accept my restrictions. *You may gather information, but you are forbidden to release any of it without explicit DOD permission.* Perhaps in a few months or even years, you can write a flash-back story on her maiden voyage.

The admiral knew how to play me. An offer like this is like dangling a goldfish in front of a cat. His message concluded: If you wish to join CAPT Russell contact Admiral Davidson who will let me know and we'll set up a helicopter transfer shortly after your Singapore visit is completed. Regards, Bernie.

Making that decision didn't take long, and I headed immediately up to the Flag Bridge for a very brief conversation with Admiral Davidson. After saying he'd take care of everything, I made time to file something back to Ben for his weekend use.

BATTLE GROUP CARRIER VISITS SINGAPORE
CHINA PROMISES MAJOR BLUE WATER NAVY
U.S. SAILORS RECALL CHOPSTICKS WAR

By: Dan Lincoln

The Republic of Singapore, Saturday January 19, 2002 (Pacific and Asia News Service):

A shore side band played as the huge 97,000 ton aircraft carrier USS CARL VINSON pulled into Singapore Harbor today. The centerpiece of the U.S. Navy's regional Carrier Battle Group anchored at this popular Asian port for a three day visit. After the recent battle with the PRC over Taiwan, the few days ashore will be welcomed by the 5,000 men and women on the carrier. Other ships of the CARL VINSON battle group are still on patrol in the South China Sea.

Rear Admiral Theodore R. Davidson, USN, commander of the group, said this visit to Singapore had been set up well before what has now become known as the Chopsticks War.

More stories keep coming from those U.S. sailors and airmen who fought in war. LT Jon

Lindeman, Weapons Officer on the cruiser USS LAKE ERIE, told me how his ship had been ordered to fire two of its Tomahawk missiles against targets in mainland China after the shooting resumed on New Year's Day night. The LAKE ERIE, an Aegis guided missile cruiser, can put a missile within feet of its target. Lindeman was called on to plot the course for two such missiles, one to land at an air base outside Beijing and the other to hit a Navy base on the northeast Chinese coast near North Korea. Both missiles hit within three feet of plotted map coordinates.

-end-

The long weekend in Singapore was just what the ship's crew needed; lots of exotic meals, shopping, sunning on Sentosa Island beaches and of course some imbibing.

On Tuesday the departure day, the flotilla sailed several hundred miles north to our station, and life was back in routine. My routine, however, was about to go upside down. Reporting to Admiral Davidson, he held a message from SUBPAC ordering me to TAD on USS JAMESTOWN, effective Friday January 25th.

"Boy, you really hop around this Navy," the admiral laughed. "You must have something big on someone back in Washington."

Come Friday I said so-long to a few of the chiefs I had gotten to know and told them I was off for more ship-hopping. Not naming any particular ship, I left the carrier for the short ride to what would become the most bizarre chapter of my already weird world.

As it worked out I didn't see the light of day for another ten days, and what would happen in between would make my spy ring story look like feature material for the Family/Home Section.

CHAPTER 118 - SQUIDY PROVES HERSELF

January 28, 2002: South China Sea

On the JAMESTOWN diving planes were forward on a squid-shaped hull. Motion was activated via water forced through the engine blades like an airplane jet engine, allowing *Squidy* to move fast or slow in total silence. She really was a stealth submarine! All of Bernie Sharpe's work and dreams were now fulfilled and I was getting to experience it even before he did.

Chief Sonarman Jack Smart was showing me control room operations Monday afternoon the 28th, when he suddenly held his hand up for silence. Into his mike he whispered: "Conn, Sonar. New contact 30 thousand yards off our starboard quarter."

"Conn, Aye. Monitor his movements and advise if he changes course."

The captain approached the chart table telling the navigator to pinpoint the contact in relation to our current position. "Right here, skipper," he said pointing to a spot off the Red Chinese coast.

"Thanks, NAV. Start tracking him."

"Aye, aye, sir."

"Conn, Sonar. Contact beginning a starboard turn steadying up at 30 degrees."

"OOD, Conn. Come right 30 degrees, maintain speed."

In my bones I knew it was Captain Wong and his rebels. Must be the skipper agreed because at 1500 he requested permission from Admiral Davidson to relinquish his screening duties for the battle group and engage the contact.

At 1700 Buzz addressed his crew: "This is the Captain speaking. We've been tracking a contact we believe to be a hijacked Chinese Navy submarine under the control of a group of officers and civilians led by the former Chief of the PRC's U.S. Intelligence section."

There was total silence aboard ship as each member of the crew strained to hear CAPT Russell's every word.

"We'll continue tracking trying to get a positive ID. It has been reported her crew is out to avenge the loss of the Taiwan battles. I am now designating this contact as *Red Star*. Keep your eyes and ears open, and good luck."

Hurrying to my quarters to make notes I passed Buzz's cabin and he waved me inside. "We may be in for a fight, Dan. I know you have submarine experience but are you ready for whatever lies ahead?"

"Are you kidding? This is a reporter's dream come true. You couldn't get me off this boat even stuffed into a torpedo tube!"

"Fine. But remember, you cannot tell anyone about any of this."

I could feel tension rising within the crew as the evening passed and they went methodically about their duties. In my quarters I opened a laptop file, named it Red Star, and entered some random thoughts.

Action sped up when we go close enough to make a positive ID. "Conn, Sonar, *Red Star* has slowed to ten knots and appears to be searching for us. She's 20 thousand yards off our forward port quarter and she is a HAN. Without any screw sounds from us she probably won't know we're here, even underway."

"Good job, Chief. Keep listening and let me know when she changes course or cruising speed."

Buzz left the control room but I stayed, eyes glued to the sonar screen. "Chief, how did you know she's *definitely* a HAN?"

"Easy," he replied, pointing at a different screen. "This oscilloscope shows sounds emitted by specific sources we've already identified. I'll put a CD track of HAN footprints on this meter above *Red Star's* signals and watch what happens."

He pushed a couple of buttons and the images on both screens matched! All peaks and valleys on the audio meter were exactly the same, proving we had a HAN. This info I *could* use in future stories.

After dinner the next SitRep came in: "Conn, Sonar. *Red Star* is now 40 thousand yards to our northwest. Course zero-one-zero at a speed of 20 knots."

Climbing into my berth, I felt the boat shudder slightly as we resumed cruising speed of 20 or 25 knots. I fell into a troubled sleep, dreaming of combat with *Red Star*, and I didn't have a station to man. I felt totally useless, and all I could do was wait for the outcome. I was shaken awake at 0600 by several *booms* from depth charges.

Aboard USS BUFFALO

Twenty miles from *Squidy*, the early morning sonar watch on USS BUFFALO also heard depth charges. Captain Bob Gruenwald knew all about David Wong, his rebel sailors and their goal of taking out the American battle group.

"Conn, Sonar. Target has just turned, gone to 30 knots and is heading away from the DDG that dropped the candy bars on her."

"Conn, Aye. Stick with her and let's see if we can give her a few more presents."

What Captain Gruenwald didn't know was that Buzz Russell's sub was also in the area; because of her unique construction and propulsion system the JAMESTOWN could not show up on his boat's sonar.

Aboard USS JAMESTOWN

Buzz duplicated the target's path but increased *Squidy's* speed to 30 knots. By early afternoon we were close enough for Chief Smart to re-identify the rebel boat. In the control room the skipper said to his team: "What do you say we give Captain Wong and his men a gift of JAMESTOWN's finest colonial weapons, one of our highly polished pewter torpedoes! WEPS, let me know when we're in firing range. OOD, open outer doors on tubes one and three and prepare to fire two conventional torpedoes."

"Aye, aye, skipper!" came the thumbs-up response from LT Bemus and his team.

On Board the PEOPLE'S VICTORY

In a similar space on PEOPLE'S VICTORY, Wong smiled while watching the sonar dot he believed to be USS BUFFALO nearing his position.

"The rat has taken our bait, Comrades. It's an American nuclear attack submarine and she's just about where we want her. Mister Chen, open *our* squid box and let the fish swim out to greet the great U.S. Navy!"

"The Americans are about to be given a big dose of their own medicine." With his entire crew listening, Wong added: "And Lieutenant Chen, make sure you also release our Beluga whale."

Aboard USS JAMESTOWN

Everyone on the JAMESTOWN was following PEOPLE'S VICTORY's face-off with one of our SSNs. Standing behind Chief Smart I watched and listened as we approached *Red Star*, but when in range Smart frantically adjusted his sonar and tapped his earphones as if he couldn't believe his ears. Through my headphones I didn't hear a sub, I heard lots of very strange noises.

"Conn, Sonar. Tell the skipper something real weird is happening here."

Within a minute Buzz Russell was at the console wearing the earphones I offered him. "I can't believe this! Are you getting the same sounds Chief?"

"Yes sir, and I'm pretty sure I also heard a Beluga whale. Or it could be a giant squid but that's too much like our own...." He stopped in mid-sentence as the captain finished it for him. "...Navy Squid Box system, the one Admiral Sharpe thinks the Chinese stole from us, is that what you were going to say?"

The chief sonarman was speechless. Russell said it for everyone: "Gentlemen, *we* cannot be detected by enemy sonar. Captain Wong and his avengers obviously have a copy of the Navy's new acoustic stealth system, nicknamed the Squid Box, and we're now finding out just how good it works. The problem is the USS BUFFALO is on the receiving end of what was supposed to have been used by American submarines *against* the enemy."

"OOD, come right to course one-nine-five, all ahead full. Set evasive maneuvering plan. Let's get away from this area and work out a battle plan to relieve Wong of his new advantage and help Captain Gruenwald on the BUFFALO. Perhaps together we'll get the PEOPLE'S VICTORY off our sonar scopes forever."

Knowing when to stay out of the way I returned to my quarters. I felt Buzz would work something out, but knowing the rebels had our secret sound system rattled me.

Simon had said something was fishy and when Admiral Sharpe suggested the Chinese had all our secrets I didn't make any connection with poor Simon and just passed it off. He was right all along; there was a Pentagon mole.

Was this mole the same American the old Chinese man told me about in Honolulu? Was he part of the PRC spy ring in Washington or was he someone long since replaced by Beijing? And where in the Pentagon was this person hiding? The mole had lived through the 9-11 attack so I figured he had to know all the right ways to hide.

CHAPTER 119 - PUSH COMES TO SHOVE

February 1, 2002: Undersea, Near the Spratlys

Aboard USS JAMESTOWN

Buzz Russell did not plan on being odd man out. He and his officers had a scheme to blast Wong and his rebels out of the sea. With *Squidy's* ability to go undetected, she would monitor the other two subs waiting for the right moment to attack.

Aboard USS BUFFALO

Captain Bob Gruenwald headed south at flank speed, intending to let the enemy sail to him. He set his op area 20 miles north of the Spratlys, covering his rear and effectively reducing Wong's attack options. At midday on Friday February first, BUFFALO came to a full stop.

The Captain told his crew: "Gentlemen, we're making our stand right here. All of you know China has our Squid Box technology but we can whip them anyway. Today you'll need to be at your absolute best. May God bless us all."

On Board the PEOPLE'S VICTORY

This is the Captain speaking: "We have them where we want them, Comrades. The American submarine is the USS BUFFALO. They think they can dodge our torpedoes by putting the Nanshas behind them, but that won't work. They think they are in a safe spot, but we will attack from their backside, the south; sink the boat and then have a clear shot at their mighty aircraft carrier battle group."

Aboard USS JAMESTOWN

Squidy was at dead stop, same as BUFFALO, when things got a lot hotter about 1420.

"Conn, Sonar. Target back on the screen, heading is two-six-five, at 25 knots."

"Conn, Aye. Standby, skipper's coming to you."

Buzz looked at Jack Smart's sonar screen, asking: "Where's he headed?"

"They have a base about here, but they don't need replenishing," the chief replied pointing to the edge of mainland China.

"Watch them like a hawk, Chief, and let me know if there's any change in status."

On Board the PEOPLE'S VICTORY

At 1700, LCDR Leong told Captain Wong: "We're 30 miles below the north coast of the Nanshas and ready for your orders."

"Very well, XO. Take us slowly up behind the enemy. Begin emitting fish noises five thousand yards sooner than normal to give the Americans a false read."

As activity picked up in the control room, Wong added: "Have all torpedo tubes loaded for immediate use. Use the conventional warheads so we don't waste nukes on just one submarine; we'll save those for the carrier battle group."

By 1830 the Chinese boat was 10 miles astern of the BUFFALO launching her version of the Squid Box.

Aboard USS JAMESTOWN

Jack Smart was finishing a cup of coffee when the phone rang. "Chief, it's PO-2 Aldinger. There's something really weird on my sonar. Could you take a look?"

"On my way. Have the OOD ask the skipper to join me.

By the time Smart reached the sonar room the captain was already at the petty officer's scope and listening on headphones to what Aldinger was hearing. The chief motioned the PO-2 to get up as he slid in behind the sonar screen.

"It's definitely Squid Box sounds, Captain, but look where they're coming from." He pointed to an area just off the coast of the Spratlys, 12 to 15 miles south of the BUFFALO's position.

"Oh, crap! The sneaky bastard circled around and came up behind us."

"Chief Smart, two can play this game at the same time. If Wong is the least bit uncertain we may be able to get the upper hand, ping on them, and send a couple of our big fish to pay them a call."

On Board the PEOPLE'S VICTORY

Like heavyweight boxers, the opposing Officers of the Deck busied themselves preparing for the fight. The Chinese OOD loudly proclaimed: "Contact believed to be the American sub, 15 thousand yards ahead, Captain. It appears he's dead in the water."

"Good. We haven't been spotted. Open outer doors on starboard tubes and prepare torpedoes for launching."

"Aye, aye, Comrade Captain."

"Sonar, advise when we're in firing range."

David Wong smiled the sinister smile only he could make and told his brother-in-law: "Let's make sure we accomplish this historical moment, XO, since another loss of face for China at this time would be totally unacceptable."

Aboard USS BUFFALO

Everyone in the control room was ready. "Conn, sonar. We have contact with the HAN. She's off our port quarter about 12 thousand yards astern."

"Conn, aye. WEPS, make tubes one and two ready in all respects, and make sure they're reloaded ASAP. OOD, stand-by to come to course two-seven-zero and make your speed 20 knots. We'll wait until she's just out of the box before we make our final move."

"WEPS, aye. Outer doors open, tubes one and two ready."

"Conn, OOD. Standing-by to come to new course two-seven-zero at 20 knots.

It took several minutes more before Bob Gruenwald felt the distance between the two boats was perfect for his attack.

"WEPS, fire tubes one and two. OOD, make your course change now!"

"WEPS, aye sir. Torpedoes away!"

"OOD, aye. Bring the boat to new course two-seven-zero and make turns for 20 knots."

The captain turned to his XO and said: "Rocky, we may be just a tad off in our timing so get us ready for a direct hit."

Unfortunately, the submarine skipper's prediction came true.

Aboard USS JAMESTOWN

Everything around us on *Squidy* seemed to change with the moment. I stayed in a corner of the sonar room in view of everything the crew was doing. If I hadn't been on U-boats for years and gone through drills almost as real as today's live action I'd have peed my pants by now.

"OOD, come left to new course heading two-six-zero and make turns for 5 knots. WEPS, get a firing plan for *Red Star*, now heading zero-eight-five degrees at a speed of 20 knots."

All of a sudden Sonar blared out: "Captain. We're in the box and still haven't been pinged by the enemy boat. The BUFFALO is about 8 thousand yards behind us and off our starboard side, but we're below her and can get a clear shot the rebels."

"Very well. It's now or never, gentlemen. WEPS, prepare to fire tubes one and three, and reconfirm torpedoes in those tubes are armed with conventional warheads."

"WEPS, aye. Torpedoes *are* conventional types."

"Very well." Buzz quickly checked the range to the PRC boat and then said: "WEPS, Conn: Fire tubes one and three."

On Board the PEOPLE'S VICTORY

"We are within firing range of the American submarine Comrade Captain. All tubes are loaded and outer doors open, sir."

"Very well. We are beginning our Motherland's return from that embarrassment at the enemy dog's hand. No one shall ever again tarnish our great name or question our role as a major international force. OOD, fire tubes two and four at those pushy Americans."

The torpedoes sped off toward BUFFALO's current position. The crew of PEOPLE'S VICTORY began applauding, congratulating each other, and in a few moments gave their leader a rousing cheer: "Wong! Wong! China Forever!"

Aboard USS JAMESTOWN

The PRC attack must have begun within seconds of BUFFALO's action. Chief Smart yelled: "Two incoming torpedoes, running hot and fast from *Red Star*."

"OOD, dive the boat to 300 feet. Release metallic chaff forward and increase speed to 10 knots," the skipper barked out.

The OOD transmitted the orders and the boat was just beginning to dive when Chief Smart said: "Twenty seconds to impact, Captain."

Buzz yelled into the 1 MC: "This is the Captain.

Incoming enemy torpedoes. ***Take cover, now***."

Within seconds Smart heard the two torpedoes passing down JAMESTOWN's starboard side and yelled: "Captain, the *Red Star's* fish aren't aimed at us they're headed for BUFFALO, *above and astern of us!*"

Aboard USS BUFFALO

KA-BOOM. The USS BUFFALO went pitch black, shaking throughout. Emergency lights flickered to life revealing half the control room crew sprawled on the deck, many bleeding. The remainder scrambled to regain control of the tossing boat.

"Damage Control. Damage Control. What's the situation? Report ASAP" barked Lieutenant Commander Rockwell, one of the few officers still standing. Chief Sonarman Morton continued manning his screen for any other incoming torpedoes or missiles. In seconds he saw a second torpedo racing by their position and a few hundred yards later it left the screen. His headphones confirmed an explosion. Explosion? What did the fish hit?

BUFFALO's two torpedoes zoomed toward the Chinese sub, but Bob Gruenwald would have no way of knowing if they hit their target. He lay crumpled on the control room deck, blood streaming from a head wound and a shattered right forearm. A corpsman arrived with a first-aid kit, but the skipper looked like he'd need a whole lot more than a Band-Aid.

"This is Chief Cash, Damage Control Party #2. We've taken a torpedo in the crew's forward port side berthing area, near the bow planes. We've got six dead but there has been no, repeat no compromise of our nuclear warheads or the vertical launch tubes. We're trying to plug the hole in the hull but water's coming in pretty fast. If you can do it, we'd be better off closer to the surface. That would reduce incoming water pressure and give us a better chance to shore her up."

"Chief, this is Commander Rockwell. I've taken

command; the captain has been seriously wounded. Do you have enough people to patch the bulkhead into the torpedo room and still keep a crew working on the hull?"

"Could be a problem, XO, but we'll try to work on both."

"Do that, Chief, but if push comes to shove stopping the water into the boat is your first priority. Keep me posted."

On Board the PEOPLE'S VICTORY

The applauding and cheers from the crew on PEOPLE'S VICTORY lasted but a few seconds because Captain Wong's sonar operator screamed out: "Incoming torpedoes, Comrade Captain! They're running straight for us, not a minute to impact."

"Release counter measures immediately. OOD, come right 90 degrees."

"Aye, aye, Captain."

"How could they have gotten off a shot when they haven't even pinged on us?" Wong said under his breath. "How did they know where we were?"

As the crew stood by for the torpedoes from BUFFALO, sonar showed both torpedoes missing them by 50 yards.

"Our joss is great," Wong yelled. "We've sunk the enemy submarine and can now head north to their Carrier Battle Group. We will give them a dose of just what they deserve."

Aboard USS JAMESTOWN

If Wong had known we were seeing the action he would have thrown-up. The sonar screen showed Gruenwald's torpedoes barely missing *Red Star,* just as Buzz Russell ordered *Squidy* to counterattack.

"Conn, WEPS. Tubes one and three are fired."

"Conn, aye. Sonar, release a little of that ink you keep for special occasions. I think this is special enough."

"Conn, Sonar. Aye, aye Captain. Ink away!"

CHAPTER 120 - RED STAR FALLING

February 2, 2002: On Board the PEOPLE'S VICTORY

Clueless to JAMESTOWN's presence, a smug David Wong hung on his periscope, looking for damage he had inflicted. Swinging about he noticed a dark cloud in the water and was about to ask his XO to take a look when the sonar operator yelled: "Torpedoes in the water, five thousand yards. Captain, they're coming from two miles *away* from the BUFFALO!"

"What!?" Wong stammered. "There isn't another ship any-where near here. You're mistaken!"

"We have only seconds to go, sir."

Wong grabbed the mike and in machine-gun like delivery commanded: "All compartments rig for incoming torpedoes. OOD, change course to zero degrees true north. Increase to flank speed. Release decoy...."

His sentence went unfinished; the first American torpedo ripped in and spoiled PEOPLE'S VICTORY and Captain David Wong's great dream. Two square hits and his boat was immediately reduced to a snarled mass of metal.

One of a lucky handful of survivors, Wong suffered some cuts and a major gash in his left leg, but he wouldn't be stopped. With LCDR Leong, LT Chen and two chiefs he groped through the smoke-filled hull, stumbling over equipment and debris, seeking the storage chamber for the SCUBA gear. LT Chen grabbed some face masks and oxygen tanks and the frantic party clawed its way to an escape hatch. As they pushed themselves free, PEOPLE'S VICTORY began her final trip to the ocean floor below.

Aboard USS BUFFALO

Meanwhile, the BUFFALO struggled to reach the surface, but with her forward diving planes useless it was tediously slow going. Medical aid was being given, while the XO and COB oversaw the damage control efforts to patch the hole in the hull.

An emergency SOS had been sent just after they took the Chinese torpedo, and five minutes later the communications officer received a reply from the CVBG that a helicopter and two destroyers had been dispatched. Two jet fighters scrambled to be on site if there happened to be any more Chinese Navy ships or subs waiting and hoping to finish off the BUFFALO.

"XO, this is Chief Cash; hull's plugged for now and you can use the starboard tubes. The bulkhead to the torpedo room is being held steady by a triple layer of mattresses kept in place by good sturdy timbers, and pumps are sending water into the bilges."

"Great job, Chief. I'll get a relief crew down there within a half hour so your boys can get some warm chow."

It looked like things were finally stabilizing on the ship when the XO picked up the 1 MC: "Attention all hands. This is the XO speaking. The damage to our hull has been shored up. The rest of the boat is secure. Captain Gruenwald has suffered a major blow to his head. He's in a coma. The Doc says he's in critical but stable condition. He'll be helicoptered to a destroyer for further treatment.

"We've lost six shipmates, but everyone else is accounted for and the injured are being taken care of. You all did a superb job at your assigned tasks and I compliment each one of you. We don't know all the ramifications of the battle we've just gone through, other than to confirm that the rebel Chinese submarine has positively been sunk. That is all."

As BUFFALO struggled to the surface, the two F/A-18s streaked by, just above the deck. The wounded submarine limped along at five knots but still intact. By end of day, the count of fatalities had grown to nine.

Emerging through the hatch to the flying bridge Rocky and COB Adams sucked in the cold fresh air.

"What's next?" the master chief asked.

"When the destroyers get here, and none too soon for

485

me, we'll transfer the captain and the rest of our wounded. Admiral Davidson has ordered us to Singapore for repairs, and then we'll return Stateside. For now, we're out of the game."

"How's the captain doing?"

"Still critical, but the Chief Corpsman says he'll pull through in a couple of days."

"That's good news, sir. If you don't mind my saying, you did a damn good job taking command!"

"Thanks, COB. I guess we all earned our fabulous pay today."

CHAPTER 121 - ALL QUIET ON THE FAR EASTERN FRONT

February 5, 2002: U.S. Seventh Fleet

My notebook filled rapidly with *Squidy* activity, so I took a break and headed for the Mess. COB Esterhaus sat down next to me and asked: "Did you get your message?"

"Nope. What was it about?"

"CVBG wants you to chopper to one of the DDGs at 1600 and Vice Admiral Sharpe wants a call from you ASAP. I gotta say, you run with the big dogs, don't you? Use the scrambler phone in our Comm shack."

I rushed to Comm Central where a petty officer dialed a number and gave me the hand set. In a matter of seconds I heard a familiar voice say: "Good Afternoon, Admiral Sharpe speaking."

"It's Dan Lincoln, Admiral. I got your message."

"Are you okay, Dan? From what Admiral Davidson has told me, several of our shipmates are damned lucky to be alive!"

"That's very true, sir, but I'm fine."

"I want you here in Honolulu as quickly as possible. Have you filed any stories since the attack?"

"No sir, I haven't filed anything since we left Singapore."

"Good. And don't release anything until you and I meet. So far the press knows nothing, and they won't if you don't tell them. This time I have to claim national security and order you to not release anything about the BUFFALO or the PEOPLE'S VICTORY, let alone the JAMESTOWN which you know is an unknown entity to the world. You do understand the importance of what I'm saying, don't you Dan?"

"Yes sir, I do, but even if this battle never hits the front pages there's still the matter of Mr. Penole and who's behind the Squid Box aspect of the overall story."

"We'll discuss that and other topics when you get back here. Admiral Davidson will get you on flights that should put you in Honolulu before next Saturday. Rest up over the weekend, but I want you in my office Monday at 0800. See you then, Chief."

I went to the control room looking for Captain Russell. "He's in the Wardroom, Chief Lincoln, and you're to join him there," said the OOD LT Clawson.

Buzz sat at the head of the long green felt covered table, reviewing a clip board full of messages. "Sit down, Chief. You don't have much time left on *Squidy*."

"I just talked with Admiral Sharpe and he tells me I'm to be choppered to CARL VINSON before catching a flight to Hawaii. I want to thank you and everyone for your hospitality and kindnesses. This is one hell of a submarine, and whenever they let me write about it I'll be able to say I was on board during her first enemy encounter. Can't say I expected all the shooting you organized these past few days but it certainly was the experience of a lifetime!"

"Good luck Dan. I don't except to see a story about all this, or about our new toy, but I would love to see how you describe a day in the life of a nuclear submariner if you do write that story."

"You'll get the second copy, skipper, right after the one for Captain Gruenwald. Give me a call if you're ever assigned to Washington again. I can always use a good Navy source at the Pentagon."

At 1600 I hopped a chopper that whisked me to the VINSON, plopping down on her giant deck. A young seaman escorted me to my quarters, asking if I wanted chow. "Nope, just sleep," I sighed.

Slipping between the cool sheets I thought: Lincoln, you old cat. You just used up one more, if not two or three of your nine lives, but you'll have a hell of a story to tell some day.

A bright sun greeted me on Sunday of my last week at sea. After ten hours of sack time I was ravished so I headed for the Mess, filling a tray with just about everything on the line. Geez, how I'd missed the wonderful chow on the flat top.

Several of the chiefs I'd met when I first sailed on CARL VINSON asked where I'd been.

"Just riding a few tin cans and the LAKE ERIE, looking for human interest stories, like a day in the life of an E-3 kind of stuff."

Like the rest of the carrier crew I spent Sunday doing as little as possible. I e-mailed Ben, advising I'd be in Honolulu over the weekend, meet with Admiral Sharpe, and start hitching hops back to D.C. I spent the afternoon in the Chief's Mess watching a rerun of the NFL Pro Bowl from Aloha Stadium. God, the weather looked good. I couldn't wait to get back to Hawaii.

While watching the game a young petty officer came in and handed me a note from Admiral Davidson. He wanted to see me tomorrow at 0830. Has to be about my flight to Honolulu, I figured.

My knock on the CVBG commander's door the next morning was answered with a pleasant "Come in."

"Morning, Admiral. I sure am happy to be back with you."

"I've read the preliminary reports from the XO on BUFFALO and assume he and his crew did a spectacular job under what must have been extreme circumstances. Dealing with that madman Wong, who had to be mentally unstable at best, must have been the maximum challenge for professional submariners." "It did get a bit hairy, sir, but all's well that end's well. I hear you've been able to get me on my way back to Pearl."

"That we have, Chief. Here're your orders and tickets. First a COD flight for Manila Thursday at 1100. Then Singapore Airlines non-stop to Honolulu arriving at 0630 that same day, Hawaii time.

"Admiral, I got more than I ever bargained for on this trip. I got a lot of human interest stuff and some good feature material from crewmen on the BUFFALO, the LAKE ERIE and the RUSSELL that can be used when I get back. Don't worry about reading any stories from me about the engagement with Captain Wong and his men. I still can't get over the fact that he spent over a week showing me around Beijing and Shanghai under the guise of being a Chinese Navy tour escort."

The admiral stood up, shook my hand again, and wished me well. "I know we'll meet again. Have a safe trip and let me know if you ever want to go to sea again."

Thursday morning, with my bags stuffed to bursting with souvenir Navy blue baseball caps and coffee mugs from each of my ships, I climbed aboard a helicopter and it immediately rose from the flight deck. Looking down I saw a small group of sailors saluting my departure. I returned their salute with pride and hoped they were able to see it.

CHAPTER 122 - DEBRIEF TO CIVILIAN LIFE

February 11, 2002: Hawaii

Approaching Hawaii by air is always a surprise because there's no other land between the west coast and the Islands. I cleared Customs and curbside sat a Navy car. The driver held a card with my name on it. I identified myself and said: "Please take me to the BEQ at Pearl." The driver said: "Admiral Sharpe told me to take you to the Royal Hawaiian Hotel." I thought to myself, cool.

When I registered at the Pink Palace the desk clerk handed me an envelope with three gold stars embossed at the top left. In my room overlooking the hotel's lush-green palm tree garden, I opened it and read: Welcome home to the Ernie Pyle of the Chopsticks War. Enjoy your weekend and my car will pick you up at 0645 Monday. You're invited to dinner that evening, and Barbara can't wait to hear all about your adventure. Aloha, Bernie.

I left my room and hit the beach. I swam a few yards, turned on my back and looked at the Royal and started to laugh. Three months in the middle of the Pacific Ocean and not one desire to take a dip. Right now I couldn't get enough!

Friday and Saturday I played tourist and Sunday was back in the sand, watching all those teeny bikinis strolling by. "Guy could go blind doing this," I muttered to myself, still staring. My mind wandered to Janice who would look stunning strolling this famous beach. I wondered if we'd get together when I got back to D.C.

On Monday traffic to Pearl was the usual stop and go, but we arrived in plenty of time for my 0800 meeting.

"You're damned lucky to be alive, Chief Lincoln, I hope you realize that!"

"Yes, sir, and good morning to you too, Admiral." Thanks for the special treatment with the car and driver, plus the weekend at the Royal."

"You're more than welcome. The car was my contribution, but the Royal is on Ben Huntley. I called him to say that you'd be on your way home soon and that you'd decided this was as much sea duty as you needed for quite awhile. He has no idea about how you spent your last week at sea, but says he'll be glad to have you back, assuming you'll have a good story for next weekend."

"I was able to get lots of interviews, enough for three or four feature stories at least. And I can do another three pieces on the PLA Navy."

"Since your encounter, as you call it, there's been a big shakeup in the Chinese Navy and it may lead to bigger things for the old men in Beijing. Admiral Ho went down with the QINGDAO. Rear Admiral Kwock was relieved of his command of the Shanghai Navy base and shipyard and is on shaky grounds. A group of active duty and former Navy officers and civilians said to have supported Captain Wong, were rounded up over the past weekend and shot to death. Just like the old days of Chairman Mao."

I whistled quietly, and said: "Was anything released by the Chinese regarding their stolen submarine or Wong's attempted revenge for the Chopsticks War?"

"Nothing in the Chinese papers or on TV and radio. Whatever they know about the PEOPLE'S VICTORY is being kept as quiet as we're doing with JAMESTOWN's story. Ours has been classified top secret and ordered frozen for 20 years. But then, you expected that."

"I did, and hope I'm still a working journalist then so I can fill in all the provocative details of those 72 hours playing cat and mouse with the Red rebels. But, as I told you from the boat, I know the rules of the game and I've agreed to live by them, at least until 2022."

"I know you'll keep your word. Okay, so much for PEOPLE'S VICTORY and Wong's Red Dragons which, we've learned, is what he called the crew. What you and I need to discuss now is how we're going to find Mr. Penole."

Admiral Sharpe relaxed in his chair and continued: "Since you found the old Chinese man during your last visit here, why don't you try finding Penole when you get home. I can arrange to have some Pentagon intelligence types help you and grease the skids within the system. Janice Cannon knows almost everything about my research into the stealth projects, both in N-771 and at Milsoftel, so she could be a big help to you."

"Thank you, sir. Let me know who to contact at Navy Intel." Sharpe sat up as if to suggest the meeting was over but then continued with a new idea: "Also, try to spend some time with Dr. George Mason at Milsoftel and a retired Senior Chief named Don Logan, who was a major player in developing the Squid Box chips. Mason will know where to find him."

"You know, Dan, the shoot-out between Buzz Russell and Captain Wong was certainly a major incident in our relations with the PRC. With him out of the picture what's in that little box of fish noises may still give us the upper edge for some time to come. If Wong kept the info from the PLA, what he stole may have gone straight to the bottom of the ocean, along with him and his men."

"Good point, admiral."

"The stealth sound system works," Bernie continued, "and not only in our own tests but under very tough combat conditions. How long we can keep it secret is pure speculation."

"Let me take it from here, Admiral Sharpe. I'm sure Ben will have a ton of things for me to do, and I need an updated backgrounder about the PRC Navy, post-Wong rebels."

"There's a sharp new two-star, Rear Admiral Jimmie Benjamin, who's just been promoted and assigned to CNO's intelligence branch. I'll advise him that you'll call in a couple of weeks."

"Much appreciated. I'm sure with that kind of help we can find Mr. Penole in the near future."

"You've done a superb job, Dan, and I'm thrilled you're on my team. I must admit I feared for losing a member of my family when I learned the JAMESTOWN was engaging the Chinese. I should have known that you'd make it through.

You're always telling me you know how to cover your six and now I'm a believer! We'll see you tonight for dinner."

I stood at attention and gave COMSUBPAC a snappy salute.

That evening during dinner Barbara asked about the shipboard 24/7 TV and newswires. "I give them my stories from PANS and they run them. In return, they help me get crewmembers to tell their stories hoping they'll make hometown papers," I explained.

"So how's the romance going with that lady commander?"

"Well, I just don't know what to do about Janice. Most of the time when we're together life's great, but then she seems to freeze me out for weeks. I don't know what to do. What do you think?"

"I remember that age; not too sure of what she wants, and maybe she's afraid to fall for you. I mean, getting married and all that."

After dinner and a round of port wine, Barbara excused herself to clean up the dishes, and the admiral suggested the two of us take a walk around the neighborhood. We walked as far as the battleship USS MISSOURI and then headed back to the SUBPAC Flag Quarters, enjoying the night air and the view of the mountains and the aroma of plumeria.

My ride was waiting when we returned, so I thanked my hosts for their hospitality and bid them a fond Aloha.

CHAPTER 123 - HOME SWEET HOME AGAIN

February 14, 2002 - Washington, D.C.

Thank God Ben didn't expect me at the office my first day back. Instead he sent a limo to Reagan National to meet my Continental flight and take me home. After arriving at my place and unloading everything, I offered the driver a tip but he waved me off saying: "No tips from you, Mr. Lincoln. PANS has already paid me very handsomely."

I took a quick shower and rolled into my very own bed. When I awakened I felt great and decided to go down to the C-C for a drink and dinner.

Force of habit took me straight to the rear of the Capitol Connection, and the Roundtable that was so much a part of my Washington routine. My answers to the barrage of questions resulted in several free rounds of drinks from my envious colleagues. I got to go to the Far East while they got more Capitol slush of both kinds.

Navy Times said kind things about my war stories and that the PRC appeared to roll over quickly, something he had not expected. Complimenting the reportorial work NBC got off a few barbs saying he felt sorry for me that I wasn't a TV journalist with the assistance of a video crew to shoot the war the way people wanted to see it, on TV.

While explaining how the Navy CVBG operated, from the corner of my eye I spotted Sung Jiang quietly climb aboard the last open barstool and listen intently to my every word. I looked squarely at him and he bowed his head ever so slightly. At the first break in the conversation, Jiang said: "Welcome home, Mr. Dan. We have been reading all about your adventures and your encounters with my countrymen."

"Good evening, Jiang. I observed your country's uncalled-for attacks on Taiwan, and also saw how fast your PRC buddies ran away when push came to shove. Perhaps the western world has been right all along; the People's Republic of China is a braggart not a world class nation with a blue-water Navy. What I saw looked more like a paper tiger dragging a wanna-be flotilla of outdated ships, with a bunch of poorly trained pilots and sailors."

His reply came like a well-rehearsed speech: "It was unfortunate that our President did not present a full-scale attack on Taiwan on New Year's Eve. He was ill-advised by staff that did not know about the FBI-taped conversations between Mrs. Shin and our Embassy, or so that's what I read in your stories, if I recall correctly."

"Your memory is fine, Jiang, but even with knowledge of the anticipated attack the PRC Navy was less than first class during the battles on New Year's Eve and immediately thereafter. To lose your best AKULA submarines, two of your own LUHU class destroyers, a HAN and perhaps two KILO submarines, plus over a dozen airplanes, is not the mark of a world-class anything!"

Jiang attempted to push aside my rationale: "We'll see what happens when the U.N. begins debate on the matter next week. And remember, one or two battles do not make a war, as you well know. We are prepared to wait a little longer to get what we deserve, and this minor set-back will not deter our leaders' efforts to claim their rightful place in the management of today's world."

Half an hour later I was out of the C-C, back to the apartment, and a night's sleep that would provide me with the energy I'd need for the kind of day I was certain lay ahead. I thought of calling Janice but for some strange reason, I didn't. Was I afraid she might not want to see me?

PANS offices. Ah, home at last! Every available inch of wall surface was plastered with newspaper front pages carrying my stories. All the biggies: New York Times, Washington Post, Los Angeles Times, Chicago Tribune, San Francisco Chronicle, London Standard, and some that I had already seen from Singapore, Hong Kong and Tokyo.

My return was almost like being a war hero. Everyone came to shake my hand and add a pat on the back except Ben who stood anchored in his doorway. Like a teacher to an errant student he coaxed: "Come on in here, my boy. We've got a lot of catching up to do."

"Most of these messages and e-mails are just congratulatory, but some you may want to answer. I know you'll be busy for awhile but I want you to know how proud I am of you and the job you did for PANS out there. Now, get out of here!"

Unexpectedly, a closure to part of my spy ring story came from President Crane. On February 26th he held a news conference that I wasn't cleared for. I had been tipped to watch it by one of my fellow C-C buddies.

President Crane told the gathered reporters: "After reviewing an FBI investigation into the activities of Sung Jiang, Washington correspondent for New China News Agency, I have today ordered Mr. Sung deported to Beijing for his well documented spying efforts on behalf of the People's Republic of China and its Washington ambassador. With that expulsion I am saying to the leaders of China we know who your spies are and if your government persists in trying to place them in our country don't count on the cover as a Communist news agency reporter to work again, ever."

With a big smile on my face, I said to myself: Now that's a president with some balls.

CHAPTER 124 - AND THE WINNERS ARE

April 10, 2002: Washington, D.C.

I wrote so many stories during March I thought my fingers would fall off! My favorite was the feature about spending a week with today's typical submariners while I rode the USS BUFFALO. I got wide circulation and some very nice reviews from it. Feeling heady, I called that new admiral Bernie referred me to, planning on asking about the PLA Navy post-Chopsticks War. A chief in his office said he'd get back to me shortly.

Okay, I'll admit my love affair with Janice seemed to be in the deep freeze. All I had managed to accomplish on that front since my return was two measly dinners at local cafes. She still looked stunning, but try as I might I couldn't get her to bed. Perhaps I'd be better off just walking away. Sure, tell that to my aching heart.

Fortune smiled on me a few days later when Ben said PANS leaders wanted me in Afghanistan, looking for stories about al Qaida and the remnants of the Taliban.

"What'd you tell them?" I asked anxiously.

"That you're far more valuable here." He paused, then continued: "Now listen, don't let this go to your already swelled head but I also said you had a chance of getting a Pulitzer, meaning you had to be here to accept it on behalf of Pacific & Asia News Service."

"And?"

"Took 'em about two seconds to drop Afghanistan."

"Thanks for big, big favor."

We lost a great friend and fellow Roundtabler on April 1st when Ray Kinny of Navy Times retired. The boys at the table couldn't believe it when Ray said he'd been covering this bloody town since 1982, and that the time had come for him to leave all this bullshit and go fishing down in the Carolinas.

By the 10th of April I was a basket case. That's the day

498

the Pulitzers are announced, precisely at 3 pm. I had my fingers and toes and anything else that could be, crossed.

The September 11th terrorist attacks had to be the story of the year. But it was something that just crashed onto the news scene and didn't have to be investigated, researched or massaged for weeks and months. Any prize that came out of that tragedy would be in the categories of Public Service or International Affairs, not Investigative Reporting. The attack would also qualify for most every other category, especially Breaking News and News Photos.

On this mild early April evening before the Pulitzers were made public, the Roundtablers were talking about the American they called Rat Boy, that scruffy bearded kid from Marin County found in the middle of an al Qaida training camp in the Afghan war zone. He was flown back to the U.S. and charged with aiding the enemy. I contributed to the conversation for awhile, finished a second drink and then said so-long, heading for the short Metro ride home.

After dinner I turned on the computer. My quest to learn more about Pulitzer Prizes was running rampant, so I went to Yahoo.com and entered: Pulitzer. Dozens of choices on the topic appeared in a few seconds and I picked one randomly, learning that:

Twenty one awards are given annually, including seven for works in music, poetry, literature and drama. Fourteen of them are for excellence in journalism. A group of over 100 distinguish-ed judges reviews approximately 2,000 entries, and just three in each category are nominated for a Pulitzer. One is chosen.

More good information, I said to myself. Hope it will come in handy some day. I watched the late news on WRC-TV and went to bed. Tomorrow would either be a super Wednesday or just another busy day at PANS. It would never, however, be a routine day for journalists all across the nation. It was Pulitzer Prize day.

After three cups of morning coffee, at least two trips to the head, an unsuccessful attempt at drafting a story about huge new military budget increases and a lousy lunch, the word finally came. It was the middle of the afternoon and I was on the phone with Janice when the story began to clear our A-P machine. Ben ran to my door signaled me to join him and said: "It's 3 o'clock and the Pulitzer list is coming over the wire. Get out here now!"

Jack O'Neill was right on top of the wire and first to yell out: "There it is! Dan Lincoln of Pacific & Asia News Service, for a distinguished example of investigative reporting by an individual or team presented as a single article or a series. You did it! You've won a Pulitzer."

The office erupted. I could hardly believe it. Me, a Pulitzer Prize winner! Suddenly champagne corks were popping and bubbly was flowing freely.

"I knew you could do it, Dan," Ben said to me and the entire office staff when everyone calmed down. "No one deserves it more than you, and your fine writing has brought great honor to PANS." Ben toasted: "To Dan Lincoln, our spy ring breaker. And a not too bad war correspondent either. Cheers!"

I was soon being hailed with calls of "Speech, speech." Fighting back tears I spoke words straight from my heart.

"It is absolutely wonderful to have been selected and winning in the category of investigative journalism is even sweeter for me. My days on the paper in Honolulu gave me the confidence to know I was doing the right thing for me, and since joining PANS, you Ben and all the rest of you, I've come to know there's no greater service I can perform than what I'm doing right now; being a working journalist in the best news town in the world."

Most of the rest of the afternoon is still a foggy memory, but I recall phoning Janice with my good news. She was genuinely impressed and said she would let Admiral Sharpe know about it.

Ben and Jack O'Neill had no problem closing the office early and even invited a couple of the other staff writers to join us at the C-C Roundtable. Within a few minutes there wasn't a person in the entire pub that didn't know what the big celebration was all about. Drinks for those lucky enough to be there that evening would flow until well after 7 pm, and no one paid for a single round but Ben.

About 7:30 pm I said I should be getting home, as well they should. A simple thank you couldn't express what feelings I had in my heart for my boss at that moment. He was the man who gave me the leeway I needed to do my thing. We gave each other a manly hug, a couple claps on the back, and I left the C-C for the Metro station. April 10th, 2002. What a day in my life.

CHAPTER 125 - SEARCH AND YE SHALL FIND

April 19, 2002: Washington D.C.

Walking into my office I noticed the light blinking on my answering machine. The first caller said: "This is Chief Snodgrass Admiral Benjamin will meet with you Wednesday the 17th at 1100 in his office, 4th deck E-Ring. Two officers from the CNO Intelligence Division will attend. Please confirm. Also, please plan on having lunch with the Admiral."

I immediately called the chief, confirming the date and time. I asked him to advise building security that I'd be coming in the North entrance about 1030 and he said all would be taken care of.

Rear Admiral Jimmie Benjamin looked to be in his early 40s; about five foot eight, lean and trim. He welcomed me into his office after Chief Snodgrass made the introductions. Two other officers got up from their chairs and shook my hand. Admiral Benjamin said: "Mr. Lincoln, this is Commander Ed Rindosh and LT Marcia Brinck. They're with CNO's Intel section assigned to the China desk. Admiral Sharpe suggested they might be helpful and add to this briefing."

"I'm very pleased to meet you all. I knew if I wanted an update on China and her Navy, Admiral Sharpe would set up the best team possible."

The admiral motioned for us to take chairs at a small conference table in one corner of his office.

"We know about your recent visit to the Seventh Fleet and your time on JAMESTOWN. Have you had a chance to see any of the Chinese or Asian papers since you've been home?"

"No sir, I haven't. Admiral Sharpe indicated that nothing about our encounter with Captain Wong is ever expected to appear in any Chinese newspaper."

"Very true, but there was a small piece in the South China Morning Post over the weekend that I'll ask Commander Rindosh to share with you."

"We didn't think much about it until LT Brinck started putting some dates and timeframes to the details." He slid a laminated copy of the news item across the table to me and said: "Read this first and then LT Brinck can amplify."

CHINESE FISHING BOAT SURVIVORS RESCUED
SPRATLY ISLAND SOLDIERS FIND VICTIMS
OF LIGHTNING STORM
THREE MEN LIVE FOR TWO WEEKS
ON RAINWATER AND RAW FISH

Hong Kong, February 22, 2002 (New China News Agency):

Three men, whose fishing boat apparently sunk when struck by lightning during a violent storm almost three weeks ago, were rescued yesterday by Taiwanese soldiers from their Spratly Islands base. The men, all from the Shanghai area and crew members on a private boat doing long-line fishing in the South China Sea, were flown to Hong Kong by a Philippine military helicopter.

According to one man, identified as David Leong the ship's captain, their 40-foot boat had been fishing an area about 50 miles north of the Spratly Islands when the storm hit on February 1st or 2nd, he didn't recall which. The boat sank almost immediately and five of the twelve-man crew survived.

Leong said two of the men lasted only a day or so before passing out and falling off the piece of the ship's deck to which they had all been clinging. The remaining men were able to find additional wood from the boat, and enough rope to lash it together, to float at sea for nine days, living on rain water and fish they could grab.

Their make-shift raft drifted close enough to the eastern coast of the northern-most Spratly island for them to paddle/swim ashore and find shelter under some large trees. A fresh water pond was located nearby and they ate tree fruits and plants available to them.

The group was found by a passing patrol from the Taiwanese Army, now occupying the island group. The Air Force helicopter was called in from their Philippine allies since no such transportation was available on island.

Leong declined to discuss the incident upon the trio's arrival in Hong Kong. The men were examined and treated at a local hospital. They asked to be allowed to return to Shanghai as soon as possible.

I put the clipping down and said to the commander: "Are you telling me this fishing boat captain and the other survivors have something to do with the PRC submarine we figured was on the bottom of the ocean?"

"That's exactly what we're saying, Mr. Lincoln." The young female officer took some paper out of a file folder and continued: "The captain said his boat was hit on either the 1st or 2nd of February. It was actually late on the night of the 1st that you folks had it out," she said, looking up from her notes.

"We've also learned, through reliable sources in China," the commander interjected, "that a PLA Navy Lieutenant Commander named Hiram Leong is one of Wong's most trusted insiders. Commander Leong was XO on PEOPLE'S VICTORY and is the brother of Wong's wife Lily Shin, with whom I know you're very familiar, thus making him a brother-in-law of the rebel captain."

I let out a chuckle, shook my head showing my incredulity, and said: "So, If Captain Leong the fishing boat survivor is in fact Navy Captain David Wong the rebel commander, it would appear that he and a few of his mates made it out of PEOPLE'S VICTORY and have survived."

LT Brinck continued her interpretation of the clipping: "Since Wong's boat was astern of your position he could very well have floated for a week before getting close enough to swim to land. The part about living on rain water and fish at sea, plus fruits and plants ashore, is all believable. In their condition after 12 or 14 days it's no wonder they welcomed being found, even though it was by Taiwanese soldiers. Frankly, they're lucky they weren't shot on the spot."

She then said something that made very good sense: "You see, when you check certain dates against known events you're trying to place or resolve, the answer comes back: David Leong is really Captain David Wong. He and two of his men survived an accident at sea, but it wasn't a fishing boat being hit by lightning."

Admiral Benjamin intervened in at this point and said: "Thank you Commander, Lieutenant. I appreciate your joining us and passing along this information." The two officers got up, excused themselves, and left the office.

The admiral suggested I move to a chair across from his desk. "I was almost as surprised as you are now about the probability of survivors from PEOPLE'S VICTORY, but the evidence our people have pieced together would seem to be a very likely scenario. And now, back to your backgrounder."

I turned on my tape recorder and took out my little blue book. "As best we can figure out, it looks like Red China is again on the brink of another major shake-up in its political leadership. That business President Zemin pulled on New Year's Eve, granting Taiwan 24 hours to consider surrender, cost them millions of dollars worth of military hardware, not to mention loss of face. I am absolutely convinced that Captain Wong went after any American submarines he could find solely for revenge of the January war battles, and probably as an overture to attacking the entire CVBG."

"Being there I agree 100 percent with your conclusion."

The young admiral continued: "It is our belief that Zemin will retire by this summer, fall the latest, but we don't know as of now who will replace him. Things are very fluid in Beijing within both the military and political circles."

Admiral Benjamin went on with details for another ten or fifteen minutes, and by the time he finished I was nodding in agreement with his every point. What I could write about was of course limited to things that would not jeopardize national security, but I came away with more than enough detailed material to do a major feature story for the next three Sundays' weekend editions.

Our lunch in the Flag Mess was excellent, and I can honestly say that I had never seen so much gold braid in any one location in my entire life! By the time we finished our desserts I was ready to take my lowly civilian and part-time CPO self back to the modest digs of PANS.

The first draft ideas of my update story on China took shape upon my return to the office, but by late afternoon I tired of that and decided to call Janice and set a date with her for the weekend. I caught her just before she headed out of her office: "I'm in a big rush, but yes let's plan on dinner Friday night." She agreed after I suggested: "My place at 7 if you don't mind driving over."

Ben was still at his desk and invited me to come in. Not wanting to get into something that might take awhile, I leaned on his door jam and told him: "Had an excellent backgrounder at the Pentagon today; new admiral with the latest developments in China. I should be able to have a good feature for us to run on our weekend wire the 26th."

"Excellent. Your stuff is pretty popular these days so keep grinding it out. Have a good night." He waved at me and I took the hint heading straight for home.

The business about David Wong surviving the attack kept coming back to me. Also, one of the things young LT Brinck said stuck in my mind. Something about piecing together known dates with happening or events you're trying to resolve. I was now more determined than ever to uncover the Pentagon mole. At this point the name Mr. Penole was tired shorthand for a killer. I wanted to know right now who was regularly stealing our military secrets that went straight to Beijing or Shanghai and who was responsible for ordering Simon Cardigan's murder.

I vowed to spend enough time in the next day or two to create a factual layout, similar to what Ms. Brinck did to figure out how a seemingly routine fishing boat accident was anything but. With her logic she was able to prove it was merely a cover-up of the survival of three rebel Chinese Navymen from a torpedo attack on their hijacked submarine by the crew of an American U-boat.

The next morning I turned my attention to the major job at hand: putting dates to paper to see if there was a pattern. Start with known events, back them up with dates and then try to find players who may have a motive and possible involvement. Where were they on the date in question? Did they have any connection at all with the event? What could they have gained?

There's usually a clear beginning to these searches. Mine went back to my last days on the Honolulu Times, when Simon confided in me that he had discovered a spy ring working for the PRC and trying to steal secrets from Pearl Harbor. He told me about it in early 1998. He'd been working on the story for over a year so that event had to go back to the start of 1997, now my Date #1.

My next exposure to Chinese spying came during my second year at PANS after I'd met Admiral Bernie Sharpe. Date #2: January 1999.

Upon my return from China after the May Day ceremonies the admiral was livid about President Zemin referring to stealth gel in his speech. How the Chinese leader knew about what was until then considered top secret could only have come from someone spying for the PRC. That's when Hank Anderson entered the equation. His final outcome was now known, but it was from this time he would be used by the ring as a source for the information they sought. Date #3: May 1, 1999.

Then there was Lily Shin. She had to be directed to get involved with Senator Anderson. Was there an intermediary in that connection? He told me he met her at an after work drinking party that he was invited to attend by his aide Tom Carlson. At that party he ran into Senate committee intern Cheryl Leong, and began his involvement with her mother, who he then knew only as a Georgetown Chinese antiques dealer. Date #4: October 10, 1999.

I was on a roll now and as I reviewed my notes from Hank's confession I could see that LT Brinck's method was a winner.

What was Tom Carlson's role in all of this? Did he even play a role? He hadn't been named in any of the FBI or Navy investigations, and wasn't an unindicted co-conspirator. So, where did he fit? I'd have to work on that.

There had to be someone at the Pentagon or Milsoftel who was leaking secrets that ultimately got to Lily Shin and on to her husband in China. Could it have been that girl Samantha Wing? She worked at the Virginia lab but was she privy to hard details of the work actually being done there? Date #5: June 14, 2000.

Captain Wong had indicated on more than one occasion that the quality of info coming via Senator Anderson was poor and already known by his people. Admiral Sharpe said he felt the Chinese also knew about our work on the stealth fish noises audio system and our trials with it off Norfolk. For that to have happened there had to be an insider, one who was well connected militarily.

Then it hit me.

CHAPTER 126 - SPY CURTAIN GOING DOWN

April 26, 2002: Washington, D.C.

"No! No! I don't believe it," I said out loud. Luckily my office door was closed. I thought: There's only one player in this entire game with contacts that fit the old Chinese man's description of the Pearl Harbor spy.

As clear as a bell, his words came back to me: One tall American. I blurted out loud: "It's got to be Janice."

I sunk back in my chair: God, no, not Janice!

Dates, events and people's names darted across my mind; our first meeting when she told me she grew up in China and then moved to Hong Kong where her father worked for some big American company with plants in the PRC.

She knew Tom Carlson, who was brought up in Beijing where his father was attached to a U.N. Trade Mission. Tom could have alerted Janice to the China-loving senator. From that point on it was as if I had opened a flood gate and the water came rushing at me in titanic waves.

The date/event theory worked well. In Janice's case, too well. I started by analyzing the period from January 1997 through April l998. I was on the Honolulu Times and Simon was getting too close to the Pearl Harbor spy ring. Janice was a COMSUBPAC staff planner at Pearl Harbor. She could have headed the base espionage efforts for China, and could have ordered Simon's murder. The old Chinese man never said the person was male or female, just tall.

First there was the 1999 May Day ceremony in Beijing where President Zemin mentioned stealth gel in his speech. Hank Anderson may have let that slip during a visit with Lily Shin, because it most likely came from a *For Senators Only* briefing where Admiral Sharpe mentioned the importance of the gel. That was also a session attended by then Lieutenant Commander Janice Cannon.

Then came the October 1999 visit to the Maryland gambling club, with Hank escorting Lily Shin who had been introduced to him earlier that evening by Tom Carlson. Was there something developing here? It kept getting better as an emerging pattern, but worse for the tall American lady.

Janice worked for Admiral Sharpe in the early days of the Skunk Works, when initial research on all sorts of submarine developments, including stealth, was being done.

She had access to the Squid Box project via her position at N-771. She knew about the Virginia Capes sea trials, and she may have had access to all my calls to Bernie via the scrambler phone over the past two years.

If Janice knew Lily, and was perhaps controlling her spy operation, she obviously knew about Captain Wong and his rebellious crew. She may not, however, have know the Squid Box info was Bernie's decoy plan.

My God; could she have played a role in my Fourth of July near-death hit-and-run accident or that Christmastime drive-by shooting attempt? Did she set up the knife mugging?

One thing I knew for sure I'd have to face Janice with this tomorrow night. I kept shaking my head, wondering why she would do this if she really did. The circumstantial evidence put her in the middle of events leading up to the Shin Leong arrests and the charges against Senator Anderson. It all seemed to fit, everything except what her motive could have been.

"Well you'll know tomorrow, Mr. Investigative Reporter," I said to myself. "And I hope you're not as good a private eye as you think."

That night sleep was difficult for me. Throughout the next day I accomplished almost nothing. All I could concentrate on was Janice and her role in a Chinese spy ring. Was I way off base? Were the dates and events I assigned to her casual coincidence?

Five o'clock finally came and Ben wished me a good weekend. I skipped my Friday drink at the C-C. I took a crowded Metro train and during the ride I tried to work out how I was going to confront Janice with my findings. This was the woman I had thought I wanted to spend the rest of my life with, and now I was about to accuse her of treason.

At home I checked the place over to make sure it was ready for company, especially this lady I had come to love so very much.

I heard the door buzzer just after 7 pm. I greeted Janice with a big hug and kiss. "I've missed you and it's only been a week." "Same here," she responded, but I got the feeling she didn't mean it. Something was wrong. We chatted about work and my recent visit to the Fleet. "Your stories were great," she said, "but when are you going to do that day-to-day submarine life feature?"

"It's in the works but Ben wants an update on China, post-Chopsticks War. I'm writing that and it should run next weekend. Actually, I got great background info from a new admiral I met last week over at your place."

"Oh, and who might that be?"

"A young rear admiral named Jimmie Benjamin."

She didn't respond to my mention of Admiral Benjamin's name, although I knew she worked in the division he headed.

Dinner was excellent and I got kudos for the grilled steaks. "You'll have to come and be a chef for my next party!" Janice said with a big smile on her face. "What do you charge for an evening?"

We sat down in the living room after I put in a couple of my Hawaiian CDs. Bruddah Iz, Israel Kamakawiwoole, was the featured singer on the first disc; I couldn't help but remember that gentle giant of a man who sang so beautifully, had such a big heart, and died so young. While he sang his signature song Over the Rainbow, I decided it was time to come right out and ask Janice if she was who I now believed her to be.

I jumped right in, laid out my evidence and asked: "Are you the tall American who's been responsible for giving Navy secrets to the Chinese?"

She stunned me: "Yes. I am the one and I'm damned proud of what I'm doing for world peace."

"What can you possibly be talking about? World peace? Janice, you've just admitted you're a spy and a traitor to your own country. You're also the first female U.S. Navy officer in our history to sell out her own nation."

"I am and I'd do it again. America is the richest and most powerful country on Earth and has been exploiting the rest of the world for years. What we need is a level playing field among the superpowers, so that no one country and no single military establishment can threaten the others."

Her voice was rising now, sounding like a Hyde Park Corner preacher on a London Sunday afternoon. "We've gone through Hitler and his desire to rule the western world, and Khrushchev almost led us into a nuclear world war."

"Chairman Mao killed millions of Chinese and barely allowed his country to escape from feudalism, but now China is experiencing a new beginning. Their people see hope ahead and they're enjoying the fruits of their labors in a market economy. The PRC stands ready to accept a greater political and military role in the new world order, but only if it can maintain an equal balance with the U.S. That's why I've been helping them for over eight years, and that's why they're now on a par with us."

I interrupted her diatribe: "What about the people who have been killed along the way? What about my friend Simon Cardigan? Did you order his murder? Was it you who sent the anthrax threat letter to PANS right after 9-11? Did you order a sniper to take pot shots at me, try to have me killed by that crazy driver last July 4th and what about the mugger?"

"Yes, and lucky for you my mugger was scared off by the cops before he could give you his full message. Those things had to be done for the good of the cause."

I sat expressionless, hearing these words tumbling from the woman I loved. Janice sped on: "I am your Pentagon mole code name Fortune Cookie, and I passed as many secrets and as much info as I could, straight to the PRC via their Georgetown embassy."

"You've not lived in China as I have. You haven't seen the dedication of the people and the strides they're making.

The government needs to make a few more changes in the area of human rights, but these things take time. After all, China is a culture that goes back 4,000 years, so what are a few more decades to reach total harmony between the government and its people?"

She was nearly screaming at this point and I couldn't believe this was the same Janice I was ready to consider marrying.

"China has been put down by the rest of the world, America in particular, and it's time for that to change. You and your friends on the *Squidy* had better consider yourselves lucky; David Wong should have sunk you when he had the chance! But, as you now know, he's still alive and I'm sure he will figure a way to haunt your aircraft carrier battle groups once again. I've been in the right places and in the right jobs to be able to contribute my small share to this great effort. And I might add I've been paid handsomely for my efforts."

She stopped her ranting and went to the bar where she poured herself a large brandy. She returned to the sofa and said in a soft voice: "You think you're such a hot-shot journalist just because you won a Pulitzer exposing my friends Lily and Cheryl, and destroying a good man, Senator Anderson. And you're so proud of your hob-nobbing with the Navy brass, but they're only using you to get their stories reported."

"You're an intelligent man, Dan Lincoln. I enjoyed my time in bed with you; as a lover you're first class. But as they say: I've made my bed, I have to sleep in it, and for the future it doesn't include you."

There was nothing anyone needed to add to that statement. Here was the whole story. How would I handle it? Janice bent over kissed me on the lips and said: "So Mr. Lincoln; or should I say Chief Lincoln? What are you going to do about all you know?"

"I'm not sure. I'm in shock. You injured me but I'll get over it. I'm pissed at what you've done to our country and right now I'm of the belief you should be sent to prison."

Choking off tears I continued: "For the time being, however, you ought to think about spending time over the weekend asking yourself some tough questions about the direction of your future, Commander Cannon."

She got up headed for the door and slipped into her coat. "Au revoir, Dan. It's been fun knowing you and I do wish you all the success you deserve."

There were no tears streaming down *her* face, just a smug little smile. She almost waltzed through the door and sauntered down the flight of stairs to her car. I heard her engine start and the tires squeal as she sped out of my life.

My sleep that night was filled with visions of Janice skulking about, peeping into submarine planning offices, then meeting sinister characters under dim streetlights exchanging secret papers. At no time did I see us together romantically, but I did see her standing over me as I laid against that curb where she tried to have me killed.

Reluctantly leaving my comforting bed the next morning, I put off breakfast and went downstairs to get the Saturday Post newspaper. I came back to the apartment and started making a cup of coffee as I screened the headlines. Turning pages I spotted a story in the Police Blotter portion. Stunned, I read:

NAVY OFFICER DIES IN LATE NIGHT CRASH

Arlington, VA. April 27, 2002 (Associated Press):

U.S. Navy Commander Janice R. Cannon, 37, of Alexandria, Virginia, was killed instantly when her late model two-door sports convertible crashed into an I-395 freeway abutment at about 1 am this morning.

Virginia State Police say the female was the only occupant, and it appeared that she lost control of the vehicle just prior to hitting the concrete overpass column. Speed is believed to have been a major factor in the accident, according to the first police officer at the scene of the crash.

CDR Cannon was assigned to a staff position in the office of the Chief of Naval Operations at the Pentagon. She was a veteran of over 15 years in the Navy, and has been in the D.C. area for the past four years.

She is survived by her father Nelson Cannon, a retired Navy officer and businessman, now living in Hong Kong. A Navy spokesman said funeral arrangements would be forthcoming.

The paper slipped out of my hands and I began to cry. "God, Janice," I blurted out loud, "why couldn't you have waited until we talked this thing through one more time? You didn't have to go like this."

She was an excellent driver so I knew she hadn't accidentally hit anything. My late friend and lover had just killed herself.

It took me until well into the afternoon to get over the shock of her death. About 2:30 pm I went into my office to use the funny phone and got Admiral Sharpe on the third ring. "It's Dan Lincoln, Admiral. Yes sir, I'm fine, but ..."

"I've just heard from Admiral Benjamin, Dan. I'm so sorry."

"Janice and I were together last evening and I'm probably responsible for her death since I confronted her with accusations that she led the Chinese spy operation and was our Pentagon mole. And, she admitted it. She was the one who ordered Simon Cardigan murdered and almost had me killed as well."

"I know, Dan. We've had her under suspicion for several months and were about to do just what you did last night. She would have been charged with treason and given a formal court martial in a matter of weeks. You merely facilitated what was already slated to happen, although we didn't figure she'd take her own life."

Running my fingers through my tousled hair, I sighed: "God, what a year this has been. First the spy ring, then the war, and now this business with Janice. What's next?"

"For you, I suggest an updated story on the current status of China and its leaders, and then a nice long vacation."

"I'll give that some thought, Admiral." I waited a moment and then said: "I assume the story about Janice is classified the same as the JAMESTOWN file?"

"Correct assumption, but it will be up to JAG and maybe even the Justice Department to make the final call, because of her involvement in the Lily Shin matter. She might be publicly exposed, but I wouldn't put any money on it. The Navy tends to avoid any bad publicity it can and her story would definitely be considered bad."

There was nothing more to say so I terminated the call to Hawaii. "Mahalo for being so understanding, sir. Give my best to Barbara and keep in touch. Aloha."

"So long, Dan, and thank *you* for everything."

The C-C was pretty empty when I walked in. Being Saturday the regulars were missing in action so I grabbed a stool at the main bar. Before I could order Archie came over.

"Are my days messed up? What brings you to this humble establishment on a Saturday afternoon, Danny?"

"Just out taking a bit of a walk to clear my head, Arch. Did you see the story on the I-395 accident in today's paper? That lady Navy commander who died was a dear friend."

"Yeah, I did. Sorry to learn she was close to you. Look at it this way; what happens is usually meant to happen; her death was probably in the cards."

"I agree her number was up."

Thanking Archie for his kind words, I walked out of the C-C. Not feeling like walking home I hailed a cab and was dropped at my building five minutes later.

Back in the apartment I closed the door, kicked off my shoes and went to the bar. I poured a hefty shot from the same brandy bottle Janice chose for her last drink with me. Stretching out on the sofa we shared during last night's shootout, I thought about things that could have been. It seemed like so much had happened in such a very few hours. I'd get over it. I had to.

It was then I realized I'd never gotten to the mail picked up with the paper this morning. Going through the stack one envelope caught my eye. It had a Navy Department return address. I ripped it open and what awaited me was beyond my wildest expectations.

Dear Chief Lincoln:

 It is a pleasure to advise you of your promotion to the rank of Master Chief Petty Officer (E-9) with an effective date of 1 May, 2002. Your outstanding service to your country while on active duty from 1976 to 1980, your subsequent reserve service, and recent Temporary Assigned Duty has resulted in substantial contributions to the U.S. Navy and to the defense of our country. Your dedication to providing quality performance on your every assignment reflects greatly on your character and devotion to duty.

 It is also noted that you have ample years of credited service to qualify for retirement, and because of certain medical problems you developed while on active duty, the Navy will certify you for full medical benefits in addition to your monthly pension payments, beginning 1 July, 2002.

Respectfully,

E. Thomas Wetzel
Secretary of the Navy

LIST OF CHARACTERS

United States Government:

President Jefferson C. Williams (D-TN) Elected in 1992
President John Paul Crane, (R-OH) Elected in 2000
SEN. Donald M. Walther, (R-AZ) Chairman, Senate Armed
    Services Committee
SEN. Henry B. Anderson, Jr. (D-MN) Minority Leader,
    Senate Armed Services Committee
Hon. Robert L. Bass, (CA) Secretary of State
Hon. James A. Gaston, (VA) Secretary of Defense
Hon. E. Thomas Wetzel, (NJ) Secretary of the Navy

United States Navy:

ADM Edgar R. Lynch, USN, Chief of Naval Operations
ADM Thomas J. Darcy, USN, Commander in Chief,
    U.S. Pacific Fleet
VADM R. Bernard Sharpe, USN, Commander,
    U.S. Pacific Fleet Submarine Force
CDR Janice Cannon, USN, Assistant to Bernie Sharpe.

Nuclear Submarine USS BUFFALO (SSN-737):

CDR Robert Gruenwald, USN, Commanding Officer
LCDR Timothy J. Rockwell, USN, Executive Officer
Master Chief Terry Adams, USN, Chief of the Boat
Senior Chief William Morton, USN, Lead Sonarman

Experimental Submarine USS JAMESTOWN (SSX-1):

Captain Frank B. Russell, USN, Commanding Officer
CDR Ellis Sherman, USN, Executive Officer
LT Bill Bemus, USN, Weapons Officer
Master Chief Harold B. Esterhaus, USN, Chief of the Boat
Senior Chief Jack Smart, USN, Lead Sonarman

Peoples Republic of China Government:

Hon. J.C. Wu, People's Republic of China Ambassador to the
United States, Washington, D.C.
Fred Tong, Cultural Attaché, People's Republic of China
Embassy, Washington, D.C.
ADM W.H.C. Ho, Commander-in-Chief, People's Republic of
China Pacific Fleet, Shanghai
Captain David K.Y. Wong, Director, Red Chinese Naval
Intelligence, and later skipper of the rebel Chinese Navy
submarine PEOPLE'S VICTORY
Ms. Lily Shin, Owner of the Chinese antique & art shop
Ming & Ching Things, Washington, D.C.
Ms. Cheryl Leong: Lily Shin's Daughter, Capitol Hill Intern
and Georgetown University Student

U.S. Government Contractors:

Milsoftel, Military Software & Electronics, Arlington, VA:
Dr. George Mason, CEO; Donald Logan, Lead
Computer Programmer; Samantha Wing, Lab
Assistant.
Mescod, Military Engineering Systems & Computer
Operations Design, Inc., San Diego, CA: CEO Arthur
Humphries, & Chief Engineer, Dr. Lloyd Davidson.

The Press Corps:

Dan Lincoln, Pentagon and Military correspondent, Pacific &
Asia News Service, Washington, D.C.
Bennett Huntley, Editor and Bureau Chief, Pacific & Asia
News Service
Jack O'Neill, Staff Reporter, Pacific & Asia News Service
Ray Kinny, Washington correspondent, Navy Times
Rick Davis, Talk Show Host, Radio Station WALX
Sung Jiang, Correspondent, New China News Agency
Bruce Ferguson, City Editor, Honolulu Times
Simon Cardigan, Reporter, Honolulu Times

TERMS & ACRONYMS

ADM	Navy Rank of Admiral
AKULA	A class of Russian nuclear powered submarines
BEQ	Bachelor Enlisted Quarters
BOQ	Bachelor Officers Quarters
Bubbleheads	Submarine sailors
CAFS	Chinese American Friendship Society
CAPT	Navy Rank of Captain
Cat	Bulldozer built by the Caterpillar Corp.
C-C	The Capitol Connection, A Washington Pub
CDR	Navy Rank of Commander
CHINFO	Chief of Information (Navy Public Affairs)
CIC	Combat Information Center on ships
CINCLANT	Commander in Chief, U.S. Atlantic Command
CINCPAC	Commander in Chief, U.S. Pacific Command
CINCLANTFLT	Commander in Chief, U.S. Atlantic Fleet
CINCPACFLT	Commander in Chief, U.S. Pacific Fleet
CG	Guided Missile Cruiser
CNO	Chief of Naval Operations
CO	Commanding Officer
COB	Chief of the Boat (Submarines)
COD	Carrier On-Board Delivery
COMSUBLANT	Commander, Submarine Forces, U.S. Atlantic Fleet, Norfolk, VA
COMSUBPAC	Commander, Submarine Forces, U.S. Pacific Fleet, Pearl Harbor, HI
CONN	The officer currently controlling the ship
CPO	Navy Rank of Chief Petty Officer
CVBG	Carrier Battle Group
CVN	Nuclear Powered Aircraft Carrier
DCFD	District of Columbia Fire Department
DCPD	District of Columbia Police Department
DDG	Guided Missile Destroyer
DOD	Department of Defense
ECHO	A class of Russian built diesel powered subs
EEZ	Exclusive Economic Zone
ENS	Navy Rank of Ensign
FBI	Federal Bureau of Investigation
FLOTUS	First Lady of the United States
Goat Locker	CPO Quarters

GPS	Global Positioning Satellite
GQ	General Quarters (shipboard battle stations)
HAN	A class of Chinese-built nuclear submarines
HKSB	Hong Kong & Shanghai Banking Corporation
HPD	Honolulu Police Department
ICBM	Inter-Continental Ballistic Missile
INS	Immigration & Naturalization Service
JAG	Judge Advocate General (Navy Legal Corps)
JCS	Joint Chiefs of Staff
KILO	A class of Russian built nuclear submarines
LCDR	Navy Rank of Lieutenant Commander
LT	Navy Rank of Lieutenant
LTJG	Navy Rank of Lieutenant (Junior Grade)
LUHU	A class of Chinese built destroyers
MCAS	Marine Corps Air Station
MESCOD	A civilian business called Military Engineering Systems & Computer Operation Design, Inc.
MILSOFTEL	A company called Military Software & Electronics
MFN	Most Favored Nation
MGD	Miller Genuine Draft beer
MING	A class of older Chinese built diesel powered submarines
MOMA	Museum of Modern Art
MWR	Morale, Welfare & Recreation
NCNA	New China News Agency
NIMBY	Slang saying: 'Not In My Back Yard'
NIS	Naval Investigative Service
1-MC	Shipboard public address system
OOD	Officer of the Deck
ONR	Office of Naval Research
OPNAV	Office of the Chief of Naval Operations
PANS	Pacific & Asia News Service
PAO	Public Affairs Officer
PEM	Proton Exchange Membrane
PLA	Peoples Liberation Army (China)
PMP	Permanent Magnetic Propulsion
POLAD	Political Advisor
Port	The left side of a ship
POTUS	President of the United States
PRC	Peoples Republic of China (Beijing)

PS&S	Politics, sex and sports
RADM	Navy Rank of Rear Admiral (Upper Half)
RDML	Navy Rank of Rear Admiral (Lower Half)
ROC	Republic of China (Taiwan)
ROMEO	Older and smaller class of Russian built diesel powered submarines
SEABEES	U.S. Navy Construction Battalions
SEAL	Navy Sea, Air & Land commandoes
SEATO	South East Asia Treaty Organization
SECDEF	Secretary of Defense
SECNAV	Secretary of the Navy
SOP	Standard Operating Procedure
SOVREMENNYY	A class of Russian built, 8500 ton conventionally powered destroyers
SSBN	Nuclear Powered Ballistic Missile Submarine
SSN	Nuclear Powered Attack Submarine
SSX	Experimental Submarine
Starboard	The right side of a ship
TAD	Temporary Assigned Duty
VADM	Navy Rank of Vice Admiral
WEPS	Weapons Officer
WWF	World Wrestling Federation
XO	Executive Officer, ship's #2 in command

To order additional copies of RED SKY AT NIGHT, at $24.00 per book, contact the author, Bill Bigelow, directly. His mailing address is:
P.O. Box 240666, Honolulu, Hawaii 96824,
or you can E-mail him at:alohabilly@yahoo.com.
His phone number is: 808-223-8838.

Please indicate the name of the person to whom you would like Mr. Bigelow to autograph the book. If the person is an active duty military person, let him know to what branch of the service he or she is attached. If a veteran, some information about the vet's service, dates of active duty, wars, etc. would be helpful.

A special price if offered for active duty, veterans, and to people who have veterans in their families. Ask for this discount when you order your books. Discount price is $21.00 plus shipping via USPS Priority Mail.

Send a check for the price of the book, whether the full $24.00 or the discounted $21.00 per book for active duty military, veterans and current or former Guard and Reserve members, PLUS $4.00 for priority mail, made payable to: The Blue Anchor Co., and the book or books will be sent to you within 3 business days.

Mahalo and Aloha from Hawaii!